Praise fo

"★★★★★"
—*The Orphan*, publication of Desolation Row

"*The New Punk!* Sounds too much like the New Deal to me and socialism makes me sick. Now don't forget to vote Republican in the upcoming primaries and remember 'you got a pal in Al.'"
—Albert Sharp, Mayor, city of Detroit

"Bleep-%$#@-bleep-&%$#@-bleep-bleep!"
—Potty Mouth, orphan, Desolation Row

"I don't do much reading—none actually now that I think about it—but when I do read I prefer to do it with a fresh Mickey's Malt Liquor. It looks cheap, tastes cheap, and *is* cheap, which is why I drink it. After four or five you won't taste a thing. So try a Mickey's, the cheap maker! It's also the drink of choice in my new, upcoming movie—coming straight to a video store near you— *Sherlock Homeless*, the tale of a down-on-his-luck detective trying to solve the mystery of who killed the butler living in the cardboard mansion. With his sewer-dwelling sidekick, Ratson, the two embark—oh right, sorry . . . read *The New Punk*, I hear it's good."
—Tom Travolta, B-movie actor extraordinaire

"You have a 99.99—repeating of course—
percent chance of enjoying *The New Punk*."
—The Wiz, orphan, Desolation Row

"Reading *The New Punk* is like digging through the dumpster
and finding a half-filled bottle of the good stuff."
—Stinky Pete, vagrant, city of Detroit

"*The New Punk* filled in me the hole of
never actually meeting my father."
—Bob Lennon, musician,
illegitimate son of Bob Dylan or John Lennon

"I eat *The New Punk* for breakfast!"
—Sergeant Breakfast, Triad of Terror member

"You don't need a pair of binoculars to see that
The New Punk is good."
—Ray Charles, orphan, Desolation Row

"*The New Punk,* now I can dig that!"
—Brown Sugar Man, mysterious street musician,
city of Detroit

THE
NEW PUNK

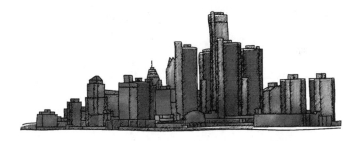

Zev Lawson Edwards

The New Punk
by Zev Lawson Edwards

ISBN: 978-0-9963116-1-8

Editing: Helena Mariposa
Cover and Interior design: NZGraphics

First Edition

Printed in the United States of America

For my mom and dad

CONTENTS

1

Desolation Row

AN ORPHANAGE CAN BE many things, but it is most like an attic where all the leftover, unwanted possessions of a person's life go to take up space and disappear. It exists solely because some belongings are too precious and sentimental to be taken out with the trash. In that regard, all orphanages stand as a testament to the fact that some things in life are more easily forgotten than remembered.

Such a place existed in the heart of America's most neglected metropolis, the city of Detroit. By fate, destiny, irony, or some poet's ill-timed sense of humor, it came to be that the all-boys orphanage on 2959 Douglas Street, Detroit, Michigan—a one-time Historical Center, Social Services Office, Public Library, Performing Arts Theater, School, Fire Department—was rightly named Desolation Row, though referred to as simply "the Row" by the many orphans who took up residence there.

The orphans, like the orphanage itself, were relics of lives never lived. They came from all walks of life, representing the many different fabrics of America's quilt. Equally unwanted, neglected, and alone, they shared a common identity and background. Born at a disadvantage, lacking in opportunity and birthright, their lives were spent looking up and asking why, while the rest of the world looked down and asked why not.

"Look sharp, men," T.W. said, the Row's oldest and most recalcitrant orphan. "I want roll call in 1300 hours. We have two Charlies en route as we speak. Scissors, I'll need a status report. Ray Charles, I want a coffee, on the double, with a splash of milk. Heavy on the sugar. I repeat *heavy* on the sugar."

"Roger that, sir," Ray Charles said, a small lad of eight, weighing no more than fifty pounds soaking wet. He left T.W.'s office, the command center of the orphanage, with such haste that he forgot to close the door.

"*The door*, Ray Charles, the door," T.W. called after him.

"Oh, right, sorry, *sir!*" Ray Charles said, putting an added emphasis on the "sir." All of the orphans addressed T.W. as sir though they had never been asked to.

With the door closed, T.W. was able to resume pacing the space of carpet between his desk and the chair that contained his second-in-command, Scissors, age twelve. Scissors held a number of titles, such as editor-in-chief of the Row's monthly publication *The Orphan*, treasurer of all financial assets related to *The Cause*, secretary of T.W.'s War Council, barber in charge of all haircuts at the Row, and gardener responsible for the well-kept lion-, elephant-, and turtle-shaped hedges displayed out in front of the Row.

With a pair of scissors in his hands, he was an artist— a real Michelangelo—like his idol, the fictional *Edward Scissorhands*. His own Afro was kept so petite and perfectly round that his head resembled a black bowling ball. Whenever orphans needed a new trim they came to Scissors, who fashioned their hair in the latest—and sometimes not so latest—trends. His proclivity for experimentation was the reason why some of the orphans had their hair styled in chic fashions popular in the distant lands of Paris or L.A., but not so much in Detroit. He was the orphan most likely to grace the cover of *Vogue Magazine.*

"Now, where was I?" T.W. mused to himself, continuing to walk holes in the carpet of his spacious office. Both sides of its walls were lined with bookshelves containing everything written by Hemingway, Shakespeare, Steinbeck, Dickens, Marx, Nietzsche, Rimbaud, T.S. Elliot, and many others. Believing that there was no greater or more loyal friend than a book, T.W. took to books like a cow took to grass. He stopped in front of one of the shelves, pulled a book at random, and thumbed through its pages.

"'There is nothing to writing,'" T.W. read. "'All you do is sit down at a typewriter and bleed.'"

"What's that, sir?" Scissors asked.

"Oh, nothing, just something Hemingway said."

T.W. returned the book to the shelf and took a seat behind his giant mahogany desk. On one end of the desk sat a large globe of the Earth, while on the other was a black Remington Standard typewriter, one of the first items scavenged from the massive dump behind the Row, which then had been repaired by The Wiz, the Row's chief technician and scientist. On the wall directly behind T.W.'s chair hung a rather large framed portrait of Che Guevara. It had a quote inscribed on the bottom:

"The Revolution is not an apple that falls when it is ripe. You have to make it fall."

For T.W., those were words to live and die by. As a self-proclaimed anarchist, he was the orphan most likely to start a revolution, overthrow the government, and organize a new regime. He was the illegitimate child of anarchy, the devil of Douglas Street, the master of alchemy, the fire of discontent, the ambassador of hip, the messiah of punk, and only thirteen years old.

By age and appearances alone he was not a very imposing figure. His hair was as black as a starless night, slicked back in the style of James Dean, the ultimate representation of rebellion. A lone cigarette sat wedged behind his left ear. His eyes were the green of a stop-and-go sign, but since they were always hidden behind dark black sunglasses, no orphan had ever peered into them. The sunglasses never left his face, even when he slept and showered.

His face had the confidence of a rock star who didn't want to be bothered and couldn't care less about being understood. His attire was of a time long before his—black motorcycle boots, tight blue jeans folded up at the bottom like he was expecting a flood, a white T-shirt topped with a black leather jacket. His stature was short, but the way he carried himself made him appear taller.

T.W. leaned back in his chair, put his feet up on the desk, and retrieved a switchblade from his side jacket pocket. He clicked it open, revealing not a knife, but a comb, which he ran through his hair once, twice, three times then folded it shut and returned it to his pocket. He started to say something, but then paused and took the cigarette from behind his ear and brought it to his mouth. Scissors was quick to stand up and light it for him.

"This is the second onslaught of Charlies this week." T.W. took a lazy drag from his cigarette. "The economy is in the slumps, so where are all of these darn Charlies coming from?"

"I don't know, sir."

The term "Charlie" referred to a potential adoptive parent. T.W. had heard the word on the Vietnam-era TV drama *Mashed*, which chronicled the life of an outcast sous-chef who worked day and night in the canteen peeling taters, while his comrades fought the tenacious Vietcong, nicknamed Charlie. Lasting sixteen seasons and starring Tom Travolta, the king of straight-to-video B-movies, it was a culinary classic.

When the economy was good, Charlies appeared like worms after a good rain. When the economy was in the dumps, like it was now, Charlies stayed well hidden underground. These particular Charlies were sprung out of the blue, like a furtive thunderstorm sneaking up on a sunny day, giving T.W. little time to prepare.

"Give me the status report, Scissors. I want an ETA, and keep it light on the details and heavy on the PIRC."

ETA and PIRC were two of the many acronyms created by T.W. ETA stood for Estimated Time of Arrival, while PIRC (pronounced perk) stood for Pertinent Information Related to the Charlie.

"Sir, the Charlies in question are set to arrive at exactly 1400 hours. Big Mama started cleaning at 0700 hours. Rec room, bathrooms, dining room, and kitchen are all checked and ready. Current location the common room. Coffee and donuts delivered at 0900 hours. Donuts number a dozen, minus one."

"*Minus one?* How's that even possible?"

"Um . . . Seafood, sir."

"Figures. After Ray Charles comes back with my coffee have him keep his binoculars on Seafood. We can't afford anymore missing donuts. Make it a TP1."

"Sir, yes, sir. A Top Priority Numero Uno, no problem, sir!"

"On second thought, as a precautionary measure have Chopsticks make Seafood a snack. That should keep him occupied and out of the SMRC."

"Sir, yes, sir. Sensitive Material Related to Charlie, no problem, sir!"

Scissors was made T.W.'s number two for the simple reason he could keep track of all of T.W.'s acronyms and recite them without hesitation at any given minute. T.W. had long lost track of the meaning behind some of the acronyms he had created to make giving orders more efficient and less verbose, which was why he had Scissors.

"If he asks any questions, just tell him it's for *The Cause*."

"Yes, sir."

The exact details of *The Cause* were classified Level 11—10 being the highest and 0 being the lowest. According to *Spinal Tap* terms, this meant that any pertinent information relating to the cause was NTKB—Need To Know Basis—and the only person who needed to know was T.W.

T.W. was about to give another order when Ray Charles, his designated runner, gopher, messenger, secretary, and do-it-all-for-nothing, came rushing into the room, nearly tripping over his own steps and spilling coffee all over the place. A loose candy cigarette hung from his mouth.

"Jeez Louise, Ray Charles, walk much?"

"Why, yes, sir. I try to walk every day."

"I didn't expect an answer, Ray Charles. I was being sarcastic. When's the last time you cleaned the binoculars on your head?"

Ray Charles scratched his head and then looked up at the ceiling pensively, as if the act could bring about a recollection. Strapped to his scrawny head and covering his eyes was a pair of black binoculars, sticking out a good four inches from his face, giving him the appearance of a Navy SEAL wearing night vision goggles. The binoculars helped with long distances, but they compromised his peripheral vision, which was why he was always walking into doors, stumbling on stairs, and causing enough accidents to be classified as a first-class klutz.

His only vice was candy cigarettes, which he consumed faster than Popeye went through spinach. At the rate he was going, Ray Charles was sure to be a diabetic by the time he was old enough to smoke the real ones. Always finding himself in asinine situations, he was the orphan most likely to go the way of the lemmings and fall off a cliff.

"Ray Charles, before you trip and hurt yourself go find Muscles immediately and have him clean those goggles on your head. Make it a TP1."

"Yes, sir. Will there be anything else, sir?"

"When you're finished seek out Seafood and tell him to report to Chopsticks. If he gives you any lip, tell him it's for *The Cause.*"

"Yes, sir. Anything else?"

T.W. took a sip from his coffee, grimaced at its strength, and waved Ray Charles away, but due to the binoculars on his head Ray Charles was unable to see the gesture and as a result stood stalwart, awaiting further orders. T.W. likewise waited for him to leave. After a brief, silent standoff T.W. ended it by saying "off with you then."

Ray Charles saluted before heading for the door, nearly running into the wall on his way out. He at least had the good sense to remember to close the door this time.

Finished with Ray Charles, T.W. turned to Scissors. "Commence with your report, Scissors."

"Yes, sir. Big Mama is estimated to be finished cleaning at approximately 1200 hours, give or take a window of fifteen minutes. Children under ten have been debriefed and suited up for contact. Children over ten are in wardrobe and makeup. They are currently being debriefed by Muscles."

"Muscles, you say?"

"Yes, sir. They are in the rec room as we speak."

"Very good. Do we have any viable Intel on the Charlies?"

"Yes, sir. The Wiz compiled a brief bio."

"Let's hear it."

"The Coopers—Mary and Peter—age twenty-eight and thirty. Residence, Royal Oak. Occupations—her, a preschool teacher and him, an orthodontist. Both originally from Illinois. Married for five years. No children."

"Hmm, Royal Oak, you say? The suburbs. Sounds like they have money. Most likely they're unable to have children of their own, have been trying unsuccessfully for the past few years, and finally decided to adopt. They're too young to be desperate, but we can't chance it. Call a Code Yellow."

"Roger that, sir."

When it came to Charlies, T.W. had organized a five-color-coded chart to represent the likelihood of possible adoption. It started with white, moved to green, then yellow before ending with orange and red. In cases of an emergency so dire and severe there was one last, hidden level—Code Black. So far since the chart's inception there had only been cause for a Code Orange and not a single incident requiring a Code Black. Such an imminent threat was why they had *The Cause* to begin with.

"Do you think they have anything to do with the Calloways, sir?" Scissors asked, checking the pages on his notebook.

"Highly unlikely, but we can't take any chances."

The Calloways were the Row's mysterious, unknown benefactors who had serendipitously stepped in to support the Row after the city withdrew its funding. Little was known of them—who they were, where they came from, or why they sent the money in the first place. But like clockwork, at the first of every month, an unmarked envelope with a check for $1500 arrived incognito at the doorsteps of the Row, delivered by a tall man in a black suit and dark sunglasses, who drove an equally black car with tinted windows.

Every time T.W. heard the Calloways' name, he would immediately take a cigarette out and twirl it between his fingers until it shredded, leaving trails of tobacco behind him as he paced the floor. Seeing this, the other orphans feared the Calloways were some kind of a threat.

"I want you to check up on Muscles and make sure everything is going smoothly. Also if you see Matches, make sure to tell him to lay off the gasoline this time around. We can't chance him lighting himself or someone else on fire or burning down the orphanage."

"Yes, sir."

"And, Scissors, one last thing."

"Yes, sir."

"Close the door behind you. I don't wish to be disturbed. I'll be in the mess hall momentarily. You can start without me."

"*Sir?*"

"It's nothing. I just need a moment to myself."

With a confused look, Scissors left the office, closing the door behind him, leaving T.W. to his solitude. T.W. took one last drag from the cigarette before depositing it in an ashtray on his desk. He got up and moved to the window, his favorite place to ponder. The outside was dreary and cloudy with the chance of rain ominous on the horizon. The street below, like most of the surroundings, was empty save for the weeds.

The neighborhood, like much of Detroit, lay in waste and abandonment, hardly the proper place for an orphanage. Douglas Street was so rundown and decrepit that even hope couldn't flourish there. The street was lined with more potholes than pavement and the sidewalks were home to a whole bunch of garbage—crumbled newspapers, scattered debris, abandoned cars, empty shopping carts—and one vagrant, Stinky Pete, who spent his days pushing a shopping cart full of discarded things.

T.W. watched as Stinky Pete picked up a bottle from the ground and raised it to his mouth for a moment, shook it, and then vehemently threw it down. Looking up, he waved to T.W. with a dirty, grease-covered hand. T.W. returned the gesture and then continued his vigil of the dirty, deserted street below.

He spotted Big Mama, a heavyset black woman and the Row's loveable caretaker and Head Supervisor, sitting on a bench, taking a break from her cleaning, and working on her favorite pastime, stitching a new shirt for one of the orphans. Her warm smile radiated optimism, being the only upbeat sign of life for miles around. "Oh, Lordy," T.W. heard her call in between stitches, "Desolation Row sure is looking good today, Lordy, yes."

From his vantage point, T.W. begged to differ.

Surrounded by abandonment, the Row was constructed in a part of Detroit not only deserted by its people, industry, and businesses but by the city itself, which had forgotten to send the Row's monthly stipend for the past year. Wedged between an abandoned pawnshop and a derelict textile plant, it was one of the few still standing and functional buildings on the block. Its red-bricked walls appeared like a fire veiled by billows of dreary, hazy smoke.

Thanks to looters, the windows of the abandoned pawnshop had been busted and boarded over, while the door was a gaping hole. The inside was stripped of anything of worth, including the copper wiring, most likely sold as scrap. All that remained of its glory days was a faded sign, reading "Open for Business." No one had bothered to turn it to "Closed."

The metal roof of the textile plant had rusted to a dull orange, while the brick walls were of such a dark gray they never hinted at a sunny day. During the late seventies the back half of the building caught fire and despite the Fire Department (the Row's third incarnation after the School and Library closed) being right next door, no fire trucks or firemen came to quench the flames. Seeing the calamity as an opportunity for cheap urban renewal, the city decided it was best for the building to burn to the ground.

Mother Nature clearly disagreed. She released such a massive rainstorm that the fire was doused in less than an hour, saving not only the abandoned textile plant, but most of Douglas Street as well. What remained were partially burned buildings, half piles of ashes and half in a state of ruin.

A massive Ford automobile plant, made vacant due to greener pastures overseas, stood across the street more like a metallic castle than a factory. Seemingly endless, it dominated the landscape, sprawling for almost an entire mile, a vast industrial emptiness, collecting debris, cobwebs, and rodents.

The only thing still open for business and within walking distance of the Row was the Detroit House of Corrections—also known as the state penitentiary or pen for short. It was not only the biggest prison in the state of Michigan, but the entire Midwest, crammed full with murderers, thieves, arsonists, substance abusers, dealers, and the pits of society, or rather the forgotten masses of Detroit. In a lot of ways, prisoners were really just grown-up orphans abandoned by society. They, like the orphans, were always there, scars pushed out of sight and concealed in darkness—the blind eye of humanity.

Despite their close proximity, neither one would have been readily aware of the other if it had not been for a technicality that resulted in large monthly shipments of supplies, originally destined for the prison, being dropped off on the doorsteps of the Row instead. The prison's address—3959 Douglas Street—was often confused with the Row's address—2959 Douglas Street. As a result, the Row often received large packages of canned goods, reading materials, bed sheets, soap, cartons of cigarettes, and stacks of letters addressed to such notorious criminals as Sonny "One-Tooth" Sullivan, Harry

"Menace" MacArthur, Mickey "No Dice" Paulson, Terry the Terrorizer, "Crazy-eye" Hopkins, and Juan "AK-47" Martinez. There were even a few addressed to the Detroit Streaker, who despite rumors of capture was still at large.

Compared to the rest of the neighborhood, the Row itself was in quite good condition. Originating from the early days of Detroit, long before its decline, it was constructed by one of the city's leading architects, a man so renowned that he was lost in the back pages of Detroit's history books and never heard from since. This unknown architect came from a time when things were built to last. The Row stood as one of his most crowning and enduring achievements, though no one bothered to notice, save for the orphans of Desolation Row.

T.W. stood erect in front of the Row's third floor window, with his right arm behind him like a general surveying the battlefield before the cannons fired, pondering the beauty hidden underneath so much wasted potential and relishing the silence surrounding him. Such a moment was a luxury seldom found in an orphanage of thirty plus orphans. As the oldest, it was his duty to look after each and every one of them. He did not think of his responsibilities as a burden or an inconvenience but rather a calling.

As he gazed off into the distance, a large flock of seagulls—also known as dumpster chickens—made their way from the dump behind the Row towards the abandoned automobile plant. T.W. pulled a watch from his jacket, looked at the time, and smiled. As always, the dumpster chickens were on schedule.

Watching them in flight always made him wonder what it would be like to fly like a bird. To have wings, to soar, to have everything below him looking up. Perhaps there was no greater sense of freedom. But, like freedom, everything came with a price, as Icarus learned when he flew too close to the sun and plummeted. The fall was something all orphans eventually faced. T.W. just hoped to have his wings long before that day came.

T.W. turned away from the window and stared down at his typewriter. He debated whether or not to attempt writing. His novel wasn't going to write itself. So far he was stuck on page 364, awaiting a major plot point to materialize. The story just wasn't speaking to him anymore. He had the characters, but not the climax, the middle and beginning but no end in sight. The way things were going, he'd be an orphan without an orphanage if he didn't find a solution.

What would Hemingway do, old boy?

"I learned never to empty the well of my writing, but always to stop when there was still something there in the deep part of the well, and let it refill at night from the springs that fed it," he thought, drawing inspiration from his mentor Hemingway.

He had tried to always follow that advice, but this time the well had gone dry.

The ringing of the lunch bell, signaling noon, broke his reverie. He released a deep breath, straightened his jacket, and stepped away from the window, deciding to save his writing for another day. He opened the door to his office and was somewhat surprised to discover he was not alone.

"Good God, Ray Charles, what in the Hemingway are you doing here? I thought I told you to get your binoculars cleaned and find Seafood."

"Sorry, sir," Ray Charles said, adjusting the knobs on the binoculars in an attempt to bring T.W. into focus. When it came to sight, Ray Charles was as blind as a mole and couldn't see more than a few feet in front of him. Lacking proper medical assistance at the Row to fix his nearsightedness, T.W. recruited his first lieutenant—there was no second—The Wiz, age eleven, to formulate a remedy.

The Wiz was the smartest orphan at the Row, with a perfect IQ of 200 and a photographic memory. He had long wild hair that clung to his head like a pile of dirty laundry. Glasses the size of two magnifying lenses sat on his small nose, making the rest of his face appear tiny. Like a mad scientist, he always wore a white apron. Its pockets full of beakers, test tubes, half-chewed pencils, and the occasional rat with its tail dangling out like a piece of string. A calculator was never far from his hand, and throughout the day he was seen punching random calculations, formulating outcomes, and figuring mathematical probabilities. He was the orphan most likely to develop a teleportation machine capable of time travel.

Within a few days, The Wiz had modified a pair of binoculars, attached a strap to them, placed them on Ray Charles's head, and then adjusted them to meet Ray Charles's ocular needs. After a quick punching of numbers on his calculator, The Wiz calculated that Ray Charles had a 74.87—repeating of course—percent chance of seeing what was in front of him.

"Can you see anything, Ray Charles?"

"No, not yet."

The Wiz turned a dial.

"How about now?"

"Sure can."

"How's it feel?"

"A little jacked up."

"You'll just have to get used to it, Ray Charles."

When The Wiz was finished, Ray Charles had the long-distance vision of an eagle, but had to constantly adjust the dials to see things up close. As a result his vision was always in and out of focus, equal parts nearsighted and farsighted.

Ray Charles was still working the dials as T.W. stood outside his office door, losing patience while waiting for a reply. "Ray Charles? What are you doing here? Shouldn't you be in the rec room with the rest of the men?"

"Yes, I know sir, but ... you see ... I was wondering ..."

Ray Charles paused and removed the binoculars from his face, revealing two rheumy eyes, dripping water like a leaky faucet. Overcome with emotion, he was unable to speak.

"Come with me into the office." T.W. motioned, looking distraught. Ray Charles followed him and closed the door.

"Well, what is it?"

"Sir, I was just thinking that, well . . . I could volunteer myself—for *The Cause*—and, you know, let myself be adopted."

It was not that Ray Charles really wanted to be adopted, but rather that he was willing to do almost anything— including taking a bullet if it came to it—for his best friend and mentor.

"Good God, man, don't be ridiculous. I wouldn't let one of those incompetent nincompoops take away one of my own. We have to stick together. It's a mad, crazy world out there. It'll tear an orphan apart. Remember what happened to Snuggles?"

Ray Charles gulped. "Right, sir. What was I thinking? Of course I don't want to be adopted."

"Good, now remember the first thing in any—" Before he could finish, Scissors came barging into the room.

"Sir, we have a situation."

"What now?"

"They're here. The Charlies. They're early, sir."

"Good God, man, put a pickle on some bread and call it a sandwich."

"What should we do?"

"Sound the alarm!"

"Roger that." Scissors left the room like a bolt of lightning.

"We'll discuss this in more detail later, Ray Charles. For now, just remember your duties and look sharp."

"Yes, *sir*." Ray Charles said, a little too forlorn for T.W.

"Can I count on you soldier?"

"Sir, yes, sir." Ray Charles said it like he had a pair.

"Alright then, help Scissors round up the troops and make sure they take up their positions. We haven't a moment to lose."

2

Tactical Engagement

"LISTEN UP, MEN. YOU know the drill. Look alive, remain sharp, and don't let your guard down. No one's left the Row under my watch and that's not going to start today. Is that understood?"

"Sir, yes, sir!" rang through the mess hall.

T.W. walked the length of the twenty-three orphans—referred to as "men" during times of conflict—in attendance, carefully inspecting each. They stood in perfect formation, in two rows of eight with a third row of seven taking up the rear. Their chests pumped forward, their heads held high, and their arms to their sides. Scissors stood in front of them, diligently marking off names on a clipboard, while Ray Charles stood beside him, a pint-sized shadow.

"More dirt behind the ears, Colonel Sanders." "Blacken that tooth some more, Snot." T.W. clasped his hands behind his back as he marched slowly down the line. "You call that a stain on your shirt, Christmas Story? Report to Chopsticks immediately." He jerked his head in Chopsticks general direction then moved on. "Open that rip on your pant leg more, Pickles, and don't be afraid to show some skin." Stopping short in front of Faygo, he said, "Is that a rash you're supposed to have or just pimples? Report back to makeup." He studied each and every man as if he were an entomologist identifying insects. "Remember, men, you're supposed to not only look sick, but contagious as well. And hey, if you're going for mentally challenged then drool more and make sure you wear your shoes on the opposite feet." He sniffed sharply. "Rub some more fish guts on yourself, Stone Age. I can barely smell you from here." "Good God, man, what are you wearing, Belch?" "That's jacked up, Marshmallow."

Having covered all three rows of orphans, T.W. stood in front of them. He adjusted his sunglasses, pulled the cigarette from behind his ear, and began twirling it from one finger to the next while examining them. "Also remember to scratch yourself at all times, especially around the head. The last thing these Charlies want is a kid with lice. And, men, remember Snuggles."

"SNUGGLES!" the men responded.

Just then Muscles, age eleven and T.W.'s third-in-command, came running into the room. Far from resembling his namesake, he was mostly skin and bones. But despite his appearance he had the strength of Superman, able to lift twice his weight and carry almost anything on his back like an ant. Such was the case, when at the age of seven, he lifted a fallen bookcase off Big Mama's leg, all without giving himself a hernia, which caused Big Mama to comment, "Lordy, that boy has the strength of Samson. Lordy, yes."

Muscles spent most of his days in the basement lifting gallon-sized cans of green beans and fifty-pound sacks of potatoes. Currently he had two ten-pound cans of sardines strapped to his arms, put there for conditioning. He was the orphan most likely to beat The Rock, Arnold Schwarzenegger, and Vin Diesel in successive arm wrestling matches.

"Sir, I have an SUC."

"Status Update on the Charlie!" Scissors shouted. The men nodded in agreement.

"Good, go ahead and give it to me."

"Charlies arrived at 1200 in a shiny new Cadillac. Their current location Big Mama's office. Door closed. Coffee and Donuts served."

"ETA?"

"Not sure, sir, but I'm guessing anywhere between five to ten minutes."

"We'll assume less. Not taking any chances. I will need everyone IPRC in two minutes."

"In Position and Ready for Combat!" Scissors shouted. The men nodded in agreement.

"Muscles lead them through the exercise."

"Sir, yes, sir."

"Scissors, where's The Wiz? I don't see him anywhere?"

"He's in his laboratory, sir."

"What's he doing there? Doesn't he know we have a Charlie in the building?"

"Sir, he told me to tell you he's working on something special for *The Cause*."

"Oh, right, of course. Did he give a number crunch for our chance of success?"

"Yes, sir, he did. The Wiz calculated that the mission has a 91.33—repeating of course—percent chance of success and a 5.29—repeating of course—percent chance of adoption."

"That's jacked up. What happened to the other 3.38—repeating of course—percent?"

"The Wiz said that the remaining 3.38—repeating of course—percent accounts for unforeseen variables and therefore remains unknown."

"I guess that makes sense. Alright, we'll just carry on without him. Listen up, men! It's time to move. Before I send you on your way we need a few distractions to buy more time. Any volunteers?"

Four hands shot up.

"We only need two, so roshambo for it. Matches you take on Bellyache and Super Soaker you take on Marshmallow."

"Best of three?" Marshmallow asked.

"No time, winner takes all, let's make it snappy."

Paper by Matches covered rock by Bellyache and scissors by Marshmallow cut through paper by Super Soaker. Matches, age ten, had long, curly red hair and freckles that dotted his face and arms like fireflies. He was the pyromaniac orphan most likely to burn down the city of Detroit. Marshmallow, age eight, was albino, his hair white as paper, and his skin so pale and lustrous he glowed like a pearl in an oyster. He was the orphan most likely to be adopted by the ghost of Hemingway, who was rumored to haunt the Row.

"Okay, Matches, you're up first. Try not to get carried away like last time and that means no homemade napalm. I repeat NO homemade napalm. Do I make myself clear?"

"Yes, sir," Matches said, somewhat disappointed. T.W. had made the mistake of loaning Matches the *Anarchist's Cookbook*, and ever since then Matches had been a fire hazard to both the Row and all its occupants.

"Okay, good, I'm glad we're clear. Now don't forget to use the birdcall if you run into any problems."

"What's the call for today, sir?"

"Scissors, what'd we use last time?"

Scissors scanned through his clipboard then shouted, "Great blue heron."

"Okay, today we're using prairie warbler."

"Roger that, sir."

Matches left the mess hall carrying his supplies—a gas can, blowtorch, and Zippo lighter. Marshmallow stood by the door, holding a brown paper bag and awaiting his orders.

"What's your story for today?" T.W. quizzed him.

"I'm a cancer patient with only a few months to live. Thanks to the chemo I have uncontrollable bowel movements and can't hold down any food."

"What's in the bag?"

"Some leftover oatmeal from a week ago. Looks just like vomit."

"That's jacked up."

"Want me to throw up on one of them?"

"Nah, shouldn't be necessary. You should be fine with just pretending to vomit in the corner. I like your spirit though, Marshmallow. Keep up the good work and remember use prairie warbler if you run into any difficulties."

"Yes, sir."

* * *

Back in the large, open common room, the Coopers had just finished their coffee and donuts and were leaving Big Mama's office, which opened into the common room. Her office was a small room crammed full of file cabinets with detailed records of all orphans, past and present, as well as any and all prospective parents. The office also led to a backroom that acted as Big Mama's bedroom and contained a small, narrow alcove that served as an infirmary, consisting of a single bed and many shelves and cabinets lined with all kinds of medicines, bandages, and medical equipment.

"Lordy, now follow me this way and I'll show y'all the grandeur of the Row, our very own rec room."

Big Mama, dressed in a purple-flowered dress, led the way with big, slow steps, her bosom and buttocks churning like pistons on an engine. The Coopers followed side by side. Mr. Cooper was tall and lanky, his brown hair just starting to bald, while Mrs. Cooper was short, just barely reaching his shoulders, with long blonde hair pulled back in a ponytail. They had on their Sunday bests. He wore a light gray suit with yellow tie and she a white dress.

Directly across from Big Mama's office they came to an open archway leading to what used to be a garage but was now a wide-open expanse of a room two stories high. A large glass chandelier hung in the center of the ceiling, while the walls were draped with massive cloth banners celebrating the sports teams of Detroit—Lions, Tigers, Red Wings, and Pistons. Crammed with desks, chairs, couches, beanbags, and coffee tables, the rec room was organized in such an arbitrary fashion that it resembled a half-played game of war, with cards strewn everywhere. Closest to the garage doors—painted shut and unable to open—was a pool table, Ping-Pong table, foosball table, dartboard, original yellow *Pac-Man* arcade, and a

TV. All leftovers from the long since retired Fire Department that fought boredom more than it did fires.

"Now Lordy, ain't this place sumthing. The orphans just love it. They—"

"Oh, my," Mrs. Cooper said, somewhat startled.

Big Mama turned to see a very enthusiastic Matches standing just inside the entrance to the rec room. His eyes blazed an overzealous welcome, while his face had the concentration of someone holding their breath. Just as Mr. Cooper was about to say something Matches lit his blowtorch, brought it to his still closed mouth, and then blew out a mouthful of gasoline. A giant fireball in the shape of a fiery rose bloomed from his mouth and warmed the white, ghostly faces of the Coopers, too stunned to do anything but stare. Matches ran off towards the common room, his giggles trailing behind him like billows of smoke.

"Oh, my!" Mrs. Cooper placed her arm beneath the protective one of her husband. Their faces ashen.

Big Mama shook her head and chuckled. "Lordy, that boy got a devilish sense of humor like ole Lucifer himself. Lordy, yes he does."

The Coopers feigned smiles, all the while eyeing the exit. Big Mama was still chuckling as she motioned them further into the rec room with her big beefy arm, acting as if an orphan breathing fire like a dragon was just a normal, everyday occurrence.

* * *

Still in the mess hall, T.W. continued his inspection of the men. He was halfway through when he noticed they were short one orphan.

"Scissors, who are we missing?"

"It appears Seafood is MIA."

"Seafood! Where in the Hemingway is he? He must have heard the alarm sound."

Seafood, age twelve, was the laziest orphan at the Row. Short and robust, he weighed under 200 pounds when not soaking wet and over 200 when soaking wet. His face was round like a pie and his stomach sloped forward like a giant teardrop. His arms hung to his sides like a penguin's and when he walked he waddled, his steps sounding like a bass drum. His hobbies included eating, sleeping, napping before sleeping, snacking before napping, gorging after napping, and eating in his sleep.

He was such a procrastinator that he often stayed in bed for days at a time to avoid getting up, went barefoot for months to get out of tying his shoes, and put off showering for so long he started to smell like his namesake. He was the orphan most likely to win a worldwide hot dog eating competition and still be hungry.

"Sir, Seafood was last spotted on the third floor eating a Twinkie near the laundry chute."

"Hmmm, Scissors organize a search party and have him located ASAP. The last thing we need is for a Charlie to spot him before we do. Wanting to adopt such a specimen as Seafood is highly unlikely, but we can't chance it."

"Rooster, Tea Bag, Ace of Spades, and Colonel Sanders, come with me." Scissors led the way out of the mess hall.

"Okay, everyone else may I have your attention. We're sticking to the plan. Take your stations and await further orders. Muscles, they're all yours. Marshmallow, you're up. Make us proud, soldier."

"Sir, yes, sir." Marshmallow left for the rec room and took his bag of oatmeal with him.

The rest of the men broke formation and followed Muscles. T.W. stood in the center of the room, surveying his troops, and pulling a cigarette from his ear. Ray Charles was quick to bring up a light, but the peripheral vision of his binoculars caused him to misjudge the distance. He held the lighter about six inches to the right of T.W.'s face.

"I'm over here, Ray Charles."

"Oh, sorry, sir." Ray Charles swayed a foot to the left.

"To your right, Ray Charles. No your *other right*. Ah, forget it just give me the lighter."

In an act almost beneath him, T.W. lit his own cigarette and blew a ring of smoke. He handed the lighter back to Ray Charles and retrieved his switchblade comb from his leather jacket, running it through his hair three times.

Over in the rec room, Big Mama was showing the Coopers the layout of the orphanage, paying special note to the vast bookshelf that lined the entire west wall (all remnants of the Row's tenure as a public library). The shelves were completely filled from top to bottom with literary classics, children's stories, encyclopedias, and how-to manuals. Other shelves were filled with every board game imaginable and a large collection of VHS movies representing every decade of film.

"Now, little Peanut Butter is our youngest," Big Mama began, taking time from her tour to give details on some of the orphans. "He's only five and a half I believe and—"

"*Wait*, excuse me, did you say his name was Peanut Butter?" Mr. Cooper asked.

"Oh yes, Peanut Butter, now he's as cute as an angel, I swear he is, Lordy. Just a little fella, hardly says a word he's so shy."

"Oh my. That sure is an unusual name for a boy."

"Yes, well, the children name themselves. A policy started . . . well, let me see here . . . some time ago, maybe ten years. I can't be sure anymore at my age, eighty-five years now," Big Mama said, not remembering she was actually eighty-seven.

"How come he named himself Peanut Butter and not something normal like Bill or George?" Mrs. Cooper asked.

"Well, I don't know. Let me think on it for a minute."

Big Mama had trouble keeping track of all of the names of the orphans, let alone the reasoning behind them—just as she'd lost track of her age. As it were, Peanut Butter, age five and a half, was named not because he was partial to the creamy gooiness, but rather because of a speech impediment that made it sound like his mouth was always full of peanut butter. His mumbled gibberish was so incoherent that no one understood a single word he said, and since he didn't know how to read or write, The Wiz was recruited to build a contraption to cipher Peanut Butter's drivel into something understandable.

It only took The Wiz a week to create a device he called the Baby-Talk. Constructed out of radio parts from five different decades, Baby-Talk was a circular contraption that wrapped around Peanut Butter's throat and connected, by a thin black wire, to a microphone strapped around Peanut Butter's right hand. Whenever Peanut Butter said something the machine processed, coded, and translated the information before transmitting it—after a one second delay—in a mono-tone, robotic voice that sounded all too much like R2-D2.

"Hmmm-mumble mumble hmmm," Peanut Butter said, which was then decoded by the Baby-Talk into "I have to pee."

Big Mama's face was still crunched in concentration, try-ing to think of the reasoning behind the boy's name, when Marshmallow, no longer carrying the paper bag, entered the rec room. Like a heat-seeking missile, he headed straight for the Coopers. He stood before them holding his stomach and making a face that suggested he had recently eaten something that didn't agree with him.

"Why, hello there," Mr. Cooper said, admiring the boy's glowing whiteness.

Marshmallow responded by spewing week-old oatmeal from his mouth. It landed on the floor in front of him with a solid PLOOMP, a few specks landing on Mr. Cooper's shoes. A line of drool clung to the corner of Marshmallow's mouth.

"Oh my." Mrs. Cooper moved closer to her husband's body as if the act of standing on her own would cause her to fall.

"He's not contagious is he?" Mr. Cooper asked.

"Oh Lordy, boy are you sick again?" Big Mama asked, ig-noring Mr. Cooper. "Come here and let me feel ya head for a fever."

She drew Marshmallow to her bosom, causing his head to be swallowed in the cushion of her chest. After about ten seconds, he was released, gasping for air. Big Mama placed her hand on his forehead and shook her plump face in disagreement.

"You're as warm as the month of July, boy. Have you been playing in the sun again? Lordy knows you got to stay in the shade otherwise the sun will fry you like a slab of bacon. Lordy, Lordy, Lordy."

Big Mama drew Marshmallow to her bosom, once more cutting off his supply of oxygen. When she released him, he was so short of breath that the only thing he could think to do besides breathe was whistle. The sound of a prairie warbler was relayed all the way to the mess hall where it reached the attentive ears of T.W.

"You hear that, Ray Charles?"

"Hear what, sir?"

"Prairie warbler. It's begun. Alright men, take your positions and commence Phase 1."

Instead of shouts of "Sir, yes, sir," the sound of prairie warbler whistled through the hall, followed by a loud explosion from the kitchen, causing the walls to shake as if in the throes of a mild earthquake. Phase 1 was underway. It involved pandemonium.

Back in the rec room, the Coopers not only heard the explosion, but felt it as well. They stared at each other with puzzled eyes. Big Mama heard the explosion too, but she was less concerned. "That washer machine must be acting up again. It always makes a racket like it's got the devil in it. Lordy knows we need a new one."

It was at that precise moment that a small group of orphans came bursting through the door, chanting like Indians on the warpath. Streaking behind them were trails of unraveled toilet paper sticking to whatever it came in contact with. The orphans circled the Coopers, wrapping them up like mummies. Another small group of orphans, with bandannas covering their mouths and wielding fire extinguishers, soon joined them. Clouds of thick fire extinguisher smoke gave chase to the trail of TP, and by the time both parties exited the rec room it was a hazy mess.

"Oh my," Mrs. Cooper said through a mouth covered in toilet paper.

"Lordy, the boys are playing cowboys and Indians again," Big Mama gasped, her chest rising and falling with laughter. The Coopers were still pulling the toilet paper from their clothes when a smell of something foul hit their nostrils. Big Mama's laughter was cut short by the wrinkling of her nose. "Whoo-ee," she said, "one of the pipes in the bathroom must have burst again. Lordy, knows we need a new one. When it snows in Detroit it sure does storm, Lordy, it sure does."

Back in the mess hall, the call of prairie warbler once again made its way to T.W.'s ears. He was about to announce Phase 2, when Scissors came back into the room with the rest of the search party.

"Sir, we discovered the whereabouts of Seafood, sir."

"Well, where is he?"

"Sir, he's sleeping in the laundry basket in the basement. We tried waking him, but he won't budge."

"Is he OSOC?"

"Yes, sir. He's Out of Sight & Out of Commission!" The men in attendance nodded in agreement.

"*Son-of-a-bee's nest!* Very well, carry on. Take positions, men. We have incoming Charlies. It's time to implement Phase 2."

Phase 2 involved "shock and awe." Most Charlies didn't make it beyond Phase 2. They were running for the doors somewhere between the shock and the awe. But just in case, there were two additional phases mapped out in T.W.'s ASP (Arsenal of Strategic Planning). Phase 3 involved "seek and destroy," while the exact details of Phase 4 were so sensitive that they were classified Level 11 and locked away in the upstairs attic. T.W. had the only key.

The Coopers approached the mess hall holding their noses and covering their mouths, while a strand of toilet paper was still stuck to Mr. Cooper's right shoe. Big Mama followed close behind with a red-and-white handkerchief held to her face. The unidentified smell only worsened as they got closer to the kitchen.

They entered the mess hall to be greeted by a war zone. All of the tables were overturned, forming barricades orphans hid behind. Bullets and bombs in the form of food came crashing down all around them. Pies of mashed potatoes and gravy were flung like grenades and exploded on the floor, tables, ceiling, and any unlucky orphan who happened to get in the way. Bottles of ketchup and mustard were used like water guns and sprayed in every which direction, while whole cans of fruit juice were upturned and emptied on unsuspecting victims. The shrieks and splats were accompanied by raucous laughter.

T.W. stood in the center of all the chaos and commotion, the only one untouched by food. Rations zinged over him, under him, just past him, and all around him, but never on him. It was as if he was surrounded by some invisible force field that kept everything out. He paced back and forth, relishing in the anarchy and giving praise when necessary.

"Nice throw, Belch."

"Way to get 'em, Poop Stain."

"You got mashed potatoes in your hair, Faygo."

"Work on your form, Toaster, you missed him by a mile."

"That's jacked up, Tea Bag."

"Dear God, man, don't hide there like a child, Mike Tyson. Grow a pair and go get some."

Before Mrs. Cooper could utter "oh my" she was hit square in the face with a mashed potato grenade. It covered her face like a facial mask at a beauty salon. Mr. Cooper was about to come to her aid when his gray suit was splattered with ketchup and mustard, making him look like a human-size hot dog minus the onions and the bun. Big Mama was hit on the front of her flowered dress with something a dark reddish brown. She brought a finger of the unknown substance to her nose and took a deep sniff before bringing it to her mouth.

"Hmmm, must be sloppy joe Tuesday."

The Coopers had enough. They made for the door while a handful of orphans chased after them flinging sloppy joe meat. Big Mama turned around to ask them if they were hungry and was surprised to find an empty space. "Oh Lordy, they must've had some other bidness to attend to. Hey, you boys, stop rubbing mashed potatoes in that lad's face. Can't you see he's had enough already? And I hope you plan on cleaning this mess up because I sure ain't, Lordy knows I ain't."

With that proclamation, she folded her arms and shook her head. Orphans will be orphans, she thought.

Outside, the Coopers leapt the three stairs of the porch in haste and hopped in their brand new, shiny Cadillac, indifferent to the fact that they were both covered in food and grime. With a squeal of tires, they left Desolation Row and the city of Detroit in such a rush that they did not stop until they were once more in the safety of the suburbs.

Back in the mess hall, the show was over now that the Coopers were gone. T.W. stood in the center of it all, surveying the damage, while Scissors stood next to him jotting down notes on his clipboard. Ray Charles walked around like a lost puppy.

"Alright, men, mission accomplished," T.W. announced. "The Charlies have left the building. Take five."

A loud hooray sounded from the men, all covered in filth from head to toe. T.W. was the only one unsoiled. He ran his comb through his hair three times and retrieved a cigarette from behind his ear. Before he had time to bring it to his mouth Scissors was there with a light, Ray Charles a close second.

"Sir, is it possible for me to have one of those?" Ray Charles asked, putting the unused lighter back into his pocket.

"One of what, Ray Charles?"

"A cigarette, sir."

"Good God, man, no! You're way too young."

"Yes, sir. I guess you're right."

"I know I'm right. Stick to candy cigarettes, Ray Charles. Take one from Scissors. You've earned it. Scissors, give Ray Charles one of your candy menthols."

"Yes, sir." Scissors handed a chalk white candy cigarette with a pink tip to Ray Charles who put it to his mouth and pantomimed smoking a real one, even coughing after taking a particularly long drag.

"Attention, men," T.W. said. "Time to begin the cleanup phase. Orphans under ten, report to the showers. Orphans over ten start in the mess hall. I want this place spic-and-span by 1500 hours. Chopsticks, a word alone, please."

Chopsticks, age twelve, nationality Korean, was head chef at the Row. Garbed in all kitchen whites and a big chef hat, he was a heavyset boy, more thick than obese. His eyes, nose, and mouth were just tiny toppings on his doughy, pizza-shaped face. Black hair, cut in a fashion popular during the British Invasion, topped his head like a black hat.

Despite never once meeting his Korean parents or another Korean for that matter, and the fact that there wasn't a single book on how to speak Korean in the Row's vast library, Chopsticks spoke fluent Korean, which he used almost exclusively when angry. But after being infatuated with the Tom Travolta Indy-Grunge flick *Seattle Jones and the Temple of the Dog*, more specifically Seattle's eleven-year-old Korean sidekick, Short-Order Cook, Chopsticks took to speaking English with a more distinct Korean dialect, Konglish. His dialect was so strong that he mixed up his /r/ and /l/ sounds, butchered the /v/ and /z/ sounds, and seldom used the articles "a," "an," and "the." He was the orphan most likely to have his own cooking show on the *Food Network*, with subtitles of course.

Unbeknownst to Chopsticks and most of the orphans, he was also T.W.'s unspoken fourth-in-command, though T.W. never acknowledged such a rank existed. After reading *Catch-22*, T.W. believed that some military classifications were best left in the mystic.

"You caw me, sir? Something I help with?"

"I just wanted to congratulate you on a job well done. That

explosion, the stench, and of course the sloppy joes were all well played. You've earned four marks today."

"Thank you berry much, sir, it nothing."

The use of marks was a rewards system created by T.W.— kept track of course by Scissors—used to give distinction and rank to the orphans (*ahem*, the men). They were distributed in the form of tiny squared pieces of metal the size of stamps forged from scrap metal scavenged at the dump. On the front was a simple inscription: *In The Cause We Trust.* On the back was another: *Cause for All & All for Cause.*

All marks were produced by Stone Age, age eleven, who thanks to a rare medical condition looked like an old man, despite being only a child. He had gray, balding hair and so many wrinkles on his face that it looked like a raisin. With a hammer in his hand, he was a master blacksmith, a real Thor. He was the orphan most likely to end up in a nursing home before being adopted.

The value of the marks was based on the Row's Bottle & Can Standard. All bottles and cans—worth a ten-cent deposit—were stored away in the basement and saved for a rainy day for *The Cause.* Anytime an orphan found a can it went straight to the large storage room set aside for bottles and cans. Scissors was in charge of the Treasury. He calculated that each mark was worth its weight in bottles and cans by a ratio of 1 to 7. With the number of marks in circulation related to the number of bottles and cans in storage, this meant that each mark was worth roughly seventy cents. Of course the weight of bottles and cans fluctuated with the market. The Wiz really made a killing when the ratio was 1 to 15. He cashed in over 200 marks, earning a profit of a 150 dollars, which went right back to *The Cause.*

Over the years, T.W. had lost track of all the ways an orphan could receive merits or demerits, and so like most things done at the Row, the marks system was calculated holistically, to T.W.'s discretion. So far, Scissors had the most marks with 2,311, while Seafood had the least amount with –37.

"Scissors, remember to add four marks to Chopstick's tally, also subtract three marks from Seafood—one for roll-call violation, one for failing to follow a direct order, another one for sleeping on the job, and one more for insubordination."

"Sir, that's four marks."

"Yes, of course it is. Isn't that what I said before?"

"No, sir, you originally said three marks, not four."

"Well, make it four, he deserves it."

"Yes, sir."

"Chopsticks, where was I? Oh yes, you did a fine job today. Are you still planning a commemoration cake for the troops?"

"It cook as we speak. Berry dewicious."

"Very good, Chopsticks. Carry on. I will see you in 1900 hundred hours."

"Berry good, sir."

By 1900 hundred hours, the entire mess hall was transformed to its former self, with twenty twelve-foot tables running in two rows of ten, and so completely spotless that any trace of a food fight could not be detected, save for a few clumps of mashed potatoes still stuck to the ceiling. The orphans were all seated at their tables, including Seafood who had awakened shortly after the cleaning was finished and was so famished he was in danger of eating the table. As always he was first in line for dinner, which included pork chops, garlic herb potatoes, applesauce, and a homemade horserad-ish sauce made from scratch by Chopsticks who described it as berry, berry spicy, but berry berry dewicious.

"Well done, men," T.W. called from the front of the room. Chopsticks and Scissors stood on either side of him. "We've showed those Charlies whose boss, upholding our perfect re-cord of—what's the latest tally, Scissors?"

"Charlies zero, orphans twenty-nine, sir."

"Yes, twenty-nine consecutive victories. Very impressive and hopefully we will have a nice, long break before our thir-tieth. Let's hear it for Snuggles."

"SNUGGLES!" the men sounded.

"As a special reward, Chopsticks has prepared a nice cake, a chocolate peach—"

"No, no, no &$%#@& (random Korean)," Chopsticks in-terrupted. "It hasselnut mousie wound cake with apicot and peach-ie cuwwent sauce."

"Right, a hazelnut mousse cake with apricot-and-peach currant sauce. Sounds delicious. Let's give Chopsticks and ourselves three loud cheers for a job well done."

Three cheers of victory sounded through the old brick walls of the Row's mess hall and cut through the silence of the abandoned city of Detroit. Big Mama heard their triumphant ovation as she sat on the front bench knitting a sweater. A warm smile spread across her large face like the wings of a bird in flight. Her smile was big like her heart. Without a family to call her own, she had devoted everything to the place most people had seen fit to devote nothing. It was in her nature. The Lord had given her the gift of love, one she shared on a daily basis. Directly behind her stood the Row. Three-stories high, its red bricks faded like red watercolor paint saturated with more water than color, its appearance no longer kept up by the long since departed Fire Department. Two giant garage doors, large enough for fire trucks to roll through, ran to the east of the building. The three hedge animals—a lion, elephant, and turtle—trimmed to lifelike precision by Scissors, stood on either side of the doors and occupied the space between. The front entrance, a small concrete porch with only three steps, hugged the west. High above it were the discolored black letters of the orphanage's namesake, standing straight, save for the W, which tilted on a severe angle so that it resembled a crooked letter E.

"Lordy, Lordy, Lordy, keep the poor souls of Desolation Row in your thoughts and prayers." She stared off into the sunset that had broken through the gloom. "Show them the righteous path and deliver them from the evils of this cold and tired city. Be especially mindful of that boy T.W. He seems the most troubled of all. Show him the light you've shown me, Lordy."

With that she folded her callused black hands into her lap and took a break from her stitching to admire the sun's last streak as it sank behind the abandoned Ford automobile plant. Above her, the shadow from the letters of Desolation Row stretched along the cracked brick exterior, with the crooked "W" trailing behind.

3

The Proletarian Pistol-Swinging Punks of Detroit

WITHOUT THE INTRUSION of Charlies, life at the Row remained fairly uneventful. The men had their chores, schoolwork, and hobbies to keep them occupied, but in times of peace there was also plenty of time for leisure, which gave an orphan ample opportunity to cause trouble. To combat transgression and the temptation of reckless rebellion and youthful angst, T.W. devised *The Cause*, the invisible binding that kept the Row together.

The exact nature of *The Cause* was classified 11. No one at the Row, save for T.W., knew the how or why of its implementation or even when and if it would ever be executed. The men never questioned why *The Cause* was there to begin with nor asked for details pertaining to its exact nature. They simply took solace in its existence, relished in its intangible tangibility, and appreciated having something to strive for even if that thing was as unclear as the future itself. *The Cause* represented the comfort and security that the orphans desperately needed but didn't recognize they needed because they were so used to taking care of themselves. Their future—bleak at best, a hole in the fabric of society—was exemplified by what lay just down the street, the state pen, which was, in a way, no more than an orphanage for adults.

Thanks to *The Cause*, the orphans shared a common camaraderie and stuck together, which was precisely why T.W. had a big wooden sign hung in the rec room with the motto "No Orphan Left Behind" inscribed in bright red letters for everyone to see. The Row was an orphanage, but for T.W. it was much more. It was his place, his institution, his opus, and most importantly, his *home*.

As such T.W. did everything within his power to keep the men from lapsing into transgression. Sometimes this included sending an orphan on classified missions that served no purpose but to keep them occupied, as was often the case with Ray Charles.

"Ray Charles, I need you to find the ghost of Hemingway. I can feel its presence. It's hiding here somewhere. It might help with my writing. Are you up for it?"

"The ghost . . . of Hemingway." Ray Charles gulped and then raised his binoculars high. "For you, sir, *anything*."

Under T.W.'s leadership, the Row functioned like a first-class boarding school where everything ran like clockwork—unlike the tall grandfather clock that stood in the common room, which gave the time, making a thunderous racket at the hours of noon and midnight, but not always accurately, chiming every other hour, but for some reason skipping both the five and the seven, while only occasionally neglecting the nine, and having no qualms with the even numbers. Ray Charles spent over an hour binoculars deep in the clock's gears, attempting to seek out the ghost of Hemingway. The only thing he found was Seafood's secret stash of Twinkies.

T.W. ran the Row so efficiently that it practically ran itself. This left very little for Big Mama to do besides tend to her favorite pastime, knitting. To date she had made hundreds of shirts, hats, mittens, and scarves. As adolescent outcasts, outsiders, delinquents, misfits, hoodlums, and exiles, the children of the Row were cut from many different clothes, but knitted together into one collective unit—The Proletarian Pistol-Swinging Punks of Detroit: Douglas Street Affiliation, Charter #1.

At the request of T.W., Scissors had thrown together a few dozen patchwork biker-gang vests made from pieces of leftover leather jackets scavenged from the dump. Stitched on the back in white letters was the Row's insignia, "PPSP Douglas Street Affiliation" with a picture of a punk rocker with a red Mohawk, sunglasses, and a cross-shaped earring. Once an orphan pledged allegiance to *The Cause*, they were given a vest with their name stenciled on the front, marking them forever a member of the PPSP Douglas Street Affiliation, an orphanhood of thirty strong. Their motto (adapted from The Who) being *I hope I die before I get adopted*, and their pledge *I swear to light my own fire, be my own light, wander the streets far past the place where the pavement ends, play my music loud, wear my hair long, color outside the lines, think my own thoughts, seek answers while questioning everything, shoot from the hip, stick it to The Man, be more punk than norm, and above all else stay true to The Cause.*

The vests, like official uniforms, were worn only on special occasions such as military operations, training exercises, and all matters involving *The Cause*. When not in use they were stored in the orphans' individual lockers on either the second- or third-floor bedrooms. Orphans under the age of ten slept on the second floor, while orphans over the age of ten slept above. Both floors were identical in design, consisting of a large open area that contained two rows of ten bunk beds each. Located on the north end of each floor were large, communal bathrooms, containing five showers, four sinks, three urinals, two stalls, and one long mirror that ran the length of the sinks. On the south end of each floor was a large private bedroom with its own bathroom. T.W. occupied the third-floor room, while the second-floor room was reserved for Scissors.

Ray Charles searched high and low on both floors for the ghost of Hemingway, checking underneath each bunk. He even investigated every square inch of both bathrooms. However, his pursuits ended in vain. The only thing he discovered were cobwebs on his binoculars.

There were two ways to reach the upper floors and three ways to leave them. The easiest method up was by way of a rickety gated elevator that ran sparingly and was prone to stoppages that could last anywhere from a minute, to an hour, or worse, a whole day. While in pursuit of the ghost of Hemingway, Ray Charles was trapped for six hours, causing him to miss both lunch and dinner. As a result, he had to settle for eating a stale Twinkie he had pilfered from Seafood's hidden stash.

The men never used the elevator. They preferred the second route that involved running up one of the two flights of L-shaped stairs that framed both sides of the elevator. However, the men seldom took the same way down as they went up, almost all chose to slide down the two sets of fireman's poles that connected the second- and third-floor bedrooms to the center of the mess hall below. This made for an easy descent whenever the breakfast, lunch, or dinner bell rang, causing a stir of commotion as the men took to the pole like monkeys to a vine.

It was only when the kitchen bell rang consecutively three times—signaling an emergency roll call—that the men took their vests from their lockers, slipped them onto their young shoulders, and then sprang into action. There was only one thing an orphan longed to do besides wear their PPSP-Douglas-Street-Affliction vests and that was grow a thick mustache like Tom Travolta, who according to *Stache Magazine* had a mustache so fine it made his acting look good no matter how poor the performance.

When the men weren't engaged in *The Cause* they were busy having fun. Without the supervision of adults they were free to do what they pleased, all within the confines and limits of *The Cause*, the Row's unwritten doctrine that empowered their rejection of society, kept the chaos of growing up at bay, and prevented the future—that great dismal abyss—from getting in the way of being an orphan.

To bring some order to life's disorder, T.W. instituted daily routines. Meals were served three times a day, Monday through Sunday, with breakfast starting promptly at eight a.m., lunch at noon, and dinner at five p.m. sharp. This schedule was so regular and ran so efficiently that the kitchen bell rang, without exception, on the exact hour, minute, and second of each and every meal call, except, of course, when the men were under lockdown or expecting a Charlie. On such occasions the Row ran on what T.W. coined "military time," also known as T.W. time or TWT for the acronym friendly.

In charge of the kitchen bell was Big Ben, age ten and a half, master of logistics. Unlike his name, Big Ben was not big at all. What he lacked in height, he made up for in his affinity for all things time-related, specifically watches. Both of his arms, from wrist to shoulder, were covered in watches. Pocket watches hung from his belt like a chain. He even wore a giant clock around his neck Flavor Flav style.

The watches were of all sorts, shapes, sizes, brands, and colors, all scavenged from the dump. Big Ben restored, repaired, and synchronized them by the hundreds. The ones he couldn't fit on his body were strewn over his bunk bed, stored in his locker, and tucked away in his dresser. They were gold, silver, pink, blue, and the colors of the rainbow. They came in various sizes, including square, heart-shaped, rectangular, and circular and all makes, including digital, windup, solar, and even calculator.

When Big Ben was not manning the kitchen bell he was out scouring the endless dump for more watches to add to his staggering collection. He was the orphan most likely to have more bling than the entire entourage of local rapper The D, who reportedly had more gold in his mouth than Fort Knox and sang such hits as "Drivin' Down Douglas Street Wit My Shorty," "I Ain't Afraid To Get Mine With A Nine," "I Sing It Like I Bling It," and "Detroit's Down Wit Da D."

Each day Big Ben painstakingly made sure that all his watches ran on the same time, spending the better part of his morning winding, tuning, adjusting, and tinkering the forty plus watches of his wardrobe. Unfortunately, he never bothered to sync all their alarms and as a result a part of him was constantly ringing or sounding off throughout the day.

While on the hunt for the ghost of Hemingway, Ray Charles was startled not once, but twice, by the ringing of Big Ben's alarms, causing him to jump with fright. "Jeez Louise, Big Ben! You scared the Hemingway out of me."

All the men were homeschooled by T.W., attending classes in the morning from nine to noon and in the afternoon from one to four, Monday through Thursday. As an avid supporter of the proletariat, T.W. was a firm believer in a three-day weekend. All time outside of class was dedicated to chores, character building, playing games, and independent study or what T.W. liked to call AFTC—Activities For *The Cause*.

Big Mama had originally taught the classes, but since she was unable to read anything other than the Bible and had trouble counting past her fingers, it fell to T.W., an ardent scholar, well-read poet, and aspiring writer. His first order of business was reformatting the curriculum, adding to the basics of reading, writing, and math a few courses more befitting *The Cause*.

Such pedagogy included Armaments, Practical Uses of the *Communist Manifesto*, How to Chuck Norris Your Way Out of Any Situation, What to Expect When You're Expecting a Revolution, An Orphan's Guide to *The Art of War*, How to Dismantle Societal Norms, A Braver Brave New World, Civil Disobedience Obeyed, Revolution for Dummies, An Orphan's History of the United States, Chicken Soup for the Soldier, Starting Fires with Imagination and Burning Down Walls with Discontent, and Hemingway— The Man, the Myth, and the Model in Which to Live by According to *The Cause*.

These classes were seen as electives and each orphan had to attend at least one per semester. Only one student had taken all possible classes related to *The Cause*, the ever steadfast Scissors, who as T.W.'s second-in-command also took charge of monitoring grades, tallying marks, and tracking progress of the men. A close second was Ray Charles, who blithely struggled with his basic studies, let alone the advanced ones, but would not be slowed by reason, caution, or in his case, common sense when it came to all things academic, doubling, sometimes tripling his course work, and as a result, spent most of his free time with his binoculars in a book.

Even while chasing the ghost of Hemingway, Ray Charles never faltered from his studies. He read and walked at the same time, which caused him to run into multiple orphans, who responded with shouts of "Hey, watch where you're going Ray Charlies!"

Since T.W. taught all classes he was the only orphan exempt from taking any. It was only his junior officers, namely Scissors, Muscles, Chopsticks, and his first lieutenant, The Wiz, who, after meeting T.W.'s approval, were also given the freedom to teach a class of their own creation, only after it received T.W.'s official seal of approval, of course.

Scissors developed a class solely devoted to all 457 and counting acronyms developed by T.W. It was appropriately called ARPP—Acronyms of the Row: Past and Present. So far in its creation, only one student besides both Scissors and The Wiz had come close to mastering the entire content. That was Ray Charles, who after taking the class four times, broke the 400 mark but got hung up on the likes of CUBAN, Charlie U

Better Avoid Now and CIGAR, Charlie in Guise and Ready.

Sometimes Scissors and T.W. spoke only in acronyms, much to the confusion of the men. "Scissors, TMO PFD UFN," which translated to "Scissors take the men out, practice formation and drills until further notice."

Muscles created a weight-lifting/fitness class. Lacking the proper equipment, he fashioned his own using household supplies and scraps from the dump. Dumbbells were made by duct-taping two gallon-sized canned food containers to a broken broom handle. Squats were accomplished by lifting a pulley attached to a motor of a '57 Chevy. Exercise bikes were created from, well, actual bikes. Used telephone lines became jump ropes, the rims of large bike tires became hula hoops, and discarded monkey bars became pull-up bars. Muscles also developed his own unique exercises that included the couch roll, bowling ball shot put, the tractor tire toss, the refrigerator lift, and the ever popular junkyard dog sprint where orphans raced from one end of the dump to the other while avoiding the snapping jaws of the four Dobermans—Rabies, Sick Boy, Snaggle Tooth, and Sir Barks-a-Lot.

Chopsticks organized his own culinary class that most of the orphans avoided because it was so demanding and involved more cleaning than actual cooking. Lacking an ounce of patience in his bones, Chopsticks was quick to give harsh criticism, with both his tongue and his wooden spoon. Orphans often left his class with low self-esteems and bruised, battered hands, arms, and the occasional face.

"I cook, you chop. I fwy, you cwean. Understand?"

A misunderstanding resulted in a swipe from his wooden spoon—*Whack Whack.*

"You burn macawoni. Unbewebable!"—*Whack Whack.*

"You call that omewet!"—*Whack Whack.*

"I say Balsamic Binegar, not sweet and sower!"—*Whack Whack.*

"I say two cup fower, not one!"—*Whack Whack.*

So far the only student to make it more than halfway through Chopsticks's course was Ray Charles. This only after receiving 321 whacks and breaking two of Chopsticks's wooden spoons on his binoculars. Seafood lasted only a day and was banned from the kitchen forever—"foweber"—for eating more than he was chopping.

The Wiz didn't really teach any classes, but his laboratory, located on the third floor above the rec room, was always open to any orphans willing to dedicate themselves as test subjects for experiments aimed towards the betterment of *The Cause.*

Much to his disappointment, Ray Charles was not allowed access to The Wiz's lab while in pursuit of the ghost of Hemingway. He tried sneaking in through the ventilation system, but The Wiz was one step ahead of him and had electrified all vent grates. Ray Charles brushed against one with the ends of his binoculars and got a terrible shock. After that, he started to think perhaps some ghosts were best left undiscovered.

The Wiz's most loyal test subject was Crash Test Dummy, aka Crash, age nine and a half. Keeping with Row protocol for safety, Crash always wore a thick helmet but still suffered multiple concussions. The exact number of them unknown thanks to concussion-related memory loss. Crash was the orphan most likely to forget that he was an orphan.

Crash was always the first to volunteer for anything dangerous and *Cause*-related. This included being shot out of a homemade cannon, jumping off the roof while wearing a pair of shoes with springs attached to the bottoms, firing the first ever semiautomatic potato gun, and eagerly drinking The Wiz's first batch of Super-Orphan Serum and doing the same for the second batch, despite the first one making him break out in hives and swell up like a balloon.

Since no classes were held on Friday, it was reserved for chores. They were upheld on an honor system and maintained by bartering marks. Every Sunday of every week, Scissors clipped various clothespins, each with the name of an orphan stenciled on it to a specific chore posted on a giant billboard. The chores were rotated on a weekly basis so that no orphan was stuck doing the same job consecutively.

The men often traded their marks to get out of an undesirable chore like dishes, cleaning the bathrooms, or the least favorite of all, sorting socks. This unflattering chore was done in the sock room, located in the basement next to the laundry room. It contained the world's largest pile of unmatched socks, numbering in the tens of thousands and coming in a myriad of colors, shapes, styles, and sizes. Once displaced at the dump, the socks were now stacked on top of each other like massive piles of leaves. It was the orphans' job to sort through their numbers in the hopes of finding mates to be put aside for *The Cause*.

There were so many socks that it was possible to get lost crawling through the endless mounds, which was exactly what happened to Ray Charles while trying to find the ghost of Hemingway. He managed to get so buried and turned around that it took him twelve hours to find his way out.

Scavenging the dump was the favorite chore of all. Normally it was a three orphan job, but could easily employ a whole platoon if needed. One orphan was the designated lookout, keeping a keen eye out for the troublesome Dobermans who threatened to make dog food out of an unsuspecting orphan's behind. Another orphan was the seeker, always looking for new treasures, loot, junk, or anything worthy of *The Cause*. The third orphan was the mule, in charge of retrieving the loot and carrying it back to the Row.

Most of the discovered loot was either broken or didn't work properly. These were taken immediately to The Wiz's lab. Next, they were restored, patched up, and renovated by The Wiz before being inspected by T.W., who decided whether something was to be donated to the rec room or put aside in the attic for *The Cause*.

All men who brought back loot worthy enough were given marks for their efforts, with an emphasis on quality, not quantity. At the end of the month, Scissors tallied up all marks, and the orphan who received the most marks was named Orphan of the Month (OM)—all commanding officers, including T.W. himself, were exempt.

The perks of being Orphan of the Month included getting first dibs during all mealtimes, being excused from all chores, having access to The Throne, the most comfy and sought after recliner in the rec room, and, most importantly, permission to wear their PPSP-Douglas-Street-Affiliation vest at all times for the entire month.

So far, since its conception, Crash had held the title of Orphan of the Month the most, with a grand total of five, none of which he had any recollection of thanks to multiple concussions, while only three orphans had yet to esteem to such a level of distinction. Seafood because he was too lazy and didn't care, Peanut Butter because he was too young, and Ray Charles because he tried too hard.

Ray Charles had come close on many occasions but was always outdone by other orphans. One time Crash volunteered to test-drive The Wiz's first ever rocket-propelled skateboard and succeeded in being the first orphan to top 100 mph, before crashing into a row of trash cans and receiving concussion number thirty-something. This trumped Ray Charles's effort of taking inventory of the entire kitchen and pantry. Ray Charles desperately hoped that turning up the ghost of Hemingway was his golden ticket to the top.

The Orphan of the Month competition provided much needed distraction, but it was the dump that provided the Row with many of its necessities. When things went out of style in the rest of America, they went in style at the Row.

The advent of DVDs and CDs created a large stockpile of bulky VHS videotapes and cassette tapes. The rec room library was crammed full of large collections of made-for-TV movies, which were canceled shortly after production, starring none other than Tom Travolta. These hidden jewels ended up in the dump almost immediately after being released and included such classics as *Killer Cauliflower, The Prince of Tires, Nazi Werewolves in London, Triassic Trailer Park,* and *How I Met Your Mistress.*

Movies were watched through a VCR connected to twenty-four TVs of various shapes and sizes stacked on top of each other in a Tetris-like fashion so that they formed a large rectangular movie-theater-sized screen. The Wiz developed a device that synchronized the TVs into one giant screen, allowing a movie to be viewed like a large, completed puzzle.

Besides VHS movies, there were every Atari and original Nintendo game imaginable and a large collection of cassette tapes, eight-tracks, and vinyl records that included the rare catalog of Bob Lennon—thought to be the illegitimate son of either Bob Dylan or John Lennon, but named after both. His popularity in America lasted only a short while, peaking for a span of five days in the 1980s with a Hot 100 hit song "I Just Ain't That Good," which reached number ninety-nine before being knocked off the charts by an instrumental jazz number and never heard of again, at least in America.

He later went on to make it big in Iceland, where he was more popular than Elvis and sold thousands of records to a country with a population less than half a million. His twenty-seven album collection, spanning over twenty years, included *Bob Lennon Sings Christmas Songs for Hanukkah, The Crimes They Are a Stealing*, and the verbose *I Was Never One for Complaining or Crying Much But You Don't Know How It Feels to Be Me So You Got to Listen to What I Have to Say Before I Walk Away and Don't Look Back Again, Baby Blue*.

The men ate up Bob Lennon like blueberry pancakes for breakfast and were particularly fascinated with such classics as "Who's My Father," "Some Days I Feel Like an Orphan," "I Was Born and You Were Gone," and "I Grew Up Without You." Ray Charles managed to come across a limited edition copy of the bittersweet "Mama Said You Died in a Car Accident," while on the lookout for the ghost of Hemingway.

For most hours of the day, the men were free to do as they pleased. From six until midnight, midnight being the designated lights out, the Row and the rec room were alive with activity as the men played games of pool, darts, foosball, table tennis, and high stakes poker, using marks, buttons, and pins as poker chips.

The Wiz and T.W. partook in a yearlong chess match that had yet to be concluded. At a stalemate, each had lost two pawns, one knight, one rook, and one bishop, but had failed to gain an advantage. Sometimes it took a whole month for one of them to decide on a move.

On special occasions, the Row's standing magician The Ace of Spades, age eight and three-quarters, did free magic tricks. Besides the usual card tricks—almost all involving the ace of spades—he pulled a dumpster chicken from a hat, made marks appear from behind an orphan's ear, and performed outlandish escape acts. The Ace of Spades was the orphan most likely to commit the largest reappearing act ever by putting the orphan city of Detroit back on the map again.

In bouts of boredom, the men often played games of Simon Says, with T.W. acting as Simon, giving facetious commands such as "Simon says truffle shuffle" or the mundane "Simon says jump on one foot" to the grand "Simon says start a . . . *revolution*." This became troublesome when on a sarcastic whim, T.W. said "Simon says find me the fabled and rare *E.T.* Atari game." Ray Charles, who was not only born with the sight of a bat but also the inability to detect sarcasm, took T.W. literally.

Hoping to kill two dumpster chickens with one stone— seek out the *E.T.* Atari game *and* the ghost of Hemingway— Ray Charles ended up MIA for two whole days, causing everyone at the Row to fear the worst, that he had been adopted. However, Ray Charles arrived back at the Row out of breath, dehydrated, five pounds lighter, covered in grime from head to toe, and missing a chunk from his bottom thanks to Sir Barks-a-Lot.

"Good God, man," T.W. said, "you look like you've been dipped in mud."

"I suppose so, sir."

"Where have you been? We feared the worst, Ray Charles."

"Sorry, sir. I wasn't able to find the ghost of Hemingway, but I did find the *E.T.* Atari game. It took me two days, but I finally found it buried beneath a couch and next to a copy of Vanilla Ice's *Greatest Hits*, which I gathered as well despite it only having two-and-a-half songs."

T.W. having no recollection whatsoever of giving an order to find an *E.T.* Atari game was beside himself, unsure whether or not to praise Ray Charles for his valor or give him a slap upside his binoculars. He thought on it for a second before saying, "Alright then we'll take it for *The Cause*. Scissors will give you an extra ration of candy cigarettes and ten marks."

Ray Charles was ecstatic, but later disappointed when the Orphan of the Month went to Poop Stain for an individual act of bravery in the face of danger—he was the first orphan to snare a small group of dumpster chickens with a rope and use them to fly away from the dump, securing his escape from the four Dobermans who had him trapped on the roof of a VW bus.

Poop Stain got his name thanks to a large birthmark in the shape of Florida on his forehead. In fact, he had more birthmarks than skin, so many that his body appeared tattooed. He was the orphan most likely to play the role of the Soviet leader Mikhail Gorbachev in a future Hollywood biopic.

During the following month, Ray Charles looked at Poop Stain with envious eyes, wondering when it would be his time to shine—to fly as T.W. so often proclaimed—and wear the crown of Orphan of the Month.

Also disappointed in not finding the ghost of Hemingway, Ray Charles brought the matter before T.W.

"I've looked everywhere, sir. It's not at the Row. It must be elsewhere."

"Nonsense." T.W. took a seat at his desk and ran his switchblade comb through his hair three times. "It's right there, on my desk. Where it's always been."

"But, sir, I don't see anything." Ray Charles adjusted his binoculars, hoping to catch a glimpse of the ghost of Hemingway.

"It's my typewriter. Hasn't worked for me in months. I'm telling you it's haunted."

"Oh . . ."

T.W. sensed Ray Charles's disappointment. "It was a good effort, kid. Don't worry about the Orphan of the Month. I'm sure you'll get it next time."

Ray Charles raised his binoculars high and saluted. "Yes, sir!"

At the Row there was always time aplenty, mingled with a little bit of hope. But no matter how good the times were, the men had to remain vigilant and keep their eyes peeled for any possible Charlies or outsiders who might threaten their world.

4

A Day in the Life of a Revolutionary

ON A TYPICAL DAY T.W. woke up at 6:30 a.m. sharp. By 6:45, Ray Charles brought in his first cup of coffee with a fresh Danish from the kitchen. From seven until eight, T.W. wrote, or as of late, attempted to write. Suffering from a bad case of writer's block, he mostly looked out the window, staring into the empty street for inspiration, while shuffling through the 364 pages of his unfinished novel.

He was beginning to wonder if he even had any story to tell. There was something inside of him yearning to come out, but like the city of Detroit it lay dormant to greatness, a vast wealth of potential with nowhere to go. He asked himself, What *would* Hemingway do? And waited for an answer to no avail.

It was the start of the week and so far T.W. had wasted more paper crushing failed pages into tiny baseballs than anything else. He stared into his typewriter and his typewriter stared back into him. Crumbled pieces of paper filled his wastebasket to the brim. His ashtray didn't fare much better. His lack of writing led to an increase in smoking. His office filled with more smoke than the sound of clacking keys. It also left him in a mood. One that was evident on his sour, pensive face, but not apparent to Ray Charles who had an ability to overlook the obvious.

"How's the writing coming, sir?" he asked shortly after 7:30, bringing T.W. his second cup of coffee.

"How does it look like its coming?" T.W. blew smoke towards the overfilled trash basket. So far this morning he had managed to write three words and smoke four cigarettes.

"Well, I can't see all that well, sir. Let me adjust my binoculars."

"Don't bother, Ray Charles, isn't there some place you're supposed to be?"

"Well, yes, sir. I'm supposed to be right here tending to you, sir."

"Well then, Ray Charles, why don't you tend to the wastebasket and my ashtray? They both appear full and then go tend to yourself."

"Yes, sir, I will get right on it."

Ray Charles was so keen about his newfound purpose that his feet ran ahead of his binoculars, causing him to walk right into the wastebasket and spill crumbled pieces of paper all over the place so that they scattered arbitrarily on the floor like spent golf balls at a driving range.

"Good God, Ray Charles. Can't you see I'm trying to work here?"

"Yes, sir, sorry, sir," Ray Charles apologized, though he could barely see anything in front of him. He was already on his hands and knees picking up the strewn pieces of paper. With nothing better to do, T.W. pulled out his switchblade comb and ran it through his hair three times while he watched Ray Charles work, or rather attempt to work. For every two pieces of paper he deposited back into the basket, he misjudged another, dropping it back onto the floor. A job that would've taken a normal orphan only a minute to accomplish took Ray Charles ten.

By the time Ray Charles finally left his office, it was two minutes to eight, almost time for the breakfast bell to ring. With only a few minutes left of solitude, T.W. sat back in his chair and broodingly thought about what was causing his inability to write.

What would Hemingway do? Most likely go on a bender, T.W. thought, but he didn't have that luxury. He was too young for one, and two, he had too much responsibility to resort to such digressions. Some storms just had to be weathered.

T.W. stood up from his chair just as the morning bell rang. Once out the door, he placed a cigarette behind his left ear. Just outside his office he stopped next to a large, metallic door and tried the knob to make sure it was locked and secured. Behind the door was a set of stairs that led to the attic where all things pertaining to *The Cause*, the glue that kept the place together, were stored. No one had stepped foot up there, save for T.W. He had the only key. For safekeeping, it was fastened to a necklace that was wrapped around his neck at all times.

T.W. walked with a purpose towards the large open third-floor bedroom and was met by a whole slew of men finishing up the last motions of making their beds, tidying their lockers, and folding their clothes. The ones that saw him coming stopped to salute, calling out, "Morning, sir!" before disappearing down the fireman's pole to the mess hall below.

Without breaking his stride, T.W. grabbed ahold of the pole with his left arm, snaked his left leg around it, and then descended. In a matter of seconds he reached the bottom of the mess hall. As soon as his feet hit the floor he walked towards the chow line, all the while pulling his switchblade comb from his pocket and running it through his hair three times.

As he approached the line, the men scattered from his path like leaves from a leaf blower, allowing him to reach the front of the line without waiting. Chopsticks, decked out in a stained apron and wielding a wooden spoon, greeted him.

"What's on the menu today, Chopsticks?"

"Your faborite, Frenchy toast with maple sywup and bacon."

"Very good. I'll take two slices of French toast, light on the syrup and heavy on the bacon."

"Berry well, sir."

Chopsticks did as he was instructed and T.W. walked away, jabbing a piece of crispy bacon into his mouth. He picked a place to sit at random. There was no assigned seating, so the men always gravitated to where he sat. Within seconds of finding a seat, Ray Charles approached him, double fisting an orange juice and a coffee.

"Sir, here is your juice and coffee. Would you like anything else?"

"No, Ray Charles. Go get yourself some food, you look ravished."

"I didn't think you'd notice, sir," Ray Charles said, almost beside himself and beaming like a flower before the sun. As always, he misread T.W.'s offhand observation for a compliment. Ray Charles made for the food line, and before T.W. could take his first drink or first bite, both Scissors and Muscles joined him.

"Morning, sir," they said in unison.

"Morning, men. How goes it?"

"Very well, sir," they said together.

"Good, let's dig in."

Like trained dogs, Scissors and Muscles lifted their forks and dug in. Their faces hung over their plates, while their right arms worked like cylinders, stopping only to wipe their mouths with a napkin or to take a quick drink from their orange juice. While they ate like machines going through the motion, T.W. ate more gradually, savoring his food and chewing more like a marathon runner rather than a sprinter.

By the time he was on his fifth bite, Scissors and Muscles had finished and were licking their plates, and the table was completely full of men, hovering around him like humming-birds next to a feeder. Those who could not find available seating at his table overflowed to the next immediate one. The only orphan indifferent to where T.W. sat was Seafood, who always sat closest to the chow line.

"How many cans are you wearing today, Muscles?" T.W. asked.

"Four, sir—two cans of kidney beans on the legs and two cans of sardines on the arms."

"How goes the workout?"

"Very good, sir. I lifted 253 yesterday."

"Is that an OPB?"

"Orphan Personal Best!" Scissors shouted. The men nodded in agreement.

"Why, yes it is, sir."

"Very good, congratulations. Scissors, give Muscles two marks for OABO."

"Outstanding Achievement Befitting an Officer, roger that, sir!" The men nodded in agreement.

"Alright, Scissors, lay it on me. What's the agenda for today?"

Scissors put down his fork and reached for his clipboard. "Well, sir. First on the agenda, after The Pledge to the Row and The Pledge to *The Cause*, is your first lecture, Freedom Fighting Isn't Free. Will you be teaching it today or am I filling in again?"

T.W. tilted his head and took a swallow from his orange juice. He scratched his chin pensively before answering, "Take it easy today. I can handle it."

"Roger that, sir. After that is . . . let me see here . . . oh right, your next lecture, Lennon vs. Lenin, followed by Where's Walden and then lunch."

"Are we still doing the TMBA?"

"Team Morale-Building Activities, yes sir!" The men nodded in agreement.

"Good. Two Charlies in one month, the troops need a break. Besides they deserve it. Give me a rundown of the activities."

"Right. All afternoon classes are canceled. Free time from one to five. A foosball and table tennis tournament is scheduled with the winners to receive five marks each. Also a junkyard dodge ball tournament is in the works, as well as a scavenger hunt. The Wiz needs new parts for his latest invention. For dinner Chopsticks is preparing country fried chicken, mashed potatoes, gravy, collard greens, and grits, with strawberry shortcake for dessert. At 1800 hours we are to be treated with a new magic trick performed by The Ace of Spades, a spectacle involving fire—he recruited Matches—and supposedly a large cauldron of gunpowder. He wouldn't go into deals, stating the Magician's Code and—"

"The Magician's Code? What in the Hemingway is that?"

"It is a sworn pact to not give away trade secrets, sir. It's very similar to all matters concerning *The Cause*."

"That's jacked up," Muscles chimed in.

"Oh, right, very well, carry on, Scissors."

"Yes, where was I? Oh, after the magic show, Crash will perform his latest stunt. It seems he will be jumping six school buses with his dirt bike."

"Six you say? Is that an OPB?"

"Yes, sir, it is. He jumped four last month."

"Very well, be sure to give him some marks if he's successful tonight—I don't care how many—and give him a few even if he isn't. Boy's got knack and sets a good example for the others to follow."

"Very well. After Crash's stunt we will continue with movie night."

"What movie?"

"Uh, let me see, a Tom Travolta one, I believe."

"Is it *Farmer Without a Crop*?"

"No, sir we watched that one two months ago. I'm pretty sure it's *RoboDoc*."

"A classic, good choice, Scissors."

"Thank you, sir. Chopsticks is popping 10,000 kernels of popcorn as expected and has prepared homemade vanilla ice cream—*baniwwa* as he calls it—for a special late night snack. Shall we have a pillow fight afterwards?"

"Of course, but make sure Big Ben remembers to remove his stash of watches from his pillow. Last time he about blinded—I know poor choice of words—Ray Charles with a smack to the face. Those binoculars are the only thing that saved him. Also remind Crash to wear his helmet. He suffered a concussion last time, number forty-something I believe."

"Will do, sir." Scissors made a note in his clipboard.

"Is there anything else, Scissors?"

"No, sir. That is all for the dailies. Will you like me to take your tray?"

"No, Ray Charles will get it. The lad's as reliable as he is blind."

As if on cue, Ray Charles appeared, standing in formation at the end of the table with a line of maple syrup running down his chin.

"Sir, you called me?"

"Not exactly, but you can take my tray when you're ready and by the way, Ray Charles, they invented napkins for a reason."

"Sir, yes, sir," Ray Charles said, taking T.W.'s tray. He came back a minute later with a stack of napkins and an apple. T.W. took the apple, but gave the napkins a second look. "What in the name of Hemingway are these for Ray Charles?"

"For you, sir. You said napkins were invented for a reason so I brought you some."

"I was referring to *you*, Ray Charles. It looks like you have a maple syrup mustache."

"Oh." Ray Charles smiled at the prospect of having an actual mustache, but frowned when he realized he was the one needing a napkin. He quickly turned around and headed straight to the bathroom, nearly running into two other men on his way.

"That lad sure is *something*," T.W. commented. "Alright, Muscles, in five lead them through the morning pledge. I have a class to teach."

"Yes, sir." Muscles saluted, working on a plate of thirds. Five minutes later he stood up with his chest pointed forward like a gorilla on its hind legs and shouted, "UH-TEN-SION!" At his command, all of the men stood up straight and in perfect formation.

"Prepare for the morning pledge," Muscles belted. Thirty chests swelled and thirty hands shot up to thirty chests, moving in perfect accord like the hands on a clock. Muscles looked to T.W. He nodded his approval.

"Begin the morning pledge."

I pledge allegiance to the Row
To take up arms if it comes to blows
To keep on firing even when out of ammo
To keep my head held high when the fighting is low
To lead while others choose to follow
And to stand my ground, never letting go

I pledge allegiance to The Cause
To be the fastest when it comes to draws
To take it to The Man with fists to jaws
To dig in deep with toenails and claws
To do it for duty not the applause
And to be an outlaw amongst outlaws

With the morning pledge drawn to a conclusion, T.W. broke file and stepped on the table to walk between the rows of his men. He sauntered with his head held high and his right arm behind him so that it was parallel with his shoulders. His black motorcycle boots made low clacking sounds against the silence of the mess hall.

"Alright, men, before I dismiss you I want to share a word. I'm very proud of your efforts of late both for the Row and *The Cause*. These are trying times, with Charlies coming at us in every direction. Each and every one of you has shown a lot of gall and fortitude. So much so, that Hemingway himself would be proud. Now a ten-second moment of silence for Snuggles."

The men lowered their heads. Ray Charles was so worked up that a tear formed out of the corner of his binoculars. After ten seconds, T.W. continued.

"As a show of my appreciation, all afternoon classes are cancelled and in their stead we are having a TMBA, followed by movie night. Morning classes shall continue on schedule. Enjoy yourselves tonight. You've earned it. Muscles and Scissors, they're all yours."

T.W. stepped down from the table and headed to the basement classrooms with Ray Charles at his heels.

"Listen up, men," Muscles sounded. "Poop Stain and Bellyache you have flag duty. Seafood, Toaster, and Super Soaker report to the kitchen for dish duty. Rooster and Mike Tyson wipe down tables. Crash report to The Wiz immediately. Everyone else report to your first hour studies. You have ten minutes. Let's move people, this orphanage isn't going to run itself."

With that, all manner of orderliness collapsed as the group of men dispersed like a dandelion that had been blown to the wind. A ticking Big Ben stood by the kitchen bell, ringing the men into action while Scissors walked the rows of the mess hall taking notes, and Muscles gave shouts of encouragement to men not moving fast enough. By 0900 every orphan was in their designated place—either at their job or in class—leaving the Row as silent as a church in the middle of prayer.

T.W. walked with casual steps, tossing his apple up in the air as he went down a hallway at the rear of the mess hall and past the kitchen, which was equipped with a myriad of shelves, four full-size ovens, three sinks, two dishwashers, a double-door refrigerator, and one large walk-in freezer. At the end of the hallway, he descended down a narrow set of stairs that led to the basement, which housed the pantry where large gallon-sized cans of fruits, vegetables, and soups lined the shelves by the thousands. A wide, poorly lit hallway led from the pantry to numerous closets, a boiler room, weight room, laundry room, where throughout the Row various aluminum chutes ran through the walls like rivers (sometimes used by the orphans as a quick means of transportation) and fed into a giant basket where all dirty laundry collected, and finally the classrooms.

T.W. found his classroom, stood in front of the podium, and began his lecture. Sporadically he pounded the wooden surface for emphasis and paused only to take a bite of his apple. Sometimes he circled the room and stopped in front of one of the eleven men in attendance, staring them straight in the eye and making them feel as if they were the only orphan in the room. His disciples sat enthralled, hypnotized, and motionless in their chairs, taking so many notes that their pencils threatened to start fire to their papers.

"'A man can be destroyed but not defeated,'" T.W. quoted. "'The world breaks everyone, and afterward, some are strong in the broken places.' Now, who said it?"

Ray Charles's hand shot up.

"Yes, Marshmallow."

"Hemingway, sir."

"Very good. 'Freedom is nothing but a chance to be better?'"

Once again Ray Charles's hand shot up.

"Yes, Rooster, what do you think?"

Rooster, age eleven, had long, feathery red hair cut into a Mohawk that looked like a giant flame burning on his head. His skinny legs were like stilts. He walked head first, bouncing forward so that he chugged along like a slow moving train. He had a loud, raucous voice, sounding like a scream when he tried to be quiet and sounding like a bullhorn when he talked in a normal tone. He was the orphan most likely to go deaf by listening to his own voice.

Musically disinclined, the only instrument he played was the kazoo. As a screaming vocalist, he joined forces with Muscles, who played drums on a drum set constructed from empty cans of sardines, Chopsticks, who played spoons, and The Wiz, who played a complicated instrument he created himself that was part guitar, saxophone, piano, and accordion, to form a punk rock group called the Flex Pistols.

They played regular shows at the Row, getting assistance from Matches (pyrotechnics), Scissors (management), and Poop Stain (makeup). Ray Charles was their number one fan.

Unfortunately, the band broke up after only a few performances and cutting a single demo, featuring the track "Kick
Out The Man." Problems first arose when Rooster insisted
on having a kazoo solo after every verse, which in a punk
song meant every ten seconds. "NEEDS MORE KAZOO," he
screamed take after take. By the time they got to take 726,
tempers flared and the other band members decided to dis-
band. The Flex Pistols were officially out of ammo.

"ALBERT CAMUS, SIR," Rooster boomed, causing T.W.
to cringe and rub his ears.

"Well done. 'Freedom is what you do with what's been
done to you'?"

Ray Charles's hand was held so high that it was practically
touching the ceiling. He was squirming in his chair so much
his bottom hovered six inches above the seat.

"Okay, Tea Bag, let's hear it."

Tea Bag, age ten and a quarter, was the only orphan at
the Row not born in the United States of America. Before
crossing the Atlantic, he was one of the huddled, poor masses,
from another United—the United Kingdom—whose family
landed in New York for a better opportunity. His parents
used this newfound opportunity to abandon him at Penn Sta-
tion, where he later stumbled on a train that took him all the
way to Detroit.

At first he was devastated, going from a city of greatness
to one of despair, but after a few months of wandering the
streets he ended up at the Row, where he slowly acclimated
and fascinated the men with an eccentric British accent and
terminology that included such head-scratchers as "where's
the loo," "bugger me," "that's the dog's bollocks," "what a

jammy fella he is, ain't he," and "what a wanker, mate." A lover of Shakespeare, he organized readings, Christmas musicals, and elaborate plays performed in the Row's amphitheater. His current production was *Romeo and Juliet*, though he was still trying to fill the leads. He was the orphan most likely to be knighted and/or adopted by the Queen.

"Let's see, it's that frogger Jean-Paul Sartre, I reckon."

"Good. 'If you want total security, go to prison. There you're fed, clothed, given medical care and so on. The only thing lacking is freedom'?"

Ray Charles was now whimpering like a puppy and held both hands skyward.

"Alright, Peanut Butter, what do you say?"

"Mumble-hmmm-mumble—[one second pause]—Chuck Norris, sir."

For some reason Peanut Butter associated everything relating to freedom with Chuck Norris, who he had a strong fascination with ever since the complete collection of *Walker Texas Ranger* was scavenged from the dump.

"Nope, not quite, Peanut Butter. Anyone else want to take a stab at it?"

By now Ray Charles was panting and sweating profusely, his hand trembling.

"Anyone?" T.W. scanned the room. "Anyone?" Still only Ray Charles had his hand up. "Alright, Ray Charles."

"Dwight D. Eisenhower, sir."

"Very good, Ray Charles. Alright, Mike Tyson here's one for you. 'Real freedom is having nothing. I was freer when I didn't have a cent.'"

Mike Tyson, age seven, had a big head on a small body, so much so that he looked like one of those bobblehead dolls.

His voice was so piercing that it sounded like he had always just consumed a large quantity of helium. He was the orphan most likely to sing soprano in a musical.

"Gee, sir, I don't know." His voice screeched, reaching a decibel similar to nails scratching on a chalkboard.

Ray Charles's hand shot up again.

"Think on it, Mike Tyson," T.W. said.

"Hmmm . . . I don't know, Bob Lennon?"

"I'll give you a hint, think on your name."

This just confused Mike Tyson more. Ray Charles was a volcano ready to burst. "*Your name,* what's your name," he called.

"*Mike . . . Tyson?*" Mike Tyson said.

"Very good," T.W. said. "That's all for today, men. Don't forget your homework assignment. Explain in five hundred words or less why the notion of freedom in the modern world has become more commercialized and politicized, losing its appeal to the common working man when compared to the fervor of the French Revolution or even the highly polarized 1960s. Remember doubled-spaced and there is no excuse for poor penmanship—alright, dismissed."

The men rushed out the door, save for Ray Charles, who had his binoculars deep in his notes. "Sir, I have a few questions on today's lessons, regarding the nature—"

"Save it, Ray Charles. Not today. Go enjoy yourself. 'Any man who can drive safely while kissing a pretty girl is simply not giving the kiss the attention it deserves.'"

"Hemingway?" Ray Charles asked.

"No, Einstein, now go."

"But—"

"I said go, off with you, Ray Charles."

Somewhat disappointed and with his binoculars pointed to the ground, Ray Charles headed to his next class, the one taught by Scissors, Acronyms of the Row: Past and Present, taken for the fifth time.

With the room to himself, T.W. flicked his switchblade comb open, ran it through his hair three times, and then took the cigarette from his ear. Unfortunately, there was no one there to light it for him. It remained unlit as the first student entered the room.

Christmas Story, age ten, was at a young age when he lost his left leg from the thigh down in a car accident that also claimed the lives of his parents. He came to the Row on crutches, but thanks to The Wiz, who constructed a prosthetic leg from materials gathered at the dump, was now able to walk on his own, though with a slight limp. When finished, the prosthetic leg looked just like a lady's leg covered in black stockings. It also came with an adjustable heel that could be lowered or raised to meet his growth spurts. He was the orphan most likely to be whistled at while walking down the street.

"Morning, Christmas Story, how's the leg treating you?"

"Very good, sir. Will you be continuing your lecture on the similarities of Lenin's *The Communist Manifesto* to Lennon's *Imagine*?"

"Why of course."

"Very good, sir, looking forward to hearing it."

The room soon filled up with men and T.W. began his lecture. It went without a hitch. Afterwards, T.W.'s voice was raspy and the men's brains exhausted. Lunch followed.

The day's special was blackened snapper with a tart avocado relish, sweet potato fries, and salted seaweed soup. T.W. ate everything on his plate, save for the soup, which he barely touched. The men ate fast, and hurried to the rec room, eagerly awaiting the day's TMBA.

T.W. stayed behind, savoring his cranberry juice. Moments alone at the Row were rare, so rare that T.W. often grew restless when he had nothing to do. The distant cheers of the men made him smile. He finished his juice, deciding it was time to make the rounds.

He sought out his officers first, finding Scissors trimming the hedges out front, Muscles in the weight room doing reps, The Wiz in his lab buried in research, Chopsticks cursing in Korean as he stirred his latest culinary creation, Ray Charles in the rec room combing through the library for a new book to read, and Big Mama on her bench knitting a red sweater. T.W. looked down at his own red sweater, with the letters T and W stitched on the front in faded black. Every orphan had a similar sweater, painstakingly sewn by Big Mama, and given to him during their first week at the orphanage.

After covering most of the Row, T.W. headed to the rec room where he found three orphans—Faygo, Compost Pile, and Cup Check—playing dominos. All were decked out in their matching red sweatshirts.

"Hey, it's not your turn!"

"*I'llroshamboyouforit*," Faygo said.

Faygo, age nine, was a skinny, hyperactive lad who tweaked, jittered, and fidgeted like he was on a constant caffeine buzz, which he was thanks to a steady diet of Faygo pop. He liked the caffeinated drink so much he poured it on his cereal and brushed his teeth with it. He spoke so fast his words came together in one long train of thought with little pause or room to breathe. He was the orphan most likely to be an auctioneer.

"How goes it, Faygo?"

"*VerywellsirI'mjustplayingdominoswiththeboysnotdoingso well*"—[paused to take a drink from his Faygo Rock & Rye]—"*SurebeatsgoingtoclassthoughandI'mhavingsomuchfun.*"

"And how are you, Compost Pile?"

Compost Pile, age eight, was the dirtiest orphan at the Row. Since he refused to take a shower or a bath, stating sensitive skin as the culprit, he was always covered in dirt. His hair was so greasy and matted that it formed natural dreadlocks and left a dirty stain on anything it came in contact with, especially his pillow, which he flipped over each night. His fingernails were so caked in grime they looked like someone had drawn on them with a black Sharpie marker. His skin, normally pale, was covered in so much soot it appeared gray, as if he spent the better part of the day in a smokestack. Neglecting to brush his teeth, they were crooked, brown, and rotted like chunks of banana left out in the sun too long. His red sweater was covered in so many stains and filth it appeared more brown then red. It was because of his ripe smell and insalubrious appearance that he attracted a variety of animals from the dump, including a raccoon, opossum, and skunk that he tamed as pets. He was the orphan most likely to live under a bridge.

"Good, sir," Compost Pile said, coughing out a small gray cloud of dust.

"And, Cup Check, staying out of trouble I hope?"

Cup Check, age eight and a half, had big buckteeth, freckles, and a sense of humor best described as unique. As the standing comedian of the Row, all of his jokes had the same punch line—*Cup check!*—followed by a smack to the orphan jewels. Knock, knock. Who's there? Cup check! Why'd the chicken cross the road? I dunno, why? *Cup check!*

He was the orphan most likely to win the World Championship of Chess with a commanding *cup-check-mate.*

"Of course, sir. Wanna hear my latest joke?"

"I'm not going to fall for that one. Carry on, men."

T.W. left them to their game of dominos and circled the rec room, talking to various men. He was first approached by Wheelin' Dealin' Steven, age eleven, who wore a large trench coat and always had something to sell. A walking, talking pawn shop, the insides of his coat were lined with all kinds of gold, silver, and diamond jewelry from watches to necklaces, bracelets, earrings, and rings, all scavenged from the dump and easily available for the right price. He was the orphan most likely to be a used-car salesman.

"T.W., my man, looking good today, looking sharp, but you know what you need? You need something to go with that hip jacket, man. I mean where's the bling? You know what I'm saying? How can you lead when you ain't got nothin' that speaks of greed? You got to represent the Row with something that glows. You know what I'm saying? Now, look what I got here, I got diamonds that'll make Mona Lisa say mommy pleas-uh. I got gold so shiny that it'll make The D say 'sunglass me.' I got watches that'll make it rain like a sprinkler. You know what I'm saying? So check it out, pick something nice for yourself. No price is final and all sales are negotiable. Let's make a deal, baby."

Wheelin' Dealin' Steven then smiled, revealing a mouthful of gold, and opened up his trench coat, exposing row after row of tacky, cheap, and affordable jewelry.

"Impressive," T.W. said, "but not my cup of cranberry juice. Hit me up when you have something befitting *The Cause*, some brass knuckles perhaps."

"Sure thing, boss. I'll be on the lookout for something right up your alley. You just wait and see. Wheelin' Dealin' Steven will take good care of you, anything for *The Cause*. But, hey, by the way I got this—"

T.W. walked away before Wheelin' Dealin' Steven had the chance to rope him into another spiel. He came across the identical twins, Belch and Bellyache, deeply immersed in a game of Contra on Nintendo. With chubby faces, short button noses, and big brown eyes, they looked exactly alike. The only thing distinguishable about them was their hair; Belch had long Lionel Richie Jheri Curls and Bellyache had long cornrow braids.

Bellyache, age nine and the oldest by two minutes, was such a hypochondriac that every day he went to Big Mama or The Wiz with a new ailment. He was the orphan most likely to die of natural causes—a worrying problem. Belch, age nine and the youngest by two minutes, burped so much that he belched all of his words instead of verbalizing them. He was the orphan most likely to win *America's Got Talent* by burping the Star Spangled Banner.

"Belch." T.W. addressed the one with cornrow braids.

"I'm Bellyache, sir. That's Belch."

"Eek-hi, Eek-sir."

"Oh, right, carry on men."

Next, he came across Snot, age seven, playing table tennis with Marshmallow. Unlike Bellyache who thought he was always sick, Snot was always sick, suffering through every ailment and allergy imaginable, which was why they kept him in a white spacesuit reconstructed and modified by The Wiz. Snot always had a runny nose and a terrible cough. He sneezed so much that sticky, slimy goo was constantly covering the inside visor of his spacesuit's mask. As a remedy, The Wiz devised a small, mechanical windshield wiper to clear it away. Snot was the orphan most likely to be adopted by a hospital.

"How goes it, Snot?"

"Very good, . . . cough . . . sniff . . . sneeze . . . sir." Snot sent a fresh glob of slime into his visor. He pressed a button on his suit, causing the mechanical wiper to wipe it clean.

T.W. walked past Snot and came to the chessboard, where he noticed that The Wiz still hadn't moved yet. He was thinking of some possible countermoves when Toaster, age ten, popped out from behind a sofa and startled him. A master of disguise, gatherer of intelligence, and the Row's designated spy, Toaster was always popping out of the least expected places or blending into backgrounds. He had been at the Row for over two months before anyone even noticed he was there. He was the orphan most likely to put the CIA out of business.

"Jeez Louise you scared the Hemingway out of me, Toaster."

"Sorry, sir. I didn't mean to."

Looking for a breath of fresh air and hoping to avoid another fright, T.W. stepped outside. He found Matches hard at work in the backyard.

"My God, Matches, why are you lighting those Barbie Dolls on fire?"

"Well, it's for *The Cause*, sir."

There was no arguing with that. T.W. told him to carry on but thought better of it, and as a precaution called for Super Soaker—also known as the Human Hose—age eight and a half, to stay with Matches. With a seemingly endless supply of hydration, the young lad could spray water like a fire hydrant. His mouth was made for drooling, and he spat whenever he spoke. He was the orphan most likely to spit in the face of authority, both literally and figuratively.

"I'll get right on it," Super Soaker spat, spraying T.W. in the face.

T.W. wiped his sunglasses off as he made his way deeper into the dump. When he was alone, he stared off into the distance of the massive pile of nothing, wondering just how in the name of Hemingway a society could produce so many unwanted things. It was both beautiful and ugly in its scope and size. Somewhere out there, he mused, was a purpose, perhaps a story for him to write.

He stayed there until the kitchen bell rang. Afterwards, The Ace of Spades performed his theatrics, surrounding himself in a ring of flames before disappearing and nearly catching the mess hall on fire in the process. Eyebrows were singed and a table blackened, but thankfully no orphan was hurt. Crash's daring stunt in the junkyard was less dramatic. He easily cleared the six school buses, but crashed while attempting to skid to a halt—concussion number fifty-something.

Movie night followed. All of the tables and chairs in the

rec room were cleared away so that the men could form a giant viewing area made out of pillows. As the lights dimmed, brown paper bags of popcorn were passed around. The men quieted down as the opening credits began to roll. On the screen, RoboDoc stepped into the ER, a stethoscope around his metallic neck and a white apron strapped to his metallic body.

"Did somebody call for a doctor?" he asked in a sexy robotic voice.

"Yes," said a beautiful blonde nurse clad in a uniform showing way too much skin. "Do you need a scalpel?"

"No, I brought my own." RoboDoc lifted his index finger. A scalpel shot out of its end, much to the delight of the men.

"That's jacked up. Tom Travolta sure is something, ain't he Scissors?" T.W. tossed a piece of popcorn into his mouth.

"Sure is. It's a darn travesty he hasn't won an Academy Award."

"I'll second that."

The movie ended in climatic fashion with RoboDoc completing two open-heart surgeries and a liver transplant, while also performing an amputation and delivering a baby. The men gave a thunderous applause—one that woke Big Mama from her slumber. She mistook the commotion for an actual thunderstorm.

"Oh, Lordy, sure is stormy tonight," she whispered then turned over and returned to sleep.

A pillow fight followed. Feathers took to the air and drifted down like lazy snowflakes, while the men rained laughter. The exuberance went on well past midnight and ended only when a pillow filled with Ray Charles's stash of marks connected with Crash's head, giving him his second concussion of the night. T.W. ordered the men to bed, signaling the conclusion of another day. While the men readied for bed, T.W. stayed awake and attempted to write. He did more staring then typing, insomnia another symptom of his writer's block.

5

A Brief Interlude:
In Which Enters The Man

MEANWHILE, IN ANOTHER PART of town, a much more affluent neighborhood, the mayor of Detroit, Albert Sharp, aka The Man, sat alone in his office nursing a glass of scotch. He too, like T.W., suffered from a bad case of insomnia, but not from writer's block. No, it was ambition that kept him awake late at night.

As the Republican (one-time Democrat) mayor of Detroit, it was he who had stripped the Row of its funding, all in the name of budget cuts and a conservative approach to government. Running on the platform of "less dumb government with more *Sharp* business sense," Mayor Sharp was not only pro-business and pro-life, but like most people with a political agenda was pro more-mouths-to-feed, but not pro the-means-in-which-to-feed-them. Whereas the men at the Row were eager to avoid adoption, he was eager to be adopted, namely elected, the public's way of adopting someone to do a job they themselves preferred not to.

Besides an ambitious politician, Mayor Sharp was also a rapacious crook. Starting off as a staunch Democrat, he quickly flip-flopped when the wind favored the other direction. Political allegiances were after all like a pair of shoes, worn for the occasion, and Mayor Sharp wore many shoes. The success of a politician depended on greasing a few wheels and getting a hand or two dirty. Mayor Sharp did it with such ease, shrewdness, conniving, and panache that his crimes were often met with praise instead of criticism.

His popularity was at a steady sixty-five percent despite a recession and massive unemployment. This largely due to his kept-up appearances, outstanding rapport with the community, and innate ability to say and do all the right things while under the close scrutiny of the public eye. Having an estimated wealth close to a quarter billion dollars didn't hurt either.

But what the people loved him for were the simple things they knew about him. Like his passion for baseball—go *Tigers*; the way he demonstrated a commitment to education by being tough on lazy teachers; his appetite for good old-fashioned American hot dogs with extra ketchup, mustard, and onions; his commitment to America—he always wore red, white, and blue; his unwavering support for the church, with charitable donations totaling in the millions; and his enthusiastic, patriotic devotion to the troops whose service and sacrifice he hailed in each and every speech, despite never having served himself.

It was the things the public didn't know about him—the actual truth—that kept their admiration from turning to scorn. Un-American things such as his favorite sport being lacrosse not baseball; his favorite food being tacos not hot dogs; his family business outsourcing more jobs than creating them stateside; his charitable donations, thanks to tax loops, saving him more money than he paid; his extra three years at the university, enrolling in such rigorous programs as Outdoor Recreation and the History of Sports in Perspective, taken solely to avoid the draft of the Vietnam War; and lining his own pockets while supporting cuts to popular programs such as education, Veteran's Affairs, and the homeless.

He was elected on the promise to right the city of Detroit by sweeping it clean of corruption, nepotism, and inefficiency. However, the naive public had unknowingly elected a crook to catch one. He dipped his hand into the state cookie jar and lined his own pockets with the other, all in the name of capitalism, the free market, and the American Dream, and did it all with a smile so warm, genuine, and steadfast that his eyes shone like the sun, the whites of his teeth were like pearls on a necklace, and his face was that of a child's bliss on Christmas morning. There was never a rainy day in the optimism he permeated, only hope, promise, and a guarantee that everything would be all right. In a world filled with uncertainty, the people needed someone or something to believe in.

Ambitious, crafty, and never satisfied, the only time Mayor Sharp didn't smile was when he was alone. It was only then that his face bore the passive calm of a person in the midst of a daydream or contemplating some serious, life-altering decision. At a glance, one would think he was meditating or lost in thought, but in reality he was just plotting. With no one around to bother him, there was no putting on a show, no selling himself, no politicking, no ruse, and no deception. The truth, he was lonely, unhappy, and unfulfilled, but never would admit it.

Born from the bottom, he was always climbing. The city of Detroit would never be enough for him, especially when every four years a vacancy opened in the White House. Once he had his paws in the cash register it was hard not to want the whole bank. Being mayor was just a step towards governor, an even bigger step towards the presidency—his one and only desire. Have it all or have nothing, there was no middle ground.

It was no surprise then that Mayor Sharp's office bookshelf contained only two books. Machiavelli's *The Prince* and Ayn Rand's *Atlas Shrugged*. He read the short-paged former about as religiously as a preacher took to the Bible, but did not have the endurance for the latter. It was there for appearance's sake. A Republican without a copy of *Atlas Shrugged* was like a skydiver without a parachute.

Greed and ambition drove the wheel the world spun on, not notions of fairness. He despised the poor because of what they represented, a glimmer of his past. He hated the Calloways, despite their wealth, because they were his political rivals who represented everything good in the world. Worse than being Democrats, they were honest, guileless, could not be bought or sold, and even worse, actually cared about people, which made them even more of a threat to his political aspirations because in contrast it might become clear that Mayor Sharp cared for no one, but himself.

On the corner of Mayor Sharp's desk was a large facial sculpture of his Byzantine mentor, placed at such an angle that whenever he was in a meeting the cold, penetrating gaze of Alexander III of Macedon stared straight back at him. Dulled by the hands of man and alive only in history and past conquests, the gaze was a daily reminder that power resided in the illusion of people's thoughts and impressions. Alexander the Great carved his empire with his sword. Mayor Sharp did it with his pen.

It was his gold-fitted, felt tip pen that did the stripping of Desolation Row's funds, a bit ironic considering Mayor Sharp was once an orphan himself, the one truth he kept well hidden from the public, doing everything in his power to keep what he perceived as his Achilles' heel a secret. There was only one person who knew the truth about his lineage, Big Mama. In his mind, this knowledge made her a potential threat. A smooth path to the presidency more than likely depended on removing her from the picture. So he decided her time would come.

Thus shortly after he had been elected mayor of Detroit the funds slowly tapered away from Desolation Row to eventually end completely. The money still appeared visible on paper in the form of ink, but in actual monetary purposes went straight to Mayor Sharp's reelection campaign, unbeknownst of course, to the taxpayers, the orphanage, or anyone else not associated with his inner circle.

As a millionaire, Mayor Sharp didn't really need the money, but he took it anyway. It was just part of the job he told himself. Getting to the White House was not cheap and along the way sacrifices had to be made for the greater good. Alexander the Great did not forge his vast empire on the principle of giving without taking. No, he took what was there for the offering and gained control of the world in the process.

In his own way, Mayor Sharp intended to do the same.

6

Out of the Woods
There Came a Squirrel

HE WAS NOT ALWAYS a Squirrel, but it was a name that quickly stuck. Born Earl Leonard Gapinski, it wasn't until the age of three, after his parents decided parenthood was not in the works for them, that he received the name that would remain his calling card.

His parents, Dale and Sunshine, suffered from a disorder known as selfish stupidity, a condition enhanced by the use of LSD and copious amounts of Pabst Blue Ribbon. Both had big ambitions, none of which involved raising a three-year-old. A child like Earl only got in the way of their hopes and dreams of living in a 1956 VW van down by the river. To solve their quandary, Dale came up with the bright idea of leaving poor, young Earl in a dumpster, but in a moment of humanity uncharacteristic of her, Sunshine thought it better to leave the boy in Detroit with her senile grandmother, Maege Mackie.

Dale and Sunshine showed up at Maege's dilapidated brown-and-yellow trailer, hoping to find her out playing bingo or doing whatever it was that seventy-year-olds did for entertainment. Unfortunately for them, Maege was at home, sipping a Stroh's, her beer of choice. Suffering from the early stages of Alzheimer's, Maege was pleasantly surprised to discover she had a granddaughter, let alone a great-grandson.

"Sara, you say?" Maege asked, answering the door.

"No, *Sunshine*, Grandma. This here's Earl." She pushed the boy forward. He was just barely three, dressed in a dirty diaper and nothing else.

"*Squirrel*! Where? Don't let 'em in the house. I'll get my broom."

"No, no, *Earl*, your great-grandson."

"Oh, why didn't you just say so?"

Maege let them into the house, offering fresh Stroh's, even to Earl, who declined but accepted some milk instead. Sunshine didn't stay long, citing an emergency (they were out of Pabst Blue Ribbon). When she didn't return hours later, young Earl became agitated and started to cry. As the tears fell down his cheeks, he comforted himself by sucking his thumb.

Maege, who had a memory with more holes than Swiss cheese, took no notice and had completely forgotten about her granddaughter ever being there. She mistook Earl for her long deceased husband, Marty.

"You need to fix the dishwasher, Marty. It's making funny noises again."

"Marty, get me another Stroh's from the fridge, will ya?"

Earl, who was told to be quiet at all times by his parents, had yet to develop a talkative spirit. His articulation was on par with a dog's. He attempted to mumble his name Earl, but it sounded more like his great-grandmother's earlier mispronunciation.

"A *Squirrel* you say? Where? Let me get my broom?"

The boy shook his head and pointed to himself.

"Oh, you're Squirrel. Shucks, why didn't you just say so?"

The name stuck, and it was a fitting one seeing how squirrels gathered nuts and Maege, suffering from a mild case of dementia, was a little bit nuts herself. She was not the most qualified person to raise a young boy like Squirrel, but compared to his parents she was considered an upgrade.

Through the years, old age had caught up with Maege. Her toothless grin now filled with yellowed dentures, her pasty skin covered in liver spots, her hair a botchy white, sparse and permed, her face a desert of wrinkles, and her skinny frame a stack of bones and skin. Years of smoking left her lungs black and drinking left her liver a dried out sponge.

Despite having to breathe out of an oxygen tank and repeated warnings from her doctor to quit smoking, Maege still huffed a pack a day, using her left hand to remove the mask from her face and the right hand to jab a cigarette into her mouth, all the while completely unmindful of the explosive oxygen tank at her feet.

Arthritis had done a number on her bones and joints, making movement a painful endeavor. To compensate, Maege rode everywhere in an electric scooter, mostly to the corner store to get her medication in the form of Lucky Stripes (her pain reliever of choice) and a case of Stroh's (her water of choice).

She spent most of her time in front of the TV, her only hobby, watching her soaps, the news, commercials, and sitcoms she found funny, despite not getting most of the jokes. Her daily exercise involved walking to and from the refrigerator and occasionally the bathroom, depending on whether or not she wore her Depends.

It was from Maege's hobby that Squirrel became well versed in the English language. Every day he sat in front of the screen, absorbing the words and honing his vocabulary. Within weeks he put his new found language to practice, fetching various items from the fridge he learned from commercials—Stroh's being the most frequent. He also became adept with the microwave—Maege's form of cooking—learning how to heat up Tombstone Pizza, Campbell's Tomato Soup, Oscar Mayer Weiner's, Chef Boyardee Ravioli, and making Spam sandwiches.

By the time he was six Squirrel was self-sufficient. Doing all of the cooking and household chores including laundry, dishes, vacuuming, sweeping, and dusting. Some days, he even went to the corner store to buy Maege more cigarettes and Stroh's, using her driver's license for an ID.

Besides trips to the corner store, life was pretty uneventful. They watched TV and ate microwavable dinners and hardly ever left the house save for once a month to cash in Maege's Social Security check and grocery shop at Save-a-Lot. It was only when Squirrel discovered Marty's old paintbrushes and oil paints put away in a shoebox buried deep within the closet that life became interesting.

Marty was never much of a painter. His artistic ability fell somewhere between scribbles and stick figures. He only came across the paint supplies after winning them in an all night poker game, defeating some artist—a then unknown Bob Lennon—hitchhiking his way to New York City. After finding little success in trading the supplies for beer—Marty's preferred currency—he stuffed them in the closet, where they collected dust until Squirrel stumbled upon them many years later.

He found them by accident, digging through the closet only because he was in need of a metal hanger to place on the TV antenna, which had lost its signal. After pushing aside a pair of bowling shoes, Squirrel found a black cardboard shoebox gray with dust. He wiped the filth off with his hand, coughed when it spread to his nostrils, and then opened the box with a sense of wonderment.

A tingling sensation, like electricity coursing through his veins, ran up his hand as he grasped one of the wooden brushes. Without his even realizing it, his hands acted with an intrinsic will of their own and began to open containers of paint. Soon a rainbow of colors covered the lid to the shoebox. From there, he moved to the closet, and then the rest of Maege's bedroom. He soon forgot all about fixing the TV and entered his own world filled with colors and alive with imagination. A good two hours had passed, when Maege finally realized the boy was missing. This only because her Stroh's was empty and her throat thirsty.

"Squirrely, where ya at? I need a new Stroh's. Squirrely?"

When the boy didn't respond, she waited a few minutes before getting up and fetching one herself. Feeling the need to make water and not wearing a Depends, she made her way to the bathroom and was surprised to see a mural of gaudy butterflies on the door. She discovered the painted green face of a crocodile on the toilet seat. "Oh my." She looked down at her Stroh's. "I must've had more than I thought."

She found Squirrel standing on her bed, painting birds on the ceiling fan.

"Squirrely, what in the world are you doing?"

"Oh nothing, just adding some color to the place."

"Well then, why didn't you just say so?"

She returned to her soaps, leaving Squirrel to his paints. He painted for the next three days straight, covering all of the walls, doors, and ceiling of the trailer with vivid images and colorful backgrounds, only stopping when he ran out of paint. Sometimes Maege took a break from TV to stand in such awe of his work her dentures nearly fell out of her mouth. She was so inspired that she took to doing all of the cooking and chores herself, even spoon-feeding Squirrel, so he could continue painting without any intrusion.

When both of them finally ran out of supplies—her Stroh's and him paint—they decided to make a special trip to Save-a-Lot to stock up. Maege left her frugal side at the trailer door, drawing some money from her beer-for-a-rainy-day-fund, so she could buy Squirrel all of the paints he desired, a whole shopping cart's worth.

Squirrel now had all of the paint he needed, but soon ran out of canvas. With every square inch of the inside of the trailer covered, he moved on to appliances and furniture, painting the washer into a pink hippopotamus, the couch into a train, the oven into a fire-breathing dragon, the teakettle into a fiery sun, and the kitchen cupboards into tiny homes for elves who appeared whenever the cupboards opened. After that he moved to the outside, transforming the ugly yellow-and-brown trailer into an ocean of colors. The door became the mouth of a giant whale, the windows the eyes of an octopus, and the front porch part of a wooden ship set to sail between dozens of fish of all shapes and sizes.

Maege sat outside on her electric scooter, watching him work and sipping her Stroh's. Occasionally a car stopped to gaze at the majesty that overtook her rundown trailer. Sometimes three or four pulled over at once.

"Watcha gawkin' at?" Maege called to them. "I don't see a fire!"

The cars sped away, leaving Maege to reflect that she hadn't seen that many people in the neighborhood since the police discovered the Detroit Streaker lived in a trailer just down the street. He was never caught and eventually the crowds dissipated. That wasn't the case for Squirrel. The more he painted, the more the crowds grew.

"Watcha gawkin' at?" Maege asked one particular bystander.

"The house, it sure is beautiful. Whoever painted it did a wonderful job."

"Well, why didn't you just say so?" Maege finished off another Stroh's. The crowds of people continued to grow. In one day alone she counted over twenty cars. It was on her tenth Stroh's of the day that she came up with the bright idea of charging people.

"Gawking ain't free." She held out a tin coffee can with "dough-nations" painted in white paint on the side. "Either pay up or move along."

Soon after, coins and dollar bills poured into her tin can. The money went straight to her beer-for-a-rainy-day-fund, as well as Squirrel's new paint-for-a-rainy-day fund. Business was good, so good that the entrepreneur in Maege decided to expand, charging people a dollar to tour the inside. "Think the outside's an eyeful, wait to you get a load of the inside. No using the toilet though, that'll cost you another buck."

Business was booming and within no time the fridge was stock full of Stroh's and Squirrel had enough paints to cover the entire neighborhood. As Maege put it, life was "flowing like a cold Stroh's on a hot day."

It was only after the trailer was completely plastered in new paint that Squirrel moved on to the abandoned tire factory down the street. He painted the images in his head, the images not in his head, and everything in between, developing a rigorous schedule that included painting four hours in the morning, taking an hour lunch break; painting four hours in the afternoon, taking an hour dinner break; painting four hours in the evening, and then watching a few hours of TV for added inspiration before finally heading to bed.

Maege kept her own daily schedule as well, taking donations and drinking Stroh's in the morning, afternoon, and evening, all before passing out around nine with a half-lit Lucky Stripes in one hand and an half-empty Stroh's in the other.

They would have made a career out of it if not for Social Services, who got a complaint of unsolicited child labor. Maege's short-lived enterprise was shutdown, and Squirrel, at the age of seven, was required to attend school at Detroit Public, the lowest ranking school in not only the state of Michigan, but the country as well. After missing both kindergarten and the first grade, he started the second grade two years behind his peers and unable to read or write.

What he lacked academically, he made up for in confidence and the ability to articulate his thoughts both verbally and artistically. In that regard, he was light years ahead of his classmates, who could read and write, but didn't have the thoughts or ideas to go behind them. He excelled when it came to art and creativity, but as an illiterate he failed miserably at his tests, quizzes, and written assignments, which he completed with elaborate and detailed drawings but no words.

His teachers, dealing with overcrowded classrooms, budget cuts, pay freezes, and a lack of resources, overlooked his deficiencies and pushed him ahead to the next grade each year, regardless of his inability to read or write or perform basic math. So it came to be that at the age of thirteen, Squirrel found himself in the seventh grade as a creative genius with the literacy level of a five-year-old.

Squirrel was far from an exception at Detroit Public, a school so run down and so overcrowded, it even had a combined middle school and high school. Most students suffered terrible test scores, fell below the poverty line, and had only three economic opportunities in the city of Detroit, all beginning with the letter W: welfare, Wal-Mart, or bearing the last name of Wilson. However, he did stick out by appearance's sake.

His only set of clothing was put together from thrift store finds and his deceased grandfather Marty's wardrobe. It involved a plain white-buttoned shirt, a brown paisley-patterned vest, gray trousers, black suspenders, and a bright red bow tie. On his head he wore a black bowler's hat with a white feather in its side. His shoes were buckled loafers, one black and one brown. As a hipster candidate he might have been popular in a fashionable city such as New York or Paris, but in Detroit, a blue-collar city that took hockey more seriously than fashion, he was more of an untrendy misfit.

Despite dressing in the wrong decade, Squirrel carried himself well. His face was dapper and his dark, long straight hair fell past his shoulders. His skin was olive, giving him the look of a young Johnny Depp. He carried in his back pockets his most prized possessions, his paintbrushes. Wherever he went, his right hand cradled a black sketchbook, while the left hung in his vest pocket with only his thumb visible.

At Detroit Public, he was an instant outcast. Boys saw him and laughed, thinking him a freak, while girls saw him and giggled, their eyes and hearts heavy with Hollywood effectuation. Neither one attempted to befriend him. His sketchbook and his paintbrushes were his only companion in the lonely classrooms and hallways of Detroit Public. While other students attempted to take notes or were busy at horseplay, throwing spitballs and paper airplanes at each other, Squirrel covered his black sketchbook in realistic portraits of his fellow classmates.

His most frequent object of affection being a skinny redheaded beauty named Demmie, who sat directly across from him in math class. She was not only beautiful but smart and active, participating in Girl Scouts, the National Honor Society, choir, student senate, math club, the debate team, and running the school newspaper, *The Detroit Public Daily*. Her passion was journalism, her hero Upton Muckraker, chief editor of the *Detroit Free Press.*

As a staunch advocate of reform and harsh critic of nepotism and cronyism, Muckraker had failed for years to stick anything to the very slippery Mayor Sharp, who he suspected of embezzlement and making large illegal profits by importing trash from all over the Midwest and neighboring Canada and using it to fill the rundown and abandoned neighborhoods of Detroit. Demmie hoped to someday follow in his footsteps and work for a big-name newspaper.

Demmie's beauty flowed from her red hair. It was long and curly, stretching down to the middle of her back. When she pushed it over her shoulder it was like watching the wind tangle with the flames of a fire. A small patch of freckles dotted the bridge of her nose and just below her eyes. Her smile was all teeth, plush pink lips, and dimples, while her high cheekbones made her face appear like a tree ripe with apples. Her dazzling blue eyes were like rivers emptying into an endless pool.

Squirrel knew her physical features like he knew the colors of his paint, but he knew nothing of her as a person, having never spoken to her. When around her, it felt like his tongue had been swallowed all the way down to the depths of his stomach, where it jumped about like a fish out of water, rendered useless. He longed to talk to her, but didn't know how.

They passed each other in the hallways and sat close to each other in classrooms, all the while not saying a word and sharing only smiles. Two young love birds unaware of the silent song they were singing.

With only his sketchbook to keep him company, Squirrel was about as popular at Detroit Public as a request for "Free Bird" at a Bob Lennon concert. He sat alone at lunch, rode the bus home alone, and did more sketching than he did talking. It seemed most students preferred detention than being caught socializing with him.

If only his last name was Wilson.

There were so many Wilsons at Detroit Public that it was hard to keep track of them all. They came from a Catholic rich neighborhood where families numbered in the hundreds, reproduced like rabbits, and had an affinity for the letter b, which resulted in a whole slew of b-named offspring. There was Billy, Bobby, Benny, Bob, Bill, Ben, Benjamin, Brandon, Braden, Brian, Blake, Boris, Barry, Barney, Buck, Burt, Buster, and Bird, just to name a few.

All Wilsons, both young and old, had one distinguishable characteristic: they thought themselves better than everyone else. If you weren't a Wilson or related to one, then you might as well not exist. This mentality was passed down from the parents, who thought they owned the city of Detroit, to their children, who thought they owned Detroit Public.

Wilsons came in all shapes and sizes, but shared the same blonde hair, blue eyes, matching crew cuts, athletic builds, and menacing scowls. Each grade at Detroit Public had at least two of them. They dominated all sports team rosters, making radio broadcasts of basketball games a confusing affair.

"Wilson passes to Wilson. Wilson drives in for a layup, misses but Wilson gets the rebound and puts it in. At the other end, that was some good defense by Wilson who passes it down to Wilson who passes it to Wilson who shoots and scores! Looks like we have a substitution, Coach Wilson puts Wilson in for Wilson."

Their political connections in Detroit ran deep. All Wilsons were directly or indirectly related to Mayor Sharp, who married into the family. His wife Betty was the youngest of a family of nine, with eight brothers. Bartholomew, the oldest, was Mayor Sharp's campaign manager. Barton, second oldest, was judge of the Detroit Circuit Court. Brett, third oldest, was chief of the Detroit Fire Department. Byron, fourth oldest, was a member of the Detroit Board of Education. Barret, fifth oldest, was the warden of the Detroit Pen. Baxter, sixth oldest, owned the dump. Beasley, seventh oldest, was the principal of Detroit Public. And Benedict, eighth oldest, was on a Special Task Force for the Detroit Police Department.

The eight brothers all did their part to help grease Mayor Sharp's political machine and all pocketed something on the side. While the city of Detroit suffered, they prospered, creating their own little slice of *Wilsonia* in the suburbs where they had a handful of cruel, unruly, and spoiled children, all attending Detroit Public, with the worst of the litter being Principal Beasley Wilson's own son, Buck. Standing at six foot six and weighing two hundred pounds, he was more giant than boy. Big in body, but small in brains, his greatest achievement at Detroit Public was holding every single record for the Presidential Challenge that included seventy-five push-ups, thirty pull-ups, and one hundred twenty sit-ups per minute.

His teachers were too scared to flunk him, so he skated by on Cs and Ds, most unearned. His highest grade was a B in gym class, which would have been an A if not for failing to keep score in bowling, spending too much time in the penalty box in hockey, and receiving too many yellow cards for flagrant fouls in soccer.

Self-centered and absorbed, he preferred to speak in the third person, saying such things as "Buck don't like you," or "Buck think you stupid," or his personal favorite "Buck gonna pound you into hamburger." He was followed religiously by his four biggest cousins Buster, Burt, Blake, and Bird.

Buck and his minions dished out daily doses of punishment to students not named Wilson. It came in the forms of wedgies, bruises, bloody lips, ripped clothes, and broken bones. Students feared them and did their best to avoid them in the hallways. Squirrel was such a nobody that he wasn't even on their radar. That was until he made the mistake of correcting Buck during history class by stating that President Harry S. Truman used the phrase "the buck stops here," not Woodrow Wilson (a fact he learned while watching *Jeopardy* with his great-grandmother).

When Mr. Brown, the history teacher, backed Squirrel's claim, Buck called him a stupid, unpatriotic moron, who couldn't teach a fish to swim. Buck was given detention. A few weeks later Mr. Brown was denied tenure and asked to seek employment elsewhere.

In one swift motion, Squirrel went from nobody to somebody, all for the wrong reasons. From that day forward, Buck made it his personal mission to harass Squirrel as much as Wilsonly possible. He and his cohorts called Squirrel names, poked fun at his unique fashion sense, covered his hair in spitballs, pushed him into lockers, and knocked his books to the floor. They were as persistent and ruthless as bullies could be, but failed to get a single reaction from Squirrel, who ignored their jabs and physical confrontations by finding shelter in his art.

He retaliated with his pencil, making the Wilsons into humorous caricatures. In comic strip form, *The Wilsons-of-Witches* were a family of fools, a horde of Sloths, a tribe of trolls, and a pack of inbred simpletons who were always outwitted by the protagonist, Super Squirrel and his sidekick Red. This he kept hidden from everyone, especially the Wilsons, who would surely have hung him by his underwear from the school flagpole as they had threatened to do so on many occasion.

As a result, Squirrel kept to himself and his art, that was, until the fateful day that changed everything. The day, like most days of significance, started like any other. Squirrel took the bus to school, thinking it just another uneventful day, while his great-grandmother Maege took her electric scooter to the corner store to pick up more Lucky Stripes and Stroh's.

Maege was in good spirits, having five Stroh's for breakfast. She got her usual case of Stroh's and pack of Luckies and left the store humming a song she no longer remembered the lyrics to. She was halfway home when she lit up a Lucky Stripes, unaware of a tiny hole that had worked its way in the tubing of her oxygen tank. It was on her third pull, and only a block from her home, when the escaped oxygen touched lips with the lit cigarette, causing a massive explosion that shook the entire neighborhood.

One moment Maege was sitting on her electric scooter and the next she was a ball of fire shooting towards the sky. All that remained of the electric scooter was a charred seat and two smoking wheels. All that remained of Maege Mackie was her dentures. Completely unscathed by the explosion, they were sent flying fifty feet, landing on the sidewalk, later to be retrieved by a fireman. It turned out her Lucky Stripes weren't that lucky after all.

Squirrel was in his second to last class of the day when he was called down to the office. Expecting to be greeted by Principal Wilson, he was somewhat surprised to see Chief Wilson of the Fire Department holding a paper bag.

"I'm sorry for your loss," Chief Wilson said, handing Squirrel the bag. "There was an explosion. Your great-grandmother has passed. I'm afraid this is all that's left of her."

He walked away without saying another word. Squirrel reached into the paper bag and pulled out the dentures—all that remained of his great-grandmother. He held it in his hand as tears streamed down his face.

With nowhere to go, Squirrel stayed with Detroit Public's secretary, Ms. Mouse, until Social Services decided what to do with him. Since he didn't own a suitcase, he packed all of his belongings in a pillowcase. The funeral service was short, with only four people in attendance besides Squirrel. The pastor, Ms. Mouse, the liquor store owner, and Douglas Street's own vagrant, Stinky Pete, who looked like he had just climbed out of a dumpster.

After the pastor's words, Stinky Pete poured some of the contents from his paper-bagged bottle in her honor. He even insisted on giving a speech.

"Maege was a good lady. Could drink a case of Stroh's with the best of them. She gave me my first paper bag. I even dated her once in high school, or maybe it was grade school, can't really remember which, but anyways I always thought Marty was the luckiest guy in the trailer park to meet a gal like Maege." He paused to take a pull from his bottle. "It's a shame what's happening to the city of Detroit, Maege. A homeless person can't even be homeless any more thanks to that uppity mayor. The shelter's been closed for over a year now. They're trying to kick us out. I got my second eviction notice on my cardboard box. You believe that? Where's a homeless man to go? The way things are heading I may have to leave the city, take a train south. Lord knows I've been an outsider all my life, but this is almost too much. Oh, well, that's just alcohol out of the bottle. May you rest in peace, Maege. The city's gonna miss you." Stinky Pete finished his bottle and walked back to his shopping cart.

With no immediate family or living relatives, it was decided the best place for Squirrel was Desolation Row. A few days after the funeral, he returned one last time to the multi-colored trailer to pack up the rest of his belongings. He didn't have room in his pillowcase for the large supply of paints so he left them behind, taking his one article of clothing, his collection of paintbrushes, sketchbook, and Maege's dentures, which he placed in an empty glass pickle jar as a keepsake.

He spent one last night at Ms. Mouse's before taking the city bus to the Row. As a parting gift, she gave Squirrel a fresh sketchbook and a card from a student at school. Having no friends, Squirrel assumed it was from the faculty. Since he couldn't read he had Ms. Mouse read it for him.

Squirrel,
I know we've never officially met, but I just wanted to say I'm sorry for your loss. I hope you are doing well. Just remember to keep your head up. If you ever need someone to talk to I'm here whenever you need me. I look forward to seeing you back at school.
Your friend,
Demmie

Squirrel was surprised she even knew he existed. It was a bit ironic. He had finally found a friend, but had lost his family and his home and would be leaving soon to a place he'd never been to be with people he'd never met. Never had his life felt so dismal, very much like the city of Detroit. For the first time in his life, the future was a very scary place.

7

A Meeting of Two Teenagers

"HE'S FIVE MINUTES LATE." T.W. looked out his office window, his agitation clear on his face. Ray Charles stood beside him, adjusting his binoculars. "How are we looking, Scissors?"

"Sir, everything is in order. We received another large package postmarked for the prison—the usual canned goods supply as well as a stack full of letters. Also, the check from the Calloway Estate arrived on schedule and in the usual manner."

T.W. scrunched his face at the mention of the Calloway Estate, the Row's mysterious benefactor, and yanked the cigarette from behind his ear and started twirling it as he paced back and forth.

Scissors exchanged a worried look with Ray Charles and asked, "Do you want me to have The Wiz make a tracking device to put on the Calloway car?

"No. I don't want to spook them yet. We still need their money." T.W. stopped pacing, brought the remains of the cigarette to his lips, thought better of it, and threw it into the trash. "Now, where's Big Mama?"

"Still outside, sitting on the bench and waiting for the newbie."

"Where is he? He should be here by now."

T.W. paced the room. He became antsy whenever things didn't go according to schedule. He was about to pull another cigarette from his other ear but then remembered he didn't want to smell like smoke for the newbie. Good impressions were everything. He pulled his switchblade comb out instead and ran it through his hair three times then said, "Ray Charles!"

"Yes, sir, what is it?"

"Go check on Muscles in the mess hall and make sure he's up to speed with the arrangements for the luncheon. Also, have Chopsticks stock the fridge with lots of Faygo, all kinds of flavors too, tell him it's BTBPTS."

"Better to Be Prepared than Sorry!" Scissors shouted.

"Yes, sir, right away," Ray Charles said.

"Also, make sure to snag a fresh copy of this month's *The Orphan*."

"Sir, yes, sir."

"Scissors, give me another rundown on The Wiz's Intel report."

"Yes, sir. Orphan's birth name is Earl Leonard Gapinski, but he goes by Squirrel."

"*Squirrel* you say? *Like the animal?*"

"Yes, sir."

"Good God, man, with a name like that we won't even have to rename him."

"Yes, sir. Let's see, he's from Detroit. Age thirteen and—"

"*Age thirteen?* When's his birthday?"

"Uh . . . March 12th, sir."

"Good, I thought for a fast minute there he was older than me. Holding rank over someone older would have created a real CCC."

"Contradictory and Conflicting Conundrum, right, sir! Let's see here, Squirrel was raised by his great-grandmother, Maege Mackie, who was recently deceased after a tragic explosion caused by her oxygen tank. No immediate family. He currently attends school at Detroit Public."

"Detroit Public you say? What a joke."

"You know of it, sir?"

"Heard of it," T.W. said, though, hidden beneath his glasses, his eyes begged to differ. "It's a shame about his great-grandmother, though. Perhaps Colonel Sanders can be of assistance."

Colonel Sanders, age twelve, was the Row's chief philosopher and psychologist. Where most people had only five senses, Colonel Sanders had six, his Orphan Sense. He could smell out an orphan just by looking at them. Whenever an orphan needed someone to talk to they came to Colonel Sanders. He took his role so seriously he even superglued strands of white dumpster-chicken feathers to his face to resemble a scholarly beard and wore thick bifocal glasses despite having near perfect vision.

Looking like a younger version of an older Freud, he was always dressed in a brown suit with patches on the sleeves. He was the only orphan besides T.W. who smoked, his preference a corncob pipe. He contributed regular articles to *The Orphan*. Most of his days and nights were spent working on research for a future dissertation on his pending PhD that examined a new subject of study he had created called *psycho-orphanology*. He was the orphan most likely to win a Pulitzer or Nobel Peace Prize or both.

His Orphan Sense was almost always spot-on, though some orphans were harder to spot than others, especially T.W. For some reason Colonel Sanders's nose never itched or twitched when around the Row's fearsome leader. Hoping to dig deeper, Colonel Sanders often asked T.W. if he wanted to talk about his father. To which T.W. replied, "Good, God, man, no. Get a grip."

"Something's off with him," Colonel Sanders mentioned offhand to Ray Charles on one afternoon. "I'm not getting anything with my Orphan Sense."

"Of course not," Ray Charles said, with a self-assured raise of his binoculars. "He's more than just an orphan, he's *The Man*."

"I thought we were supposed to be sticking it to The Man, Ray Charles."

Ray Charles's self-confidence faltered, his binoculars lowered. "Well . . . well . . ." His binoculars rose as the proper response came to him. "He's The Man who sticks it to The Man."

Colonel Sanders let the matter go, but there was a part of him always a little suspicious of T.W. His Orphan Sense never lied.

"Shall I contact the Colonel, sir?" Scissors asked.

"Not yet, we'll wait until after the MG and IAN."

"Roger that sir, Meet and Greet and Initial Analysis of Newbie. I'll—"

Just then Toaster emerged from the office window,

decked out in red-bricked camouflage to match the front of the building.

"Sir, he's here."

"About time. Alright, Scissors, you man the Row while I step outside. If you see Ray Charles tell him to bring me two Faygos on the double and have him make sure they're ice cold. Job well done, Toaster, two marks."

Both Toaster and Scissors saluted T.W. as he walked out of his office. T.W. hurried down the steps and met Big Mama outside. The sun glinted off his sunglasses. Together they watched as a tall, skinny lad with long black hair stepped off a big white bus carrying a pillowcase, sketchbook, and pickle jar.

"Lordy, you made it." Big Mama extended her big, plump hand. "Let me—"

"Here, let me help with your things." T.W. stepped in front of Big Mama and took the pillowcase from the newbie. "Welcome to the Row. The name's Teenage Wasteland, but everyone calls me T.W. That there's Big Mama, the standing adult at the Row. What's your name, kid?"

"Squirrel," he said, taking a bow and giving a curtsy with his bowler hat.

"Well, Squirrel, it sure is nice to meet you. Let's get you inside so I can stow away your things and give you a proper tour of the place." T.W. slung the pillowcase over his shoulder. "I got it from here, Big Mama."

"Lordy, you sure are a go-getter. Thank ya, T.W."

"No problem, Big Mama."

"I got me some stitching to finish up anyway. Don't forget to give him a fresh towel and show him where to put his dirty laundry. That Compost Pile ain't found the washroom or shower yet, and he's been here for over a year now, Lordy."

Compost Pile had actually been there for over four years, all without showering. T.W. motioned for Squirrel to follow him, and together they descended the steps. Squirrel couldn't help but notice the crooked W.

"Is she in charge of the place?" he asked as they entered the Row.

"Who Big Mama? Are you kidding? No way, kid. I'm in charge here."

"But you're not an adult."

"*So what*? I've been taking care of myself since I was old enough to comb my own hair. Just because I'm not an adult doesn't mean I can't run a place. If most adults acted responsibly there wouldn't be a need for a place like this now would there?"

Squirrel nodded in agreement.

"So, this is the common room," T.W. said. "That's Big Mama's office over there and straight ahead is the elevator, but it doesn't work worth a Hemingway so I would use the stairs if I was you. Besides, a little exercise goes a long ways towards *The Cause*."

"*The Cause*? What's that?"

"Yes *The Cause*. Don't worry about it right this second. You'll catch on soon enough. Just know that *The Cause* is the single most important thing at the Row, it's what keeps it all together if you follow what I'm saying."

Squirrel didn't, but he followed T.W. into the rec room regardless. They were joined by Scissors, carrying his clipboard, and Ray Charles, with a candy cigarette in his ear and two Faygos in his hand. He eyed the newbie with suspicious binoculars.

"Squirrel, this is Scissors, my number two." Squirrel nodded and tilted his hat as an introduction. "If you have any questions or concerns, he's the man to see. He'll make sure you get situated and take care of all your needs. He's our most reliable orphan."

"Thank you, sir," Scissors said.

"Don't mention it. Alright then let's continue the tour."

"Ack-hmmm," Ray Charles coughed. He held out two cans of Faygo in what he thought was the direction of T.W., but was in fact a foot to the right.

"Oh, yes, this is Ray Charles, my runner. I hope you like Moon Mist, all we got in these parts is water and Faygo pop."

Squirrel nodded and tilted his hat. Since all Maege had in her trailer was water and Stroh's, he never had the luxury of sweets. He eagerly took the can, his first soda ever. It was sweeter than expected and so tasty he finished it in three swallows, showing his approval with a loud burp.

"Good God, man, you sure were thirsty. Didn't they have anything to drink in your neck of the woods? Ray Charles, take Squirrel's things up to the third floor and when you're finished retrieve another pop for our new recruit."

"But, sir, I—"

"The only butt I'm concerned about is yours moving to the third-floor bedrooms with Squirrel's things, understood?"

"Yes, sir," Ray Charles said begrudgingly.

"And take that candy cigarette out of your ear, it looks ridiculous."

Squirrel kept his sketchbook and pickle jar, while Ray Charles took the pillowcase. It was heavier than expected, causing him to slouch over on the right side and hug the ground like a large, fat child on the low end of a seesaw. He walked away slowly, half-dragging and half-carrying the pillowcase and threatening to fall over with each step. T.W. motioned for Squirrel to follow him, but stopped when he noticed what was in his hand.

"Good God, man, what in the Hemingway is in that pickle jar?"

"My great-grandmother's dentures. It was all that was left of her."

"That's jacked up, but hey, I'm sorry for your loss. What do you plan on doing with them anyways?"

"I dunno, hold onto them I guess. It's all I got to remember her by."

"Right on, follow me."

Squirrel held the jar close to his chest as T.W. led him into the rec room.

"This is the rec room where we keep all the fun stuff like games and whatnot. Feel free to look around during your leisure time. I recommend perusing through the records. We got the best collection of Bob Lennon this side of Chicago. We share everything here so don't worry about putting your fingers on something that's already claimed. There's only one rule we have at the Row and that's there isn't an 'I' or 'me' in orphan."

"You sure could fill a lot of paint on that ceiling," Squirrel observed.

"Sure could. What are you some kind of interior decorator or something?"

"No, I just paint," Squirrel said, removing his paintbrushes from his back pocket. "It's a hobby of mine. I draw or paint most of the time."

"That's good to know, we could use some color around this place. There's not a single artist amongst our ranks. Poop Stain is the closest, but the kid's only specialty is fake tattoos and fake mustaches."

"How many are you—I mean how many orphans are at the Row?"

"Well, with myself included, we're thirty strong."

"Wow. That's a lot. It was just me and my great-grand-mother before."

"All of us have been alone at one time or another, but we're all in this together now. In fact, we're thirty-one strong now with you in the ranks. Say, kid, what kind of painting do you do?"

"A little of everything I guess, but unfortunately, I couldn't bring my paints with me. I guess that pretty much makes me a car without gasoline."

"Very poetic, but nonsense. Paints you say? What kind do you need? We can get just about anything at the dump."

"Really? I mostly use oil, but I can make do with pretty much anything."

"Of course, just make a list of colors and I'll get the men right on it. *Scissors!* Come here, I have a DOFA I want you to write up immediately."

"Direct Order From Above, yes, sir!"

T.W. pulled Scissors away, out of earshot from Squirrel. "Tell Muscles to organize a search party, make it at least ten men strong. I want him to scour the dump for anything that can be used as paint. I don't care what kind or how much, but tell him not to come back empty-handed and I want it OTD."

"On The Double, roger that, sir!"

"And tell him it's for *The Cause*, he'll understand, and as an added incentive throw in a few marks as well, that should keep the men's eyes peeled."

"Yes, sir! Anything else?"

"No, that's all. I'll see you in the mess hall for lunch."

T.W. walked back to Squirrel. "Let's continue the tour shall we?"

Scissors ran off with orders in hand while T.W. led Squirrel back to the common room and into the mess hall where they ran into Belly Ache, complaining of all things, a sore stomach.

"Sir, I don't feel so swell?"

"Well, what is it, Belly Ache?"

"I think it was something I ate or maybe food poisoning or a bacterial infection or worse yet, a tapeworm," he whispered the last part, fearing if he said it loud enough it might actually be true.

"It's most certainly not that serious, probably all in your head. You're going to give yourself an ulcer if you keep this up. Report to The Wiz, I'm sure he's got something he's willing to test on you."

"Yes, sir."

"I tell you that kid is something else. Last week he thought he had Tuberculosis. Turned out to be he had nothing more than a common cough."

"Why do you call him Belly Ache?"

"Why? Because it's his name."

"That's kind of a strange name isn't it?"

"Nah, his name's actually pretty normal compared to some of the other yahoos we got running around here. We name ourselves, just like we take care of ourselves. Why bother keeping a name given by somebody who gave you away in the first place? Doesn't make a lot of sense to me, which is why I'm Teenage Wasteland. You can change your name too if you want, but then again Squirrel's a pretty cool name, even if it is a bit jacked up."

"I think I'll stick with Squirrel. It suits me. What's your original name?"

"Original name—*ha*. I don't have an original name, and even if I did that'd be classified."

Squirrel looked around the mess hall and felt his stomach grumbling. He had not eaten much since his great-grandmother's passing. Before he could inquire about lunch, an almost clairvoyant Big Ben started to ring the bell. It was followed by the sound of shoes pounding on floor and men screeching down the fireman's pole. Squirrel was almost run over by Seafood who beelined towards the front of the line, sending three men flying.

"Hey, I hope you're hungry kid," T.W. said. "We got all kinds of grub lined up for you, let me introduce you to our chef and get you a hot plate of chow."

They walked over to the mess hall counter, cutting through the line of men with pleas of "make way." Chopsticks greeted them, decked out in his usual grease-stained apron and using a knife to shave slices of prime rib.

"Chopsticks, say hello to Squirrel, our newest recruit."

"Huwo," Chopsticks said, brandishing his knife. "Ah, Newbie, you wook more like noodle than meatball. We need fatten you up. Here, take this, Pime Wib, doubwee-baked potato, and gween beans. I hope you like bwoody."

Chopsticks handed Squirrel a plate stacked high with food, the prime rib pink in the middle and dripping with juices. T.W. took his equally full plate and led Squirrel to a table near the back. They were soon joined by a handful of men.

"Don't be bashful," T.W. said. "Dig in. The food's not going to eat itself."

Squirrel didn't need to be told twice. Having never eaten a home-cooked meal that didn't involve being heated up in the microwave first, he was surprised at how wonderful it tasted. He didn't pause from chewing once, only stopping when there was nothing left on his plate to eat.

"Good God, man," T.W. said. "Didn't they feed you where you came from? Don't worry we got plenty more. *Ray Charles!*"

When Ray Charles failed to materialize, T.W. looked around bewildered. The boy had never failed to be by his side when called. "Ray Charles, where in the world are you? *Ray Charles!*"

"I'm here, sir!" Ray Charles raced into the mess hall, covered in sweat and out of breath, his binoculars fogged from exertion.

"What took you so long, Ray Charles? I've been calling all over for you."

"Sorry, sir, I was preoccupied."

He was preoccupied with Squirrel's pillowcase, which took him fifteen minutes to drag up just one flight of stairs. It was so burdensome that Ray Charles could only manage to haul it up by walking up the stairs backwards, using both hands to lift it up a step, and then pausing to catch his breath before moving on to the next step. By the time he reached the second floor, he was so exhausted he almost passed out, but was saved by Muscles who took the pillowcase in one hand and carried it the rest of the way like it weighed no more than a feather, despite having gallon-sized cans of sardines strapped to both his arms and legs.

"Well, now that you're here, go fetch Squirrel another plate of food and a Faygo from the fridge. Make sure it's ice cold and a flavor other than Moon Mist. He's had that one already."

"Yes, sir," Ray Charles said, his chest heaving. He gave Squirrel a dirty look before hurrying away.

"That kid needs to lay off the candy cigarettes, he can barely breathe."

"What's with that thing over his eyes?" Squirrel asked.

"Oh, Ray Charles, right. Kid can't see two feet in front of him so The Wiz—who you'll meet later—strapped some modified binoculars over his eyes and presto, problem solved."

"Hmmm," Squirrel said, eyeing the other men, who quickly redirected their attention to their food. Ray Charles returned with a new tray and a Faygo Root Beer before disappearing without saying another word. Squirrel ate his second helpings about as fast as he ate his first, pausing only to gulp his Faygo.

As soon as he was finished, another orphan carried away his tray, this one decked out in what appeared to be a spacesuit. T.W. caught his look of amusement and said, "That's

Snot, the sickliest orphan you'll ever meet. We keep him in that suit as a safety precaution. The kid's allergic to practically everything, himself included, I reckon."

They got up from the table and were about to leave the mess hall when they were stopped by Wheelin' Dealin' Steven.

"Hey, newbie, you need a watch—*Rolex, Timex, you-name-ex*—or how about some bling to go with that fancy hat of yours, you know what I'm saying, baby?"

"Not now, Steven." T.W. pulled Squirrel away. "I know it's a lot to process, being new and all. I'll lead you to your bedroom and leave you to yourself for the remainder of the day."

T.W. led him up the stairs to the third-floor bedrooms. Squirrel's pillowcase was waiting for him on his bed, along with a fresh towel, toothbrush, bar of soap, a copy of the latest edition of *The Orphan*, with Crash on the cover discussing his latest concussion or rather what he remembered of it, and a folded red sweater with a black S on the front.

Before he left, T.W. gave Squirrel a quick tour of the third floor, pointing out the bathrooms and his office, while neglecting to mention the locked door leading to the attic.

"I'll be in here if you need me." T.W. took a seat at his desk, his eyes focused on the typewriter.

"What's in there?" Squirrel pointed to the large metallic door next to T.W.'s office.

"Oh, that. Sorry, kid, that's classified. Once you earn your stripes, I'll fill you in."

"When will that be?"

"Soon enough, once you get settled in."

"But what if I don't fit in and don't earn my stripes. I've always been sort of an outcast, no family besides my great-grandmother. I guess I just don't belong anywhere."

"Well you're in the right place then, kid. We're all outcasts here. This is your new family. At the Row, everyone belongs."

Squirrel nodded and left the office. Clacking sounds from a typewriter followed him all the way back to his bed. Squirrel unpacked his meager belongings and stretched out on the bed. He stared up at the ceiling, wondering if this weird, wild place would ever feel like home. As he closed his eyes, holding back the tears, his mind was doubtful.

8

A Second Interlude:
In Which The Man Reflects

IN THE HEART OF DOWNTOWN Detroit, Mayor Sharp, an orphan in denial, sat in his office, reading the daily paper. His mind was hopeful, fixated on the future—*his future*. The latest polls showed his approval ratings were now at an even seventy percent, an all time high. He chuckled at his success, a smile spreading on his face.

The smile lasted for only a split of a second before being replaced by a serious frown. No matter how successful he was there was still one little matter that gnawed at his insides—his past. It was easy to sway public opinion, but the past was always there, buried within, an insidious parasite. No matter what he did, he could never escape the fact that he did not come from a well-respected lineage, but rather a discarded bundle on the front steps of an orphanage.

The orphanage in question was not Desolation Row—still a library at the time—but rather Hope's Promise, located in the outskirts of the city of Flint, a place that shared the destitution of its southern neighbor, the city of Detroit. For the first five years of his life, Mayor Sharp was raised in Hope's

Promise, an institution that failed to live up to its namesake and closed its doors in the eighties when the economy took a turn. Mayor Sharp—Businessman Sharp at the time—had it demolished shortly after and converted into a vacant lot, currently occupied by forgotten dreams.

Mayor Sharp had arrived at the orphanage as a month-old baby left by his parents, names unknown, in a wooden basket at the doorstep. A single note had been attached with a solitary word, no contact information, no please, and no thank you, just a name—Albert. The two old nuns who had run Hope's Promise, Sister Alice and Sister Katherine, had been used to such unexpected guests. Through their years of servitude they had seen their share of parents lacking adult accountability, but none with the gall to leave a child without so much as a hello or explanation. Such devious souls were the recipients of their nightly prayers. Unfortunately, there just weren't enough prayers to go around, and as a result, unwelcomed children like Albert showed up all the time.

"Well, we have to give him a last name," Sister Alice said. She was the oldest by four years. "He can't go through life as only Albert."

"What should it be then?" Sister Katherine asked.

"Let us pray on it."

Lacking a creative bone in their combined aged and fragile bodies, the two nuns prayed on it and when their prayers weren't answered, they left the name to their assistant, a young thirty-something black woman named Big Mama, who called the baby Albert Godson because she believed all children who found their way to their doorsteps were God's sons.

The name remained with him for five more years, until the fortuitous day when a wealthy and prominent family—the Sharps—adopted him. After years of unsuccessful pregnancy attempts, followed by extensive doctor visits equally unsuccessful, the Sharps only option was to adopt. Deeply devote Christians, they felt it their duty to raise one less fortunate than themselves and so settled on Hope's Promise, the lowest and poorest of all orphanages.

They arrived in the downcast and derelict city of Flint driving a brand new BMW convertible and decked out in their Sunday bests—she in a blue dress with a yellow hat and he in a dark gray suit. They approached the wobbled, uneven steps of Hope's Promise with the air of royalty. Their heads raised high, their clothes tidy from dry cleaning, and their noses somewhat shriveled and unaccustomed to the stench of poverty.

The nearly two dozen orphans stood before them unkempt, soiled, and dressed in rags appearing more like bullet ridden flags left over from a battlefield than clothing. The children, so embarrassed by their sullied appearances and sad dispositions, did not meet the warm, friendly stares of the Sharps or bother to smile, save for just one.

What compelled a young Albert Godson to be uncharacteristically daring and bold, even forcing a smile, was a mystery even to the boy himself. He had, in fact, just recovered from a nasty case of the flu that had left him bedridden for almost two weeks. His only source of sustenance had been a few tablespoons of chicken broth and some stale pieces of bread, all fed to him by Big Mama, who soothed his warm, feverish head with a cool, damp washcloth. During his bed rest he had lost close to ten pounds, and as a result was so skinny that the only way to keep his pants up was by tying a thin piece of nylon rope around his waist.

Fortunately for him, his fever broke just the day before the arrival of the Sharps. If his fever had held out for just one more day, young Albert Godson would have stayed in bed and missed his dance with destiny. But life has a way of putting shoes on a person's feet even when they are just barely able to stand on their own.

When Sister Alice called the orphans down to the foyer to greet the prospective parents, Albert's legs had almost failed him as he stepped out of bed. He came lumbering down the stairs just as Sister Alice gave out one last call. He was in such good spirits to finally be out of bed that he couldn't help but smile when the door opened, revealing something he had not seen in nearly two weeks of despair—the sun. He was still smiling when two darkened figures closed the door behind them.

"Oh, look, Peter, it's an angel," Mrs. Sharp said.

At that moment all of the children looked up and smiled, for Elizabeth had not made it clear which orphan was the angel. By then it was too late. It was Albert's smile, and his alone, that got her attention.

"Oh, yes, it most certainly is," Mr. Sharp replied.

"Can we have him? Oh, please say yes, Peter."

"Yes, dear, we can have him."

It was then that Mrs. Sharp rushed over and scooped Albert Godson into her arms, causing his bones to creak and crack like dry wood burning in a woodstove. While she gushed and cried out, the rest of the children let out a collective sigh of disappointment.

In his last moments as a Godson, Albert packed his meager belongings into a pillowcase. They included a box of matchsticks, a scruffy teddy bear, two nickels and three pennies, a spare shirt, a red toy car missing a black wheel, and a comb with so many missing teeth it resembled the black keys on a piano.

Pillowcase in hand, he hopped in the backseat of the shiny BMW. With the top down, the breeze ruffled his hair like leaves on a tree. As the car sped away from the driveway, leaving nothing but a trail of dust behind, the newly transformed Albert Sharp did not look back once. His final image of Hope's Promise had been a teary-eyed Big Mama waving goodbye, a large smile on her face.

The years after Hope's Promise had been good to him. What he had lacked at the orphanage had been bestowed on him at his new home. He had never gone without, indulging in toys, clothes, leisurely activities, and his favorite—food.

Albert was a skinny lad when he left the orphanage, but it didn't take long for him to grow into a big, strapping boy. His appetite never faltered, only mounting through his teenage years, and as a result he became a large man who had all the girth and build of a wrestler mixed with all the charm and charisma of Santa Claus. More elliptical than round, more solid than soft, more SUV than car, more alpha bull than cow, he cut an imposing figure. Whereas before he needed a strap of nylon rope to keep his pants from falling down, he now needed a pair of suspenders to keep them up.

His biggest draw was not his size, but rather his face. Pudgy, round, and so like a baby's that if not for his beak-like nose one would have thought it was made of putty instead of flesh and bone. He smiled like a salesman interested in buying just as much as he was selling. When in full bloom, his double chin all but disappeared. His eyes sparkled bright blue, two oases in the pale desert of his face. They were topped with a crop of blondish-brown hair that was always slicked back.

It was this same happy face that adorned all of his campaign posters and TV commercials, pledging to the public that they had "a pal in Al." His looks spoke of wealth and prestige, not a humble background with roots buried deep in an orphanage, much to his relief.

The only thing remaining of Albert's days as an orphan was the tiny toy red car with the missing black wheel that had left Hope's Promise in a pillowcase. It was now on his desk, just in front of his homage to Alexander the Great. The reason he hung onto this relic of the past was as lost to him as his early memories.

Sitting in his office, pondering his future, Mayor Sharp's eyes fell to the empty gap where the one wheel remained vacant like the missing tooth of a smile. A somewhat intrusive, uncharacteristic pang of nostalgia swept over his heart. He quickly dismissed it and returned to the paper, shuffling through it with mild interest. He eventually came to the obituaries and was about to dismiss them as well when something towards the bottom caught his eye, something about an explosion.

"Son-of-a-Calloway!" Mayor Sharp stood up, balled his hands into fists, and pounded them on his desk. His anger flashed red on his face. Someone has some explaining to do, he thought. Someone needs to pay.

9

It's a Hard Knock Life

"LOOKS LIKE THEY'RE at it again." T.W. stared out his office window.

He was joined by Scissors and Ray Charles who watched workers from the Calloway campaign put up signs supporting local Democrats, which would be taken down minutes later and replaced with signs supporting local Republicans by workers from the Sharp campaign who were led by a menacing looking fellow dressed in army camouflage. Knowing this was a daily ritual, the three of them could not help but smile at the foolishness of The Man.

The gubernatorial race, still well over a year away, was looking to be a heated one. Leading in the Democratic primaries was the Row's mysterious benefactor, Calloway. Unlike Detroit, with the four seasons always in flux, the political season seldom changed. It was never ending, always in motion since someone somewhere was always up for reelection.

Big Mama sat outside on her bench, knitting a sweater. She recognized one of the faces on a poster, having never once forgotten a face of her many children, and commented, "Lordy, there's that Albert Godson. Got himself a new name, but my Lordy has he ever filled out. Good for him. Lordy, knows he deserves all his successes. Amen, Lordy."

"Which party are you rooting for, sir?" a blithe Ray Charles asked, hoping to unearth a little personal information from his fearless leader and mentor.

"Neither. I'm an anarchist."

"Oh, right," Ray Charles replied, scratching his binoculars. He quickly excused himself to go off in search of a dictionary to look up the word, but due to bad shortsightedness caused by his binoculars, he accidently came across the word analogy instead. By the time he wrapped his binoculars around the meaning of analogy he was more confused than anything, coming to the conclusion that T.W. was more of an anomaly—another word he had accidentally stumbled upon while trying to navigate back to analogy.

"How are we looking on Charlies this week?" T.W. asked, running his comb through his hair three times. Scissors studied his clipboard.

"So far none. However, we do have reports of Tag Police activity all over Douglas Street. It seems they are closing in on the Row. Toaster has also spotted lots of suspicious characters in the neighborhood clearing out the homeless, as well as numerous dump trucks coming and going at odd hours of the night. They mostly go to the vacant lots near the dump, which has grown exponentially, according to The Wiz, almost doubling in size."

"Interesting," T.W. said. "But not our concern. Our only focus is to keep our men from being adopted. But just in case there's something happening beneath our noses we must be on guard, remain vigilant, and as always remember Snuggles."

"Yes, sir, of course."

"On a side note, how's our newbie holding up?"

"He seems to be fine, a bit taciturn, but I guess that's expected for a newbie. Ray Charles has his suspicions. He even offered to spy on him."

"Ridiculous. Squirrel just needs time to acclimate."

"Right, sir."

"Now, if you will excuse me, Scissors, I'm going to attempt to write."

Scissors gave a salute and left the office, closing the door behind him. T.W. stared at his typewriter. A blank page (number 364) stared back at him. He sat behind his desk with a sigh, resisting the urge to smoke and attempting to put up the good fight against writer's block.

He remained in his office for the better part of the morning, managing to type just a single sentence and not a very good one at that. A knock at his door roused him from his daily battle with the typewriter.

"Yes, come in."

The door opened, revealing Squirrel, his face downcast. So far, his first week at the Row had done little to dissipate his uncertainties and feelings of being all alone. He missed his great-grandmother and little trailer home more than ever. "I hope I'm not interrupting anything."

"Nonsense, of course not. How can I be of service?"

"Well, you see, I've been meaning to ask," Squirrel said, his head lowered. "How soon do you think before I'm adopted?"

"Adopted, ha. Nobody get's adopted around here."

"Why what do you mean? I thought the whole purpose of an orphanage was to get orphans adopted by a real family."

"Not here at the Row. You see we don't wait around for a real family, we create our own. Out there in the real world we're nothing. But in here we're everything. You see we are family, a brotherhood of the forgotten, the Proletarian Pistol-Swinging Punks of Detroit."

"But what if a good family comes along? Wouldn't you— you and the other orphans—want to have the opportunity for a better life?"

T.W. sighed and folded his arms. "There was a time at the Row when the men dreamed of being adopted, but that all changed after Snuggles."

"Who's Snuggles? I've heard him mentioned before, but none of the other orphans like to talk about him much. They always grow silent whenever I inquire."

"And for good reason. What happened to Snuggles was a real setback for the Row, a tough time for all of us, but it's too soon to give you all the details just yet. You should talk to the men, ask them to share their stories first, and when the time's right I'll fill you in all about Snuggles. You have my word on it, swear to Hemingway."

Squirrel nodded and did as instructed, spending a few days observing the happenings of the Row and getting acquainted with the men. The first thing he noticed was how close and disciplined they all were, very much like the tight-knit, wayward gang of the Tom Travolta not-so-classic film *Hooked*. Set in the fictional Never Never Read Land, it was about a gang of illiterate misfits who overcame the odds and learned how to read despite the determined efforts of Captain Crook (played by Tom Travolta, sporting a mustache so thick and big it could be viewed from space), who banned *Hooked on Phonics* and any form of literacy. It was a box office calamity, but a major literary success because all the people who paid to see it thought it so bad they lost faith in cinema and took to reading books instead.

Day in and day out, the men ran through drills and practiced formations, all of which Squirrel was exempt from since he didn't have his stripes yet. He watched in wonderment as the men roshamboed for marks, went to class, did their chores, and took care of themselves without any adult supervision. Everything ran like clockwork. It seemed change was the only thing the men feared more than being adopted.

"What are *they* doing?" Squirrel asked Muscles, who was busy multitasking—standing on watch duty while also curling a large can of sardines. They were standing in front of a small group of men—Peanut Butter, Marshmallow, Belch, and Compost Pile—who were busy pounding the chests of mannequins scavenged from the dump.

"Oh, they're getting their OCPR certification?"

"What's that?"

"Orphan Cardiopulmonary Resuscitation!" Scissors shouted, coming up beside them. Muscles nodded in agreement.

Squirrel made the rounds and talked to as many men as possible. He learned that before Toaster showed up at the Row, he had been so used to being unnoticed at home that his parents had forgotten all about him when they had moved away. He had spent six scary weeks alone, living off crackers and hiding from homeless home invaders before Social Services had found him and had shipped him off to the Row. It was good practice for his future career as a spy.

"It was very much like that old Tom Travolta movie back when he was a child actor and could only grow half of a mustache," Toaster said. "You know, the one where he gets left alone on the range and has to fight off Indians and Chinamen and robbers and thieves? *Home Alonesome Dove*, I believe."

From Snot he learned that his parents abandoned him because, "Well, you see [sneeze] they said [sneeze] my medical [sneeze] expenses was cutting in [sneeze] to their bar funds [sneeze] so they left me [sneeze] in a dumpster [sneeze]."

By the time Snot was finished with his short narrative, the wiper in his suit was working overdrive to clear the mucus from his visor.

Crash didn't remember much of his childhood before the Row, citing concussion-related memory loss as the culprit.

Tea Bag explained how it was tough making it in an entirely new country. "You see I about killed myself crossing the street. How was I to know you drove on the bloody wrong side of the road? It was tough enough not having me mum and dad, but no designated teatime or biscuits and all that bloody coffee. It was mad I tell you."

When he first came to the Row, Christmas Story not only lost his family, but his leg as well. "I was so devastated with grief that I thought I'd never stand on my own foot again. It was real bad for a few years, but then The Wiz made me a new leg. Sure it's fashioned like a lady's, but I kind of like it. People used to stare at my stump and give me looks of pity, now they see my leg and whistle."

Overall, Squirrel gathered that the men weren't upset at all about not having a "normal" family, one with a mother and a father. Abnormal was the norm for them. It was something they accepted and lived with every day. All of them were happy with their circumstances and had complete trust in their leader, T.W. The only thing questionable in their lives was the outside world, which they all mistrusted with good faith.

"You should have seen the place before T.W. showed up," Scissors said. "It was in complete disarray. Beds full of lice. Brown water coming out of the faucets. Rats in and out of the walls. Big Mama tried her best, but there was no money or support to go around. The city had abandoned us. Heck, they even sent us to public school. That was the worst. Every day the men were tormented by bullies and beat up by gangs, the worst being a bunch of blonde-haired hooligans in varsity jackets. They made fun of Marshmallow because he was too white, took to calling him an albino wino. Harassed Christmas Story because of his missing leg, calling him One-Leg and saying he was missing something like Lance Armstrong. Laughed at Belch and Bellyache because they were too black, calling them the Turd Twins. Poked fun at Chopsticks because he was Asian, calling him Eggroll. Tortured Muscles because he was too skinny, calling him String Bean. Ridiculed Faygo because he talked funny, calling him Speech Impediment. Shamed Stone Age because he looked so old, calling him Nursing Home. Mocked Rooster because of his red hair, calling him Ginger Ale. Teased Seafood because he was too fat, calling him the Human-Whale-Who-Ate-A-Shark. Thank Hemingway T.W. got us out of that cesspool and away from all those tormenters. He saved us, but he couldn't save Snuggles. That was the worst thing to ever happen at the Row."

"What happened to him?"

"It's not for me to say." Scissors had a forlorn look on his face. "You'll have to ask T.W. He's the only one who can tell you the whole story."

Squirrel decided it was time. He had seen and heard enough. He went to T.W.'s office to learn the truth about Snuggles.

"Come on, kid, follow me," T.W. said

"Where are we going?"

"To the majesty of the Row. It'll blow your mind. When we get there I'll tell you all about Snuggles."

Squirrel never had his mind blown and was curious as to what it would entail. Together they walked down the stairs into the rec room and out the door that led to the massive dump. Having lived his entire life in the flatlands of Detroit, Squirrel had never encountered a mountain before, or at least, one not seen on TV. What stood in front of him was the largest man-made mountain range in the Midwest. As far as the eye could see massive five-storied piles of junk and mounds of derelict rubbish towered in the air. Piles and mounds built with abandoned school buses, tractors, automobiles, trailers, boats, refrigerators, washing machines, couches, tires, toilets, and millions upon millions of garbage bags.

Through the years the dump had amassed a century's worth of forgotten belongings, making it a living, breathing museum of the developments of capitalism through the years. Generations of junk were piled on top of each other in almost chronological order so that if one wanted to know what was popular in the fifties all they had to do was sift through all of the junk from the nineties, eighties, seventies, and sixties.

The dump was also home to one of the largest flocks of seagulls—also known as dumpster chickens—in the Western

Hemisphere. Numbering in the thousands, they gorged on the leftover and rotting food of Detroit's millions.

"In a way, it's kind of beautiful," Squirrel said, plugging his nose from the smell.

"That's one way of putting it," T.W. said. "Here, take this."

T.W. handed him a clothespin. Squirrel noticed that T.W. had already placed one on his nose, and so he did the same.

"Rumor has it that half the junk in Canada is shipped here by way of Windsor." T.W.'s voice sounded nasal from the clothespin. "The Wiz has found license plates from Toronto, Ontario, Montreal, and Quebec. Even stateside ones including Indiana, Illinois, Ohio, and as far away as Florida. Somebody's sure making a lot of dough taking in all of Canada's and America's unwanted things. We've only mapped out a fraction of it."

"You mean you guys actually go out there?"

"Of course, where else would we find all the treasures you saw in the rec room? There's a gold mine out there if you know what you're looking for. We've got a dozen men out there right now, scouring through its depths."

"But isn't it dangerous?"

"Comes with the territory, but we've got a good system going. No orphan goes out there alone. Biggest thing to worry about is the four Dobermans—Rabies, Sick Boy, Snaggle Tooth, and Sir Barks-a-Lot. Stay away from them. They'll take a bite out of your behind if you're not careful."

Squirrel looked everywhere for any sign of the dogs, but saw none.

"Come with me, kid. Let me show you something."

T.W. led him to the edge of the Row's backyard—what remained of it—and removed a long wooden board with the words "Keep Out" written in red paint. What lay beyond was a large tunnel clear of debris.

"This is *Dante's Descent*, leads right into the heart of the dump. Come on, follow me. It's safe."

The tunnel was wide enough for them to walk side by side and tall enough so that they didn't have to worry about bumping their heads. It went on for the length of a football field before opening to a wide open valley of garbage that was condensed, flattened, and covered in so much dumpster-chicken poop it looked like a stony beach. Near the exit of the tunnel was a garbage barrel stuffed full of umbrellas.

"Here take one of these." T.W. handed Squirrel an umbrella.

"Why? It doesn't look like rain today."

"Trust me, you'll see."

Squirrel opened the umbrella and placed it over his head. Within seconds, two clumps of goo that were too heavy to be raindrops hit the umbrella and slid down the curvature of the umbrella like slow moving tears. T.W. stood next to him with his own umbrella released. Before he could say a word it was hit with three successive clumps.

"Flipping dumpster chickens," T.W. said.

"*Dumpster chickens?*"

"Oh, right, seagulls. Thousands of them in the dump, perhaps a million. All they do is eat, fly, and *poop*. The Wiz thinks they serve a purpose, but I think they're just a nuisance."

"That's jacked up," Squirrel said, borrowing from T.W.

"Exactly, you're a quick learner." T.W. removed the cigarette from his ear and placed it in his mouth. He looked around for Ray Charles, but after realizing he wasn't there, looked to Squirrel instead. "Say, kid, you got a light?"

"No and besides you really shouldn't smoke those things you know."

"Why not?"

"Because they'll kill you."

"Says who?"

"Says me. My great-grandmother blew herself up smoking one of those. If it wasn't for her Lucky Stripes, she'd still be alive today and I wouldn't be here."

"Oh, right." T.W. removed the cigarette from his mouth and placed it back behind his ear. "Sorry, kid, I forgot all about that. I'll do my best not to smoke around you."

"It's alright. I'm sorry. I shouldn't be preaching to you, sir," Squirrel said, not realizing he had picked up the habit every other orphan who came before him had. "I guess I'm still a bit sore about losing my great-grandmother."

"Don't worry about it." T.W. ran his comb through his hair three times. "You don't have to explain yourself to me. I get it. Here at the Row, we've all lost something."

T.W. stared off in the distance, his demeanor quiet.

"I guess it's time you learned about Snuggles."

"Yes, I think I'm ready. Who was he and what happened to him?"

"Snuggles was the only orphan to ever be adopted under my watch." T.W. paused to run his comb through his hair three times. "You should have seen the men before I showed up. No discipline. No direction. The only place they were heading was the state pen, where most outcasts and orphans end up anyway. When you're at the bottom there is no easy way to the top, just a lot of hard work or a life of crime.

"By the time I arrived, the men were battered and beaten, couldn't even read or write. Most of them hadn't been outside the city of Detroit. The ghetto was the only existence they knew. They spent their time sitting around feeling sorry for themselves, hoping against hope that some rich family would adopt them and save them from this life. They were lost souls, going through the motion of this life. You know what The Wiz, our chief scientist, was doing with his life? Burning paper with a magnifying lens, that's what. Stone Age was making license plates. Big Ben couldn't even tell time. Chopsticks couldn't cook. The only thing he could manage was heating up cans of soup on the stove. And Seafood, well, Seafood . . . he—"

Just then they came upon Seafood passed out in a tattered recliner, a half-eaten Twinkie in each hand and a small pile of empty wrappers stacked on his stomach.

"Well, Seafood is pretty much the same, but the point is most of the men weren't living up to their potential. Their talent wasted. The first thing I did when I took over was come up with *The Cause* to give them hope, something to believe in. The next thing I did was teach them how to read and write. Poverty's a wheel at times and the only way to keep it from spinning is to reinvent it through the basics of education. I got the men to learn by starting out with the easiest book in the world to read, Bob Lennon's one and only children's book, *Imagination*. It wasn't always easy, but through hard work and discipline the men came around, one by one. In no time we were a brotherhood, forging the one thing the world had taken away from us, a family."

T.W. paused, a bittersweet half-smile playing on his face.

"Snuggles, age seven, was one of the sweetest and kindest orphans I ever met. The kid had a big heart, just like Big Mama. He had real potential too. He was Orphan of the Month on multiple occasions. Nice as well, would go out of his way to help anyone and outgoing, with an easy smile, and an affable personality. Whenever an orphan was down or feeling lonely, Snuggles was there to give them a hug or word of encouragement. Sometimes he'd sit on the corner of Douglas Street with a cardboard sign, advertising "Free Hugs." As an avid thumb sucker, he enjoyed the simple things in life, like a nice warm blanket fresh out of the dryer, smelling like fabric softener. He carried this soft, blue blanket with him wherever he went. It was a keepsake from his mother, before she died from cancer, which led him here. He was the orphan most likely to give the world a hug just because he could.

"You should have seen how happy he was on the day of his adoption. Biggest smile you ever saw. Adoptions were a rarity back then. Times were hard. Detroit was just going through its third or fourth recession. If any orphan deserved to be adopted it was Snuggles. We were sad to see him go, but also happy to see him get the one opportunity orphans seldom got. He stayed in touch with us through letters via dumpster-chicken carrier. Things started out well, he said he was happy, his new parents were great, but then something happened. Snuggles stopped sending and responding to messages. After about a month of nothing, we got a dumpster chicken back with an SOS. It couldn't have come at a worse time. We were neck deep in Tag Police, and the city was in the process of shutting us down, cutting our funding. It was hectic. We were fighting for our very livelihood, very much like Tom Travolta in his action-packed karate masterpiece *Enter the Drag Queen.* By the time we were able to put together a rescue party to come to his aid it was too late, the damage had been done."

T.W. paused to adjust his sunglasses and took a deep breath.

"When we arrived at his new home there were no Charlies in sight. We found Snuggles holed up in a closet in a catatonic state, sucking his thumb and staring off into nothing. His tiny body was malnourished and covered in bruises and cigarette burns. After some investigation we discovered his Charlies had used his adoption as a front to collect money from the state. It seemed the city had cut their unemployment, welfare, and disability funds, so they adopted Snuggles for the extra income. We never discovered why the Charlies beat and mistreated him so. They were long gone, taking with them our chance of revenge. Snuggles wouldn't say a word. Just sat there sucking his thumb. After some forensic work, The Wiz discovered that his blue blanket had been burned in a metal barrel outside. Only a small corner, no bigger than a stamp, was all that remained. We tried giving it to Snuggles, hoping it would snap him out of his trance, but nothing happened. Snuggles was lost to us. For weeks, we tried everything to bring him back. Colonel Sanders attempted every psychology trick in the book, even hypnosis, but they all failed. In the end, Big Mama had no choice but to have him institutionalized."

"That's terrible, I'm sorry," Squirrel said. "I had no idea. I don't know what to say."

"After that I said no way, never again. We can't control the outside world and the people living in it, but in here we at least got a fighting chance. Here we make the rules, control our own destiny. No one can take that away from us. We stick together no matter what. That's why we don't allow ourselves to be adopted. I can't let what happened to Snuggles happen again, not on my watch."

T.W. turned to Squirrel and placed a hand on his shoulder.

"I can't make you join our ranks, live by our code, Squirrel. So if you want to be adopted that's up to you, but if you're going to be one of us, you have to be all in and that means no adoption. We're your family now. You can accept that or go your own way. Either way I will support you. I know it's a lot to consider, so I'll give you time to think it over. Just let me know when you've made your decision."

T.W. turned to go back in the direction of the Row, but Squirrel stopped him.

"No, wait, sir. I'm in, *all* in. Just tell me where to sign."

T.W. smiled and clapped him on the back. "I had a feeling you'd say yes. Welcome to the ranks. Say, can I ask you something?"

"Sure, what?"

"Can you fly?"

"Can I *what*?"

"Can you fly?"

"No, of course not. How could I possibly fly?"

"Well, there are flying squirrels you know. I guess it doesn't matter. Someday I'm going to fly, once I get my wings, of course." T.W. paused to gaze up at the sky. "Alright, let's go. I have a surprise to show you."

"A surprise f—"

Before Squirrel could finish, the distant arguing of two men cut him off.

"What in the Hemingway is going on?" T.W. and Squirrel walked off in the direction of the disruption and found Ray Charles and another orphan inspecting a large red couch that appeared in decent condition despite a missing cushion.

"Don't remove the tag!" Ray Charles said with his binoculars up in the face of the other orphan.

"The *what*?"

"The tag, Jeez-Louise, Pickles. The *tag*!"

Pickles, age ten, was always in a pickle, having an uncanny ability to be in the wrong place at the wrong time. This was evident by the unforeseen circumstances that led to his arrival at the Row. Originally born into a family of great wealth, Pickles had the misfortune of being accidently switched at birth with an unwanted baby headed straight to the orphanage. Instead of being a trust-baby worth millions, he became an orphan worth nothing.

It was this same kind of bad luck that stuck with him throughout his youth. At the age of six he was trapped in the laundry chute for two days after a game of hide-and-seek that was more hiding than seeking. At the age of seven he was caught in a game of tug-of-war between two of the four Dobermans—Snaggle Tooth and Sick Boy—that resulted in seventeen stitches. At the age of eight he was accidently mailed to the state pen where he spent a week sharing a cell with "Crazy-Eye" Hopkins. He was the orphan most likely to misplace the winning numbers for a billion dollar lottery ticket.

"What's going on here?" T.W. asked.

"Pickles here was about to cut off the tag of this here couch, sir."

"What tag?" Squirrel asked, thinking perhaps it was the price tag.

"The security tag," T.W. said. "In the state of Michigan it is illegal to remove the consumer information tag from a couch or mattress. The state pen is full of convicted offenders, some serving life sentences for multiple offenses."

"Geez," Squirrel gulped. "What's so wrong with pulling a tag?"

Ray Charles laughed derisively. "What's wrong with pulling the tag? You really don't know shoes from Shinola do you? Haven't you ever heard of the Tag Police?"

"The Tag Police?"

"Yes, the Tag Police," T.W. said. "They take the cutting of tags very seriously in these parts. We had a run in with them a few months back. It wasn't pretty, The Wiz almost had to gas one of them with Forget Me Juice, some guy named Wilson, but thankfully we handled the situation before it came to such measures."

"Did you say Wilson?"

"Yeah, I believe that was his name. Why? Have you heard of him?"

Squirrel gulped and nodded.

"Tag Police are everywhere just like those darn dumpster chickens," Ray Charles piped in with a smug smile.

"Enough brownnosing, Ray Charles. Pickles, you should have known better. We don't cut the tags off until after The Wiz has inspected them. You could have caused a real pain in my Hemingway. A good thing Ray Charles was here to set you straight."

Ray Charles beamed at hearing praise, but was somewhat disappointed it didn't include any marks. He was determined to win this month's prestigious Orphan of the Month. The only problem was he had yet to earn any marks, despite volunteering for every possible side mission and running on only four hours of sleep a night. This down from his normal five and a half. He decided he would just have to work harder, while keeping his binoculars on the newbie.

"Carry on, men," T.W. said. "This way Squirrel."

T.W. led them deeper into the labyrinth of junk. They stopped a few minutes later in front of a large fishing boat so gutted it looked like the fossilized bones of a beached whale. T.W. pursed his lips together and cupped his mouth with his hands. A high-pitched whistle—prairie warbler—sounded from his mouth. He whistled again, but no response.

"What in the Hemingway," he called. "I told them to come after hearing prairie warbler—wait that was last week's call. That's right. This week is, let me see here, oh yes, eastern yellow robin."

T.W. changed his tune and was immediately answered. Within seconds, Muscles and his ragtag scouting team emerged from all corners of the rubble.

"You called, sir?" Muscles said.

"Yes, how goes the search?"

"Very well, sir. Belly Ache hit the jackpot. He stopped to take a rest on a wooden crate, complaining of a tummy ache. When his brother Belch came upon him, he was surprised to see he was sitting on just what we were looking for."

"How much did he find?"

"Over thirty cans and all kinds of colors. Rooster and Cup Check found some containers as well, not sure how many. They're still scavenging."

"Very good, give all of your men a mark and give an extra one each to Belly Ache and Belch. Tell the men to start hauling the loot back to the Row. I want them cleaned up and ready for dinner. Good work, as always, Muscles."

"Yes, sir."

"What were they scavenging for?" Squirrel asked.

"Supplies for you."

"Supplies for *me*?"

"Yes, your paint. You can't be a very effective painter without any paint."

"But why go through all of the effort? You barely even know me."

"It doesn't matter. You're one of us now and we take care of our own."

They headed back to the Row. Squirrel was too overcome with emotion to say anything. After days of feeling alone, he was starting to feel a part of something again.

10

Duke Day

SQUIRREL WAS ONLY at the Row for a little over a month before he got to partake in his first official orphan holiday. May 26th signaled not only the last day of school at Detroit Public, but also the birth of a great icon, The Duke himself, John Wayne. Many considered him outdated and asinine, but he fit right in at the Row, where the men cherished everything behind the times and forgotten.

To commemorate such an occasion, T.W. marked it the official Duke Day of Desolation Row. By his decree all men were granted permission to wear their black PPSP-Douglas-Street-Affiliation vest. Wearing only his new red sweater—having not yet earned his stripes or vest—Squirrel spent the days leading up to the big event settling in and returning to school, both having their own setbacks.

The first difficulty lay in continuing to get to know all of the men and remembering their unique names. He could only tell the twins, Belly Ache and Belch, apart when they spoke; he had a ringing in his ears after a brief conversation with Rooster; he had been spit in the face by Super Soaker, he had been swore at in Korean by Chopsticks for taking too long to decide what he wanted to eat; he had been coerced by Seafood into giving him his dessert; he had mistook Faygo's name for an actual Faygo; he had been requested to rub suntan lotion on Marshmallow; he had been talked into buying a second-hand watch from Wheelin' Dealin' Steven; he had agreed to switch chores with Crash so he could practice his latest stunt; he had been asked by Matches if his paint was flammable; he had been scouted by Tea Bag to act in the Row's production of Shakespeare's *Romeo and Juliet*; he had been cup-checked so many times by Cup Check he avoided the boy whenever he saw him; and was followed so closely by Ray Charles it felt like he had grown a second shadow.

"Are you following me, Ray Charles?"

"Who *me*?" Ray Charles adjusted his binoculars. "Why no, of course not."

"I'm not stupid, you know. I see you hiding around corners and lurking about the bookcase in the rec room while I draw."

"I . . . I . . . never mind. I don't have to explain myself to you."

Ray Charles raced away before Squirrel could say anything else. He didn't stop until he came to his locker. He tore it open, grabbed a bookcase-camouflaged jumpsuit that he had bought for six marks from Toaster, and grumbled, "Gosh darn it, Toaster you said this would make me invisible." He was so furious that he tossed it down the laundry chute and walked right into a wall on his way out.

Squirrel attempted to befriend Ray Charles on numerous occasions, but the more he tried the more Ray Charles loathed him. It seemed the lad was binocular-bent on trying to one-up him or shame him in the process. One time Squirrel came out of the bathroom only to find Ray Charles in the middle of doing some push-ups, a candy cigarette dangling from his mouth.

"One ... hundred ... and ... fifty-seven ... one hundred ... and ... fifty-eight ... one hundred ... and ... oh, it's you, *newbie*."

"Hey, Ray Charles, how are you?"

"Oh, I'm fine. Just, you know, doing some light cardio. I got to stay in shape being T.W.'s runner and all. I'm gonna go for a light ten-mile run, if you want to tag along and see what you're made of."

"Sure," Squirrel said, much to the surprise of Ray Charles, who paused in his attempt at a one-armed push-up.

"You'll probably just slow me down anyways." Ray Charles took off and nearly ran into a wall in the process. After that he hardly said a word to Squirrel, except for insults or to laugh at his ignorance when it came to the Row's many acronyms and anything related to *The Cause*. Squirrel didn't know what he did to ire the boy so much and even brought the matter before T.W.

"Ray Charles like most orphans just doesn't like change. Doesn't help that he can't see what's in front of him, which makes it hard to distinguish friend from foe. That's his biggest problem. Don't worry about it. He'll get over it eventually. Something similar happened when I made Muscles my number three. Ray Charles challenged him to an arm wrestling match and wouldn't go near him for a month after Muscles almost broke his arm off. Now they're the best of pals."

Squirrel didn't know if he and Ray Charles would ever be friends. Instead of worrying about it, he focused on earning his stripes. Row protocol called for all newbies to get a fresh haircut as part of the initiation. Squirrel went to see Scissors about a trim.

"What can I do for you?" Scissors asked. "I can cut just about any style you want, from the traditional buzz cut to the crew cut, bowl cut, classic taper, fade, faux hawk, high and tight, flattop, layer cut, pompadour, shag, texture, Caesar, ivy league and with your long hair I can make you look like any celebrity—the DiCaprio, the Clooney, the Sinatra, the Elvis, and of course, the Tom Travolta. What do you say kid, what will it be?"

"I don't know. I've never had a real haircut before."

"*What*? Not even a trim?"

"Nope, nothing."

"Geez-Louise, what rock have you been hiding under? Alright, I'll just take a little bit around the edges and keep it shoulder length until you figure out a look that fits. How's that sound?"

"Sounds good."

A little around the edges translated into about four inches. Squirrel stepped out looking pretty much the same. With his haircut out of the way all that remained for him to do was find a hobby befitting *The Cause*. T.W. decided to put his natural talents to use, recruiting him to give the interior of the Row a much-needed makeover.

"Feel free to paint whatever you want. I'll leave it up to your discretion. This place needs some new color, so any bare, available wall or ceiling is yours to do as you please. However, I have a favor to ask of you before you begin."

"Sure, whatever you need, sir."

"Do you think you could paint a portrait of me, one to hang in my office? All great men have one done at some point of their career. It's been on my Orphan's List for some time now."

The Orphan's List was a list of all things T.W. wanted to do before he grew up. So far he had completed number four (running an orphanage) and number sixteen (learning how to ride a motorcycle), and was currently working on number one (writing a novel) and number three (flying), while number two (starting a revolution) and number ten (making a run for office) were still works in progress.

"Not a problem, sir. When would you like me to begin?"

"It's up to you, whenever you're free."

"Well, how about now?"

It only took Squirrel a few hours to complete a portrait of T.W. They used the time to get to know each other better. Squirrel talked about his days in Maege's trailer and how he transformed it into a living, breathing colorful work of art. "We didn't have much, but we had each other, which is sometimes all you need in life, sir."

While he posed, T.W. confided his beginnings at the Row, how he started out as a quiet, reticent boy who eventually took over after the oldest orphan, a big, hefty twelve-year-old named Tonka Truck, was sent to a juvenile detention center for punching a Charlie.

"As I was saying, it wasn't easy in the beginning. I was green in the ways of running an outfit, but I was tough and resilient. My first challenge was the Teepee War. Our supply lines were running short thanks to budget cuts, and we were down to our last few rolls before we had to start wiping with tidbits and trinkets from the dump. I made the boys ration out our last rolls, only a few sheets per number two. It didn't go over well, and I almost had a full-blown mutiny led by Seafood on my hands. That son-of-a-Hemingway must have sat on the john three times a day and used a whole roll himself. The rations didn't sit well with him—*literally*—and he soon formed a small alliance, the Teepee Party. It got to the point where I had to give away my own rations, using pages from that bore of a writer Faulkner instead. I was about halfway through *The Sound and the Fury* when the Calloways stepped in and delivered a big shipment, allowing me to restore order. The Teepee Party disbanded, and all of the men fell back in line, each and every one of them. I got through the Teepee War by leading through example. As the Duke always said, 'If you got them by the balls, their hearts and minds will follow.' It took both hands, but I eventually got there."

"But why burden yourself, sir? Why not just let Big Mama run the place?"

"It's my duty and besides 'there are some things a man just can't run away from.'"

Squirrel had seen enough John Wayne movies to recognize a Duke quote when he heard one. It seemed T.W. knew them all. He was about to say one of his own, when out of the blue T.W. pulled a knife from a drawer and threw it at the closed door of his office. It struck with a thud and vibrated like a plucked guitar string.

"Ray Charles, what are you doing standing by the door?" T.W. hollered. There was a small crash from behind the closed door, followed by a short cry of pain.

"Oh nothing, sir. I was just . . . just . . . just—"

"Just come in already. I can't hear you very well with a wood door between us."

Ray Charles opened the door and stepped in. Unsure of what to say for himself, he just stood adjusting his binoculars.

"*Well?*"

"I was just . . . uh . . . uh . . . waiting to speak to you, sir. How did you know I was there anyways?"

"I didn't. I was assuming and knew I assumed correctly when you made that commotion. Now what is it, can't you see I'm busy?"

"Oh, I was just wondering if you needed anything. A pop? Snack? Breath mint? A light for your cigarette?"

"No, I'm perfectly fine, Ray Charles. If I needed anything you'd be the first to know. Now leave us. Squirrel and I were discussing important business."

"Does it involve the Orphan of the Month?"

"Don't overstep, Ray Charles. Now off with you before I decide to demote you to second runner."

Ray Charles gasped and left the office in a hurry. As he walked away, his sweaty hands turned to fists. He didn't like the fact that T.W. was spending so much time with the newbie, who he feared was a spy, which was precisely why he spied on him.

Back in the office, Squirrel wrapped up the last touches of T.W.'s portrait and showed him the finished product. "Good God, man you sure know how to paint. You're a true artist, a real da Vinci, a Hemingway of the brush, a . . . a . . . ah forget it, you're in a class of your own, kid."

"Thank you, sir."

T.W. walked to his bookcase and pulled a book from the shelf. "Here take this, I want you to have this as a show of my appreciation."

"What is it?"

"Hemingway's *The Old Man and the Sea*, one of his finest. This one's a rarity, a first edition."

"I can't take this, sir."

"Why not?"

"Well for starters I don't know how to read."

"You got to be kidding me?"

"No, sir, it's the truth."

"Now that's jacked up. How's that even possible at your age? Haven't you been going to school for the past few years."

"I have, but—"

"You don't have to explain yourself. It's that darn Detroit Public. They might as well turn that place into a broom factory for all the good it doesn't do." T.W. scrunched his face in concentration. "Look, kid I want you to have the book anyway. It's a gift. If you like I can teach you how to read and write."

"Really? But you're not a certified teacher, sir."

"Certification, nerdification, who needs it! I've been reading and writing since I could walk, which for your information was a few months after being born. I'll have your eyes glued in a book in no time."

"When do we begin?"

"Right now. We'll start with Dr. Seuss, he's not a real doctor, but he's got a PhD in imagination that's for sure."

Squirrel's first book was *The Cat in the Hat*. It took them over an hour to get through the whole thing. It was painstakingly slow work, with T.W. correcting more than Squirrel read. When they were finished, Squirrel used his new found inspiration on a wall of the second floor bedroom, painting a giant picture of the funny feline.

T.W. was inspired himself. He hung his painting next to the door so that the mirror-like image of himself, wearing dark sunglasses and revolutionary garb, stared back at him. For the first time in months, he began to write. Filled with the creative spirit, he hunched over the typewriter with his hair in disarray and an unlit cigarette drooping from his mouth like a tree branch laden with snow. The sounds of clacking keys once again filled the third floor of the Row.

The Cat in the Hat was followed by *Green Eggs and Ham*, which was used to decorate the walls of the kitchen. *Horton Hears a Who* became a bathroom. *The Lorax* set up shop in the laundry room. *How the Grinch Stole Christmas* filled a hallway. *One Fish Two Fish Red Fish Blue Fish* covered a set of stairs.

More books followed. *The Very Hungry Caterpillar* devoured the second set of stairs, *Where the Wild Things Are* lurked in the elevator, *Curious George* discovered Big Mama's office, *The Giving Tree* found a home in the common room, *Cloudy with a Chance of Meatballs* covered the mess hall, and *Puff the Magic Dragon* terrorized the weight room.

In a few short weeks, Squirrel moved on to a bigger canvas, the large ceiling of the rec room to paint what he hoped to be his opus, a night sky filled with nebulas, galaxies, planets, stars, suns, spaceships, extraterrestrials, and everything yet to be discovered in the depths of space. It was a recommendation of T.W.'s, who said the men needed something to look up to, since there wasn't much in way of inspiration in Detroit. The only roadblock was reaching the two-storied ceiling.

"Go see The Wiz," T.W. instructed.

Squirrel found the door to The Wiz's lab closed and locked. He knocked twice and waited for a reply. He was about to knock again when the door burst open, spilling out a jumpy Ray Charles who almost ran into him.

"What are you doing here, newbie?"

"I'm here to see The Wiz."

"Well whatever it is I'm on to you. You just better watch out because I have my binoculars on you."

He didn't. They were pointed six inches to the left of Squirrel. Ray Charles turned away, almost tripped over his own feet, and then shook a fist at Squirrel before running off. Squirrel, unsure of what he had done to deserve the watchful eye and indignation of Ray Charles, shrugged his shoulders and entered The Wiz's domain. The lab was dark and shadowy. It took his eyes a few seconds to adjust to the windowless gloom.

"Hello," he called.

"Over here," a voice responded. Squirrel looked to his right and saw a long table stacked with beakers, graduated cylinders, flasks, and test tubes of various shapes and sizes. Most were filled with an assortment of liquids in a variety of colors, giving off hazy, translucent vapors.

"No, over *here*," the voice called again. Squirrel turned to his left and saw more tables. These ones piled with all kinds of junk and scrap metal scavenged from the dump. On one was an engine assembled with gears and belts from various appliances. Another was covered with a cloth, obscuring what appeared to be a large flying machine. On a third was the frame of a human-shaped robot. A work in progress, its head was missing and its lower body was a mess of wires and circuits.

"No, *here*," the voice called a third time.

Squirrel looked straight ahead and spotted The Wiz, decked out in a black apron and wearing a dark welding mask. He stood over a table that was covered with a myriad of old radios, transmitters, wires, and antennas. Surrounded by shadows, The Wiz was illuminated by a bright blue flame that shot out of the end of a narrow gun held in his right hand. A red, snaking hose connected it to a black box on the floor.

"I wouldn't stare too long into the flame if I was you. The only person foolish enough to do that is Ray Charles, and he's already half blind as it is."

Squirrel averted his eyes and carefully walked towards The Wiz, mindful of all of the junk lying on the floor, hanging from the ceiling, and threatening to spill over the tables.

"You're Squirrel, right? I believe we haven't met, I'm The Wiz."

Squirrel nodded and tipped his hat as a curtsey. The Wiz put out the blue flame and pulled back the mask so that it rested on his large flock of curly hair and divulged the thick glasses that covered half his face.

"So I hear you are in need of my expertise. What can I make for you?"

"Why, yes I am. But how did you know I needed something made?"

"I know everything. Now tell me what it is. Time's a wasting."

Squirrel handed him a sketch of the contraption he needed and explained its purpose, while The Wiz listened with his head cocked.

"Hmmm. I see. It can be done, but it will take some time. I will need to organize a search party for supplies and then recruit Stone Age and Muscles to help with the heavy lifting and construction. I am currently busy with a few other projects, but I should be able to get to yours in a week or two. Now about my fee."

"Your *fee*?"

Yes, my fee. This first one is free, but after that I am required to charge you marks or request favors for services rendered. You can also roshambo me for it, but just so you know, I've never lost a two-out-of-three match, not *once*. My record stands at 284–0."

Squirrel gulped. "Sure. That sounds fair to me."

"Good, but before I commit to a project, I have to ask, does it serve *The Cause*?"

"What do you mean?"

"All things must serve the betterment of the Row. Does your request meet such a requirement?"

"Yeah, I think so. I mean, I need to paint the ceiling of the rec room."

"Very well. Expect a message from Ray Charles within a few days." With that, The Wiz dropped the mask back onto his face and resumed his work.

With time to kill while he waited for The Wiz to build his contraption, Squirrel decided to make portraits for the remaining twenty-nine orphans. Scissors told him to pay close attention to his hair. Muscles insisted on flexing during the entire pose. Chopsticks thought his was "berry good." Compost Pile refused to shower or comb his hair and was thrilled by Squirrel's added touch of gluing pieces of garbage to his face and clothing. Marshmallow's background had to be painted black to contrast his color. Pickles dropped his right away and had to duct tape it back together. Toaster was adamant about wearing camouflage and having a matching camouflage background so that the only things distinguishable were his eyes. Belch and Bellyache asked to be painted together. Faygo drank a Faygo in his. Big Ben insisted that his included real, working watches and made ticking sounds. Wheelin' Dealin' Steven demanded his bling be painted with real gold. Rooster thought his needed more kazoo. Stone Age appreciated how the paint erased the lines on his face and made him look younger. Peanut Butter appreciated how the paint made him look older. Colonel Sanders analyzed his for a whole week, realizing that an orphan's perception related directly to his adoptability. Matches immediately set his on fire. Tea Bag thought his was "jolly good, mate." Christmas Story wanted a full portrait to include his leg. Ace of Spades made his disappear so that it was never seen again. Poop Stain thought his birthmark on his forehead was too glaring and overshadowed the rest of the portrait. Snot persisted on his being of a moon landing, with special attention paid to his suit. He also sneezed so much that Squirrel had a hard time seeing his face. Mike Tyson insisted on making his head smaller. Cup Check said his reminded him of the punch line to his latest joke. Seafood's took the longest because he needed a snack break every five minutes. And Ray Charles, well his was . . .

"*Crap*! Look, you got my binoculars all wrong!"

Big Mama was the most appreciative of her portrait, pressing Squirrel to her bosom and causing him to hold his breath for twenty seconds. "Lordy, Lordy, Lordy, you're a true angel you are. Lordy knows you are."

The portraits sealed Squirrel's fate at the Row, going a long ways towards earning his stripes. All of the men liked him, save for Ray Charles who still had his suspicions. For the first time in his life, Squirrel had more friends than enemies. Unfortunately, it didn't change anything at Detroit Public, where he was still nobody.

T.W. tried convincing him to be orphan-schooled.

"You know you don't have to go to that stupid school if you don't want to. We're an accredited academy here. I'm certified to teach all subjects, and I can do a Hemingway of a better job than those morons they call teachers at Detroit Public. I bet they couldn't even teach a dumpster chicken how to poop all over the place."

Squirrel wanted to take T.W. up on his offer, but then thought of Demmie and her act of kindness. She was the only friend he had besides the men, and he still hadn't written her back or talked to her yet.

"Sorry, sir, but I have to go back."

"Unfinished business I take it?"

"Well, sort of, sir."

"No need to explain, just remember one thing."

"What's that, sir?"

"Don't let The Man get you down, kid."

Squirrel didn't have to worry about letting The Man get him down when he had the Wilsons to contend with. They had not forgotten him in his short hiatus, especially Buck, who always started in on him first, while his lackeys added a chorus of laughter.

"Hey, turd brain, where ya been the last week? Searching for nuts because you don't have any?"

"Hey, hippy, why don't you get a haircut? Buck thinks you look like a girl."

"Squirrely's a girlie. Squirrely's a girlie."

Thankfully most of their abuse was verbal, and Squirrel was able to avoid them as much as possible, sneaking in the hallways and hiding in the art room during free periods. This also meant that he inadvertently avoided Demmie as well.

Not being able to write didn't help matters either. He longed to tell her how he felt but was handicapped by his inability to form words around her, both vocally and written. His only viable option was to seek counsel with T.W.

"What's that you say? You need help writing a letter?" T.W. ran his switchblade comb through his hair three times. "Well, kid you came to the right place. Who's the letter for?"

"A girl." Squirrel felt a bit squeamish.

"A love letter, even better. Let me get my collection of Shakespeare."

"Well, you see, it's more of a thank-you letter, not a love letter."

"Nonsense. Thank you? Love? What's the difference? Either way you want to melt this girl's heart, right?"

"Well . . . I guess so."

"I know so. Come on. Let's go write some beautiful prose for this dame without a name. With my help she'll be your gal in no time."

It took days of editing and reediting before Squirrel finally had his letter.

Dearest Demmie,

Thank you for the letter. I apologize for my leisurely response. I wanted my words to match my thoughts because your beauty could make Picasso paint straight, Einstein forget relativity, and Bob Lennon skip a verse and move straight to the chorus. It even makes a guy like me shy. Whenever I see your face, my insides turn to jelly and my tongue becomes tied in knots of licorice. So please forgive me for not reaching out to you earlier. This poem is for you.

Roses are red
Violets are blue
Your hair is the fire
That has me burning for you

Yours Truly,
Squirrel

He slipped it in the narrow slits of her locker, sealed in a red envelope. Included inside was one of his better sketches of her.

The days leading up to the last day of school and Duke Day were painstakingly slow for Squirrel. Every day he checked his locker for a response and every day he found nothing in return. With each passing day his hope dwindled until the last day of school when the last bell rang and any trace of optimism gave way to trepidation as he approached his locker.

He opened it with a sigh and felt like someone kicked him in the stomach after he discovered only his books and no letter. He closed it shut with his head down.

It was only because his eyes were averted to the floor that he was able to see a soft, pink hand holding out a white envelope. Squirrel raised his eyes and met the sparkling blue of Demmie's. A sensation of drowning overcame him as air escaped his mouth and failed to return. Unable to speak, he just stood there.

Demmie smiled, placed the envelope in Squirrel's hand, and kissed his left cheek before walking away. Squirrel watched her hair bounce with her steps as his breath slowly returned to him. She turned a corner and was gone for the summer, all before they could say their first words to each other.

The bus ride back to the Row felt as long as a rainy day. Squirrel held the envelope the whole way, caressing it with his finger and eagerly waiting to know its contents. When the bus finally arrived at the Row, Squirrel jumped off and sprinted up the three steps, passing Big Mama seated on her bench, stitching away.

Big Mama watched him run and shook her head. "Lordy, that boy running like his britches is on fire."

Squirrel didn't stop until he reached the third floor and burst through the door of T.W.'s office, much to the chagrin of Ray Charles who was in the process of snooping through Squirrel's locker for condemning evidence.

"*She wrote back.* It's here. Right *here.*"

"Slow down, man. Get a grip."

"Quick, you have to read it to me."

T.W. extracted a knife from his desk drawer and slit open the top of the envelope. He leaned back in his chair and ran his switchblade comb through his hair three times while he read.

"*Well,* what does it say?"

"Why don't you read it yourself?"

"But, I can't read."

"Sure you can. Give it a try."

T.W. handed the letter back to Squirrel. He held it in his sweaty palm and looked at it with apprehension.

"Go on, you can do it."

"It says, 'Dear Squirrel, I have w-w-waited for your resp-sp—"

"Response."

"I have waited for your response for some time now. It was g-g-good he-*ring*—"

"Hearing."

"Hearing from you. I have w-w-wanted to talk to you for some time, but was too scarred."

"Scared."

"I was too scared. Please write me back over the s-s—"

"Summer."

Squirrel looked up with a smile. "There's an address and a postscript. The p-pic-*picture* you sent me was the b-b-best gi-gift I ever re-re...re—"

"Received."

"The best gift I ever received. I love it."

Squirrel put down the letter and stared out the window. "She wants me to write her over the summer. Can you believe it? And she loves the picture."

"Sounds like true love, kid."

"But what will I say to her? How can I write her back? I can barely write a complete sentence."

"Don't worry about it. Just leave it to me, kid. We'll double our efforts. This calls for a celebration. Let's have a toast of the good stuff."

"*The good stuff?*"

"Old-fashioned, rich chocolate Ovaltine. I got a can dating back to World War II I've been dying to try. I'll have Ray Charles fetch us some warm milk. *Ray Charles*, get in here!"

The door burst open and Ray Charles came tumbling in. He adjusted his binoculars as he said, "Yes, sir, what is it?"

"I need two warm milks on the double . . . no make it three, on the double."

"Yes, sir." Ray Charles ran from the room. T.W. went to pull the cigarette from behind his ear, but remembered Squirrel was there and pulled out his comb instead. After three quick swipes it was back in his pocket.

"Now I know the reason why you wanted to go back to that god-awful school. She must be quite a beaut."

"She is, sir."

"I look forward to meeting her someday. And just for your information I am an ordained minister in the state of Michigan, certified to marry couples."

"How'd you manage that, sir?"

"*The Cause* works in mysterious ways, kid."

Squirrel nodded. Ray Charles came back into the office carrying a tray with three steaming cups of milk. He attempted to set the tray on T.W.'s table, but miscalculated the landing zone, nearly placing it on thin air. Thankfully T.W. was adroit enough to catch it before it crashed to the floor.

"Jeez-Louise, Ray Charles. Watch what you're doing."

"Sorry, sir."

"Don't be sorry, be more careful."

T.W. opened the tin can of Ovaltine and put two spoonfuls into each cup, stirring each briskly before moving on to the next. When he was finished he handed a cup to Squirrel first and then Ray Charles who took his with a fulsome salute.

"Okay, boys, let's have a toast before we drink up. 'Courage is being scared to death—but saddling up anyway.' To young love, Squirrely getting his stripes, and the Duke, may he rest in peace."

They clasped cups. Both Squirrel and Ray Charles took a big swallow. T.W. took a small sip and immediately spat it out.

"Holy mackerel, Ray Charles. You can't use condensed milk on Ovaltine. What in the Hemingway happened to the fresh stuff?"

Ray Charles didn't have an answer, only a thick Ovaltine mustache.

They finished their Ovaltine in silence before heading downstairs for the Duke Day festivities. Down in the rec room the men were halfway through *The Green Berets*. It was part of their John Wayne marathon, having already finished watching *The Shootist, The Man Who Shot Liberty Valance, Red River,* and *She Wore a Yellow Ribbon*. After dinner, the marathon was to be concluded with *McLintock, Sands of Iwo Jima,* and the orphan favorite *True Grit*.

"I love this movie." T.W. took a seat on the pillow pile. "'Out here, due process is a bullet.'"

The ending credits were received by the dinner bell and then a procession of black vests moved towards the mess hall to devour a meal fit for the Duke, consisting of steak grilled medium rare, baked beans and bacon, and a mac-and-cheese casserole, with chocolate cake for dessert. At the conclusion of the meal, the men pounded their tables with forks and spoons, calling, "Speech, speech, speech."

T.W. waved them silent and stood on top of a table near the front.

"On May 26, 1906, a great man came into the world. And though he was not an orphan by birthright, he was a man who all orphans could strive for, a man who stood for all we believe in, a man who blazed his own trail and understood what *The Cause* was all about, a man known simply as the *Duke*."

The men banged their silverware on the table. With a brush of his hand T.W. painted them into silence. "Today not only commemorates the birth of the Duke, but also the induction of our newest member, making us thirty-one strong. As the Duke said, 'A man has to have a code, a way of life to live by,' and it is with great pleasure, honor, and duty that I hereby name Squirrel a member of the Proletariat Pistol-Swinging Punks of Douglas Street. May he wear his stripes with pride and never stray from *The Cause*."

The men gave a thunderous applause. All save for Ray Charles, who kept his arms folded and his binoculars out of focus. Squirrel walked up to the front of the mess hall, where he placed one hand on a copy of Hemingway's *For Whom The Bell Tolls* and swore the vows of both the Row and *The Cause*.

Afterwards, he was handed a black PPSP-Douglass-Street-Affiliation vest from Scissors, his name stenciled on the back. T.W. helped Squirrel put the vest on, officially joining him to the ranks of the Proletariat Pistol-Swinging Punks of Douglas Street.

* * *

Mayor Sharp sat on a sofa in one of the many rooms of his large, spacious suburban house, sipping a Scotch and watching a John Wayne rerun. Ever since a kid, he had been a big fan of the Duke, though for different reasons than the orphans of Desolation Row. What Mayor Sharp liked most about the Duke was the fact that it was all a ruse. John Wayne, real name Marion Mitchell Morrison, was just a stage name. On screen he portrayed rugged American individualism, but in truth he was just an actor, very much the way Mayor Sharp was a politician on stage, posing like he cared, when in truth, he cared only about himself. He was just an orphan who started with nothing and came to have everything. Well, nearly everything. There was still the presidency to be had.

Mayor Sharp finished his scotch and then pulled two folders from the coffee table. One was labeled Cottonmouth, the other Black Mamba. He started with his nemesis first, then moved on to the second, his obstacle, trying to devise a way to resolve two problems with one solution.

11

Orphan of the Month

SQUIRREL'S FIRST PRIORITY of the summer as a new member of the PPSP Douglas Street Affiliation was to compose Demmie a letter. Unsure of what to write, Squirrel decided to indulge her with the daily happenings of the Row. Five rough drafts later (with T.W.'s assistance) he had a finished copy.

"Dearest Demmie," T.W. read. "Life at the Row (what we orphans call the orphanage) begins at 8 am, with the ringing of the breakfast bell. Classes follow, but since I am on summer vacashun my days are spent reading and painting the walls. So far I have most of them complete, but I need help from The Wiz (the smartest orphan) before I can start the ceiling of the rec room. After lunch I continue to paint and with the help of T.W. (our fearsome leader) I am learning to play chess, though I am not very good. Every night we have dinner at five, which is usually a deleshus gormet meal prepared by Chopsticks (our cook). After dinner is free time. Orphans either play games in the rec room or scavenge the dump for supplies. Sometimes I just paint or stare at the stars. Lights out is at 11 p.m. sharp, sometimes later if it's a holiday or special ocashun. I like the summer, but can't wait to go back to school so that I can see you again. Included is a picture I drew of the Row. I hope you like it and I look forward to hearing from you. PS I got my stripes and I am now an oficial member of the PPSP (Proletariat Pistol-Swinging Punks) of Douglas Street."

T.W. folded up the letter and handed it back to Squirrel. "It looks good, but you misspelled gourmet, delicious, vacation, and occasion. Also there are two f's in official, not one."

Squirrel circled the words while T.W. spoke.

"Also be careful with your run-ons. Use a period instead of using *and*. And don't forget to write the Row's address on the bottom of the letter. That way she knows where to mail a response, just in case something happens to the front of the envelope."

"Will do, sir."

"You should also include another poem. Girls eat that stuff up like chocolate-covered strawberries."

"Yes, sir, will do. How much is the postage?"

"Don't worry about it. The Wiz has trained some of the dumpster chickens to act as carrier pigeons. Don't ask me how he did it, but believe me they're as reliable as Big Ben's kitchen bell. The Wiz even managed to send one of them all the way to Philadelphia. It came back two weeks later with a signed receipt and a half-eaten Philly cheese steak. Seafood ate the rest. I guess The Wiz was right about those stupid birds serving a purpose."

"Very well. I'll make the corrections and it should be ready for delivery tomorrow."

The letter was sent out the next day, attached to one leg of a dumpster chicken, while a small tracking device was pinned to the other. The Wiz tracked the bird's movements with a large black remote-control box with a silver antenna as thin as a pencil stretched two feet in the air from its top. On the front of the box was a small screen with one tiny dot marking the location of the Row, another marking the coordinates of Demmie's house, and a third transmitting a green halo that marked the progress of the carrier bird, beeping every second. By the controller's current calculation, it was still three miles from the Row, with another seventeen to go.

"She should have it sometime tonight." The Wiz kept his eyes on the green dot.

"Great, thank you."

"No problem and about that other thing—you know what you asked me about—expect an update from Ray Charles within the next few days."

It only took one day. Squirrel was in the middle of painting the last remaining wall of the second-floor bedrooms—drawing inspiration from Roald Dahl's *The BFG*—when Ray Charles interrupted him.

"Hey, newbie, got a message for you."

"From The Wiz?"

"Who else would it be, newbie?"

"Why are you still calling me that, Ray Charles? I've earned my stripes now."

"Whatever. Do you want the letter or not?"

Squirrel took the envelope from Ray Charles. Almost immediately, he couldn't help but notice that it had been opened and carelessly put back together with tape and glue. There were even powdered candy-cigarette marks on it as well.

"Have you opened this letter, Ray Charles?"

"Nope, it was like that when I got it. Can't blame me, I'm just the messenger."

It wasn't like that when Ray Charles first got it. After receiving the letter, Ray Charles hid himself in the laundry room to read it in private. It took him only a minute to read through its contents, but over an hour to try to seal it again.

Squirrel tore the envelope open and read through the letter quickly, his reading ability having come a long ways since his first lesson with T.W.

Squirrel smiled when he was finished. According to the letter, The Wiz had gathered all of the supplies and was set to begin construction. It would be ready within a week.

"Very well, thank you, Ray Charles."

"So why do you need a Mobile Elevation Contraption anyways?"

"How did you know I needed a Mobile Elevation Contraption, Ray Charles? I don't remember sharing that piece of information with you."

Realizing he was caught red-handed Ray Charles ran away as fast as his feet could carry him, which turned out to be too fast for his binoculars. He tripped on the stairs and went binoculars over heels, tumbling all the way to the first floor, thankfully avoiding any serious injury. Unfortunately, the same couldn't be said for the pack of candy cigarettes in his front pocket. They were crushed and the chalky sticks were reduced to tiny chunks the size of Tic Tacs.

The summer was not going well for Ray Charles. Disappointed with not making last month's Orphan of the Month, he redoubled his efforts, making him a camel with many straws on his back. Besides spying on Squirrel and being T.W.'s runner, he was now The Wiz's full-time runner as well, helping scavenge new parts from the dump and inadvertently helping with the construction of Squirrel's Mobile Elevation Contraption, whatever that was. Thanks to the added stress, he was now up to two packs of candy cigarettes a day.

The opposite was true for Squirrel. His summer was filled with leisure. He read on a daily basis, continued to cover the walls of the Row with paint, and eagerly waited for a response from Demmie. Whenever Scissors called "mail call," Squirrel was the first to greet him with "anything for me?"

Most days it was no.

"Sorry, nothing, Squirrel. Just a cooking magazine for Chopsticks, a *Pyromania* magazine for Matches, a letter from the Psychology Department of Stanford University for Colonel Sanders, a box of allergy medicine for Snot, and a bunch of letters—mostly rejections I surmise—from the Governor's office for T.W."

Every day he waited for mail call and everyday received the same thing—*nothing*. One day, as he was walking through the common room with his head down, he was startled by Toaster who popped out from behind a plant, wearing camouflage green and fake leaves glued to his hat, shirt, and face.

"Hey there, Squirrel. I can spy on that gal of yours if you want me to. I'm a master of disguise. Just give me an address, an objective, and consider it done. She won't even know it's stalking. But it'll cost you ten marks, plus travelling expenses."

"Thanks, but no thanks, Toaster."

"Hey, suit yourself." Toaster disappeared back behind the plant.

Squirrel didn't bother to ask Toaster what he was doing hiding as a plant. He just assumed he was on some special assignment for T.W. or The Wiz. The end of the month was a busy time at the Row, with men doing whatever they could to get more marks for the Orphan of the Month competition.

Peanut Butter volunteered for dangerous late-night scavenging missions at the dump, resulting in Sir Barks-a-Lot chewing out the backside of his jeans. Compost Pile volunteered as a Guinea Pig for The Wiz, resulting in his body breaking out in red hives for a week. As an incentive to participate in his showing of *Romeo and Juliet*, Tea Bag offered marks to anyone willing to play the female lead of Juliet—a part that involved a kissing scene and dressing in drag. He was hoping for Mike Tyson because of his soprano voice, but so far his only volunteer was Ray Charles, who declined the part once he learned Squirrel was playing the lead of Romeo, stating irreconcilable differences. Cup Check was giving away marks to anyone willing to listen to his latest comedic repertoire. Ray Charles could only handle four jokes before walking away cupping his orphan jewels and grimacing in a voice matched only by Mike Tyson. "Come on," Cup Check said. "That wasn't even the end of the first act." Seafood didn't have any marks to trade, but he was willing to roshambo any orphan for their dessert. Wheelin' Dealin' Steven was having a special: buy any two pieces of jewelry and get an added mark; buy any three pieces of jewelry and get two additional marks; and the topper, buy any five pieces of jewelry and get five marks. Ray Charles tapped into his college fund to purchase two necklaces, a gold watch, a silver ring, and a bracelet. It took all of Stone Age's efforts to keep enough marks in circulation, his hammer pounding day and night.

Feeling that this was his month to shine, Ray Charles also participated in counseling sessions with Colonel Sanders, traded aspirin to Belly Ache, suntan lotion to Marshmallow, and broken watches to Big Ben, gave all of his Faygos to Faygo, assisted Stone Age in forging marks, traded flammables with Matches, peeled potatoes for Chopsticks, worked out with Muscles, graded papers for Scissors, volunteered for sock sorting in the Sock Room, and helped Big Mama with the never ending laundry pile, washing and folding so many clothes that Big Mama told him, "Lordy, boy, you starting to smell like Downy Fabric Softener."

By his calculations, Ray Charles figured he had well over a hundred marks, an easy shoe-in for Orphan of the Month. As the end of the month approached, Ray Charles shined his binoculars with a triumphant smile.

Squirrel was too preoccupied with painting to really care about the Orphan of the Month competition. He had a large pile of marks next to the pickle jar containing his great-grandmother's dentures. He didn't bother keeping count and would have gladly given them away if one of the men had simply asked.

Two days before the big announcement of this month's winner, Squirrel's Mobile Elevation Contraption was finally complete. It was good news, considering he still hadn't heard back from Demmie and continued to write her on a weekly basis.

"You don't look too excited," T.W. said as they walked to the rec room to inspect the new device.

"I am, sir, it's just that I haven't heard back from Demmie."

"You know, when I first started writing letters to the Governor's office to secure more funds for the Row, they never wrote me back. Not a single letter. It was only when I doubled, tripled, and quadrupled my efforts, sending them letters once, twice, three, even four times a week before writing them on a daily basis that they started to take notice and pay attention. *Numbers*, I tell you, that's all those darn politicians care about. Strength in numbers, there's truth to that saying, Squirrel. The more letters you send that dame, the more likely she'll respond. Besides it's good writing practice."

That it was. Squirrel was far from becoming a scholar or poet, but he was becoming less and less reliant on T.W. It was only the big words that slowed him down.

They entered the rec room to find The Wiz there waiting for them. "Well, what do you think?"

"You really outdid yourself this time, Wiz," T.W. said.

"It's beautiful." Standing in front of Squirrel was a seven-foot tall wooden, rectangular platform, the size of a bunk bed, folded like an accordion. A ladder ran up the backside with four rubber wheels attached to the bottom.

"How high up does it go?" Squirrel asked.

"Hop on and see for yourself." The Wiz handed Squirrel a small black remote control. "The *on* switch is located at the top. The controls on the right control the boom, while the dial on the left moves the ME. It's pretty self-explanatory, even that daredevil, bonehead Crash figured it out."

"What's 'ME'?"

"I took the liberty of renaming it the Mobile Elevator, ME for short."

"Right, good one." Squirrel started to climb the ladder.

When he reached the top, he was pleased to see it was as soft as a bed, even coming with a pillow for extra comfort. He lay on his back, taking in the ceiling.

"Wow, this feels like a real bed."

"It should, we used a Tempur-Pedic mattress."

Squirrel's hand fumbled to the side and discovered a retractable table for his palette and various holders for his paints and brushes.

"The table's a good touch too."

"Alright, try the boom."

Squirrel flipped it on and then moved the dial for the boom. His stomach filled with a sensation of movement as the boom lifted and the ceiling slowly crept closer. He released the dial only when he was close enough to the ceiling to reach up and touch it.

"This is fantastic," he called down to The Wiz. He removed one of his brushes from his pocket and stroked it against the rough texture of the ceiling. In his mind, he envisioned how the paint would transform the dull gray into a mosaic of night.

He looked over the left side. Farther up than expected, he was surprised at how small everyone appeared below.

"What do you think, Squirrel?" T.W. asked.

"It's great."

"Try moving it," The Wiz said.

Squirrel worked the controls on the left side and felt movement as the ME lurched forward.

"It's perfect. Thank you, Wiz."

The Wiz smiled and nodded. "It appears my job here is done."

He walked away, leaving T.W. to run the switchblade comb through his hair three times. Squirrel lowered the boom and climbed down the ME.

"What do you say, kid, up for a game of chess?"

"Not today, sir. I want to start painting right away."

"Get to it then. You're excused." T.W. waited until he was out of the rec room before he retrieved the cigarette from behind his ear and placed it in his mouth. Toaster popped out of his hiding place to light it for him.

"Thanks, kid, carry on." T.W. headed up the stairs to his office. Expecting to have some much needed time to himself, hopefully to put some ink to paper, he was surprised to find his first officers seated at his desk. Scissors, Muscles, and Chopsticks all stood up and saluted as he entered.

"You're on time, sir," Scissors commented. "That's a first."

"On time for *what*?"

"The officers' meeting. We need to discuss this month's Orphan of the Month recipient."

"Oh, that again. Where's The Wiz? Isn't he supposed to be here?"

"Duty calls, sir. He's still working on a modified tracking device and sends his regards."

"Figures, alright, take a seat and let's get started. Muscles, we'll start with you. What are your thoughts for Orphan of the Month?"

"It's a tough call, sir. The men have been working extra hard this month."

"They work extra hard every month. Who stands out?"

"I have to say Ray Charles, sir. He's worked out with me every day this month and claims he's up to one hundred push-ups, an OPB."

"And you believe him? Have you seen him complete one hundred push-ups with your own eyes?"

"No, not exactly, sir. Well, *almost*. I came into the weight room one day and he was sounding off from seventy-something."

T.W. smiled. "Alright, Chopsticks what about you?"

"Way Chawle. He peel hundred potato for mashy potato night."

"Now, I can believe that. What about you, Scissors?"

"I have to agree with the others and say Ray Charles. According to my calculations he has 107 marks, which is 60 more than the closest candidate. The boy has proven himself busy as always, and besides he's due, having yet to receive the honor."

T.W. paused and brought his hand to his chin.

"I'm not sure if he's ready yet. A boy like him always needs something to strive towards otherwise he'll end up lost. I don't want him—to quote the Boss—to be 'blinded by the light.' I know I've been holding out on him for some time now, but I want to make sure it's the right moment, that he's completely ready."

"How much longer would that be, sir? The Wiz fears he is overworked and close to the breaking point. He believes there is an 85.27—repeating of course—percent chance that Ray Charles could breakdown from exhaustion."

"Nonsense, he just needs to learn how to pace himself. We'll wait a few more months before we give him the honor, by then he'll be ten—

"Nine, sir," Scissors said.

"Whatever, by then he'll be ready for the responsibility that comes with Orphan of the Month. Give him some more rations of candy cigarettes to hold him over for now."

Scissors made a note on his clipboard.

"Alright, who else do we have for a candidate?"

They deliberated for five more minutes before coming to a decision. T.W. sent them out afterwards. Scissors was the last to leave, closing the door behind him. T.W. sat in his chair and read through the last paragraph he wrote the day before. In no time he was clacking away, losing all track of time.

Sometime later a loud knock broke him from his typing trance. "Sir, it's time," Scissors said, bringing him a fresh cup of coffee. T.W. stood up, adjusted his sunglasses, ran his comb through his hair three times, and pulled on his black PPSP-Douglas-Street-Affiliation vest, and took a sip of the coffee. He stared at the picture of Che Guevara and gave it a curt salute before leaving his office.

By the time he entered the mess hall, it was full of seated men, teeming with excitement. Whispered voices crackled like electricity, only to be hushed as T.W. marched through their ranks.

"Attention men," T.W. called from the front of the room. Thirty orphans stood up in place with their hands at their sides, facing forward.

"At ease."

The men sat back down.

"It has been a very busy and productive month at the Row. Everyone has done his part for *The Cause*, and I'm proud of each and every one of you. However, only one of you has gone beyond the call of duty, done more than the common orphan, and shown initiative above all others. Only one of you stands alone."

Ray Charles heard these words and swelled with pride. He was practically bursting with dignity, valor, and a sense of duty.

"Only one of you can be Orphan of the Month."

At the mere mention of Orphan of the Month, Ray Charles stood erect in his chair. His binoculars held high and his chest pointed forward.

"And now for the moment you've all been waiting for. Drum roll, please."

The men pounded on the tables, creating a cacophony of noise equivalent to rain falling on a metal roof. Ray Charles gripped his acceptance speech in his hand, waiting to walk up and claim his prize.

"This month's Orphan of the Month is . . ."

Ray Charles held his breath.

"Squirrel!"

All the men broke out into a loud applause, all but Ray Charles. His lower lip trembled and a tear rolled out of the left side of his binoculars. As Squirrel stood up to accept his award, Ray Charles slipped away unnoticed from the mess hall.

"That does it," he cried. "There's only one thing left for me to do."

* * *

In another part of town, Mayor Sharp was having a clandestine meeting with his crew, nicknamed the Dogs, who used fear and intimidation whenever bribery and cronyism failed to get his intended results.

"How are we looking men?"

Their leader, a big hulk of a man dressed in camouflage, stepped forward. His voice boomed like a bullhorn. "SIR,

WE'RE AHEAD OF SCHEDULE. TAG POLICE ARE STILL GOING DOOR TO DOOR. CITY BLOCKS ARE CLEARED AS EXPECTED. DUMP TRUCKS RUNNING NIGHT AND DAY. ONLY A FEW HOMELESS HOSTILITIES REMAIN."

"Good, very good. I have a special mission for you and your crew. A reconnaissance mission. I need you to get whatever Intel you can find on the person in this folder. Use any means necessary. Also plant some evidence as a contingency. Do it ASAP and await further instructions."

Mayor Sharp handed the big, bulky man a manila folder. On the front it was marked in big black letters. The top line read "Target: Big Mama, aka Black Mamba" and the line underneath it "Location: Desolation Row, aka Future Carwash."

12

The Unthinkable

THE REST OF THE SUMMER went slow for T.W., so slow, in fact, that despite a few intrusions by the Tag Police, the Row practically ran itself. He used the spare time to focus on his novel, while the men came and went as they pleased, Big Mama napped more than she stitched, blaming late summer humidity as the culprit, and Squirrel busied himself painting the ceiling of the rec room while also enjoying his tenure as Orphan of the Month.

The threat of adoption was just as sluggish. It had been months since an unexpected Charlie. T.W. wasn't sure whether to be joyful or suspicious. At an orphanage, times of tranquility were usually followed by times of despair. Hope for the best, expect the worst, it was all an orphan could do. Yet, he couldn't shake the feeling that a storm was brewing just over the horizon. What it entailed, he didn't know.

As a precaution he added more watch duties and met with his officers.

"There's been an awful lot of Tag Police activity in the neighborhood." T.W. paused to run his comb through his hair three times. "I don't know who keeps tipping them off.

We need to keep an eye out for them. It's only a matter of time before they come in force."

"Do you think they're related to the Calloways? The check came in on time and in the usual way this week."

"Maybe, but not entirely sure. We'll meet on it again tomorrow. Meeting dismissed."

The officers left, leaving T.W. alone. He brushed away his premonitions like he did stray hairs with his switchblade comb then turned to his writing. So far he had surpassed the 400 page mark. He was starting to think he might actually finish the darn thing. Thanks to the removal of his writer's block he had even managed to cut back on cigarettes, much to Squirrel's satisfaction.

"You should just switch to candy cigarettes, sir," Squirrel said. "You know the ones Ray Charles always has in his mouth."

"Nonsense, those things taste like cardboard. Besides I had my sweet tooth removed years ago."

Things were going so well that T.W. was beginning to think that the outside world had forgotten all about Desolation Row. But that was hardly ever the case. A dump was never short on garbage and an orphanage was never short on orphans. In the middle of July the Row received three additional orphans, a trio of brothers.

The youngest brother, Monster, age seven, was far from a monster, but had a phobia of nearly everything known to orphan. Just to name a few, there was agliophobia, fear of pain, which was why he wore football pads in his clothing, gymnophobia, fear of nudity, which was why he always showered while wearing his underwear, and chaetophobia, the fear of hair, which was why he didn't have any. Prone to randomly fainting and wetting his pants, he wore a black bicycle helmet wherever he went and had two drawers stocked full of underwear to replenish the ones he accidently soiled.

He was so timorous that he jumped at the sight of his own shadow and slept with a light on. It was because of him that Muscles had to organize a special task force whose sole purpose was to investigate the Row for possible bogeymen, ghosts, and monsters. Every night before lights out they swept the Row and every night they came back declaring "all clear."

Monster met with Colonel Sanders every day to discuss his fears, their sources, and possible remedies. However, after only a few weeks he developed a phobia of psychiatrists and had to cancel his appointments. Since he had a fear of adoption, T.W. never had to worry about him being adopted. He was the orphan most likely to never leave the city of Detroit, or the Row for that matter.

The middle brother, Duct Tape, age nine and a half, was a jack-of-all-trades who could fix anything with a roll of duct tape, including his clothes, which were patched all over in gray tape. His shirts and pants were as stiff as burnt toast, causing him to walk around like a robot, while his shoes squished with every step. The Wiz took a special interest in him and recruited him for his lab. There he fixed appliances and performed general maintenance. He was the orphan most likely to star on the *Red Green Show*.

The oldest brother, Potty Mouth, age eleven, had the mouth of a sailor. Every other word was a curse word. When he spoke, the younger orphans had to cover their ears with pretend earmuffs—their hands—and hum the alphabet. T.W. was the only one who could make any sense of his cursing.

"Bleep-%$#@-bleep."

"Oh, right, Potty Mouth, of course it's for *The Cause.*"

"Bleep-%$#@-bleep-&%$#@-bleep-bleep."

"No, Potty Mouth, the towels for the showers are over there."

"Bleep-%$#@-bleep-bleep-&%$#@-bleep."

"That's not a very nice thing to say about Ray Charles, Potty Mouth."

His mouth was so dirty that brushing his teeth with Colgate, followed by swishing with Listerine didn't make it any cleaner. He was the orphan most likely to live in New Jersey.

The three brothers quickly took to the Row. Monster made friends with Snot and Belly Ache. Together they formed their own self-help therapy group, discussing all the ills of society and how they were better off staying inside, away from the outside world. Duct Tape became good friends with Stone Age. Together they became the right and left hand of The Wiz, duct taping and hammering all kinds of inventions for *The Cause.* Potty Mouth took to playing dice with Belch, Faygo, and Peanut Butter. Together they shared speech impediments and barely understood each other.

"*WhatyousayPottyMouth?*" Faygo asked.

"Eck-what-eck?" Belch asked.

"Bleep-%$#@-bleep," Potty Mouth responded.

"Did he say what I think he said?" Peanut Butter asked, his Baby-Talk relaying the message in a smooth robotic tone.

Four new orphans, including Squirrel, in three months and no new Charlie made T.W. nervous. As a precaution, he decided it was time for an addition to his cabinet of officers. He only had one orphan in mind.

"A second lieutenant?" Squirrel asked. "What does that even mean?"

"Well, it's a leadership role. You'll be a part of my War Council and have a say in how things are run around here."

"I don't know what to say, sir."

"Say *yes*, for Hemingway's sake."

Squirrel paused to think. "But what about my painting, sir? Won't it take time away from that?"

"Not necessarily. You'll only have to attend meetings and fill in for The Wiz when he's busy. Besides you've been painting nonstop for over a month now. Aren't you almost finished with the place?"

"I know, sir, but I'll find something else to paint. I always do."

"Well, just think it over, kid. I don't need an answer now."

Just then an out of breath Scissors ran into the office.

"Sir, there's been another report of a monster."

"Let me guess, the newbie again. Where was it spotted this time?"

"The sock room, sir. Monster claims he saw a tail the size of a boa constrictor slithering through the pile of socks."

"Could have just been Seafood looking for that Twinkie he lost last week. We better follow up on it so the boy can sleep at night. Have Muscles organize a search party."

"Roger that, sir. And have you seen Ray Charles? He's been acting funny of late."

"No, I haven't. How so?"

"Well, yesterday after class he asked for a whole carton of candy cigarettes."

"Yeah, so? The kid goes through candy cigarettes faster than Monster goes through clean underwear."

"That's true, but he's been cutting back these past few weeks. I hardly see him with one in his mouth. Also he no longer asks questions in class. In fact, he skipped today. The first time ever, I believe. Last semester he attended class when he had a temperature of a 104 and had to carry around a paper bag to spew in."

"Hmmm . . . I guess you should keep an eye on him. Part of Ray Charles's problem is that he's trying to fill ten pounds of orphan in a five-pound bag. Oh well, if you see anything else suspicious recruit Toaster. The boy doesn't miss a thing."

It was just then that the ventilation grate above T.W.'s door popped open, followed by the emergence of the dust-covered face of Toaster.

"Did you call for me, sir?"

"Jeez-Louise, Toaster! How long you been up there listening?"

"Oh, not long, sir."

"Who authorized you to be up there anyways?"

"Why, you did, sir. You told me to check out the ventilation system for bugs and see where it went."

"Oh, right. Carry on then."

Toaster's face disappeared, closing the ventilation grate behind him.

"Where was I? Oh yes, keep an eye on Ray Charles. Maybe monitor his movements with one of The Wiz's tracking devices. It's operational, right?"

"It is and will do, sir. I'll get right on it today."

Scissors left the office, scribbling notes on his clipboard.

"You see what I have to deal with on a daily basis, Squirrel. An orphan like you would make my job a whole lot easier."

"I've only been here a few months, sir. I'm not sure if I'm ready for a leadership role."

"Nonsense, you were born ready, just haven't realized it yet. Go paint, think on it, and get back to me. I have some writing to do. Chess game later?"

"Sure. See you later, sir."

Squirrel left the office and closed the door behind him. T.W. sat in his chair with his feet up on the desk. Alone with his thoughts, he could not escape the cloud of his intuition, an impending storm was on its way.

T.W. spent the next few days pondering all the things that could go wrong and would go wrong. He was so caught up in what hadn't happened yet that he completely missed what was happening in front of him. As a result, towards the end of August the unthinkable occurred. Another orphan was adopted on his watch.

It took a day before anyone noticed that Ray Charles was missing. Scissors came bursting into T.W.'s office screaming, "Sir, we have a situation."

"*What*? A Charlie?"

"Worse, I think something is wrong with Ray Charles."

"What do you mean?"

"I did as you requested. I put a tracking device on him, and well, he's been at the dump all day and all night. But the thing is, I went to the dump, to the spot where he was supposed to be, and he wasn't there."

"Interesting. Explain yourself, Scissors."

"You see, I checked the control of the tracking device before I went to bed last night, and Ray Charles was in the same exact spot he had been in earlier in the afternoon. When I woke up this morning he was still there, so I went out to see if I could find him, but he wasn't there, only two bags of garbage, like he just vanished into thin air."

"Hmmm," T.W. said, biting his nails. "Show me the spot."

It was drizzling outside when they came to the backyard. The ginormous junkyard steamed with condensation. Scissors held up an umbrella as T.W. studied the trash bags that sat just to the left of the sign proclaiming *Dante's Descent*, the spot where they placed trash from the Row to be taken further into the dump and where Ray Charles should be.

"This was yesterday's trash, correct?"

"It appears so, sir."

T.W. pulled a knife from his back pocket and sliced open the two garbage bags. Various pieces of trash, debris, and food spilled out like fish guts. T.W. used his knife to dig through its contents, his hands pausing when they came to something solid and black.

"What is it, sir?"

T.W. handed him a pair of binoculars.

"*Holy Hemingway!* Why are Ray Charles's binoculars in the garbage?"

"Why exactly? This is worse than I expected. Go ring the kitchen bell, call a Code Red. Hand out walkie-talkies. I want every available orphan on the lookout for Ray Charles. Meet back in my office in fifteen. I want all officers present, including The Wiz, *especially him*. Hurry, Scissors, the Row's under MELD until further orders."

"Mandatory Emergency Lock-Down, roger that, sir!"

Within minutes the kitchen bell rang through the Row, followed by the commotion of running footsteps. T.W. hurried to his office, opening the safe behind the portrait of Che Guevara. He took out its contents—a black Luger pistol and a stack of documents lined in a plastic baggie. He placed them on the desk and then rubbed the key hanging from a chain around his neck.

Squirrel came bursting into the room with a look of surprise on his face. "What's going on, sir? The men are running all over the place. It's total chaos down there. What are—"

It was then that he noticed the Luger. His look of surprise grew into one of complete shock. "Is that a real pistol?"

"Of course it's real. We got a situation on our hands. Could be SDPOT. I'm not taking any chances."

"Serious, Dangerous, and Possibly Orphan-Threatening," Squirrel muttered, having learned it from Scissors just the other day. He gulped as T.W. tucked the Luger in the back of his pants and proceeded to unseal the documents on his desk.

"What are those papers for, sir?"

"Ray Charles has gone missing. We're still assessing the situation. These papers are contingencies, specifying what to do in such matters. They're classified, officer eyes only. If you are going to stay than I need you to accept my offer, otherwise I have to ask you to leave."

Squirrel could tell by the look on T.W.'s face that he was serious. He had no other choice. "Alright, sir, I will be your second lieutenant."

"I'll need you to shake on it and swear an oath."

T.W. spit into his right hand and offered it to Squirrel. Squirrel did the same before accepting T.W.'s handshake.

T.W. held his grip. Squirrel could make out his ashen face in the reflection of T.W.'s dark sunglasses.

"Do you swear to give your life to *The Cause* and the Row, to always follow orders, and stand true to your fellow men, take a bullet for them if need be, and whenever possible stick it to The Man?"

"I do, sir."

"Welcome to the club."

Just then Scissors rushed into the room, followed by Chopsticks and The Wiz.

"Where's Muscles?"

"He's organizing the men, putting them in groups of three to search every inch of the Row. Each squad leader has a walkie-talkie turned to channel three. They're using mallard duck as a back-up call."

"Very good. Be sure to fill him in when the meeting's over. Also, Squirrel is a new member to our council. I just swore him in as my second lieutenant."

The officers nodded in agreement.

"Alright where are we? What do we know? What are our options? Scissors, fill everyone in from the beginning."

Scissors told them about Ray Charles's strange behavior and how he skipped multiple days of class, which resulted in him placing a tracking device on Ray Charles's binoculars. He ended by rehashing how they found the binoculars in a garbage bag by the dump.

When he was finished, T.W. spread out a folded map of the Row on his desk. He circled a spot near the backyard to indicate where Ray Charles's binoculars were found.

"Interesting," The Wiz said.

"Berry interesting," Chopsticks said.

"Alright we need to figure out where Ray Charles went from here." T.W. pointed to a place on the map.

"Ray Charles's last known whereabouts were two days ago. He was working with Stone Age in the lab but was spotted the day before last by Pickles, leaving the second-floor bedroom dressed in his Sunday's best. His binoculars unaccounted for."

T.W. drew a line from the dump to the lab to the second-floor bedroom. Next, he gave the pen to Scissors. "Circle the locations of the search parties."

Scissors circled them, while T.W. concentrated on the map.

"Get Muscles on the mike."

"Breaker, breaker," Scissors called into his walkie-talkie. "This is HQ, calling attention to Bravo Company, over and out."

There was a sound of static, followed by a crackle. "Breaker, breaker, this is Bravo Company, over and out."

"Breaker, breaker, what's your current location Bravo Company? Over and out."

"Breaker, breaker, the Southwest . . . (*static*) . . . quadrant of the dump, over and out."

T.W. took the walkie-talkie from Scissors. "Breaker, breaker, Bravo Commander, this is Wolf Pack Leader. I need you to redirect back to Base Command, immediately. We believe clues to the Tango's whereabouts are within the perimeters, not outside. Rendezvous and scour the second-floor bedrooms. Leave no bed left unturned, HQ over and out."

"Breaker, breaker, roger that . . . (*static*) . . . Bravo Company over and out."

"Hmmm," T.W. said, pacing the room. "The kid was blind when whatever happened to him happened. But what would anyone want with a blind orphan? Perhaps he's just lost. It's happened before. However, the timing isn't good, especially with so many Tag Police scouring the neighborhood. This just doesn't make any sense. He doesn't go anywhere without those goggles on his head."

"This makes perfect sense," The Wiz said. "I don't think Ray Charles is missing, sir. I think he was adopted."

A hushed silence fell over the officers.

"How is that even possible?"

"By my calculations," The Wiz said, pulling his calculator from his shirt pocket. "Out of all of the men, there was a 66.44—repeating of course—percent chance that Ray Charles was most likely to be adopted."

"*Son-of-a-Hemingway!*"

"That is not all," The Wiz said, rubbing his big glasses clean. "Ray Charles was due for a breakdown. According to Chaos Theory, he had a 73.32—repeating of course—percent chance of doing the unthinkable. He was a time bomb waiting to blow. Colonel Sanders said he even showed signs of POTS, sir."

"Post-Orphan-Traumatic Stress!" Scissors said. The officers nodded in agreement.

"Nonsense," T.W. exclaimed. "What is this *Vietnam*?"

"His symptoms have only increased with the arrival of Squirrel. His chances of doing the unthinkable spiked to 82.67—repeating of course—percent chance once Squirrel entered the equation."

"Why wasn't I informed of this?"

"Sorry, sir, I've been busy."

"This is all my fault, sir," Squirrel said.

"Bologna. Ray Charles just doesn't take kindly to change. He's always been touchy. I still think adoption seems unlikely. We haven't had a Charlie in months. Do we have any other leads?"

"None, sir," Scissors said. "All we know is that Ray Charles has left the building, sir."

"He's not Elvis." T.W. sighed. "Alright, I need answers. I want to know how this all happened. If he was adopted, why wasn't I made aware of any possible Charlies? Wiz, you're on the case. I want a report by 1500."

The Wiz nodded, taking his leave. T.W. pulled the cigarette from behind his hair. Scissors quickly lit it. The smoke formed a question mark above his head.

"Ray Charles, where in the Hemingway are you?"

* * *

Ray Charles was long gone. Following in T.W.'s footsteps, he had his own contingency plan, one permitting adoption, not preventing it. The day after the Orphan of the Month announcement, Ray Charles spent the day crying his binoculars out. The following day, he wiped his binoculars clean, orphaned up, and got to work. He put his plan into motion.

T.W. wasn't made aware of any possible Charlies because no one knew of the Charlie, except for Ray Charles. Not wishing to wait for a Charlie to come to him, he opted to go to the Charlie instead. His first order of business was getting in good with Big Mama by offering to clean her office and reorganize her filing cabinet.

"Oh, Lordy, yes. Thanks for ya help, Ray Charles. You're an angel, a real blessing. Lordy knows you are."

Acting more like a devil, Ray Charles used the opportunity to comb through her files, looking for the perfect Charlie to contact. Since Big Mama kept a record of all possible Charlies, there were well over 200 to choose from. Ray Charles spent two full days focusing and refocusing his binoculars while digging through the files until he came to the perfect Charlie—the Wilburys, Ken and Meg, both optometrists.

He used Big Mama's phone to give them a ring.

"Yes, hello, Lordy," Ray Charles said, his voice high and affable, mimicking Big Mama's. "Is this the Wilburys' residence? Oh, Lordy, good. This is Big Mama from Desolation Row, and Lordy, I got good news for you. Lordy, you bet I do. There's a new orphan that's heaven sent like Jesus himself, Lordy yes. He'd be perfect for any family. He's so nice, charming, sweet, smart, strong, courageous, reliable, helpful, thoughtful, delightful, and just plain full of goodness that any family would want him. Lordy knows he won't last long. But I was thinking he'd be just perfect for you, Lordy yes. That is if you're interested?"

They were. For added emphasis, Ray Charles included four more Lordy's before hanging up the phone. A meeting was scheduled a week later at a coffee shop a few bus stops down the street from the Row.

With all of his Hemingway's in order, all Ray Charles had to do was lay in wait until his adoption day. He watched with clenched fists as Squirrel wore his PPSP-Douglas-Street-Affiliation vest daily and directed his binoculars away whenever he saw Squirrel sitting in the comfy La-Z-Boy Throne in the rec room. He continued to attend class and help The Wiz in the lab only to avoid rousing suspicion.

No one suspected a thing, not even The Wiz who hardly missed a thing. Only Scissors noticed something was amiss with the boy, but by then it was too late. For over a week Ray Charles played the part of the good orphan. Everything went according to plan until the day of days. Then it almost completely fell apart.

The night before the big day, Ray Charles had his bag packed with all of his belongings, save for his PPSP-Douglas-Street-Affiliation vest, which he had left in his locker. His plan was to stow his bag behind one of the animal hedges so no one would see him leaving with it. However, he didn't plan on Toaster being there.

"What are you doing?" Toaster asked, popping out from against the wall. His face, hands, clothes, and shoes were all painted to resemble faded red bricks. He was on reconnaissance duty, keeping an eye out for the Tag Police.

"What are *you* doing?" Ray Charles asked in return.

"I asked first. Let's roshambo for it, best out of three."

Ray Charles lost the first two. "Jiminy Cricket. It's for *The Cause*, alright, and it's confidential. You're interfering with official Row business. Now scram, you ignoramus."

"Jeez Louise, sorry, Ray Charles. I'll leave you alone."

With the animal hedges a wash, Ray Charles dragged his suitcase a few blocks down the street and stored it behind a shopping cart full of dirty clothes. The extra detour made him almost miss breakfast. All that was left was crusty oatmeal the color of monkey brains.

"You wate, Way Chawles, you wate." Chopsticks waved his wooden spoon at Ray Charles.

"I know, I know."

Ray Charles ate quickly. When he was finished he checked in with a ticking Big Ben to see what time it was.

"8:45 already? Jiminy Cricket!" The watch he was currently wearing was ten minutes slow, despite Wheelin' Dealin' Steven guaranteeing it was as accurate as a calendar when it came to telling time.

"What's the big [alarm from a watch sounding] hurry, Ray Charles?" Big Ben asked. The watches and clocks all over his body made ticking sounds.

"I gotta go."

He skipped morning class with Scissors and hurried to the lab. Stone Age was already distracted with work, his gray hair perspiring with sweat and his hammer swinging. Ray Charles used the opportunity to gather some supplies and his stash of marks from under a bench. By his calculations, he had close to 500, making him one rich orphan. His pockets were heavy by the time he left the lab.

He went back to his room, put on his best clothes—a suit and tie too big for his skinny frame—and tidied up in the bathroom.

"Why are you so dressed up?" Pickles asked. He had his hand caught in the drain of a faucet sink. "You look sharper than Tom Travolta in *An Orphan and a Gentleman*."

"None of your bee's wax," Ray Charles said, running a comb through his hair. "It's official Row business—*confidential*."

"Oh, gotcha. Hey, do you think you could hand me some soap? I'm trying to grease my hand. It got stuck in the drain again."

"Sorry, I gotta go."

Ray Charles only had one last errand to attend to before saying goodbye to the Row forever. He stuffed his signature binoculars into the wastebasket in the rec room. With suitcase in hand, a big smile, and red holes around his eyes where his binoculars used to be, he walked past a sleeping Seafood and headed towards the front door.

The only thing in his way was the wall, which he ran straight into. He left the Row rubbing his noggin.

Already running behind schedule, his journey towards adoption only grew more complicated once he left the safety of the Row and entered the chaotic realm of the real world. It was his first time out on his own. All he had going for him was his nearsightedness, which made the world appear blurrier than it actually was. Ray Charles was too blind to be anything but optimistic, hoping he was walking in the right direction.

He turned the corner and was surprised to see a homeless man digging through his suitcase. The man wore a tattered green army jacket and a dirty red winter hat that covered his long, greasy hair. His scruffy beard was uneven and looked like fungi growing on his face. Even worse was the smell, which was akin to a pile of dumpster-chicken poop.

"Hey, what are you doing going through my things?"

"Who says they're yours?"

"I do, it's mine."

"And who are you?"

"I'm Ray Charles."

"Name's Stinky Pete, pleased to meet ya. How bout we split the stuff? There's enough to go around for both of us."

"But it's mine. Hey, that's my carton of candy cigarettes. Put them back right this second, you imbecile. "

"Hey, little buddy. Take a chill pill. It's a free country, y'know."

"Don't make me use this."

Ray Charles extracted from his pocket what appeared to be a very large, homemade Taser—one of The Wiz's self-defense mechanisms. He pointed it at what he thought was Stinky Pete's chest but was in fact six inches to the right.

"I'll use deadly force if need be," Ray Charles said, trying to sound tough.

"Whoa, little buddy. I don't want any problems. City's rough enough as it is without anybody getting hurt over it. I just got my third eviction notice on my cardboard box. The homeless can't even sleep under bridges no more. Mayor's kicking everybody out of town, won't even put us in warm jail cells, nope, sending us all to the armpit of America, the state of Ohio. Please don't hurt me, son. I'm just trying to get by. Take it. It's all yours."

Stinky Pete fled, leaving the suitcase and his shopping cart behind.

Feeling better about the situation, Ray Charles attempted to put the Taser away, but misjudged the location of his pocket and stunned himself in the leg instead. He did the Harlem Shake then fell to the ground.

It only took him a few seconds to regain his composure, but when he stood up he realized his entire right side was numb. He grabbed his suitcase with his left hand and then began walking, half dragging his numb right foot behind him. It was slow progress to the bus stop, but he made it there just as a bus was pulling in.

"Here, keep the change." Ray Charles handed the driver two marks.

"You gotta be kidding me," the driver said. "I can't accept these."

"What do you mean you can't accept these?"

"They're just scraps of metal with a stupid logo on it."

"It's not a stupid logo, *you're stupid.*"

"You got a lot of nerve, kid. Either you pay up with real money or get off my bus and walk your mouthy little butt back to wherever you came from!"

"That's all I got."

"Hey, wait a minute that watch looks familiar."

The watch in question was the one Ray Charles had gotten off Wheelin' Dealin' Steven a month ago. The watch looked familiar because it was the exact same one that the bus driver had thrown away six years ago when the wristband broke. It was scavenged at the dump by Rooster, repaired by Big Ben, traded to Wheelin' Dealin' Steven, and then bought by Ray Charles, who was currently wearing it.

"How 'bout you give me that watch instead and we call it even?"

Ray Charles bit his lower lip before giving him the watch. He walked to the back of the bus with a smile, knowing the watch was ten minutes slow. Fifteen minutes later, Ray Charles missed his bus stop because he couldn't read the signs. Unsure of where to go, he hailed a taxi and was nearly run over in the process.

"Are you stupid or something? Whaddya doing standing in the middle of the road, kid?"

Ray Charles had seen a similar stunt done in a Tom Travolta classic, *Driving Miss Daisy Duke.* "Sir, I need to get to the Motown Mocha Coffee Shop, ASAP. I'm willing to pay you ten whole marks."

"Marks, what are those? Canadian currency or something?"

"Do you want my money or not?" Ray Charles debated whether or not he should use lethal force and Taser the guy. He thought better of it, since he didn't know how to drive a car. While he was contemplating what to do, the cab driver noticed the necklace hanging from Ray Charles's neck. It was the same one he lost a few years back. It was scavenged by Marshmallow, traded to Seafood, who exchanged it to Wheelin' Dealin' Steven for a Twinkie, who then sold it to Ray Charles.

"Gimme that necklace and I'll take you anywhere in the city you wanna go."

Ray Charles gave it to him, and five minutes later he arrived at the coffee shop. The Wilburys were already there, waiting for him. Expecting to meet Big Mama, they were somewhat surprised to be approached by a skinny eight-year-old with a suitcase. Before they could say a word, Ray Charles hugged them and said, "Hi, Mom and Dad. It's so good to finally meet you."

It took The Wiz a few days to retrace Ray Charles's steps. Thankfully the lad was as good at leaving a trail as he was blind. There were traces of white candy cigarette powder everywhere, most prominent on a manila folder labeled Wilbury.

"It's been confirmed, sir," The Wiz said, handing T.W. the folder. "Ray Charles was adopted. All of his belongings are gone, save for his vest. He even took some marks and a few other items from the lab. I believe a Charlie with the surname Wilbury adopted him. Phone records show they were contacted over a week ago. They're both optometrists, which explains the tossed binoculars."

"Good. And an address?"

"It's all there in the file."

"Thanks, Wiz. You're an orphan-saver. I'll take it from here."

The Wiz left the office, leaving T.W. with Scissors and Squirrel. T.W. fingered the key around his neck.

"Is it time to use the key?" Scissors asked.

"No not yet. We can handle this situation ourselves. We'll save that for *The Cause*." He let the key fall back to his neck and pulled out his switchblade comb.

"Sir, what are we going to do then?" Squirrel asked.

"There's only one thing to do." T.W. ran his switchblade comb through his hair three times. "We get him back."

It took a few days to formulate a plan. The men were so preoccupied with retrieving Ray Charles that no one noticed a large, bulky figure, dressed in all-black camouflage, sneak into the Row during the middle of the night and enter Big Mama's office. Big Mama was fast asleep, saying Lordy in between snores. The figure made straight for her filing cabinet, the one containing all sensitive material pertaining to the Row and the men. For every file he took, he replaced it with one of his own. When he was finished, he snuck back out, all without a trace.

13

Blinded by the Night

"WHERE ARE WE GOING?" Squirrel asked.

It was night. Douglas Street lay in darkness. All of the streetlights were permanently shut off years ago by the city in an attempt to conserve money. T.W. led the way, followed by Squirrel, Muscles, and Toaster, all decked out in their PPSP-Douglas-Street-Affiliation vests and fake mustaches. The full yellow nimbus of the moon filled the sky above, casting long shadows, none larger than the dark silhouette of the abandoned Ford plant straight ahead.

"The armory," T.W. said.

"I still don't see the point in me coming along," Squirrel said. "Ray Charles hates me. It's because of me that he left in the first place. My presence would only compromise the mission."

"Nonsense. Ray Charles needs to see the folly of his actions and that means confronting you. If we're going to get him back, we're going to get him back completely so that something like this doesn't happen again."

"But what if Ray Charles likes his new surroundings? Why take him away from a good family?"

"Because he doesn't truly want to be adopted that's why. He's doing this to spite me. Didn't you listen to a word Colonel Sanders said?"

Colonel Sanders had given a detailed lecture on the ailments of Ray Charles. He explained that Ray Charles suffered from father figure deficiency, also known as Rival Orphan Syndrome, and therefore he needed constant attention and reassurance from a paternal figure. Due to the arrival of Squirrel, who Ray Charles viewed as a threat because of his closeness to T.W., he felt deprived of that attention and reassurance from T.W., the closest thing to a father Ray Charles had.

T.W. thought all of this was total rubbish, to which Colonel Sanders offered T.W. to talk about his own father, which, of course, T.W. refused.

"But," Squirrel said. "I—"

"Save all of your buts for Peanut Butter. You just have to trust me on this."

T.W. didn't say another word. The orange glow of his cigarette pointed the way. The Row, a good five minutes behind them, remained on High Alert with Scissors in charge. Before leaving for their late night rescue mission, T.W. had briefed his small, elite team.

"Listen up, men, this is an in-and-out mission. No need to raise suspicion. We go by cover of night, complete stealth, DEFCON 4. Tonight's birdcall is Baltimore oriole. I want everyone suited up, ready, and out of here in five. That means vests, supplies, and mustaches."

"*Mustaches*?" Squirrel asked.

"Toaster, fill him in."

Toaster held out a handful of fake mustaches, various shapes and sizes.

"These are all specially crafted by The Wiz. They're perfect for espionage. Just lick 'em like an envelope and place them over your mouth. We got all kinds, including the Dali, the Van Dyke, the Zappa, the pencil, the handlebar, the gringo, the boxcar, the Super Mario, the chevron, the horseshoe, the trucker, the Kublai Khan, the Wyatt Earp, the Magnum PI, the milk-stache, the Hulkster, the Chaplin, the Zorro, the Yosemite, the Fuhrer, and the always popular Tom Travolta."

Squirrel went for the Chaplin. Muscles wore the Hulkster, Toaster the Magnum PI, and T.W. the Hemingway.

"Sir, what's the point of wearing mustaches?"

"Moral support and intimidation. The Wiz calculated that an orphan feels 75.21—repeating of course—percent more confident with a mustache and most people feel 48.83—repeating of course—percent more submissive when in the company of someone with a mustache. Can't beat the statistics, kid."

"Right," Squirrel said, feeling more confident already with his Chaplin.

They waited until Big Mama was fast asleep before exiting the Row. Behind her closed bedroom door, her loud snores sounded like distant thunder.

"What happens if she wakes up?" Squirrel asked as they climbed down the steps.

"She won't."

"But how do you know?"

"Scissors slipped two of The Wiz's homemade sleeping pills into her coffee. She'll be out for at least ten hours. The stuff's strong. One time Seafood made the mistake of taking double the allotted dosage and was asleep for three days straight."

The night was quiet and cool as they walked. The moon gave them plenty of light to go by, but it was still difficult to make out anything in the distance. Detroit at night was a ghost town with more empty buildings than people.

It was only when they were just in front of the Ford automobile plant that T.W. signaled them to halt. "Okay, we're close enough. Give us some light, Muscles."

Muscles turned on a flashlight, illuminating a rusted door, locked with four padlocks. T.W. reached into his pocket and pulled out a key ring, heavy with dozens of keys. He flipped through them quickly, found the right ones, and then unlocked the padlocks in succession.

When he was finished, he held the door open for the others to enter. Unsure of what to expect, Squirrel walked into both literal and figurative darkness. The light from the flashlight speared into the shadows, revealing little.

"Hit the light switch, Toaster," T.W. ordered.

Toaster flicked the switch. Along the ceiling industrial-sized lights turned on in sequence like synchronized swimmers jumping into a pool one at a time. It took a moment for Squirrel's eyes to adjust and take in the scope of the room.

"Wow," was all he could say.

"Impressive, isn't it?" T.W. asked.

The abandoned warehouse was the size of an airplane hangar and large enough to contain two football fields. The ceiling was twice as high as the one in the rec room. Busted windows lined the tops of the walls, allowing bats to fly in and out of the shadows. Vehicles of all different makes and models filled the entire room. There were dump trucks, bulldozers, school buses, campers, tractors, cars, trucks, motorcycles, four wheelers, and golf carts. Far from new, they were pieced together with scrap parts from the dump.

Lacking windows and paint, they appeared road ready for a demolition derby. Some were modified to look like war machines with pieces of metal welded over the windows like prison bars, makeshift plows forged to their front ends, and spikes attached to the tires so that they resembled crude, warrior-like vehicles from the Tom Travolta post-apocalyptic car-racing classic *Crazy Carl.*

"Do they all run?" Squirrel asked.

"Well, most of them do. Some are still under construction."

"What are they for?"

"Well, *The Cause,* of course."

"But you have enough vehicles for a small army. Are you expecting a war or something?"

"Something, I guess." T.W. rested his arm on a giant piece of machinery that looked like a tank with a catapult on the top. "Most of the men think The Wiz spends all of his time in the lab. But in truth, he spends most of his nights here, tinkering away with Stone Age. This is his true domain. Even I don't know what most of these machines can do."

T.W. paused, pulling a cigarette from his ear. Toaster was quick to light it. "Most of the men don't even know this place exists. Consider yourself part of the inner circle, Squirrely."

"I don't know what to say, sir. This is . . . just . . . *unbelievable.*"

"Well, believe it. In this day and age, an orphan's got to be prepared for any kind of situation, real or imaginary."

"Sir," Muscles called. "Are we bringing weapons?"

"No, just the stunner."

"*The stunner*?" Squirrel asked. "Why do we need weapons?"

"Scissors reported that a Taser was missing from our arsenal at the Row."

"So Ray Charles is armed and dangerous?"

"Not really, more like armed and a danger to himself."

"But if he's harmless why bring the stunner?"

"You don't know Ray Charles like I do. He's a loose cannon. I've scorned him, and there's no telling what an orphan scorned will do. Best to be on the safe side and use precaution. Alright, men let's saddle up. Toaster, you ride with Muscles. Squirrel with me."

T.W. led him to a tarp-covered object the size of a large desk. He removed the tarp with a quick swipe, revealing a black motorcycle with an equally black sidecar. Light flickered from the silver chrome, while red flames danced along the side paneling.

"That is Isis. Restored her myself. She rides like a dream. Do you know how to drive a motorcycle?"

Squirrel shook his head no.

"You can ride in the sidecar then."

"What about helmets, sir?"

"What about 'em?"

T.W. hopped onto Isis and motioned for Squirrel to do the same. With a kick from his boot, the machine came to life. Its loud purr resonated through the thick walls of the warehouse. Squirrel hopped into the sidecar.

"Hang on tight to your hat."

"Yes, sir." Squirrel clamped down on his black bowler just as the motorcycle leapt forward, leaving black skid marks on the concrete floor. Muscles pulled up alongside them in a large camouflage four-wheeler. Toaster sat behind him, barely visible in his own camouflage. Together they zoomed towards a large closed garage door. T.W. hit a switch on his bike and the door inched slowly open.

"Sir, I don't think we're gonna ma—"

The motorcycle whizzed through the opening, the bottom end of the garage door just brushing the top of T.W.'s hair. The bike took the corner a little too sharp, causing the sidecar to tip up on its side. Squirrel gripped the sides of the sidecar, lifting his hand only to press the bowler back onto his head, just before it had the chance to blow away. "Whoopee," he screamed as they made pavement and tore down Douglas Street.

They roared through the barren wasteland of Detroit. Large billboards showed the grinning face of Backseat Bob stating, "If life doesn't throw you a Frisbee, call Backseat Bob, and he'll help you sue the city." In the ghetto they passed rundown, empty buildings, vacant lots where broken glass grew like grass, the skeleton frames of discarded, gutted cars, and street corners with the homeless gathered around burning barrels, standing like scarecrows in torn flannels, hoodies, and parkas. Absent of light, Detroit was a Gothic landscape devoid of hope, very much a Third World Country tucked away, hidden in a modern civilization.

Despite the thickness of night, T.W. still wore his sunglasses, steering the bike around potholes the size of swimming pools and through streets people only drove down when lost. In the sidecar, Squirrel stared into Detroit's abyss, peered into its emptiness, and swam in its ugliness. He did not sink.

The scenery quickly changed once they reached the suburban hub of Royal Oak. The difference was so great that it was like stepping into a MacDonald's and entering a fancy restaurant instead. They passed streets with working streetlights, parking lots filled with working cars, and giant houses that all looked the same, as if made out of ticky-tacky. It was a world of luxury seldom seen by the eyes of an orphan.

"What is this place?" Squirrel asked, as T.W. pulled the bike along a street and killed the motor. Standing in front of them was a three-storied mansion. A mailbox the size of a dollhouse had "The Wilburys" written on the side.

"The suburbs," T.W said, "a Charlie's natural habitat."

"I've never seen anything like it before. Everything is so . . . so—"

"*The same.*"

"Yes, exactly."

"Places like this are about as entertaining as elevator music. I'll take the Row any day over one of these giant pieces of dumpster-chicken poop. At least it has character."

Squirrel nodded.

"Well, let's get this over with." T.W. pulled the Luger from the back of his pants then pulled back the chamber with a loud *chick-chick*. "The sooner we get Ray Charles the sooner we can get the Hemingway out of here. Muscles, scan the perimeter. Toaster, you're up."

"Yes, sir," they both answered, disappearing into the yard.

"What do we do now, sir?" Squirrel asked.

"We wait."

T.W. ran his switchblade comb through his hair three times while Squirrel adjusted his hat. The suburbs hummed with inactivity. Five minutes later, Muscles reappeared.

"The perimeter's clear, sir. No dogs and no alarms. The Charlies are in the living room. He's watching TV and she's reading a book. No sign of Ray Charles or word from Toaster."

"Alright, we'll give him a few more minutes."

Two minutes went by before a high-pitched whistle—Baltimore oriole—pierced through the quiet night. "That's our signal," T.W. said. "Let's move."

They walked single file, hunched over like monkeys, across the vast expanse of the yard. When they got to the side of the house, they stood against it, commando style, waiting for a signal from Toaster.

"Pssst, up here," Toaster said. They looked up to see Toaster's head appear from a second floor window. "Ray Charles is in a bedroom on this floor. The backdoor's unlocked. Just follow the rainbow." He disappeared again. Squirrel looked to T.W. for clarification, but he had already headed toward the backdoor. He shrugged and hurried after him.

They entered the backdoor, followed a green Skittle into the kitchen, went down a hallway after an orange one, and climbed the stairs in pursuit of a purple one. There was a red one in front of a closed door. Toaster popped out of a room, carrying a handful of white linen.

"Ray Charles is in there. I figured we could use these for our escape."

"Good work, Toaster. Alright, we go in on the count of three. One . . . two . . . *three!*"

They burst into the room with T.W. leading the charge. Ray Charles sat at his desk, typing away on a computer. His face seemed almost unrecognizable without his binoculars.

"Hey, guys," he said, not taking his eyes from the screen. "How's it go—*wait what the*—how did you find me?" Ray Charles stared at them astonished, even more astonishing was the fact that he was staring in the right direction.

"My God, Ray Charles, you can actually see," T.W. said.

"Yeah, contacts. Pretty cool, huh?" Ray Charles's eyes focused on Squirrel. "Wait. What's *he* doing here?"

Ray Charles jumped out of his chair, reached into a drawer on his desk, and pulled out the same Taser he had accidently used on himself two days ago. He pointed it straight in Squirrel's face.

"Ray Charles, put that away before you stun yourself," T.W. said, taking a casual seat on his bed. "See? Didn't I tell you how difficult he could be?"

"Get him out of here or I swear to Hemingway I'll tase the mustache off his face."

From downstairs came a call. "Raymond, what's going on up there?"

"Oh, nothing, Ma," Ray Charles called down.

"I thought I heard voices in your room. It's almost bedtime."

"Oh, right, sorry I was watching a movie on the computer, Ma."

"Alright, just turn it down, please. Five more minutes and then lights out."

"Sure thing, Ma."

"*Raymond!*" T.W. whispered. "What in the Hemingway happened to Ray Charles?"

"I go by Raymond now," Ray Charles said, lowering his head. "My parents said it sounds more proper than Ray Charles."

"That's a big bowl of cereal and you know it. Whatever happened to your real family, Ray Charles? The one that's been by your side since day one? What about us, your brothers? What about me for Hemingway's sake?"

"*What about you?* All you care about is that stupid newbie. Squirrel this and Squirrel that, well what about me for a change? When is it my time to shine? You couldn't even name me Orphan of the Month, even after all the work I've done."

"So that's what this is all about, Orphan of the Month? I didn't think you were ready for such an achievement and this foolishness only proves you're still not ready."

"That's horse crackers and you know it. I've proved that I can take care of myself," Ray Charles said, his voice building in a crescendo. "That I don't need you or *The Cause* or the Row or stupid Squirrel. I got everything I need right here, so *Hah.*"

"RAYMOND, I told you to turn that down! It's past your bedtime."

"Sorry, Ma. I'll get right on it."

Ray Charles redirected the Taser at T.W. "You guys need to get outta here before I get in trouble. So out now or I'll . . . I'll . . . I'll—"

"You'll do what?" T.W. stepped in front of Ray Charles so that the Taser touched his chest. "You'll Taser me? Go ahead. I deserve it. You're absolutely right."

"*I am?*" Ray Charles said, his grip loosening on the Taser.

"Yes, of course you are. You've shown that you can take care of yourself. You don't need me or the Row. You've proven yourself beyond all measure and doubt. This little stunt you pulled took great initiative and a lot of gall. You're the first and only orphan under my watch to orchestrate their own adoption. No one else has that distinction. What can I say? I'm proud of you, Ray Charles."

Ray Charles's face perked up, his chest swelled.

"I was only hard on you because I care for you. I'm sorry for the trouble I've caused by not believing in you and taking the things you've done for granted. I was wrong. Can you ever forgive me?"

Tears swelled up in Ray Charles's eyes. "Yes, of course, I forgive you, sir."

"In fact, I came here tonight to show my appreciation for all you've done and personally name you Orphan of the Month. That is, if you'll accept."

"Of course, I will."

"Well, then put that thing away before you give me a jolt."

Ray Charles placed the Taser on his desk.

"Muscles, will you do the honor."

Muscles pulled out Ray Charles's black PPSP-Douglas-Street-Affiliation vest and held it open so that Ray Charles could rope his arms through the opening. T.W. clapped him on the back. Ray Charles gave him a big affectionate hug.

"Thank you, sir, thank you."

"Don't just thank me. It was Squirrel's idea. He thought you'd be the perfect man for the job. He felt terrible accepting last month's honor because he thought you were more deserving."

"He did?"

"Yes. He even helped me see through my own arrogance. Do you think you can find it in your heart to give him a chance?"

Ray Charles sniveled and wiped his eyes. "For you, sir, anything."

He walked over to Squirrel and offered his hand. "I know we got off on the wrong hand, but I am willing to bury the machete if you are?"

"I'd love to," Squirrel said, taking his hand. Ray Charles went a step further, giving him a big hug.

"Well, I guess our job here is done." T.W. walked towards the door. "We just wanted to stop in and make sure you were alright. Best of luck with your new family, Ray Charles. We're all happy for you. You'll be sorely missed at the Row, but remember you always have a home there if you need one. We'll stay in touch via dumpster-chicken pigeon carrier. That way you can get a hold of us if you need our help. No matter how good your new parents are, always remember Snuggles, and keep your binoculars—I mean eyes on them. Alright, let's go men. We have a long ride ahead of us."

They were almost out the door when Ray Charles called to them. "*Wait,* give me a second to pack my things."

"But what about your new family?" T.W. asked.

"They're not my real family, you guys are."

"Are you sure, Ray Charles?"

"As sure as Hemingway."

T.W. nodded his approval. "Well, then you're going to need these." From a pocket of his leather jacket he pulled free Ray Charles's binoculars.

"Ah, sir, you shouldn't have."

Ray Charles tore out his contacts, tossed them to the floor, and placed the binoculars back on their rightful place, his face. It took a few turns to readjust them back into focus. After Ray Charles had packed his belongings, they left by way of window, tying the linen Toaster had confiscated into a rope and crawling down commando style. The only thing left undecided was who was going to ride behind T.W. and who was going to ride in the sidecar.

"I'll roshambo you for it, Ray Charles," Squirrel said.

"Sure, best two out of three?"

Riding on momentum, Ray Charles beat him two to one, but couldn't help but laugh at his strategy. "What were you thinking using paper three times in a row?" Squirrel smiled as he took his seat behind T.W.

"Everyone ready?" T.W. asked.

"Wait a minute," Squirrel said. "How far away is the city of Warren?"

"I don't know, not too far. Why?"

"Well, if you don't mind, I have a favor to ask."

"What is it?"

Squirrel told them and then asked, "What do you think? Is it possible?"

"Of course it is, kid," T.W. said, eyeing Ray Charles. "Sounds like a three orphan job. What do you think, Ray Charles? Are you up for a little more adventure?""

"Yes, sir, of course. Anything for the newbie—I mean Squirrel, but, sir, I have to ask, does it serve *The Cause*?"

"All things serve *The Cause*."

"Well then what are we waiting for, sir? Let's make pavement."

They waved Muscles and Toaster ahead, stating they'd meet them back at the Row, and left the Wilburys with a trail of black-tire marks. The further they got away from Royal Oak, the smaller the houses became. They soon arrived at the in-between place of Detroit, neighborhoods acting as buffers between the luxuriant suburbs and the ghetto.

They were almost to their destination when something on the streets caught Squirrel's attention. He motioned for T.W. to stop.

"What is it?" T.W. asked, retrieving the Luger.

"Look, there's a man over there selling flowers," Squirrel said.

"Where?" Ray Charles adjusted his binoculars.

The man in question had long, wavy black hair and dark skin. He wore equally dark sunglasses and a leather jacket. Next to him was a small table filled with red and white roses. A cardboard sign read "Flowers 4 Sale." Across his lap was an acoustic guitar. He appeared to be strumming a slow song.

Squirrel hopped off the bike and tipped his hat to the mysterious man. "Hey, mister, how much for a flower?"

"Depends."

"Depends on what?"

"Well, on how much you got and who it's for."

"I don't have much and it's for a girl."

"In that case, one flower will cost you nothing."

"Nothing, but how will you make any money?"

"Love's got its own currency. Besides, I'll be fine, little man. Just pick any flower you want. It's on the house."

This sparked T.W.'s curiosity. "Say, mister, can you fly?"

"Only once. In the early seventies, I flew all the way to

South Africa for a gig. I really dug the place, but ran out of money and as the saying goes there's no place like home. So I took a boat back. It was a long journey. By the time I got back it was the nineties, man. I've been here ever since playing songs and selling flowers. Sometimes I do some carpentry work on the side, but that's only in the wintertime when things get cold and the flowers don't grow so well. Say, that's a nice Luger you got."

"Thanks. What's your name mister?"

"People around these parts call me the Brown Sugar Man."

"Why?"

"I dunno, man. It stuck when I was a kid. I used to run with all these white cats, white as sugar you know, and I guess compared to them I stuck out so they called me Brown Sugar, you know like the Stones song. I added the Man. I kinda wished they would have called me Rollin' Stone instead, like the Muddy Waters song, but the Stones already nabbed that one so I guess I came too late, man. Story of my life."

"Well, Brown Sugar Man, it was nice to meet you," Squirrel said, picking a red rose. "I got to go see about a girl."

"I hear ya, man. Give her my regards. I bet she's as sweet as a song."

"She sure is."

"Well, take it easy. I walk these here streets, so I'll be seeing ya."

"And just in case you decide to get your wings again." T.W. tossed five marks into the empty guitar case.

"Wow, marks. I haven't seen those in years. Thanks, brother."

"No worries. Say, mister, were you an orphan?"

"Name a musician who wasn't."

T.W. smiled as they waved goodbye. A few minutes later they arrived at Squirrel's destination, to see about a girl.

"So what's the plan?" T.W. asked.

"I don't have one."

"So we're just going to wing it? I like it."

Squirrel nodded. They got off the bike and crept into the backyard of a modest-sized two-story house and hid behind some bushes. All of the lights were off.

"Is she even home?" T.W. asked.

"I dunno."

"Which room is hers?"

"I dunno."

"Is there anything that you do know?"

"Yes, this is exactly what Hemingway would do if he was here in our shoes."

T.W. laughed. "Fair enough. It's too bad we can't see worth a lick. I knew I should have snagged the flashlight from Muscles."

"Leave that to me," Ray Charles said. "My binoculars have night vision."

"They do? Since *when*?"

"Since forever," Ray Charles said, scanning the rooms of the house. "There, on the first floor bedroom. I see a poster of what appears to be a young Tom Travolta from his only mainstream hit, *Fitzgerald*, the sad romantic film about the sinking of the SS Edmond Fitzgerald. I must have cried twice during that movie, especially when the lead drowned—"

"Enough about the posters, Ray Charles. What else do you see?"

"Just a bunch of girlie stuff—a jewelry box, a Girl Scout dress, a stack of newspapers, and a desk with a computer."

"That's got to be her room," Squirrel said. "What do we do now?"

"Improvise." T.W. picked up a rock and chucked it at the window. It hit dead on with a loud dink. A light turned on from inside the window, followed by the movement of someone inside.

"Looks like someone's coming," T.W. said.

Ray Charles adjusted his binoculars. When they came into focus they fell on Demmie, dressed in a blue nightgown, her red hair flowing. He fell over so fast that it was like he'd been hit by a semitruck. T.W. went to his side and removed his binoculars. "Ray Charles, what happened? Are you okay?"

"Hubba, hubba," Ray Charles whispered, his eyes spinning.

Squirrel was so awestruck he was incapable of movement. "What do I do now?" he asked.

"Good God, man, go talk to her." T.W. pushed Squirrel forward. He stumbled into the open, almost losing his hat in the process. When he regained his composure, he found himself staring straight into Demmie's blue eyes. Not sure of how to proceed, he bowed his hat, gulped, and then spoke the first word to come to mind, something usually reserved for horses.

"Hey."

"Hey," she responded, not sure what to make of the oddly familiar stranger with a thick mustache standing before her.

"Say *something* you nitwit," T.W. whispered from the bushes.

"Oh right, hi, it's me, you know Squirrel, from school."

"Squirrel! What are you doing out there?"

"I-I was just . . . uh . . . in the neighborhood, you know."

"At this hour, it's almost midnight. What's that on your face? I almost didn't recognize you?"

"Oh, this?" he said, rubbing the Chaplin. "It's just a . . . you know . . . a fake mustache. I heard they're big in Japan or something."

A groan came from the bushes. Squirrel rubbed his hands together before shoving them in his vest pockets.

"That's . . . um . . . interesting, I guess," Demmie said.

"Good God, man, *the flower, the flower*," T.W. whispered.

"Oh right, I brought you this." Squirrel pulled the red rose from his back pocket. He walked to her windowsill and handed it up to her. "It's a rose. It's red just like your hair. I hope you like it."

"I see that," she said, raising it to her nose. "It's beautiful. Thank you, I love it."

"*You do?*"

"Yes, I do."

Squirrel smiled and then frowned. "Didn't you get my letters? I haven't heard back from you all summer and was beginning to worry."

"Yes, of course, I received all of them. That bird you sent was quite unusual. Didn't you get my letters?"

"No, not a single one."

"That's strange. I mailed at least a dozen, even one the other day."

"*A dozen* are you sure?"

"Yes, I sent them all to 2959 Douglas Street."

"Did you use the US Postal Service?" a voice asked from the bushes.

"Yes, and may I ask who you are?"

"The name's Teenage Wasteland, but you can call me T.W." T.W. stepped out of the bushes. "That explains it all. The US Postal Service is only good at losing mail, not delivering it. They're always sending us things meant for the state pen, which is probably where they sent all of your letters. I recommend using the dumpster chickens from now on. The Postal Service is about as useful as decaffeinated coffee."

"I'll remember that next time, thank you."

"No problem, doll. Now I hate to break up this late night reunion, but we need to be heading back to the Row, besides Ray Charles is still passed out in the bushes over there, mumbling in hubba-hubba land."

"Ray Charles?"

"He's one of us," Squirrel said. "My friends."

"Oh, I see. Will I see you at school next week, Squirrel?"

"Of course." He turned to follow T.W., but Demmie called for him to wait. "Come here, I want to give you something before you leave."

Squirrel stepped toward the window. Demmie leaned over the windowsill and planted a kiss on his lips, causing him to turn as red as her hair. "See you later alligator."

"After a while crocodile," Squirrel said. He walked towards the bushes, his lips still damp and warm from her kiss. His step had a new bounce to it, and the night suddenly felt as light as his heart.

They made it back to the Row in the late hours after midnight, about the same time that a shadowy figure returned to the secret meeting place of Mayor Sharp. He had in his hand a number of files, all of which were handed to a shaky and nervous Bartholomew Wilson.

"Thank you. Mayor Sharp will be pleased to see these. Were you able to plant the other files?"

The shadowy figure nodded. Mayor Sharp's plan was ready to be set in motion.

14

Out of the Oven
and into the Furnace

THE ROW'S NUMBERS were once again thirty-four strong with Ray Charles back in the mix. Having been the only orphan ever adopted to come back whole, he was greeted with a standing ovation upon his return. He stood in the mess hall, holding his breakfast tray, while the pounding of forks and shouts of "speech, speech, speech" resonated throughout.

"There I was surrounded by two Charlies," Ray Charles began, decked out in his PPSP-Douglas-Street-Affiliation vest. "They had me cornered, trying to win me over with all kinds of new stuff. Toys, clothes, a computer—you name it. They even tried to give me a new name. *Raymond*, can you believe that? But I wasn't fooled for one second. No sir, not me. Even without my binoculars I could see right through their ruse. They just wanted me for child labor or worse yet, to be eaten like those two kids lost in the woods, Hannibal and Grendel."

Some of the younger men gasped. Monster almost fainted.

"Luckily for me those two Charlies didn't know their shoes from Shinola, and I was able to bide my time and plan my escape. Being on the outside made me realize one thing—there's no place like the Row."

The men thundered their approval with loud whoops, while Ray Charles bowed triumphantly. He not only held the prestige of Orphan of the Month but also was more popular than Tom Travolta after starring in the action-packed trilogy *Depart Hard*. Ray Charles took to his newfound celebrity like he took to candy cigarettes. It all went to his binoculars.

His fame was short-lived, lasting only a few short days before attention was drawn elsewhere, namely to the end-of-summer extravaganza known as *The Row's Got Talent*. They held it in the Row's small, circular auditorium that was part of the Row during its one year tenure as a former performing arts theater. Its stage was constructed of solid oak and stood five feet tall. Dark, velvet curtains hugged the top of the stage like drapes. The ceiling was open and arched, consisting of a blue-and-gold tapestry that intertwined like the red-and-white lines of a peppermint candy. The walls were cut from dark gray stone. A dozen hand-carved gargoyles, with scowling faces, hung from them like numbers on a clock. Reclining seats, the color of dried blood, were placed in ten rows of eight. The lighting was poor, consisting of dim-lit lanterns pointed to the ceiling like flashlights.

The talent show held a whole slew of memorable acts. Belch belched out a version of Bob Lennon's not-so-hit song "The Long and Winding Roller Coaster," Matches reenacted a scene from the movie *Backdraft*, the Ace of Spades made Christmas Story's fake left leg disappear, Faygo recited the entire "I Have a Dream" speech by Martin Luther King Jr. in under twenty-six seconds—a personal best, Super Soaker filled up an entire glass with water from ten feet away, Tea Bag acted out *Hamlet* in its entirety, playing every single role himself, Marshmallow glowed in the dark, Colonel Sanders gave a lecture on Orphanology that put all of the orphans to sleep, save for Ray Charles who thought it brilliant and spot on, Seafood ate thirty-four hot dogs in under five minutes—not a personal best, Snot stepped outside of his space suit for an entire three seconds before a coughing fit drove him back inside, Big Ben gave the correct time for every single time zone on the planet (which took longer than expected thanks to so many alarms going off), Compost Pile did an animal show involving his tamed pet raccoon, opossum, and skunk that ended terribly when the skunk sprayed the entire ensemble, Crash attempted to ride his bike across a tightrope, but living up to his namesake, crashed to the floor instead, suffering concussion number sixty-something, Rooster performed a cover of his favorite punk song, lasting two minutes, with a kazoo solo taking up most of it, and Cup Check's comedy sketch concluded with a three-two-one punch line, all aimed at Monster, Duct tape, and Potty Mouth's orphan jewels. This resulted in Potty Mouth letting loose such a storm of swearwords and profanity that the men not required to wear earmuffs thought it great and unanimously named him the winner. His acceptance speech was less candid, but went somewhere along the lines of "bleep-%$#@-bleep-%$#@-bleep-bleep," which T.W. translated as "I thank you all very much for this award."

With the conclusion of the talent show, summer was at an end. A few warm days hung around like stragglers, the chilly nights stretched long like shadows near dusk, the leaves hinted at their change, which in a few short weeks would erupt from green to fireworks of orange, red, yellow, and the birds were eager to begin their long migration south, all save for the dumpster chickens who stuck around the dump yearlong.

Squirrel spent the last days before the start of school putting on the finishing touches to the rec room ceiling, while T.W. pined away in his office, wrapping up the final chapters of his long-awaited debut novel. On the Sunday night before the start of school, they took an afternoon break from their work to play a game of chess.

"I do have to say the ceiling is coming along nicely." T.W. said, moving a pawn forward. "Whenever I look up at it I feel like I'm standing outside, staring up at a starry night."

"Thank you, sir," Squirrel said, moving his knight.

"I still don't understand how you made that nebula so colorful. It's so realistic I half expect to see the *SS Fertilizer* fly out, steered by both Captain John Deere and Mr. Spud."

T.W. was referring to the Tom Travolta epic sci-fi series *Star Tractor*, currently in production for its twenty-seventh season.

"I was thinking of adding a few spaceships. Perhaps use the epic battle scene from season sixteen as a reference point."

"The one between the *SS Fertilizer* and the evil Insecticides?"

"Yeah, that's the one."

"Very good." T.W. moved a bishop.

"I do have to say that was quite a stunt you played with Ray Charles, sir." Squirrel moved his pawn two spaces forward.

"What are you talking about?"

T.W. used the opportunity to take the pawn with his

bishop. So far Squirrel had lost a rook, a knight, and three pawns, while T.W. had lost a single pawn.

"You know, how you suckered him into coming back to the Row."

"I didn't sucker him into anything. He came back on his own free will."

"That's what I'm saying. You made it seem like it was his idea not yours, even though that was your intention all along. Like how you gave me credit for recommending him for Orphan of the Month when I didn't."

"What can I say, kid? Sometimes a leader has to do a few questionable things—white lies I like to call 'em—for the greater *Cause*. Without such sacrifices, this place would just fall apart. It's not easy trying to keep everything together all of the time. An orphan's got to do what an orphan's got to do."

"I'm not saying it's easy or that you did something wrong, sir. I was just impressed by your methods. They were unexpected, but effective."

"Thank you. Would you have done anything differently?"

"No, but I probably would have given Ray Charles a promotion as well. He's been your runner for well over a year now. He's perhaps the most loyal orphan at the Row."

"You see, that's the thing. Dogs are loyal and obedient, but that doesn't make them smart. Loyalty can blind a person and make them good at only following orders and nothing else. I select my officers not just because they are loyal but also because they can think for themselves. 'Loyalty to the country always. Loyalty to the government when it deserves it.'"

"*Hemingway?*" Squirrel asked, moving his queen into play.

"Nope, Mark Twain," T.W. said, advancing a knight. "You see, I'm the government, Squirrel. The Row is the country. I need someone loyal to the Row first and me second. Do you think Ray Charles can distinguish between the two?"

"I think in time and with practice. He's still quite young, you know."

"Yes and *half-blind*. We can't forget about that either."

"True, he can't see very well, but sometimes you need someone who sees things differently to catch the things you've missed."

"That's exactly why I picked you for my second lieutenant."

"I don't understand, sir. I just paint and stuff."

"Nonsense, you observe things and not just with your eyes." T.W. made a final move on the chessboard. "Checkmate."

It took Squirrel a few seconds to recognize his defeat, but much longer to fully understand it. "I shouldn't have brought my queen out so quickly. It left my king defenseless. Bugger me I was really closing in on you too."

"Yes you were, but your only focus was offense. Your aggression is a good thing, but you have to remember that sometimes the best offense is a good defense. The whole point of chess is to put your opponent's king in check while also preventing your own from the same fate. You're very good at going after my king but not very good at protecting your own."

"I always thought the best defense was a good offense, sir."

"It all depends on the situation. However, it's best to be prepared for both."

"And that's why you have *The Cause*, right?"

"Correct."

"I think I'm beginning to understand *The Cause* now."

"Oh, you are? Explain it to me then."

"Well, I'm not quite there yet, but I'm close. I just can't put it to words. I'm sure I could express it artistically, but that probably wouldn't do it justice either."

"Why don't you try that first and then get back to me. The thing about *The Cause* is that it's a lot like true love or freedom or religion or anything else ethereal, in that it is felt, not spoken. Poets are life's greatest fools, always attempting to express with words what is best left unsaid. But perhaps the greatest of all fools are those who stop searching. 'I looked under chairs, I looked under tables. I tried to find the key to fifty million fables.'"

Squirrel raised his eyebrow. "Bob Lennon?"

T.W. smiled and shook his head no. "'They call me the Seeker. I've been searching low and high. I won't get to get what I'm after until the day I die.'"

"Sorry, sir, I don't know who."

"You just said it."

"I did. *Who*?"

"Exactly," T.W. said, smiling as he reached for his switch-blade comb. "That's enough life lessons for today. I have work to do."

T.W. stood up, ran his comb through his hair three times, and was about to leave when something crossed his mind. "Say, don't you have more rehearsals today? I hear Ray Charles is taking his role quite *seriously*."

Squirrel groaned as T.W. walked away. Since their late night rescue, Ray Charles had transformed from his bitter rival into his new best friend, acting overly affectionate like a lost puppy that has found a new owner. Every day he sat next to Squirrel in the mess hall, took his tray when he was finished, and gave him the apple that was normally reserved for T.W. He even went so far as to offer to do his laundry.

Squirrel was able to tolerate most of Ray Charles's idiosyncrasies, but nothing prepared him for his renewed interest in playing the female lead in Tea Bag's production of *Romeo and Juliet*. Ray Charles took his role so seriously he recruited Poop Stain to help administer make-up, Scissors to hem and cut him a dress, The Wiz to supply him with some refreshing breath spray for the big kissing scene, and Chopsticks to give him white dirty strands from an old mop to use as a wig.

Squirrel took his role more leisurely, having yet to memorize any of his lines or making any attempts at wardrobe. He simply wore his bowler hat and suspenders and attended rehearsal only after being hounded by Ray Charles. No matter where he hid, Ray Charles had a way of sniffing him out, making Squirrel wonder if perhaps his pair of binoculars gave him some sort of sixth sense.

Squirrel was halfway finished with the *SS Fertilizer*, adding detail to the rear thrusters of the tractor-shaped spaceship, when Ray Charles, dressed in drag, entered the rec room.

"Hey, buddy, it's almost time for rehearsal."

"Oh, right. I'll be there in a few minutes."

"No worries and don't forget today's the big day."

The big day was in reference to the big kiss scene between Romeo and Juliet. Having never kissed anyone on the lips besides his great-grandmother Maege and Demmie, Squirrel was a bit apprehensive about kissing anyone, let alone another orphan. The past week he had used every excuse in the book, a cold, chapped lips, bad breath, sore tonsils, orphanitis, all to no avail.

Squirrel left the rec room and entered the theater with the enthusiasm of a convict on Death Row walking towards the electric chair. He found Ray Charles on the stage, adjusting his mop top wig and applying lipstick.

"Oh there you are chap, you made it," Tea Bag said, sitting in the stands with a clipboard. "Ray Charles asked me to observe the big scene, wants to make sure it looks jolly good."

Squirrel groaned. He was not expecting an audience.

"Uh, hey, Ray Charles . . . uh . . . about that . . . uh . . . kissing scene . . . I'm not . . . really feeling up to it yet. You think we can—

He was interrupted by Tea Bag. "Alright, mates, AC-TION!"

Squirrel felt his stomach drop as Ray Charles crooned, "Oh Romeo, oh Romeo." He paused to spray his mouth with breath spray and then stood on his tippy toes, leaning in for the big kiss. Squirrel swallowed hard, puckered his lips, closed his eyes, and prepared for the worst. He leaned forward but before their lips met, Ray Charles's binoculars smacked him in the nose, causing him to kneel over in pain.

"Bollocks," Tea Bag said. "CUT, CUT, CUT!"

"Are you okay?" Ray Charles asked.

Squirrel stood up, rubbed his nose, and thanked Hemingway for the divine intervention. "I'm fine, but I think I'm done for the day. I'm heading to the infirmary for some ice."

Squirrel left the theater, smiling as he went. He had dodged a bullet, but unfortunately a nuclear bomb lay in wait for him, a WMD, Wilson of Mass Destruction.

The school year started out well for Squirrel. Over the summer he had improved greatly in his reading and writing, which made class work easier. He still lagged behind in math, so T.W. promised to switch his instruction, stating that a revolution was not won simply by numbers, but arithmetic.

Classes were rolling, and Squirrel was pleasantly surprised when he received his first ever B+ on an English paper comparing Bob Lennon's "Let It Behave" to Homer's *Odyssey*. It was placed on the fridge of the Row's kitchen for all the men to see.

Even better than his grades was the fact that he was going steady with the most beautiful girl at school—Demmie. Having already shared their first words, they quickly overcame their shyness and became nearly inseparable. They held hands in the hallways, sat together during lunch, and hung out after school at the local library where she worked on articles for the school newspaper and he worked on his sketches. Squirrel could not believe his luck that such a flower of a girl would like such a ragtag orphan as himself.

She was particularly fond of his *The Wilsons-of-Witches* comic strips.

"My god, that looks just like Buck, but better and funnier. I love how you call him Butt and his horde of cousins Buttholes. You even made his face look like a butt. You're so talented. How do you do it?"

"I don't know I just do it."

"And how do you describe him again? Big in the head department, but little in the brains department or something like that?"

"Oh, right." Squirrel raised his hand to his chin in the pose of *The Thinker*. "Butt Wilson lived up to his namesake, having a face shaped like a bottom that was good for only one thing, *excrement*. Suffering from diarrhea of the brain, he was more toilet than bathroom."

Demmie laughed. "I have no idea what that last part means, but it's hilarious. How did you come up with it?"

"T.W. helped me. He's the writer and I'm the artist."

"Well, I love it."

"Here have it. The first edition of *The Wilsons-of-Witches* is all yours. I'll even sign it."

The first edition was followed by many more, all of which were more outlandish than the previous one. There was the "Chronicles of Butt," "Butt vs. the Toilet," "I Can't Believe It's Not Butt," and drawing on Shakespeare, "To Butt or Not to Butt."

They became so lost in their own world that they didn't realize they were quickly becoming the center of attention at school. The others could not believe that a nobody like Squirrel was with a somebody like Demmie.

Their romance especially irked Buck. He felt it was his manifest destiny, by virtue of being a Wilson alone, to get whatever he wanted, including Demmie, who he saw as an object of affection more than he did a person. If he was the king of the school, then she should be his queen, not some orphan's named after a rodent.

"*WHAT'S* girlie Squirrely doing with her?" Buck said to his inner circle of minions, Buster, Burt, Blake, and Bird, all wearing red varsity jackets over black football jerseys. As starters on both offense and defense, they were the main contributors to the undefeated football team that was on track this season to win a state championship.

"Buck don't like it. Buck angry. That rodent's more girl than boy. More . . . more—"

"More orphan than ordinary," Buster blurted.

"More school than cool," Burt chimed in.

"More freak than friend," Blake uttered.

"More wimp than Wilson," Bird crowed.

"Exactly," Buck boomed. "Why Buck ought to get him real good. Buck should—"

"Punch him," Buster blurted.

"Clobber him," Burt chimed in.

"Break his bones," Blake uttered.

"Feed him to the crows," Bird crowed.

"Yeah, Buck should pound him into hamburger," Buck growled. His eyes narrowed into tiny crevices of malice as he made a fist out of his right hand and slammed it into his left, repeating the process in one-second increments. His four cronies picked up the chorus, creating a symphony of ill-intent.

"Girlie Squirrely's dead," Buck promised.

"Deceased," Buster threatened.

"Lifeless," Burt warned.

"Departed," Blake pledged.

"D-d-d-dead," Bird crowed, unable to think of any other adjectives.

"Buck said that already," Buck said, punching Bird in the shoulder.

"Ow," Bird crowed, rubbing his shoulder.

"Exactly," Buck said.

Squirrel was completely unaware of the Wilsonian clock ticking against him. He was too caught up spending time with Demmie at the picnic table outside the library.

"Sorry I'm late," she apologized, taking up a seat beside him. "I have a gift you."

"A gift?"

"Yes, a gift," she said, handing it to him. "I would have had it done sooner, but it took longer than expected to make."

Squirrel studied the multicolored bracelet curled in his hand. In its center was a heart with the letters S and D sewn in the middle.

"It's beautiful, but what exactly is it?"

"It's a friendship bracelet. We both have matching ones. As long as we both wear them we'll be friends forever. You need to tie it on your wrist. Here let me help you."

She tied it to his left wrist so that whenever he held her right hand they would touch. Just as she finished, a sound of malicious laughter sounded from behind them. Squirrel and Demmie turned to find Buck and his four minions, their arms crossed and their faces folded in malevolence.

"Buck thinks the bracelet looks stupid."

"Dumb," Buster blurted.

"Girlish," Burt chimed in.

"Ugly," Blake uttered.

"Despicable," Bird crowed.

"Go away, Buck," Demmie said. "We don't care what you think."

"Buck thinks—

"That perhaps you should stop speaking in the third person," Demmie interrupted. "Buck this and Buck that, talking in the first person would go a long way in not making you sound like a complete moron."

Buck's face reddened. He was so rattled by her words that he stammered his own. "B-Bu . . . I think it's time Bu . . . Bu . . . I taught this rodent a lesson."

"The day you become a teacher of anything, will be the day my pet goldfish learns to read, now go away, Buck."

"Or what?" Buck stepped forward and took Squirrel's sketchbook. Squirrel protested and reached to grab it back, but Buck pushed him to the ground. When Squirrel tried to get back up, Buck kicked him in the side. His minions laughed like it was the funniest thing since the Tom Travolta comedy *An Amish Called Waldo*.

Demmie stood up, her face so flushed with anger it was nearly as red as her hair. "Give that back right this instant, Buck Wilson, or I'll—"

"Do what? You're just a girl."

"Give it back or I'll scream."

"Go ahead," Buck said, with a smile.

"Make our day," Buster blurted.

"I dare you," Burt chimed in.

"Double dare you," Blake uttered.

"With a cherry on top," Bird crowed.

Demmie hesitated for a second, and then screamed. At first nothing happened. Buck continued to smile. She continued to scream. Nearby adults looked over, some even began to walk in their direction, wondering about the cause of the commotion. The unwanted attention made Buck uneasy. Silencing boys with fists was easy, but he didn't know what to do with a screaming girl.

"Stop it," he hissed, which only made Demmie scream louder.

"What's going on here?" an older gentleman called. Buck's brain froze. A single train of thought was all it could manage. His first instinct was to punch something. He panicked instead, ripping Squirrel's sketchbook and tossing it to the ground.

"This is not over," he said, stomping away.

"Far from finished," Buster blurted.

"See you in the sequel," Burt chimed in.

"To be continued," Blake uttered.

"To be concluded," Bird crowed.

"I really hate them," Demmie said, once they were gone and out of earshot. She bent down to help Squirrel pick up the scattered pieces of his sketchbook. "Why can't they just leave us alone?"

"They'll eventually grow tired of us and move on to somebody else. Bullies always do."

"You don't know Buck. He won't just go away. He always has that stupid father of his to get him out of trouble. Because of him some poor kid got sent to the psychiatric ward last year. Kid's never been heard of or seen since."

"What can I do? I'm no fighter. You saw what happened. He'll just put me in the hospital."

"Who said anything about fighting him? You're smarter than he is. Hurt him with your brains not your brawn."

"How do I do that?

"I have an idea."

Demmie smiled. She pulled Squirrel close and whispered in his ear. By the time she was finished they were both smiling.

The following Monday at school, the headlines of the *Detroit Public Daily* ran as followed: "The Butt of All Jokes."

It featured a two-page editorial of comic strips written by the Daily's own chief editor, Demmie, and illustrated by Squirrel. Over two hundred newspapers were printed and distributed throughout the school. Students humiliated and silenced for years by Buck and his cronies suddenly had a voice, one aimed at their tormentor.

At first, Buck had no idea what was going on. He was somewhat taken aback when a bunch of nobodies giggled at him and then buried their faces beneath whatever they were reading. It continued throughout the day, eventually drawing his suspicion. He grabbed some freshman twerp by the throat, threatening to pop his face like a zit if he so much as looked his way again. He was about to clobber him for good measure but then got a look at what the dweeb was reading. Buck couldn't read so well, he had trouble spelling his own name, but the majority of the article was done in pictures, no reading required.

Staring back at him was a familiar face—*his own*—but done in a fashion so that it looked more *Butt* than Buck. "Why that no good, stinky, bed-wetting, snot-eating, booger-faced, rodent," Buck grumbled. Boiling with rage, he crumbled the newspaper and went in search of the smarter of his thirty-some cousins, Benjamin, who by Wilson standards was thought of as a genius because he could write a whole paragraph.

"Read," Buck ordered. "Buck wants to know what it says."

Benjamin cleared his throat before reading. "Butt is so dumb that he makes the dumbest of the dumb look smart. So dumb in fact that he often misses the punch line to the most simplest of dumb jokes like 'How do you amuse a dummy for hours? Write *turn me over* on both sides of a piece of paper,' or 'How do you make a dummy laugh on Monday? Tell him a joke on Friday.' Buck is so stupid that—"

Buck was infuriated, not just at the fact that Squirrel had the audacity to call him a dummy, but that Squirrel was right about something, namely Buck not getting the punch line to both jokes. He visualized a paper with the words *turn me over* on both sides, but kept coming back to where he started, which only confused him more and made him angrier. Even more troublesome was the fact that it was Monday. Buck couldn't comprehend why that had anything to do with a joke on Friday. While the gears in his head turned, the fury on his face intensified.

"Butt was followed around by his even dumber lackeys— The Buttholes. I think he's referring to *me.*" Benjamin paused before continuing. "There was Butt-kisser, Butt-noser, Butt-farter, Butterfinger, Butterlips, Butterface, Butt—"

"Enough already," Buck said, seizing Benjamin by the throat. He was so incensed that he could barely speak. "Buck angry. Buck wants to destroy. Get the others. Tell them we crush the rodent after school."

"But what about football practice?"

"*What did you say?*"

"I said, what about football practice?"

"*No* before that."

"What are you talking about?"

"*You said 'but,'* don't EVER say that in front of Buck again."

"Okay, I'm sorry, Butt—I mean Buck."

Buck's fist shot forward so fast that Benjamin didn't know what hit him. One moment he was there, the next he was on the ground, knocked out cold.

By the end of the school day, Squirrel was more popular than he ever was, thanks to his contribution to the *Detroit Public Daily*. Random students congratulated him, sneaking in high-fives and thumbs up. Not knowing what to make of his new celebrity, he approached his locker with a smile.

He was halfway through his locker's combination when he noticed a shadow fall over his shoulder, followed by a sinister snicker. His first instinct was to run, but there was nowhere to go. His second was to scream, but before he could let out a breath, Buck put a hand over his mouth. The others grabbed his legs and arms, dragged him to the boy's bathroom, and tossed his bowler hat aside.

"Who's the Butt now?" Buck asked as they lifted Squirrel upside down. Before he could answer, they planted him face first in a toilet. Squirrel struggled for breath, his arms thrashed against the porcelain. After a few seconds they lifted him, his hair dripping. Squirrel gasped for air, but just before he could catch his breath, they dunked him again.

"You look thirsty, rodent. How about some fresh lemonade?"

The Wilsons took turns turning the water yellow. When they were finished they resumed forcing Squirrel's head in the toilet, using it as a plunger.

After the swirly, they continued their onslaught. They emptied his pockets, broke his paintbrushes and ripped apart his textbooks and sketchbooks. They tore Demmie's friendship bracelet from his wrist and flushed it down the toilet.

They gave him wedgies, took turns beating him, punching him, and kicking him until he was bloodied and blue. They bleached his hair so that it was the color of sand on a beach and then cut it so that it was a ragged mess on his head. Just when he thought it couldn't get any worse, they tore open his backpack, and discovered his black PPSP-Douglas-Street-Affiliation vest. It was only then that Squirrel protested.

"Please don't take my vest."

"It speaks. Buck can't hear you. What'd you say, rodent?"

"Please," Squirrel pleaded, trying to hold back his tears.

"It's mine, now, rodent," Buck said, giving him one last kick before leaving the bathroom, taking the vest with him.

* * *

Meanwhile, in his downtown office, Mayor Sharp was digging through a stack full of files, most of which proved to be nothing of interest. It was only when he came to the profile of a strapping young orphan that he paused.

"Oh, my," he said, with a chuckle. "Oh my how ironic. This is too funny. Bart, get in here, you got to come see this. BART!"

Bartholomew came barging into the office, his face slick with sweat, expecting to find an angry Mayor Sharp, especially after earlier breaking the news that Calloway was up in the polls, but was surprised to see him smiling instead. "Yes, sir, what is it?"

"You're not going to believe this."

Mayor Sharp held up one of the folders. It contained the smoking gun profile of one particular orphan, causing an even bigger smile to spread on his face. He now had all the ammo he needed to take out both his political rival and his lone obstacle to the White House. Calloway and Big Mama, two problems, one solution.

15

The War of the Wilsons

"LET ME AT 'EM, let me at 'em," a flustered Ray Charles screamed, his hands balled up into fists. "Somebody better hold me back or I'll kill 'em. I swear to Hemingway I'll kill 'em, I'll kill 'em all." To stress his point, Ray Charles threw wild roundhouse swings at the air, causing him to spin in circles, nearly falling over.

"Get a grip, man," T.W. said, tending to the wounds on Squirrel's face.

"I'm trying sir, but I'm so worked up that I'm afraid I'll explode. We got to get the sons-of-guns who did this to Squirrel. Just let me at 'em. I'll open a can of sardines on 'em."

"In due time, Ray Charles. In times of war, patience always prevails. Right now I need you to open up a can of be quiet."

"How bad is it, sir?" Squirrel asked.

"You'll live, but won't have your charming Tom Travolta good looks, at least for a little while. I'll have Poop Stain put some make-up on your face to cover up the worst of it."

Squirrel winced as T.W. applied a rag soaked in alcohol above his right eye.

"The good news is that you won't need any stitches, but it'll take a while for the swelling to go down. Wiz, how's the pain medication coming?"

The Wiz stood in the doorway of the infirmary, holding up a small vial filled with a green liquid. "Ready, sir, but I have to warn you it hasn't been tested yet, at least not on orphans. So far it appears to work on rats and dumpster chickens. However there is a 37.36—repeating of course—percent chance of negative side effects that include swelling, bloating, vomiting, and in some cases a nasty rash."

"Well it can't make me feel any worse," Squirrel said. "I'll take my chances."

"Very well." The Wiz handed the vial to Squirrel. He took it down with one swallow.

"That a boy." Ray Charles pat Squirrel on the back. "You'll be feeling better in no time."

"I sure hope so. My hair's another story though."

"Leave that to Scissors," T.W said, applying a bandage over Squirrel's left eye. "He'll straighten that mess up in the morning, but for now you need your rest. I'm finished here, so why don't you head to bed."

Squirrel got up slowly and was helped to the door by Ray Charles. T.W. stood and motioned for Scissors. "Gather the other officers. Meet in my office in T-minus five. We have preparations to make." Scissors nodded and ran off.

Leaning heavily on Ray Charles's shoulders, Squirrel made his way to his bunk. All of the men gave him a silent salute as he limped by. He collapsed into his bed and was instantly asleep. Ray Charles took off his shoes and tucked him in, bringing the blanket up to his face before saying, "Good night, sport."

He then hurried to T.W.'s office where the mood was dour.

"What do we know about these Wilsons?" T.W. asked, pacing the room.

"From my reports," The Wiz said, "they are numerous. Over thirty of them attend Detroit Public. That's just the ones named Wilson. Distant cousins make up another twenty or thirty, depending on how far down the line you want to go. Grade wise, they're about as smart as a pack of mules. Only one of them, Benjamin Wilson, has ever made the honor roll, though just barely. The others, well let's just say they can do enough to stay eligible for sports and that's about it. Their leader is Buck Wilson, a real monster on the football field. He sent seventeen kids to the hospital last season, a dozen so far this year."

"He's probably the one who did this to Squirrel."

"There's more, sir. Their parents are represented in nearly every facet of Detroit's political machine. From the courts, police, fire department, and all the way up to the mayor's office. One of them even owns the dump. Buck's father is principal of Detroit Public. They could pose a problem. All in all, this Wilson clan is a formidable adversary."

"What are our chances of success?"

"If we take on the Wilsons alone there is a 46.57—repeating of course—percent chance of victory in hand-to-hand combat, however when blunt objects and weapons are thrown in the mix there is a 53.98—repeating of course—percent chance of victory. Our numbers go down greatly if we take on the whole clan and are close to impossible if we include the parents."

T.W. pulled the cigarette from his left ear. Scissors quickly lit it.

"I like our chances. We'll need to assemble a team for combat, the smaller the better. I don't want to leave the Row undefended so we'll need reserves. Let's start with them, any suggestions?"

It was decided that Snot, Belly Ache, Monster, Peanut Butter, Marshmallow, and Christmas Story were not fit for combat. They joined the reserves, aka Foxtrot, led by The Wiz and composed of Stone Age, Cup Check, Tea Bag, Big Ben, Poop Stain, Duct Tape, Wheelin' Dealin' Steven, Pickles, Colonel Sanders, Belch, Faygo, and Mike Tyson.

T.W.'s Easy Company would lead the assault. It included Matches, Toaster, The Ace of Spades, Compost Pile, Crash, Rooster, Potty Mouth, Chopsticks, Super Soaker, Muscles, Ray Charles, Scissors, and Seafood.

"*Seafood*?" Scissors exclaimed. "But, sir, he's lazy and can't fight worth a lick."

"Doesn't matter, Scissors, with his size we can use him for intimidation."

It was close to midnight before the War Council convened. T.W. stayed up much later, alone in his office, staring out his window at the starless night with strategies and counterstrategies rolling through his mind.

Early the next morning, the kitchen bell rang three times, signaling the Row was under lockdown until further notice. Classes were canceled, everything ran on military time. The men were ordered to wear their PPSP-Douglas-Street-Affiliation vests at all times and remain vigilant. A guard was kept at every possible entrance in and out of the Row.

"Lordy, them boys is off playing war again." Big Mama shook her head and grinned.

Ray Charles ran around so much his binoculars fogged up. Muscles led formations and reviewed hand-to-hand combat, including Jean-Claude-Van-Damme kicks. The Wiz modified and passed out Double-H W's (Hand Held Weaponry) to all men in the reserve. Chopsticks sharpened his knives in the kitchen and ran sandpaper over his favorite wooden spoon. Scissors held command while T.W. took his bike on official Row business.

At a quarter to twelve, T.W. pulled his bike into the parking lot of Detroit Public. He parked just outside the front entrance, releasing the kickstand with his boot. He was displeased to notice a black PPSP-Douglas-Street-Affiliation vest hanging from the flagpole.

The female security guard was unimpressed with his parking job.

"You can't park there."

"Watch me, honey."

T.W. strode past her, running his comb through his hair three times. He walked into the office, popped an elbow on the counter, and grinned at the secretary. She was in her mid-forties, with narrow librarian glasses and a rosy face, pudgy with timid kindness and lacking make-up. Her curly brown hair was done up in a bun with two yellow pencils stuck in the back. She dressed conservatively in a flowered dress that covered everything but her face and hands.

"May I help you?" she asked coyly.

"Sure, doll," T.W. said, looking down at her nametag. "I mean, Ms. Mouse. Think you can tell me where I can find a Wilson, the biggest, dumbest one you got?"

"Oh, you must mean Buck," she said, smiling at T.W.

He gave her a sly grin. "Yeah, that's the one. Any idea where this Buck might be lurking?"

"Well it is lunchtime. He should be in the cafeteria with all the other children."

"Thanks, doll. I'll be seeing you."

He was about to leave, but paused, reached into the pocket of his leather jacket, and pulled out a small tape recorder. "Say, can you play this over the loudspeaker for me?"

"I'm not supposed to use the loudspeaker without Principal Wilson's permission."

T.W. leaned in closer to Ms. Mouse, tipping his sunglasses forward.

"What if I say please?"

"I-I could get in trouble. I could—"

T.W. placed his finger on Ms. Mouse's lips, silencing her. "Can you do it for me, just this once?"

Ms. Mouse blushed. She took the tape recorder without saying a word.

"Thanks, doll," T.W. said, giving her a nod and then took his leave. As he left the front office, his motorcycle boots clacked against the linoleum. The opening lick to The Who's "My Generation" blazed over the intercom as he made his way to the cafeteria.

The chatter of some 500 students greeted him as he entered the big cafeteria. Without breaking stride, he hopped on the nearest table, walked the length of it, sidestepping trays of food and cartons of milk. Girls turned their heads, giggling, while forks and spoons hung in mid-suspension in front of open mouths. When he reached the center of the cafeteria, he placed two fingers in his mouth and let out a loud whistle. The chatter died down immediately as all heads turned to face him.

"Which one of you goes by the name Wilson?" T.W. called. Thirty hands shot up. "Alright which one of you goons goes by Buck?"

The cafeteria remained quiet as a funeral as thirty blonde-haired Wilsons surrounded the newcomer. T.W. hopped down from the table and came face-to-face with five imposing figures, all a good foot taller than him. Buck stood in their center like the tip of a sharp spear.

"You must be Buck," T.W. said.

"And you must be dead meat," Buck said, cracking his knuckles. "Buck gonna crush you like a bug."

"A beetle," Buster blurted.

"A grasshopper," Burt chimed in.

"An ant," Blake uttered.

"A cockroach," Bird crowed.

T.W. grinned and then pulled out his switchblade comb from his pocket. The cafeteria let out a collective gasp, thinking it an actual knife and anticipating blood. Buck took a step back. T.W. let the Wilsons sweat a bit then opened the switchblade revealing the comb and ran it through his hair three times.

"Listen, Bucky boy, I hate to break it to you but you messed with the wrong orphan. Come this time tomorrow your behind's gonna be so sore you're gonna need help wiping."

Buck clenched his fists and stepped forward, but T.W. held up his finger. "I'm not finished, butt for brains. A school is no place for violence. We settle this elsewhere. Meet tonight just after dark at the abandoned parking lot, just past the railroad tracks on the north side of Douglas Street. You bring yours and I bring mine. Got it?"

Buck nodded, his head steaming.

"Alright, let's shake on it."

T.W. spit in his hand and held it out. Buck's hand was the size of a baseball mitt. It swallowed T.W.'s hand, squeezing hard enough to make orange juice. T.W. didn't wince once.

"One last thing, Bucky boy." T.W. leaned in closer. "Squirrel gives his regards."

T.W. brought his foot forward hard enough to kick a field goal, connecting with Buck's family jewels. Buck released his hand and collapsed to the floor, his face beet red and his eyes bulging like two golf balls. T.W. hopped on the table and made a quick exit, a hundred heads turning to watch him go.

He returned to the front office and found Ms. Mouse in the middle of brushing on some make-up. Her face turned red as he approached.

"Got a light, babe?" T.W. placed the cigarette from behind his ear in his mouth.

"You're not supposed to smoke in here," she whispered.

"I'm not smoking yet, but you sure are." T.W. left the office.

"But what about your tape recorder?" Ms. Mouse called after him.

"Keep it, babe."

He left the school, hopped on his bike, and kick-started the engine into life. The bike tore up the grass as he made his way to the flagpole. He was still pulling down Squirrel's vest when Demmie found him.

"T.W. is that really you?"

"Sure is, doll."

"I heard there was a commotion in the cafeteria involving Buck. When some of the students mentioned a boy they've never seen before wearing a black vest, I assumed it was you. I'm so glad I found you before you left. How's Squirrel? I haven't heard from since yesterday. Buck's been bragging all day about how he beat him up real good. Is it true? Is Squirrel hurt?"

"Squirrel's pretty banged up, but he'll live."

"I feel so horrible. This is all my fault."

"Nonsense. Buck's the only one to blame and tonight we make him pay."

"What are you gonna do?"

"It's best that you don't know." T.W. pulled the vest free from the flagpole and threw it over his shoulder. "Say, do you have a light?"

"Sorry no."

T.W. let out a sigh and placed the cigarette back behind his ear. He hopped on his bike and turned to Demmie.

"Well what are you waiting for, hop in."

"Where are we going?"

"To see Squirrel of course."

"But I have class."

"Class will be there tomorrow. Let's go, there's people coming."

Demmie turned towards the front entrance and sure enough Principal Wilson and two security guards were coming their way. Beasley led the charge, his girth bouncing and his blonde hair swaying.

Demmie hopped in the sidecar. T.W. put the bike in gear just as Principal Wilson approached. "Stop right there," he screamed. "STOP! STOP! STOP!" T.W. gave him a fist of solidarity as they spun out of the parking lot.

They arrived at the Row a short while later. T.W. led Demmie up the steps. When they reached the door, he knocked three times, paused, knocked twice more, paused again, and then knocked a final time. The door opened, revealing Potty Mouth armed with a potato gun. He saluted T.W. and then commented "Bleep-%$#@-bleep" when he noticed Demmie.

"That's no way to speak in front of a lady," T.W. said, leading Demmie into the Row.

"What did he say?" Demmie asked.

"You don't want to know."

They walked through the common room, heading for the stairs. The men, unaccustomed to such beauty, stopped and gave Demmie wide-eyed stares as if they'd just seen a ghost. Ray Charles turned a corner, nearly running into them. When his binoculars focused on Demmie, he immediately fell over and began chanting, "Hubba, hubba."

"What's wrong with him?" Demmie asked, as they continued up the stairs.

"A little bit of everything."

They found Squirrel still asleep in bed. His face had turned the brownish color of a rotting banana and his left eye was the size of a small egg. "My god." Tears swelled in Demmie's eyes. "I didn't think it would be this bad. Shouldn't he be in a hospital?"

"No, he's under The Wiz's supervision, kid's practically a doctor himself."

Demmie knelt beside Squirrel and cupped his hand. "Oh, Squirrel, I'm so sorry."

Squirrel stirred and opened his one good eye. Still clouded with sleep, he blinked, not sure if she was really there or just part of his imagination.

"Demmie," he managed. "What are you doing here?"

"I'm here to see you, silly."

Tears welled up in Squirrel's eyes. Embarrassed, he wiped them away. T.W. gave him a curt nod and slipped away.

"I wish you didn't have to see me like this," Squirrel said.

"I wouldn't have it any other way," she said, kissing his bruised cheek.

"Thank you. I don't know what else to say."

"You don't have to say anything," she said, this time kissing his cracked lips instead of his cheek. His one good eye opened wide.

"Now you need your rest." She crawled into bed with him and rested her head on his shoulder. Squirrel ran his hand through her hair, making waves of fire and eventually fell asleep, though he had no idea when.

They were awakened a few hours later by the ringing of the kitchen bell.

"What's going on?" Demmie asked.

"I don't know. Let's find out."

"Shouldn't you stay in bed?"

"I'll be fine, let's go."

Squirrel was too sore to take the fireman's pole, so they took the stairs instead. He leaned on Demmie's shoulder and took the steps one at a time. The men were already in formation by the time they entered the mess hall.

T.W. paced the ranks, while Scissors took roll call on his clipboard. The mood was solemn, save for a few men who fidgeted with anticipation. The men were given their assignments, grouped into either Foxtrot or Easy Company. Only two were unsatisfied with their allocation. Seafood who preferred the comfort of the reserves to combat and Mike Tyson who wanted to prove himself in battle.

"Permission to speak, sir," Mike Tyson called, his voice sounding sharp as a whistle.

"Permission granted."

"May I go with Easy Company, sir? I've been lifting iron with Muscles every day. I'm as ready as I can be, sir."

"Permission denied. You're too young for combat."

"But I'm almost the same age as Ray Charles and he's going."

"Ray Charles is almost an officer. It's his duty to go. Sorry, kid, maybe next time."

Mike Tyson was so disappointed that he vented his frustration by punching the air. However this happened to be the same air that was occupied by the Ace of Spades who caught the punch right in the nose. He let out a scream and began pulling foot after foot of red-colored ribbon from his nose. His next trick was no trick at all. Both eyes started to blacken.

"Good god, we got a man down and the fight hasn't even started yet." T.W. shook his head. "Ace of Spades, report to the infirmary."

Mike Tyson stepped forward. "It's my fault, sir. I deserve to be punished. Do with me what you please."

T.W. rubbed his chin. "You've got more head than brains, Mike Tyson. But you leave me little choice. Alright, kid, you can tag along."

Mike Tyson was so excited he took another swing at the air, this time connecting with Potty Mouth. "Bleep-%$#@-bleep-%$#@-bleep," he shouted, holding his nose.

"Earmuffs everyone," T.W. said. "Potty Mouth, report to the infirmary. Mike Tyson, keep those mitts of yours to yourself, otherwise there's not going to be anything left for the Wilsons."

"I can go in Potty Mouth's place," Squirrel said.

"No, you're to remain in bed until you're RTRFD."

"Ready to Report for Duty!" Scissors shouted. The men nodded in agreement.

"Sir, I want do my part. This is my fight."

"Nonsense, any fight involving one of us, involves all of us."

"But—"

"The only but I'm concerned with is your butt in bed, end of discussion."

Squirrel sighed. Demmie helped him limp towards the stairs.

"Squirrel," T.W. called to him. "One last thing, I got this back for you."

T.W. tossed Squirrel his black PPSP-Douglas-Street-Affiliation vest. "You've earned your wings, kid. Tonight we fly in your honor."

Squirrel gave him a forlorn smile and a salute before turning away. T.W. redirected his attention to the men. "Easy Company, let's move out. Wiz, you're in charge. If we're not back in 2300 hours, send in the reserves, fully armed with potato guns, Tasers, sewer-water balloons, sleeping gas—*the works.*"

"Yes, sir, will do."

"After the fight we'll set off two red flares for victory, one for defeat."

The Wiz nodded. "Hemingway speed, sir."

T.W. turned and led the thirteen members of Easy Company towards the front door. Big Ben stood at the entrance, his whole body ticking, handing out fake mustaches. Poop Stain administered streaks of black make-up under every man's eyes. Salutes were given, knuckles cracked, and black PPSP-Douglas-Affiliation vests checked.

They went by abandoned school bus. Muscles drove with two big cans of sardines attached to his arms. T.W. stood in the front, black sunglasses reflecting the fading sunlight. "Won't Get Fooled Again" blared over the radio.

They arrived before the Wilsons, the sun barely visible on the horizon. T.W. used the opportunity to address the men. "Listen up, men, you all know what's at stake here—our very livelihood. If you mess with one orphan you mess with them all."

The men nodded in agreement.

"We'll most likely be outnumbered tonight. Our enemy will be double our size, twice as tall, and meaner than those four Dobermans at the dump. The Wilsons are formidable foes, the wolves that prey on the sheep. Don't take them for granted. They'll kick you when you're down. Spit in your face. Break your bones. Eat your flesh if you let them. You all saw what they did to Squirrel."

Deep-seated anger spread through the ranks.

"No matter how many Wilsons show up tonight, do not be intimidated. They may be bloodthirsty wolves, but there's one thing they don't realize. Where there's sheep there's also the protector of sheep, *the dogs*. We're those dogs, men, and there's nothing nastier than a dog that smells a wolf among its flock. Let me hear you bark, dogs."

The men filled the night.

"*Louder*, I can't hear you."

The men pounded their chests.

"They may take our lives, but they can't take our orphan-hood! Let's do this for Squirrel and Snuggles!"

"SQUIRREL! SNUGGLES!"

"Look, they're here," Scissors said. A line of cars pulled into the parking lot on the far side of the train tracks, numbering in the dozen.

"Toaster, you're up," T.W. said.

Toaster broke rank and made for the bushes. Disguised as a Wilson, he wore a blonde wig, red varsity jacket, and black football jersey underneath.

"Everyone else, hold tight and wait for my command."

The cars pulled alongside each other, forming a dozen yellow eyes pointed straight at the men. Thirty hulking silhouettes sauntered in their direction.

"There's so many," Seafood said.

"Just let me at 'em," Ray Charles said, all revved up like a race car in neutral.

Buck gave them a wicked smile and cracked his neck. The rest of the pack stood beside him, wearing matching red varsity jackets with black football jerseys. Their collective blonde hair glowed in the moonlight. Directly across from them stood the men, menacing in their fake mustaches and black PPSP-Douglas-Street-Affiliation vests.

T.W. raised his fist and held it high in the air. The men followed suit. He looked to Scissors and nodded. Scissors reached into his vest pocket, retrieving a Twinkie. He held it up for Seafood to see. Seafood's nostrils flared. "Gimme," he moaned. Scissors tossed the Twinkie like a grenade into the horde of Wilsons. Seafood broke rank and charged forward like a raging bull, knocking Wilsons out of his way like bowling pins.

"Alright, boys, it's KBTNL Time," T.W. yelled.

"Kick Butt and Take Names Later Time!" Scissors shouted. The men nodded in agreement.

"Give them Hemingway!"

The men screamed their battle cry and charged forward. T.W. made straight for Buck. "Hey, look there's Barry Sanders," he called. Buck turned to look, and T.W. used the distraction to connect his boot with Buck's jewels for the second time that day. Buck, a slow learner, dropped to the ground. Before he could say knuckle sandwich, T.W. was feeding him lefts and rights. Buck's head moved back and forth like a windshield wiper.

Elsewhere, the men were doing their own damage. Decked out as a Wilson, Toaster reappeared, causing all kinds of havoc among the Wilsons who thought he was one of their own. He popped out here and popped out there, delivering judo chops to unsuspecting necks. Crash crashed into Bill and Ben Wilson, knocking them over (concussion number seventy-something). Super Soaker spat in Blake Wilson's face, causing him to run around blind. Compost Pile rubbed his stinky armpits into the face of Bird Wilson, causing him to vomit before passing out. Matches gave Bradley Wilson such a fierce head noogie that his hair was smoking. Muscles opened a can of sardines on two Wilsons—Burt and Barney. Chopsticks pinned Brandon Wilson to the ground and hit him over the head numerous times with his wooden spoon. Scissors had Brian Wilson in a headlock with one arm and was cutting his hair with the other. Seafood was sitting on top of Braden Wilson eating his Twinkie. Cup Check was cup-checking Wilsons left and right, leaving them on the ground holding their family jewels. The only orphan not laying the smack down was Ray Charles who thought he was fighting a Wilson, but thanks to his lack of vision, was in fact swinging at the air. He took wild punches at nothing at all and got so turned around one punch landed right in his face, sending his binoculars flying.

The fight came to dramatic close, when Billy Wilson screamed, "My ear, my ear!" and ran away holding the left side of his head. The sight of blood caused the rest of the Wilsons to retreat. The sound of barking dogs followed the Wilsons as they left the parking lot in squealing tires.

"My God, Mike Tyson just bit off part of his ear," Scissors said.

"That's jacked up," T.W. said. "Now he'll need a tetanus shot. How did the rest of the men fare? I want a full casualty report."

The men were pretty much unscathed, save for Ray Charles who had a swollen black eye and a cracked lens on his binoculars. "I don't know what in the Hemingway happened," he said. "One of them Wilsons got me pretty good, but I sure put a number on him."

The air begged to differ.

16

Cause for Alarm

MAYOR SHARP SAT in the big comfy chair behind his even bigger desk. The statue of Alexander the Great stared ahead while he stared out the window, pretending to listen to Principal Beasley Wilson of Detroit Public. Outside the city of Detroit appeared cloudy and gloomy. It matched the mayor's mood. As per usual, he was easily agitated while waiting for his plans to come together. It didn't help that Calloway had once again jumped ahead in the polls of the Democratic primaries.

"As I was saying—"

"Half of the team is in the hospital," Mayor Sharp said, cutting him off. "Yes, I heard you the first time, Beasley."

"Yes, but the half that's in the hospital is the half that plays both offense and defense."

"So what are you trying to say?"

"The season's a wash, sir. We're done. The other half can't play nearly as well as the good half and from what Coach Wilson explained there might not be a single Wilson to play in next week's big game. We need to do something to those orphan hoodlums who hurt our boys. One of them even bit part of young Billy's ear. The nerve of those punks!"

Mayor Sharp nodded and leaned back in his chair. His big stomach bulged forward, threatening to pop the buttons on his shirt.

"Well you leave me no choice but to call in the works. Get everybody, including the Dogs. We're going to bring down Desolation Row and the Calloways too. We'll even leak it to the press. It'll be headline news. A tale of corruption and negligence so disturbing that even the liberals can't ignore it."

"Genius, sir," Beasley chuckled. "Too stones with one bird."

"Two birds with one stone, you idiot." Mayor Sharp leaned back in his chair, rubbing his knuckles. The first glimpse of the sun broke through the clouds and entered his office. He allowed a smile to form on his face.

* * *

Meanwhile the men were in the midst of a weeklong celebration, completely unaware that the dumpster-chicken poop was about to hit the fan. Victory Week, as it was called, started with a Faygo shower. Over twenty cases were opened, passed around, shaken, and then opened, spraying pop everywhere like confetti. Faygo was in orphan heaven.

T.W. made a decree that all black PPSP-Douglas-Street-Affiliation vests were to be worn at all times, even to bed. Ray Charles received an Orphan Heart of Valor for injuries received while in the line of duty. He was also offered a promotion.

"You're doing *what*, sir?" Ray Charles asked.

"I said I'm promoting you. Why the long face?"

"Well, as you're well aware, sir, I'm half blind. I'm just afraid that'll get in the way of things."

"Nonsense, you'll be fine. And remember you're not an officer yet, just a senior officer's assistant. Your rank and duties will remain the same. Consider this your training wheels."

"Yes, sir."

"Any questions, Ray Charles?"

"Uh, yes, sir. Does this mean that I can finally have a smoke?"

"*Good God no*, Ray Charles. You're not even old enough to grow a mustache, let alone smoke a cigarette."

"But, sir, you smoke and you don't have a mustache."

"That's beside the point. I smoke for *The Cause*. Just stick to candy cigarettes, Ray Charles. They'll put hair on your chin."

"Yes, sir," Ray Charles said, saluting before returning to his duties.

T.W. ran his comb through his hair three times and went in search of Squirrel. He found him in the rec room, painting the ceiling.

"How are you feeling, Squirrel?" T.W. called up to him.

"Oh, fine, sir. Not nearly as sore as I was. The bruises have started to turn yellow."

"Good to hear. And the new haircut?"

"It's great. Scissors did a Hemingway of a job."

It took Scissors close to two hours to fix the mess Buck and his minions had created. When he was finished, Squirrel was left with a short military look that was made popular in Tom Travolta's not-so-classic, anticlimactic war-without-a-war film *Apocalypse Nowhere*. Little could be done about the bleach-blonde color. Squirrel would just have to outgrow it.

"And how's the redheaded dame?"

"She's good, sir. She says we're the talk of the school. All the kids can't believe the OW you put on the Wilsons."

"Yes, it was a good Orphan Whooping. When do you plan on returning to school?"

"Hopefully soon, sir. I have a lot of homework to make up, but Demmie's been collecting it for me. She's very swell, sir."

"That she is. Let me know if you need anything. I have to go prepare for tonight's festivities. Chopsticks made a cake to commemorate our victory. Also Tea Bag is directing a reenactment of the battle so that all of the reserves can see what they missed. Ray Charles is playing the lead."

"I look forward to seeing it, sir."

"Yes, should be interesting. Chess game later?"

"Sure, sir. Maybe today's the day I finally beat you."

T.W. couldn't help but grin as he ran his comb through his hair three times.

At 1700, cake was served and the men gathered in the theater for Tea Bag's latest production, *An Orphan Apart*. Morale was high. So high in fact that no one suspected anything amiss, not even T.W., who sat with his feet stretched out on the back of an empty seat. No orphan was more surprised than him, when a group of officers wielding batons and flashlights entered the darkened theater halfway through the scene involving Ray Charles opening a can of sardines on a large Wilson played by Seafood.

"Nobody move. This is the police," their leader said. Captain Cornhole was a large fat man with the face of a pig who looked like he lived on a steady diet of bacon and donuts. His chubby cheeks were lined with deep pockets of pock scars. A thick mustache covered his lips, which moved like white slugs on the four layers of his chin whenever he talked.

He waddled to the center of the theater, pulling up pants that went well past his bellybutton. His stomach was so large it looked like it swallowed the sun. The simple act of walking was such an exertion that it caused him to sweat profusely.

"Show's over!" he yelled, already out of breath and wiping his face with a handkerchief. "Nobody move a muscle."

Police officers lined the front of the stage, their batons pointed at the seated men. T.W. dropped his feet from the chair and tossed his switchblade comb and the key around his neck to Toaster, who disappeared before anybody realized he was there.

"What gives you the right to be here?" he asked, standing up.

"Official city business," Captain Cornhole said, wiping more sweat from his face. "This place is being seized by the city of Detroit."

"Under what grounds? Let me see your warrant."

Captain Cornhole laughed, his big belly shaking. "I'll show you the back of my hand, sonny. Now step aside or we'll start cracking skulls."

"Not until I see your badge and warrant. I know my rights. The Fourth Amendment says you can't be here without a warrant. Either show us or take your circus elsewhere. We have enough funny business without you clowns."

The men sounded their approval as T.W. crossed his arms and stood his ground, a look of defiance on his face. The layered face of Captain Cornhole filled the reflection of T.W.'s sunglasses.

"Now you listen here, sonny. Start cooperating or I'll stick your little orphan behinds in a jail cell faster than you can say monkey in a zoo."

T.W. put two fingers in his mouth and blew a loud whistle. Every orphan stood at attention while the police officers dug the wax out of their ears.

"*Men,*" he said, "give 'em Hemingway."

Before Captain Cornhole could say bacon in a pan, all Hemingway broke loose. The men ran in every direction, sidestepping officers. Peanut Butter crawled between the legs of one officer and made for the stage. Compost Pile raised his stinky armpits, causing officers to halt their pursuit and plug their noses. Mike Tyson took a swing at an officer but was too short to actually hit him. He was quickly apprehended and then quickly released when he bit the officer in the arm. Cup Check cup-checked any officer that got in his way. Super Soaker sprayed an officer in the face. Chopsticks took a baton from an officer and used it on him like a wooden spoon. Matches lit off some firecrackers, causing officers to duck for cover and pull out their revolvers. T.W. easily outmaneuvered Captain Cornhole and made for his office.

Other men were not so lucky.

Seafood was the first to be caught. Too lazy to run, he just sat in place until an officer cuffed him. Monster was too scared to do anything but scream. An officer came up from behind him, clamped a hand over his mouth, and hauled him away. Big Ben hid in a corner, but his ticking gave him away. Pickles almost immediately found himself trapped between two burly officers and had no choice but to throw in the towel. The Ace of Spades disappeared from the theater, but unfortunately reappeared in the back of a cop car with no chance of escape. Potty Mouth swore his way into a corner. An officer made a grab for Christmas Story and came away with his prosthetic leg, hampering Christmas Story's ability to escape. He hopped a good ten yards before another officer took him away. Snot's sneezing and space suit slowed him down. Marshmallow tried hiding in a dark corner, but his paleness gave him away. The Wiz was in the middle of calculating his chances of escape (33.33—repeating of course) when an officer handcuffed him. Ray Charles made good progress, dodging two officers, until his blindness caused him to run into the waiting arms of a third. Squirrel went willingly. He was still recovering from his wounds and not in any shape to play cop and orphan.

In the end, there were just too many officers and not enough men. T.W. was halfway up the second flight of stairs when he ran into a wall of a chest.

"AND JUST WHERE DO YOU THINK YOU'RE GOING MAGGOT?" A big man in green camouflage fatigues with Major Balls inscribed in black letters on the left side of his shirt blocked T.W.'s escape. Well over 250 pounds, he was heavy in the chest, thick in the legs, and had arms the size of orphans. His tight-fitting short-sleeved shirt showcased every curve of his muscles. His pants were tucked into big black military boots, running up to his knees. A wide jaw jutted outward from his face like the curved bill of a duck. His nose was so big it cast a long shadow over the petite mustache above his lips. When angry, his nostrils flared like he was about to breathe fire. His hair, fashioned in a short crew cut, was more skin than hair. His eyes were such a fierce, penetrating blue that they threatened to look through someone. They were topped by a heavyset brow that gave the impression Major Balls was incapable of smiling.

One of his thick hands locked onto T.W.'s arm like a vice. "GAME'S UP, YOU'RE COMING WITH ME, MAGGOT." He hoisted T.W. over his shoulder and carried him down to the mess hall where the rest of the men were detained and guarded by a group of menacing officers. The only orphan unaccounted for was Toaster.

"Well, well, well," Captain Cornhole said, twirling his baton. "Look at what the cat dragged in. It appears we caught the leader of this here rat pack. You must be Tee Dubya. We've heard of you. Got orders to pay special attention to you."

Major Balls threw T.W. down in front of the other men.

"I see you've met Major Balls, the new Headmaster of Desolation Row. He's here to restore order to this ungodly place."

"We already have order, you moron," Ray Charles said.

"Somebody smack that imbecile in the binoculars," Captain Cornhole said. Major Balls moved to do just that.

"Leave him be," T.W. said.

"You again. Major Balls show this hooligan the meaning of respect."

Major Balls grabbed T.W by the arm. His fingers dug in, almost to the bone. He twisted T.W.'s arm at an odd angle, forcing him to cry out in pain.

"Hurts don't it? Should teach you some manners."

Some of the men looked to come to his aid, but T.W. shook his head, telling them to stand down. He gritted his teeth while Major Balls kept his grip.

"What's the meaning of this?" a loud voice called.

Major Balls released T.W. and turned to face the newcomer. Captain Cornhole remembered his composure and stood up straight, adjusting his pants and wiping his brow. All of the police officers stood at attention while the men looked in wonder as a large shadow filled the mess hall.

In stepped the villain, The Man himself, Mayor Sharp, with Bartholomew close behind, scribbling notes on a pad of paper. He gave Captain Cornhole a discerning look before taking in the whole of the men.

"That there's an orphan," Colonel Sanders whispered to a distraught Scissors. "My Orphan Sense is vibrating off the charts. He's one of us, well not really *us*, but an orphan."

"Well," Captain Cornhole sputtered. "We had ourselves a little incident here and was just teaching this ruffian the meaning of respect."

"He didn't hurt you did he, son?" Mayor Sharp turned to inspect T.W. He wore a warm, sympathetic smile. The same one he used on his constituents.

T.W. shook his head no.

"He's just a boy, Captain. How much trouble can one boy really cause? And I told you this one was not to be harmed. He's special."

"You see, I told you," Colonel Sanders whispered. "There's always been something not quite orphan about T.W."

Captain Cornhole answered by wiping his face and pulling up his pants. "Yes, of course, sir. I'm terribly sorry."

"Now, give me a rundown of the situation."

"We have all the orphans in custody, except one," Captain Cornhole reported. "A boy named Toaster is unaccounted for, but I have a team on it."

"You won't find him here," T.W. said. "He was adopted last month."

"According to my list he's supposed to be here." Bartholomew checked his notes. "Says so right here, thirty-four orphans, not thirty-three."

"Big Mama's always getting the list mixed up," T.W. said. "There's only thirty-three of us, count for yourself if you don't believe me."

"Now wait just a minute," Captain Cornhole said.

"Listen to the boy," Mayor Sharp said, cutting him off. "He appears to know what he's talking about, more than I can say for you. Major Balls, how are we looking security wise?"

"RIGHT ON SCHEDULE, SIR," Major Balls shouted. "MY SECOND AND THIRD ARE SECURING ALL EXITS AND POSSIBLE ESCAPE ROUTES. SECURITY CAMERAS ARE BEING PUT IN PLACE. NEW BARBED-WIRE FENCES ARE BEING CONSTRUCTED. TRACKING COLLARS ENROUTE. NEW LOCKS FASTENED ON ALL DOORS. LOCKDOWN IS SCHEDULED FOR 2100, ONCE THE TAG POLICE FINISH THEIR SWEEP, SIR."

"Very good," Mayor Sharp said. "My campaign manager Bart will assist you if you have any questions. He will also handle the media who should be here shortly. Keep your hands off the orphans, especially their faces. *Don't* leave any visible marks until after the news reporters leave. The last thing we need is for one of them to cry abuse and then we'll have excessive force charges on our hands—*your hands.* Is that clear?"

"CRYSTAL CLEAR, SIR."

Mayor Sharp was about to give further instructions when a commotion from the common room disrupted him.

"Get your hands off me. What's the meaning of all this? Let me see my children, Lordy, yes let me see them or Heaven help you."

Big Mama came barreling into the mess hall, tears streaming down her cheeks. "Oh, children, I'm so sorry, Lordy knows I am."

She came to a startled Monster, picked him up in her arms, and pressed him to her chest, cutting off his source of oxygen. "Oh, child, don't cry. Everything will be alright, Lordy knows it will."

"Captain Cornhole," Mayor Sharp said. "Arrest that woman!"

"For what?" T.W. shouted.

"Embezzlement for starters. Bart, show them the warrant and papers."

Bartholomew pulled out a stack of papers. "What we have here is irrefutable evidence that for the past five years, Big Mama has been cooking the books at Desolation Row, lining her own pockets with money that should be going to the orphans. We also have all kinds of evidence for tax fraud and as well as stolen goods from the dump and a number of tag violations. I'd say there's enough here to put her in the slammer for thirty or forty years."

"Why I never took a cent in all my life," Big Mama said, looking mighty fierce for her eighty-seven years. "Lordy knows everything I have goes back to the orphanage. That's God's honest truth, Lordy yes."

"Not according to these papers found in your office."

"That's a bunch of bull and you know it," T.W. shouted. "This is an inside job. You set Big Mama up. You're all a bunch of lying, thieving crooks."

"Takes one to know one," Mayor Sharp said, eyeing T.W. intently. "Son, I know all about you and your little games. You and I we aren't that different. In order to have truth, we first must have some lies. Now don't take it personal. This is just business. In this life you win some and you lose some. Remember that next time you sit at the table with the big boys."

Mayor Sharp walked up close to T.W. and leaned in towards his ear. "Don't worry, son, your secret is safe with me." He grinned and then turned to face the room. "Alright, let's wrap this up. I have places to be. Get her out of here. Major Balls, the orphanage is yours."

Big Mama began to cry, her sobs sounding like a siren. As they dragged her out, she met Mayor Sharp's eyes with a look of recognition. "Why, oh Lordy, why? All I ever did was be good by you. What have my children ever done to you?"

Mayor Sharp's face betrayed no emotion. He waited until she was gone before taking his leave. Bartholomew stopped him as he headed out.

"Yes, what is it, Bart?"

"What about him?" he asked, pointing to Squirrel.

"Yes, what about him?" Mayor Sharp said, looking down at his watch.

"He's all covered in bruises. I think he's the one that Beasley's son Buck did a number on. We can't keep him here. The media will have a field day with him."

"Yes, indeed." Mayor Sharp rubbed the bottom of his chin. "Very well, he can come with me. Grab his things and escort him to the car."

"Are you sure?"

"Yes. Betty has wanted a child ever since her last miscarriage. Besides just think of the media coverage. I can see the headlines now. 'Mayor adopts troubled youth, promises better hope for not only the boy, but perhaps the city of Detroit.'"

"Genius," Bartholomew said.

"I know. Let's go. I have a fund-raising speech to write."

Bartholomew ordered two officers to take Squirrel away, much to the protest of the men.

"You can't take Squirrel," Ray Charles yelled. "He's one of ours. We're the Proletarian Pistol-Swinging Punks of Detroit and we'll open a can of sardines on you if you don't let him go. So help Hemingway we will."

Mayor Sharp stopped to chuckle at his gall. "Son, I hate to break it to you, but I'm the Anti-Punk."

With that, Mayor Sharp took his leave, leaving the men in stunned silence and in the care of Major Balls. "YOU MAGGOTS BETTER GET ONE THING STRAIGHT," he screamed. "YOU'RE MINE NOW. UNTIL YOU MAGGOTS ARE ALL PROPERLY ADOPTED, I AM YOUR ONE AND ONLY PARENT. GOT IT, MAGGOTS?"

It took the Tag Police, led by Benedict Wilson, over two hours to sweep the Row. They found twenty-seven violations of tag misconduct, namely the cutting of tags off couches and issued twice as many citations. Baxter Wilson, proprietor of the dump, and volunteer Tag Policeman on the weekends, was surprised at the amount of junk from the dump that was stored at the Row. He promised to have it all shipped back to its rightful place.

By the time the Tag Police filled out the paperwork, the construction crew had finished sealing off all exits, changing the locks, barring all windows, and building a barbed-wire fence in the backyard to keep the men out of the dump. As an added precaution they electrified it.

It was close to midnight before the men were ordered to bed. The holes over the fireman poles were boarded up, all doors leading to the bedrooms were locked, and a guard was posted on each floor. The men slept in silence. T. W. stayed up most of the night staring up at the ceiling and listening to the cries of his comrades. The Row had become a prison, and there was no escape, not even in dreams.

"We'll get you back, Squirrel," T.W. whispered. "On that I promise."

17

The Changing of the Guard

UNDER THE TIGHT REGIMEN of Major Balls, the Row was run like a boot camp, with little room for fun. One of his first decrees was to strip the men of their PPSP-Douglas-Street-Affiliation vests. He stuffed them in garbage bags and delivered them to the dump. In their place, the men had to wear matching pink prison jumpsuits. Tracking devices were placed around their necks like dog collars, worn at all times, even in the shower.

All doors in and out of the Row were padlocked shut. Major Balls had the only key. The Wiz's laboratory was closed down. All materials originally set aside for *The Cause* were labeled contraband and confiscated. T.W.'s office was converted into Major Balls's personal bedroom. The shelves were stripped of books and replaced with large protein shake containers and various weight-lifting trophies. The poster of Che was swapped with one of Napoleon.

All furniture and games were taken from the rec room and returned to the dump. Chopsticks was demoted from chef and reassigned to dish duty. Big Mama's office was converted into a jail cell, with her closet acting as solitary confinement.

The only room Major Balls didn't have access to was the upstairs attic. He tried prying it open, breaking it open, busting it open, kicking it open, and finally blowing it open with C4, all to little avail.

"Reinforced steel," The Wiz bragged. "I designed the door myself."

The sock room became a sweatshop, with men working around the clock. Major Balls sold all matched socks on the black market for a profit, which went straight to Mayor Sharp's campaign fund.

"What I would give for a break," Pickles said, well into his eighth straight hour of work and not realizing the walls had grown ears. The next day he was given a break, Major Balls broke a food tray over his head.

As a former drill sergeant for the Marine Corps, Major Balls had an authoritarian three-step discipline plan that involved one, yelling, two, beating, and three, breaking. Bullying was an unspecified fourth component. His tough regimen was based on the principle that yelling led to listening, beating led to remembering, and finally, breaking led to obeying.

As Headmaster, his voice had only one volume—bullhorn.

His commands were so loud that when he got agitated the wind from his voice caused the hair on the men's heads to fly back. He even made Rooster sound quiet. He walked with a purpose, talked like he had a pair, and was so intimidating that he caused Belly Ache to pass out, Monster to wet himself, and Peanut Butter to cry, all simultaneously.

"MY NAME IS MAJOR BALLS, AND FROM THIS DAY FORTH, IF YOU BREAK THE RULES I WILL BREAK YOU. IS THAT UNDERSTOOD, MAGGOTS?"

Maggot was Major Balls's favorite word, narrowly beating out his second favorite word, infraction. He had so many rules and infractions that it was hard to keep track of them all. Talking out of turn—INFRACTION. Shirt not tucked in—INFRACTION. Bed not made on time—INFRACTION. Sneezing—INFRACTION. Untied shoelaces—INFRACTION. Leaving the toilet seat down—INFRACTION.

To keep his many rules enforced, Major Balls ran a tight ship. The men were ordered to do fifty push-ups for minor infractions, while major infractions resulted in a boot to the behind and solitary confinement.

Only one orphan tried to escape. Crash made it half a block before an electric surge caused him to crash into a shopping cart of clothes, concussion number eighty-something. He was still writhing in pain when Major Balls came to retrieve him. With the tracking devices doubling as shock collars no one else tried to escape.

The easiest method to keep the men out of trouble was to keep them as busy as orphanly possible. Each morning, the men were ordered awake at the break of dawn and endured two hours of calisthenics and conditioning. This was followed by a plain breakfast of oatmeal and grapefruit.

"What I would give for a little brown sugar," Pickles complained. The next day he was given a bowl of oatmeal without any oatmeal.

Breakfast was followed by morning chores. This included scrubbing every square inch of the Row with a toothbrush, especially the areas covered in paint. Major Balls took exception to Squirrel's artwork, preferring white walls to anything with color. The men believed it blasphemy to destroy something orphan-made and worked at a snail's pace. This didn't bode well with Major Balls. As punishment, he cut food rations and increased hours in the sock room.

Seafood was the first to break. Threat of starvation made him scrub the walls with his toothbrush like he had a phobia against cavities. Other men followed suit and soon the Row was as plain as a blank piece of paper; all except for the ceiling in the rec room, which was unreachable thanks to the disappearance of the Mobile Elevator.

Morning chores were followed by lunch, which featured a bland meal of bologna sandwiches on plain white bread and a side of grapefruit.

"What I would give for some mustard," Pickles complained. The next day he was given a plate full of mustard.

After lunch were afternoon chores, consisting of digging trenches in the backyard. As soon as the trenches were deep enough, the dirt was shoveled back in, guaranteeing the men plenty of work the next day. This was followed by afternoon classes, all taught by Professor Bore, a ninety-year old retired economist. Standing tall and emaciated, his arms and legs were no wider than rulers. His gaunt face was covered in a thin white beard while his head was bald on top and heavy with gray on the sides. Thick bifocals sat on his long, beak of a nose.

He stood in front of the classroom, wearing a white collared shirt with a black bow tie and plaid pants held up with suspenders decorated in various fish. Each class began with him writing his name in chalk on the chalkboard and then proceeding to lecture in a monotone voice for three hours straight, never pausing once in his sermon on the pitfalls of macroeconomic investment in a microeconomic setting, which if left unchecked resulted in a whirlwind of economic upheaval and downturn.

"Now, *you see*, inflation can lead to prolonged disequilibrium in the market economy, *you see*, and possible high unemployment, *you see*, which in a stagnant market, *you see*, can be detrimental to any form of economic recovery, *you see*, possibly leading to stagflation, *you see*, which can result when the productive capability of a market economy, *you see*, is abridged by an unflattering supply tremor, *you see*, which tends to raise prices on the demand side of things, *you see*, to the point, *you see*, that an abundance of money is in pursuit of too few goods, *you see*, which in a recession is unfavorable to any form of upturn or recovery, *you see*. Now in market shares in Southeast Asia, *you see*."

The men did not *see*. Professor Bore bored them near to death. Seafood came into the classroom fast asleep before he even sat in his chair. The ends of Ray Charles's binoculars rested face down on his desk. Chopsticks snored in Korean. Compost Pile had flies swarming in and out of his mouth between yawns. Super Soaker had a puddle of drool under his mouth. Cup Check cup-checked himself just to stay awake. Big Ben slept despite a number of alarms on his watches going off.

"What I would give for a good book to read," Pickles complained. The next day he was given a good book, right upside his head.

After classes, dinner consisted of boiled hot dogs served on white bread with grapefruit for dessert. On special occasions, the men were given a baked potato with none of the fixings.

"What I would give for some sour cream," Pickles complained. The next day he was given a potato so overcooked it was hard as a rock and looked like a piece of coal. This caused Pickles to swallow hard. One of Major Balls's most strictly enforced rules was that everything must be eaten on an orphan's plate before it was taken to the kitchen, even the crumbs. Punishment was severe. Failing to comply resulted in losing bed privileges for a whole week.

"Where would you even sleep?" Pickles whispered.

One of Major Balls's many talents, besides being stronger than an ox, was an incredible sense of hearing. He was on the other side of the mess hall when Pickles made his comment.

"WHAT'S THAT MAGGOT? YOU WANT TO KNOW WHERE YOU'LL SLEEP. WELL LET ME TELL YOU SOMETHING, MAGGOT. YOU DON'T SLEEP. YOU STAND. NOW GIVE ME FIFTY."

Faced with the dilemma of eating an inedible potato or not sleeping for a whole week, Pickles once again found himself in quite the predicament.

"Give it to me," T.W. said. "I'll take care of it."

It was passed under the table between the men until it reached The Ace of Spades, who made it disappear, current location unknown.

After dinner came evening chores and conditioning. Evening chores included picking up trash around the neighborhood and delivering it to the dump. Conditioning included running up and down Douglas Street for an hour straight. The men were so out of shape that Muscles was the only man not to toss up his supper. Four passed out from heatstroke and Belly Ache complained of shin splints. Seafood had to be carried to the infirmary on a stretcher, suffering from what was originally thought of as a stroke, but was later diagnosed as a really bad cramp.

"What I would give for a glass of water," Pickles said half-way through the second night's run. Major Balls ordered him to place his mouth in front of a fire hydrant. The spray of the water sent Pickles rolling head over heels to the other side of Douglas Street.

Lights out followed at 2200 sharp. The beds were stripped of their feather mattresses and replaced with mattresses made of straw. Any talking or movement in the bed was, as expected, an INFRACTION. After a long, hard day's work, the men were too tired to do anything but sleep. Suffering from insomnia, T.W. was the only man to lie awake at night.

"What I would give for a more comfortable mattress," Pickles complained the first night. The next day his bed was stripped of everything but the springs.

Every day the rules were reiterated by Major Balls and his two lackeys, his second-in-command, Sergeant Breakfast, and his third-in-command, Gunner Grape Juice. Together they formed the Triad of Terror.

Sergeant Breakfast was the Dean of Orphans and in charge of disciplinary matters and conditioning. She carried around a thick ruler, used to whack the men into shape, and a whistle around her neck used to call the men to attention.

"Alright, move it, turds" she called in a baritone growl. "I want a five-minute mile from each and every one of you turds. And I do mean five minutes."

Sergeant Breakfast was in such good shape, she boasted of running a three-minute mile. She was not quite as big as

Major Balls, but she was just as imposing. Her legs and arms were the width of telephone poles, causing her to walk bow-legged. She had short, cropped hair that fell just above her single eyebrow. Her face was masculine and chiseled like a sculpture with a short chin and protruding nose. The thin outline of a mustache crept above her thin lips, which were always taut like a kiss.

"Move along, turd," she called. "I eat pieces of crap like you for breakfast."

"How can she eat, *you know*, pieces of crap for breakfast?" Pickles exclaimed. The next day for breakfast he was served something resembling just that. It was passed along under the table to Seafood, who ate it without second thought.

Sergeant Breakfast's favorite hobby was pulling orphans by the ear and dragging them to detention. Her other hobbies included picking her nose and weight lifting. Sometimes she would bench-press an orphan over her head. Her favorite orphan to bench-press was Pickles.

"Come here, turd, I got a use for ya."

After fifty reps, she tossed Pickles aside with a loud grunt before saying, "Yeah, that's right I eat pieces of crap like you for breakfast."

"What I would give to be invisible," Pickles said. The next day he was placed in solitary confinement where nobody saw him for twenty-four hours.

Gunner Grape Juice had two roles. He was head chef in charge of cooking all meals and chief mechanical engineer in charge of security and responsible for the large electrical fence in the backyard as well as the tracking collars around the men's necks. Not much of a cook, his specialty was boiling water.

Gunner Grape Juice was only in his forties, but looked well into his sixties with wrinkly skin that clung to his body like a loose tarp. He was as skinny as a rake and no taller than an orphan. He had a big nose and big ears attached to a small face. A big bushy handlebar mustache ran above his lips like an upside down horseshoe. His mouth and lips were in constant movement, scrunching and shifting the wad of chew from one side of his mouth to the other. He hardly said a word, choosing to spit instead.

"Why do they call him Grape Juice?" Ray Charles asked.

"Maybe he likes grape juice," Scissors said.

It was thanks to Pickles that the men all learned the true meaning of Gunner Grape Juice's name.

"What I would give for something to drink besides water," Pickles complained. Before he could move down the food line, Gunner Grape Juice grabbed an empty glass and spit in it until it was full. It looked like grape juice.

Nobody despised Gunner Grape Juice more than Chopsticks. Being demoted to dishwasher was bad enough, but turning his kitchen into an unorganized pigsty was near sacrilegious.

"Pot go there, not *there*," Chopsticks complained. "Knifey in here, not there."

Gunner Grape Juice responded with a spit on the floor followed by a smile so purple it looked like he had just eaten a whole can of beets. Missing a handful of teeth, his voice was a shrill squeal. "Don't forget to clean up that mess, Chop Suey."

Chopsticks was so flustered he stormed away, cursing in Korean as he went. Gunner Grape Juice just grinned, his mouth working the chew in his mouth.

Used to a life of leisure and freedom, the men did not take well to the new constrictive regulations the Triad of Terror exerted over the Row. Any form of rebellion was quickly doused. Something T.W. learned the hard way.

T.W. spent the first few weeks under Major Balls's regime carefully biding his time, waiting for the right opportunity to strike. Keeping his cool was harder than expected, especially since Major Balls banned cigarettes. Without his smokes, his nerves were stretched. Ray Charles had it worse. After candy cigarettes were banned, he had severe withdrawals, constantly twitching and scratching the side of his binoculars. He became so desperate that he inhaled pieces of chalk to get his daily fix.

T.W. felt just like the lead of Tom Travolta's *Cool Hand Lucifer*, a straight-to-video production about a group of convicts trying to survive day-to-day life in a hellish, inescapable prison. Every day he fought the urge to smoke and bit his tongue while Major Balls made examples out of his men.

"IF YOU DON'T FOLLOW ORDERS—INFRACTION. IF YOU USE MORE THAN ONE LENGTH OF TOILET PAPER WHEN YOU WIPE YOUR BEHIND—INFRACTION."

And so began the Second Teepee War. Toilet paper became more valuable than marks. Wheelin' Dealin' Steven replaced all watches and necklaces in his trench coat with lines of paper. They were later confiscated as contraband.

"IF I FIND SO MUCH AS A SINGLE PIECE OF PAPER ON ANY OF YOU MAGGOTS, I WILL MAKE YOUR BOTTOM SO SORE THAT YOU'LL HAVE TO STAND UP TO GO NUMBER TWO. DO I MAKE MYSELF CLEAR, MAGGOTS?"

Belch belched in response.

"WHAT'S YOUR MAJOR MALFUNCTION, MAG-GOT?" Major Balls boomed, his face mere inches from Belch's.

"Eck-I Eck-don't Eck-know, Eck-sir."

"IF YOU BURP ONE MORE TIME I'M GOING TO DRIBBLE YOUR FACE ON THE FLOOR LIKE A BASKET-BALL. YOU GOT THAT, MAGGOT?"

Fearing another burp, Belch nodded his head like he was having a seizure.

"GIVE ME FIFTY."

Belch dropped down and began his fifty push-ups. Major Balls turned his attention to Poop Stain.

"WHAT'S THAT PIECE OF DOG CRAP DOING ON YOUR FACE, MAGGOT?"

"It's a birthmark sir."

"THAT'S NO BIRTHMARK. THAT'S A GODMARK, HIS WAY OF TELLING THE WORLD THAT YOU AIN'T WORTH A POT TO POOP IN. NOW GET DOWN AND GIVE ME FIFTY BEFORE I WIPE THAT POOP STAIN OFF OF YOUR MAGGOT FACE."

Tea Bag was ordered fifty for not speaking like an American, Peanut Butter for mumbling, Big Ben for ticking, Christmas Story for limping, Marshmallow for glowing, Stone Age for not shaving, Super Soaker for spitting, Potty Mouth for swearing, Snot for sneezing, and Seafood for sleeping, but he was so lazy he couldn't even manage a single push-up.

"WHAT IN GOD'S NAME IS YOUR MAJOR MAL-FUNCTION, MAGGOT? YOU CALL THAT A PUSH-UP. I'VE SEEN BEACHED WHALES MOVE MORE THAN

YOU DO. EVEN A GIRL CAN DO AT LEAST ONE PUSH-UP. WHY YOU'RE SO FAT AND STUPID THAT A PARENT WOULD RATHER ADOPT A SHOPPING CART THAN YOU. YOU MAKE ME SICK, MAGGOT. SO SICK IN FACT THAT I HAVE THE TASTE OF VOMIT IN MY MOUTH. NOW GIVE ME FIFTY OR I'LL KICK YOUR BLUBBER INTO OIL."

Seafood tried pushing himself from the floor, but he couldn't do it. Tears ran down his chubby cheeks.

"I can't do it, sir," he cried.

"GOOD GOD ALMIGHTY. Major Balls placed his foot on Seafood's back. "SOMEBODY CRY ME A GLASS OF WATER. I BET IF THERE WAS A TWINKIE DOWN THERE YOU'D DO A HUNDRED PUSH-UPS!"

"Hey, meathead, why don't you leave him alone?"

"WHO SAID THAT?" Major Balls turned to face the other men. "WHICH ONE OF YOU MAGGOTS SPOKE OUT OF TURN?"

Major Balls walked up and down the row of men, his face so red it was almost purple and his eyes bulging with rage.

"I did." T.W. stepped forward. There was a quiet murmur through the ranks.

Major Balls stormed towards T.W. and made to grab him by the neck, but T.W. ducked and turned out of the way, leaving Major Balls's hand grasping for air. When he turned around, T.W. was waiting for him and delivered his signature move, a boot straight to Major Balls's family jewels. Expecting to hear a howl of pain, T.W. was surprised to hear laughter instead. Major Balls grabbed him by the collar and lifted him up so he was eye level.

"YOU CALL THAT A KICK, MAGGOT?"

Sergeant Breakfast and Gunner Grape Juice snickered. T.W. swung at Major Balls, but he was held too far away to make contact.

"LOOKS LIKE WE GOT OURSELVES A FIGHTER. A LITTLE FEISTY, I LIKE THAT. BUT NOW IT'S TIME I TAUGHT YOU WHAT HAPPENS WHEN YOU CROSS MAJOR BALLS. GUNNER GRAPE JUICE, GET ME SOME ROPE AND A CHAIR. SERGEANT BREAKFAST, BRING ME MY CLIPPERS."

They strapped T.W. to a chair, his arms and legs secured so that he couldn't move. The men were reduced to silence.

"HAIR LONGER THAN REGULATION—INFRAC-TION."

Major Balls ran his electric razor down the middle of T.W.'s head. Strands of his black hair fell like leaves to the floor. When Major Balls was finished, T.W.'s head was completely bare. He looked just like a—

"Cancer patient," Sergeant Breakfast exclaimed, laughing so hard it popped like a machine gun. Gunner Grape Juice spat in agreement. T.W. was untied from the chair and pushed back into formation.

Later that evening during dinner, Major Balls implanted a whole new catalog of rules to deter any other forms of insurgence. He was on infraction 176 when T.W. stood up, wound up like a pitcher, and threw a baked potato. It collided with Major Balls's face. Infraction 177.

Major Balls responded by slapping T.W. so hard he did a complete 360 before landing on his bottom, a white handprint left engraved on the side of his red face.

"GET THIS MAGGOT OUT OF MY SIGHT. PUT HIM IN THE HOLE WHERE HE'LL NEVER SEE THE SUN AGAIN. THE REST OF THESE MAGGOTS ARE ON SOCK DETAIL UNTIL FURTHER NOTICE."

T.W. was carried away by Sergeant Breakfast and placed in solitary confinement. The other men were led away by Gunner Grape Juice. When they complained too much or didn't work fast enough, Gunner Grape Juice gave their electric shock collars a zap.

Sometimes he gave them a zap just for the Hemingway of it.

T.W. fared worse. His cell was so small that he had only enough legroom to sit cross-legged on the floor. There was no bathroom, just a bucket, and no ventilation or light, just a tiny crack at the bottom of the door.

The door to his cell was secured by four padlocks, negating any chance of escape. He had no contact with the outside world. His three daily meals (a slice of white bread and half a grapefruit) were slid in through a small cubby.

With no timetable on a release, T.W. was stuck in the breaking phase of Major Balls's three-step Disciplinary Plan. But he refused to be broken. Left alone in the darkness, he sat in a Zen-like pose and mentally constructed his own three-point plan.

1. *Dispose of Major Balls*
2. *Rescue Squirrel*
3. *Revolution*

Afterwards, he rubbed his recently shaved head, feeling the rough patches where his hair used to be. In his mind, he underlined the word Revolution twice before attempting to fall asleep.

18

Living with the Enemy

MAYOR SHARP'S HOUSE, or rather mansion, was so sizable that Squirrel got lost twice while trying to find the bathroom. It was an easy thing to do, considering the place had three levels, plus an attic, a full-size basement, ten bedrooms, six bathrooms, two kitchens, a dozen closets, an indoor pool, tennis court, and a four-car garage.

His own room was so large and roomy it made him uncomfortable. His bed wide enough that he could roll over five times before falling off. The mattress so soft and comfy his body sank a good three inches, making him wonder if it was made out of quicksand. His meager belongings took up only one drawer of his ten-drawer dresser.

Squirrel thought it odd that the Sharps had so many bedrooms and no children to fill them. He surmised they had a lot of guests. There were only two other permanent residents, a butler named Mr. Tidy and a small, furry black terrier mix named Rosie. Neither of which liked the intrusion of Squirrel.

"Your room is this way," Mr. Tidy said, not hiding his disdain and pointing the way with hands covered in white gloves. His upper lip sniveled as he sniffed Squirrel's hair. "And you will be required to take a bath, *immediately.*"

Always dressed in a black-and-white suit, Mr. Tidy was as dapper as Tom Travolta in his espionage thriller *James Bondage*. Just a shade over sixty, his hair, dark like a roof, was combed to the side, while the sides, a light gray, were kept short along his ears. His face was clean shaven, save for a finely trimmed black mustache, no more than a pencil line above his lips. He kept his head held high, as if the act of looking down was beneath him.

Mr. Tidy kept Mayor Sharp's house like he kept up his appearances, perfectly clean in every sense of the word. He was so hygienic that he never wore the same pair of gloves twice, tossing them out with the trash after a day's use.

Under his command were six maids and four landscapers. Every day he made the rounds, inspecting the work of his underlings, using a black dust brush to touch up the areas they missed. His golden rule was to not touch anything, *ever*.

"Dinner is served every night at six o'clock prompt," Mr. Tidy continued. "When the Sharps have guests you are expected to eat in the servers' quarters. However, they asked for your attendance tonight." He said the last part with a sigh.

"Dress is dinner casual," he said, looking down at Squirrel's rags. "I would change into something more proper before coming down."

"But this is all I have."

"Very well, a proper suit will be laid out on your bed," he continued. "Breakfast is served at seven sharp and lunch at noon. You are expected to clean up after yourself. We're not running an orphanage here. This is a civilized place, one that is kept clean and *dust free*."

"My advice to you," Mr. Tidy said, raising his eyebrow, "is

to keep out of sight and out of mind. Any form of rubbish can be easily taken out with the trash, if you catch my meaning?"

Squirrel did. He just couldn't catch a break, attracting more enemies than Tom Travolta did Oscar snubs.

He hoped to fare better with their pet, Rosie, but the dog immediately smelled the orphan in him. Squirrel first came across Rosie on his way downstairs after having just bathed and changed into a red-and-black schoolboy uniform that had been left on his bed by Mr. Tidy. As he reached the bottom of the stairs, he was greeted by a deep growl, followed by a loud ferocious bark. Expecting to see a fierce Doberman like the ones at the dump or worse yet the evil rabid dogs from Tom Travolta's *101 Damnations*, he was surprised to find a furry critter no bigger than a cat.

Rosie's black fur was so overgrown and unkempt it looked like the hair on Tim Burton's head. The dog was completely black save for a white patch that ran on its chin like a goatee. Thick bangs covered its eyes, making it hard to see. Around its neck was a large heart-shaped name tag.

Despite having a girl's name, Rosie was actually a he— the Sharps waited until after it was a year old to have its sex checked and then didn't bother to correct their earlier assumption that it was female when it was in fact male.

"Hey, girl," Squirrel said, offering his hand for it to lick. Rosie responded by snapping at his fingers, nearly drawing blood.

"Jeez-Louise, you're not the friendly type, are you?"

Rosie responded with a snap of his teeth.

As much as Rosie loathed Squirrel, he loved his owners unconditionally, who conditionally tolerated his existence while secretly anticipating the day he keeled over or just simply went away and never came back. Much to their dismay, Rosie was the type of dog that could not take a hint, lingering around like a cat with many lives.

Every morning Rosie greeted Mr. Sharp by running around his legs and every morning Mr. Sharp kicked him out of the way. One time Mr. Sharp kicked him so hard that he was booted right out the open front window and into the pool. He came back into the house later looking like a wet rat.

As a joke, Mayor Sharp once told Rosie to go find Jimmy Hoffa. Hoping Rosie would take the hint and never return, Mayor Sharp was surprised when he returned three weeks later with the bony remains of a severed hand. After several medical examinations it was determined that the hand was not Jimmy Hoffa's, but rather D.B. Cooper's.

Rosie was told multiple times to "go play with lightning."

Always attentive to his master's command, Rosie played outside during every storm. It didn't take very long before he was eventually struck by lightning. The Sharps were somewhat disappointed when he came back with his fur smoking and singed but otherwise unscathed. Afterwards, they refrained from telling him to play with lightning, insisting instead on playing in traffic.

Rosie was so often overlooked and forgotten that the Sharps left him at the Grand Canyon during a summer vacation. They were somewhat astounded when he showed up home four months later, disheveled and looking like a critter from famine-ridden Africa. Thinking the dog was gone for good, the Sharps had celebrated by getting rid of all of his toys, food, and bed. They had even forgotten his name, calling him dog at first, until an impromptu call from the vet reminded them that the dog's name was Rosie.

They had given him away *twice*. Once as a Christmas present to Betty's brother Baxter, hoping he could use the dog at the dump, and another time as a birthday present to Bart's niece Brittany. Both times, Rosie ran away and returned with his tail wagging and his tongue rolling, happy to be home, while the Sharps cursed the ground beneath his paws.

As a joke, they often used his name as a verb, rather than a noun, like when Mayor Sharp forgot to pick up Mrs. Sharp from her hair appointment, she was Rosied, or when Mrs. Sharp became so incensed at Mayor Sharp that she threatened to "Rosie him," which meant she either planned on giving him a good kick or leaving him. Most times, they just didn't give a Rosie about anything.

Already having two members of the household against him, Squirrel had little, if any hope for his dinner with the Sharps going well. Despite his best attempts at looking presentable, he was still rough for wear. The bruises on his face had yet to properly heal, making him look like a boxer mere days after the losing end of a big fight.

He found the Sharps in the dining room, a room the length of a bowling alley and containing a table with so many chairs it was possible to seat every orphan at the Row. A giant white crystal chandelier hung from the ceiling. It glittered like diamonds in the sun and shined so bright Squirrel had to squint to look at it.

"Well, there he is," Mayor Sharp boomed. "Our guest of honor has arrived. Please take a seat and join us."

Mayor Sharp sat at one end of the very long table, while

at the other end (a good twenty feet away) sat Mrs. Sharp, wearing an orange dress and looking as plump as a pumpkin. Her pudgy, rosy cheeks beamed at Squirrel's arrival. Unsure of where to sit, Squirrel eyed the table with unease.

Mrs. Sharp raced over to greet him. With each step, her large bun of brown hair bobbled, while her short, stubby legs waddled. She was so excited to see Squirrel she had no idea Rosie was in front of her. With one quick swipe of her foot she sent Rosie flying into the wall, where he crashed and slowly slid down like a wet washcloth.

"Oh come here, you," she said. "Give me hugs and kisses."

Before Squirrel could say pickle in a jar, Mrs. Sharp had her arms wrapped around him, planting kisses on both cheeks before moving to his lips, her red lipstick leaving tracks all over his face. Squirrel felt somewhat violated.

"Enough already, Betty," Mayor Sharp shouted. "The boy's not a teddy bear."

Mrs. Sharp stepped back, taking a deep breath and fanning her hands in her face. Strands of hair had come undone from her big bun and make-up smeared across her face. Mayor Sharp raced over to save Squirrel from his wife, completely unaware of Rosie limping in front of him. His hurried footsteps sent the dog flying up into the chandelier, where he stayed until the morning when Mr. Tidy discovered him while dusting.

"Come here, son." Mayor Sharp took Squirrel's hand. His large figure towered over Squirrel. "I'm very pleased to make your acquaintance, Earl. You're a member of the Republican Party, right?"

Squirrel, looking confused, didn't know what to say.

"Just kidding." Mayor Sharp grinned, slapping Squirrel hard on the shoulder. "You're too young to vote anyways. Let's get some food in ya. You look ravished. Didn't they feed you at that orphanage?"

Squirrel was placed in the middle of the table, equal distance between Mr. and Mrs. Sharp who were so far apart that they had trouble hearing each other. He took his seat and was about to unfold his napkin when the Sharps bowed their heads for prayer.

"Thank you, Lord, for the meal we are about to receive," Mayor Sharp started. "May you bless the worthy and righteous and walk among us in the light. May you punish the wicked who walk in the darkness, just like that good-for-nothing-Calloway who just announced he was dropping out of the Democratic primary due to personal reasons. Can I get an amen?"

"Amen," Mrs. Sharp answered.

"And may you bless me on my run for governor, now that my bitter rival has been displaced, and see to it that the voters of the great state of Michigan have the wisdom to vote Republican."

"Amen," Mrs. Sharp said.

"Amen," Mayor Sharp said. "Alright, let's eat. Mr. Tidy, chop-chop."

Mr. Tidy brought out the first course, a cream of mushroom soup with a slice of French bread on the side. Squirrel couldn't help but notice his bowl was only a quarter full and his bread the hard end-piece.

"Delicious," Mayor Sharp said. "How's the soup, Earl?"

"It's Squirrel, sir, and it's delicious."

"What'd he say?" Mrs. Sharp yelled.

"It's delicious," Squirrel yelled in response.

"Oh right, very good. Will you pass me the salt?"

"Pass the what?" Mayor Sharp yelled. "Speak up, woman!"

"*The salt*. Pass the salt!"

"Lift up your bowl, Earl."

Squirrel had no idea what Mayor Sharp was talking about. Clarity came a split second later, just as Mayor Sharp slid the saltshaker in his direction. Squirrel lifted his bowl just in time, it passed right beneath and sailed across to Mrs. Sharp who caught it with her pudgy hands and shook enough salt into her soup to fill an ocean. From above, in the direction of the chandelier, came a whimper no one paid any attention to.

Squirrel was on his last spoonful of soup, when the second course arrived—a Caesar salad. He couldn't help but notice his salad was entirely green with no tomatoes, onions, cucumbers, or carrots and hardly any dressing.

"Pass me the pepper," Mrs. Sharp called.

"*The what*?"

"The pepper."

"Oh, alright. Lift up your plate, Earl."

More prepared this time around, Squirrel lifted his plate with seconds to spare. The pepper shaker slid across the table, under his plate, and right into the waiting hands of Mrs. Sharp.

The third course was Red Snapper soaked in lemon, with a side of sweet potato pudding and green bean casserole. Squirrel couldn't help but notice his fish was mostly bones, almost choking on one after his first bite. The rest of the evening was spent digging fish bones out of his mouth.

"Pass me the tartar sauce," Mrs. Sharp yelled.

"*The what?*"

"The tartar sauce."

"Oh alright."

Squirrel was ready long before the tartar sauce came barreling beneath his plate. The fourth and final course was dessert, a hot fudge brownie sundae. Squirrel's didn't have a cherry on top.

"Pass me the chocolate syrup," Mrs. Sharp yelled.

"*The what?*"

"The chocolate syrup."

"Oh alright."

Squirrel held his bowl at his chest, eating his ice cream while the chocolate syrup, caramel sauce, and whipped cream went back and forth on the table. Tea and coffee were served afterwards. Squirrel was offered a cup of hot water. Knowing that Mrs. Sharp would need the cream and sugar passed her way, Squirrel held his glass away from the table.

After dinner, Mr. Tidy cleared the table while Mayor Sharp leaned back in his chair smoking a big cigar, and Mrs. Sharp used a mirror to adjust her make-up. Squirrel twirled his thumbs, waiting to be excused.

"Well," Mayor Sharp declared. "I believe it is time to retire to bed. Big day at the office tomorrow, dealing with those darn Socialist union reps. Make yourself at home, Earl, and let Mr. Tidy know if you need anything."

"I will, sir."

"Before you go, Earl, I have a small housewarming gift for you. It should help you make sense of this crazy world." It was a copy of *Atlas Shrugged.*

"And one last thing, Earl, check in with Mr. Tidy in the kitchen. He has something for you as well." It was the dirty dishes. Squirrel spent the better part of an hour doing them before heading to bed.

The next day, Squirrel went back to Detroit Public for the first time in over a week. Instead of taking the bus, he returned in style, riding in a shiny, silver Mercedes Benz. Mr. Tidy dropped him off at the front entrance. No sooner had Squirrel shut the car door then it was squealing out of the parking lot.

Squirrel checked in at the office and was greeted with a warm smile by Ms. Mouse and a deep-seated frown by Principal Wilson.

"Welcome back, Squirrel." Ms. Mouse adjusted her glasses and blushed slightly. "How is . . . *uh* . . . that friend of yours, T.W., I believe?"

"Um, he's fine I think."

"Good. If you see him will you please tell him I said hello?"

"Will do," Squirrel said, turning to leave.

"Oh, Squirrel, one last thing. A Mr. Tidy just called and said you need to find your own ride home after school today."

Squirrel left the office and was immediately greeted by Demmie, dressed in a tan Girl Scout uniform. She threw her arms around him and gave him a big kiss on the lips.

"Your face is healing up nicely. I'm still not used to your hair though."

"It'll grow back eventually." Squirrel ran his hand on his neck, where his long hair used to fall.

"I know. Hey, I have something for you."

"What?"

"Come with me to my locker."

She led the way, holding Squirrel's hand. As they walked down the hallway, students stopped to stare. Some even turned the other way, looks of terror on their faces.

"What's that all about?" Squirrel asked.

"They heard what happened to the Wilsons. It's been the talk of the school. The word on the hallway is that you and your friends are not to be messed with. Buck no longer runs the place, not since he came back from the hospital. There's a new king in the castle."

"Who?"

"Why you, of course, silly."

They turned a corner and came in contact with two Wilsons, Blake and Bird. They saw Squirrel and took off running.

"You won't ever have to worry about the Wilsons again," Demmie said. "Those orphan friends of yours sure put a beating on them. Most of them are still pretty banged up, can't even play football. They lost the big game on Friday, first loss in five years or something. Buck hasn't been the same either. He no longer talks in the third person. Just sits in the corner and doesn't talk to anybody. Some of the teachers think he may have had some good sense knocked into him. It's a shame what happened to your friends at the Row. Have you heard anything from them since the raid? Are they alright?"

"I don't know. I've been expecting a dumpster-chicken carrier, but so far none have come. It's only been a few days though."

"Is it true that you're living with the Sharps?"

"Yeah, it's kind of weird, staying with the enemy."

"Wow, the mayor of Detroit. I heard his house is huge."

"I think it's just as big, or even bigger, than the Row."

"Do you miss it?"

"Yeah, I do. It's my home, where I belong."

"You'll get back there someday. Until then, I'm just glad you're back here with me."

They came to her locker. She had two gifts for him, not one. The first was a new friendship bracelet, which he immediately put on his left wrist. The second came in a brown paper bag.

"What's this?"

"Open it up and see."

Squirrel reached in his hand and pulled out a half dozen paintbrushes of various sizes.

"I hope they're okay. I wasn't really sure which ones to get. I still have the receipt in case you want to return them."

"No, they're perfect. Thank you."

For the first time in forever, Squirrel was happier at school than he was at home. He dreaded taking the bus back to Mayor Sharp's but was relieved when he found the place empty. Waiting for him on the kitchen counter was a butter sandwich and a note. *The Sharps are at a fund-raising function. Stay out of the cupboards and don't touch anything! Mr. T*

Squirrel took his plain butter sandwich up to his room. On his way, he heard a low whimpering from a closet. He opened the door and was startled to see Rosie locked up in a small, cramped cage, his nose pressed between the bars.

"Looks like you're stuck here too."

He unlocked the door and motioned for him to come out, even offering a piece of his sandwich. Rosie took it with a quick swipe of his mouth and then growled before running away. Squirrel did not see him for the rest of the evening.

As the days dragged on, Squirrel saw less of the Sharps. They were always busy attending some function or on the campaign trail. Squirrel had become as neglected and forgotten as their dog, Rosie. He was there, but not there, spending most of his time alone in his room painting or taking his meals in the servants' quarters while the Sharps wined and dined various guests.

The only attention Squirrel received from the Sharps was when they needed him to have his picture taken for the *Detroit Free Press*. Their chief editor, Upton Muckraker, was running an article on Mayor Sharp's charitable contributions to the city of Detroit that focused on his having adopted a needy orphan from a rough part of town. This was in direct contrast to his previous articles that only attempted to pin charges of corruption to Mayor Sharp. Due to the unexpected resignation of Calloway from the primaries for "personal" reasons—much to the surprise of the public—Upton had all but lost faith in the system and figured that if you can't stick it to The Man you might as well find something positive to write about.

After the article ran the mood in the house took a drastic turn, so drastic in fact, that Squirrel was summoned to the dinner table to have his second official meal with the family.

"We've been thinking." Mayor Sharp paused to suck meat from a crab leg. Squirrel's own crab was more shell than meat. "That it wouldn't be exactly fair of us to give everything to you on a silver platter. You see—"

"Pass me the garlic butter," Mrs. Sharp yelled.

"*The what*?"

"The garlic butter."

"Oh alright."

Squirrel raised his plate while Mayor Sharp sent the bowl of garlic butter sliding across the table.

"Now where was I?" He paused to wipe his face with a napkin. "Right, life's not easy. The real world is not going to give you any freebies. You have to earn everything out there. Otherwise you'll just live off the system, collecting handouts in the streets, sucking the country dry. You get what I'm saying, Earl?"

Squirrel didn't, but nodded anyway.

"Good, I see you've been reading that book I gave you."

He hadn't. Thanks to Rosie it had been torn to bits—the only nice thing he had done for him since he had been there. He thought sharing his food with the dog would earn him some favors, but Rosie repaid him by dropping land mines on his bedroom floor.

"Anyways, as I was saying, we need to prepare you for the harshness of reality, make you stronger for what lies ahead. In that manner, it's been decided you need to earn your keep around here. That includes doing chores and paying rent. We'll give you some time to get your feet wet, but after that you'll have to get a job and pay your own way."

Having never had a job or paid rent before, Squirrel gulped. "How much exactly will rent be, sir?"

"Well, we'll cut you a deal and make it say $150 a month, plus another $50 for utilities, so an even $200."

"But, sir, I don't have a job or even know how to get one."

"Don't worry, Mr. Tidy will take care of it. He has some job applications waiting for you."

"But what about school and my homework?"

"You'll just have to make do, son. 'Pride is the recognition of the fact that you are your own highest value and, like all of man's values, it has to be earned.'"

Having never read *Atlas Shrugged*, Squirrel had no idea what to make of the quote. After dinner he was excused to his room where he found three things: an envelope labeled job applications, a black dust brush, and a long list of chores.

His new chores included taking out the trash, vacuuming, sweeping, washing the dishes, folding the laundry, watering the plants, feeding the dog, walking the dog, poop scooping after the dog, and dusting, underlined three times.

It took Squirrel only a few days to secure a job—all of the applications were for business owned by various Wilsons. Not sure which job to choose, he decided on an internship for the Honorable Judge Barton Wilson of the Detroit Circuit Court. He was hired on the spot and began work the next day.

Even Rosie was not exempt from employment, sometimes having to fill in for a watchdog at the dump.

Much to Demmie's disappointment, Squirrel skipped their daily after school meet-ups at the library and took a bus downtown to begin his new job. Picturing the fun, exciting life of an intern for a hotshot lawyer, reminiscent of Tom Travolta's medieval courtroom drama *Knight Court*, he was dissatisfied to find himself locked away in a small storage closet, stacked high with legal documents, mostly charges of illegal removal of couch tags. His job was to sort them all.

When he wasn't sorting documents, he was licking envelopes, thousands of them. He licked so many plain white envelopes that his tongue became insensitive to taste. No matter what he ate, which was usually just butter sandwiches, all he tasted was the bland, mouth-drying tang of envelope glue.

At a measly five dollars an hour, Squirrel calculated he would need to work at least forty hours a month to break even. However, he did not include taxes in his calculations, which due to Mayor Sharp's way of doing things included taking half—all to be redistributed to Mayor Sharp's campaign funds. This meant that Squirrel had to work eighty hours a month, or twenty hours a week, just to break even.

Coupled with chores and schoolwork, this gave Squirrel little free time for Demmie or painting. Most days he woke up at 5 a.m. to start his daily chores. He was at school by 8, off to work by 4, and home by 9 to finish the rest of his chores and homework before going to bed just before midnight.

His chores normally wouldn't have taken long to complete, but Mr. Tidy was a stickler. He always double-checked, sometimes triple-checked, Squirrel's work by running his white-gloved finger over an area for signs of dust and then uttering a single, solitary dreadful word.

"Again."

Squirrel dusted and dusted again so much that he was in a perpetual dust storm, one that kept him sneezing on a regular basis. His dust brush replaced his paintbrush, so much so that the conservative Sharps were able to let go two of their six maids, savings that went straight to Mayor Sharp's campaign.

He worked day and night, surviving on only butter sandwiches, which he shared daily with Rosie. The work was so exhausting Squirrel had little time to think, all he did was sleep.

The Row and his friends became a distant memory, lost in the fatigue that overtook him.

On one particular exhausting evening, Squirrel was lying in bed when he heard a tap tapping on his window. Thinking the sound a figment of his fatigued imagination, he paid it little mind. It was only when it became louder and more insistent that he got out of bed and approached the window. He opened it and was almost knocked over by a scraggly dumpster-chicken carrier. Attached to its foot was a rolled up note. *Things at the Row are bad. Situation dire. We need your help immediately. Meet me at the dump tomorrow. Toaster*

Squirrel smiled for the first time in weeks. A new surge of energy and purpose filled him, his exhaustion forgotten. He raced to his dresser and packed his things into a pillowcase. He made a quick stop in the kitchen to load up on food, dismissing Mr. Tidy's golden rule of not touching anything.

The night was quiet and cool as he snuck out the front door. As he left the Sharp's estate, he did not realize he was being followed.

19

Reclaiming the Throne

"I'M STARVING. What do you have for food?"

Toaster was so hungry he was shaking. His hands fidgeted with the ends of his red sweater. His face was covered in grime. It looked like he had been through the thick of it, just like Tom Travolta in his epic World War II saga, *Saving Ryan's Privates.*

He sat next to Squirrel on the doorsteps of an abandoned warehouse a few blocks from the dump. It was early morning and neither one of them had slept much the night before. Dark lines hung heavy beneath their eyes.

"I have some granola bars." Squirrel reached into his pillowcase, which was half-full of snacks from the Sharps' pantry.

"Perfect," Toaster said. He would have eaten the wrappers if Squirrel had not opened them for him.

"What happened to you?" Squirrel opened his own granola bar. A steady diet of butter sandwiches and walking for most of the night had left him famished. Toaster's mouth was too full of food to answer.

"It was . . . (chew) . . . terrible . . . (munch) . . . I had to . . .

(swallow) . . . spend the better part of a month hiding in the ventilation system. All I had to eat . . . (chew) . . . was some stale crackers . . . (munch) . . . and some cheese . . . (swallow) . . . from a mousetrap."

"Why didn't you sneak some food from the kitchen?"

"The whole place is under lockdown. It has tighter security than a bank. It took me a few days just to escape and make it to the dump. I've been scavenging food ever since, almost had to eat a dumpster chicken to keep from starving."

"That's jacked up."

"Tell me about it. It took me another week to finally catch one of those stupid birds. I would have eaten it, but it was one of The Wiz's old carrier pigeons. I thought it best to get ahold of you and sent a message right away. We're the Row's only hope."

"What happened to the rest of the men?"

"All held captive by Major Balls and his Triad of Terror. They keep the men locked up in their rooms at night and use them for slave labor during the day. The Wiz's lab has been dismantled. Everything has been returned to the dump. The rec room is completely bare—no games, books, or nothing."

"Son-of-a-Hemingway! What about Big Mama? What happened to her?"

"Not entirely sure. As far as I know they took her to the state pen. I didn't see it, but heard them dragging her away outside, talking about charges of neglect, child abuse, tax fraud, and recklessness just to name a few."

"Oh the audacity of those scoundrels! This smells like a set up."

"Tell me about it." Toaster paused. "You're not going to like this next part, Squirrel. They . . . *uh* . . . even wiped away all of your paintings. Made the men do it too, threatened to starve them out. The Row is as plain as toilet paper right now."

"I can always paint it again. What about *The Cause*? They didn't open the locked door did they?"

"No. It's the only place they haven't got their filthy paws on yet. Thank Hemingway, otherwise we'd be USWC."

"Up a Sewer Without a Clothespin." Squirrel stared off into the distance, thinking of Scissors. "They infiltrated every other place. How did they manage to stay out of there?"

"The Wiz made the door orphan-proof, besides I have the only key."

"How'd you swing that?"

"T.W. gave it to me just before all Hemingway broke lose."

"How is he?"

"That's right, you don't know."

"Don't know what?"

Toaster swallowed hard and lowered his head. "T.W., they, uh, cut off his hair and stuffed him in the hole. He's been there for over a week now. I have no idea how he is or if he's, you know, still alive. There's no telling how bad a shape he's in."

"We've got to do something."

"I know, but getting in can be tricky. I've been on the outside for a while now. It's pretty quiet in there, kind of like a funeral home. No word in or out. When it comes to intelligence, we're completely in the dark. Their security's tight—cameras, electrified fences, tracking collars, the works."

"What about the abandoned Ford factory? It's stockpiled for a war."

"It's mostly vehicles and weaponry. That won't do us a lot of good in this situation. They'll just call in the cops or worse yet the National Guard. We need to work in stealth and release everyone from their tracking collars."

"Right, I forgot about those. What are we going to do then?"

"I dunno. It's just the two of us."

"Actually it's the three of us." Demmie stepped around the corner carrying a large bag. "I got your dumpster-chicken carrier, Squirrel. Sorry it took me so long to get here. I'm not too late am I?"

"Not at all," Squirrel said. "We were just strategizing."

"Good. What's the plan?"

"We don't have one. We're just going to have to wing it. Are you in?"

"Of course," she said with a smile. "Are you guy's hungry? I brought Girl Scout Cookies."

Toaster ate a whole box by himself, while they sat together and drew up a plan to reclaim the Row. They were not alone. Out of the shadows of an abandoned building, a fourth kept a watchful eye.

* * *

Back at the Row, Sergeant Breakfast was in the middle of browsing through the illustrations of *Steroids Magazine* with one hand and lifting a fifty-pound weight with the other when someone knocked on the front door.

"Son-of-a-Chuck-Norris," she growled, getting up from the chair and strutting over to the door, all the while still working the weight in her hand. She unlatched the half dozen locks on the door before opening it. Standing in front of her were two girls dressed in tan Girl Scout uniforms. One was tall with red hair done up in two pony tails, Pippi Longstocking style, while the other was of the same height, but with short blonde hair and heavy make-up.

"What do you turds want?" Sergeant Breakfast asked.

"We're selling Girl Scout Cookies," the redheaded one said. "Would you be interested in buying any?"

"I don't eat Girl Scout Cookies for breakfast."

"Did I mention that each purchase comes with a free subscription to *Buff and Tough Magazine?*"

"*Buff and Tough Magazine* you say? Well come on in."

Sergeant Breakfast led them into the common room. The door remained open long enough for a shadow to slip in. It blended with the walls and slowly crept towards what used to be Big Mama's office, now a holding cell. While the two Girl Scouts and Sergeant Breakfast took a seat to conduct their business, the shadow slipped unnoticed into the office.

T.W. sat alone in solitary confinement. He was on his knees, in a meditative pose when he felt a folded piece of paper touch his knee. The little glimmer from the bottom of the door provided enough light to read the message. It contained only five letters: BRFTC.

"Be Ready For *The Cause,*" T.W. whispered.

Out in the common room, Sergeant Breakfast concluded her business with the two Girl Scouts, coming away with two boxes of cookies and a free subscription to *Buff and Tough Magazine.*

"You sure are a quiet turd, aren't you?" Sergeant Breakfast asked the blonde-haired one.

The blonde-haired one nodded, quickly turning away.

"Is that an Adam's apple in your throat?" Sergeant Breakfast bent down to get a better look. "Sure is. I have one too. In fact, I used to eat a lot of apples for breakfast, but gave them up when I discovered they weren't a very good source of protein."

"Hm-hmm," the blonde-haired one said.

"Right, well we better get going," the red-haired one said. "Lots of cookies to sell, as you know, the early orphan gets the worm."

"*Wait*, what did you say?"

"Oh nothing, just that the early—"

The blonde-haired girl gave the red-haired girl a sharp kick to the shin. "—the early dumpster chicken gets the worm."

"Oh, right." Sergeant Breakfast scrunched her face in concentration. "Say how much do you weigh turd?"

"Who me?" the red-haired one asked.

"No, the other turd. It doesn't matter. I can figure it out myself."

Before the blonde-haired girl could say ice cream in a cone, she was lifted up over the shoulders of Sergeant Breakfast and then bench-pressed five times before being placed back on the ground again.

"I say you're about 105 pounds. A little heavy for a girl."

Sergeant Breakfast flexed, her biceps looking like they swallowed two softballs. "Alright, off with you two turds. I got things to do and pieces of crap to eat for breakfast."

The two girls were escorted to the door. The shadow did not follow.

The time for *The Cause* came a few short hours later. It all started with the unplanned ringing of the kitchen bell three times, one right after the other.

All Hemingway broke loose afterwards.

Major Balls heard the bell ringing and stormed out of his office. His face was so red it looked like it was on fire. A thick vein bulged from the center of his head like a well-fed tapeworm. He entered the mess hall ready to smash heads. Sergeant Breakfast was close behind, her ruler in hand, ready to whack turds.

"WHAT IN THE NAME OF GOD IS GOING ON HERE? WHO RANG THIS BELL? I WANT ANSWERS AND I WANT THEM NOW."

The men scrubbing the floor with toothbrushes paused in their work to look up.

"WHICH ONE OF YOU MAGGOTS DID THIS? RINGING THE KITCHEN BELL EQUALS INFRACTION."

Major Balls was about to strangle an orphan, when Gunner Grape Juice appeared from the kitchen carrying a tracking device.

"Sir, we have a problem." To reiterate his point he spat to his right. A spray of purplish goo landed on Pickles's face.

"WHAT IS IT?"

"An orphan escaped and is outside the perimeter. He appears to be out of commission and holed up in the dump."

"DON'T THESE MAGGOTS EVER LEARN? ALRIGHT LET'S RETRIEVE HIM. SERGEANT BREAKFAST YOU COME WITH ME. GUNNER GRAPE JUICE YOU HOLD DOWN THE FORT. LET'S MOVE PEOPLE."

"Roger that, sir." Gunner Grape Juice turned around and spat to his left, covering Pickles's face again.

* * *

In solitary confinement, T.W. heard the kitchen bell ringing three times in a row, like it did to warn the men that Charlies were coming, and knew the time had come. He stood up and stretched his legs, waiting for the next signal. A few minutes later, he heard the sound of locks being unlatched then the door opened and white light flooded his cell. Thankfully he had his sunglasses on.

"*Toaster*, good God, man, it's good to see you."

"It's good to see you too, sir," Toaster raised his arm in a salute. "Let me get that tracking collar off you, sir."

T.W. leaned his head forward, while Toaster used a device to unfasten the collar. It only took a few seconds before his neck was free. T.W. rubbed his neck and grinned at Toaster.

"How'd you manage that?"

"The Wiz, sir. He's been on it for some time now, made it himself and calls it the Orphan Wrench. Before I forget I have something for you, sir."

"What is it?"

Toaster handed T.W. his key, his switchblade comb, and the Luger. T.W. placed the key around his neck and the Luger in his back pocket.

"Where'd you get these?"

"I found them in Major Balls's office in a drawer marked contraband. I also got these."

He handed T.W. a pack of smokes. T.W. put one behind his ear and another in his mouth. Toaster quickly lit it.

"That really hits the spot." T.W. ran his comb three times through the space where his hair used to be. "How are the men? Fill me in on what's going on?"

"Situation is not good, sir. I've only managed to make contact with The Wiz. He's organizing the men and removing their tracking collars. We just completed phase 1, Infiltration. I don't know how long until the rest of the men will be ready for phase 2, but preparations are in order. The Wiz figures we have a 42.77—repeating of course—percent chance of success. We're just waiting on him before we launch a full-scale assault. Squirrel and Demmie are distracting Major Balls and Sergeant Breakfast as we speak."

"*Wait* did you say Squirrel? How'd he get here?"

"I contacted him via dumpster chicken. He arrived today with Demmie. The three of us organized Operation Reclaim The Row, ORTR for short."

"Good, what phase are we currently under?"

"Phase 2—extraction, sir. Awaiting word for phase 3."

"What's phase 3?"

Just then an explosion sounded from the mess hall.

"All out war, sir."

* * *

At the dump, Major Balls and Sergeant Breakfast had tracked the signal to the electrified fence. Two blackened smoking Girl Scout uniforms had caused it to short-circuit. At the bottom was a small gaping hole, big enough for an orphan to crawl through.

"WHY THOSE LITTLE SONS-OF-MAGGOTS. I'M GOING TO SQUEEZE THE ORPHAN OUT OF THEM."

"Wait a second," Sergeant Breakfast said. "I recognize those uniforms. Those two turds from earlier."

"WHAT TWO TURDS?"

"The turds who sold me Girl Scout Cookies. They probably lied about that subscription to *Buff and Tough Magazine*. Darn it all! Why those stupid little turds! I'm gonna—"

"ENOUGH ALREADY. WE'VE BEEN INFILTRATED. LET'S RETRIEVE THIS LOST MAGGOT AND GET BACK TO HEADQUARTERS ASAP. I DON'T LIKE THE SMELL OF THIS."

Sergeant Breakfast grabbed one end of the gaping hole and tore the rest of the fence open so that there was a gap big enough for both of them to walk through. They hurried along towards the dump, the tracking device beeping in tune with their steps. Thirty seconds later they came to the spot. There was no orphan in sight, only a solitary tracking collar. It lay in a pile of something brown and gooey.

"WHAT THE?"

"It appears to be a pile of turds." Sergeant Breakfast ran a finger through the mound and then brought it to her mouth. "Nope just canned dog food."

"THIS DOESN'T MAKE A MAGGOT OF SENSE. WHY WOULD A MAGGOT PUT THE TRACKING COLLAR IN A PILE OF DOG FOOD?"

As if in response, they heard deep low growls behind them. They turned around and came face-to-face with the four Dobermans—Rabies, Sick Boy, Snaggle Tooth, and Sir Barks-a-Lot—their mouths foaming and looking like they hadn't eaten in days.

Before Major Balls and Sergeant Breakfast could say turd in a toilet, the four Dobermans were on them, gnashing, biting, and tearing away skin. Their screams coincided with the explosion in the mess hall.

* * *

Inside the Row, T.W. and Toaster rendezvoused with the men in the rec room. *The Orphan* Wrench was passed around and their necks freed. In no time, T.W. was surrounded by his War Council.

"That was a Hemingway of an explosion, wasn't it?" Matches's face beamed with pride. "I can make a bomb out of just about anything."

"Sure was," T.W. said. "Job well done. You earned yourself ten marks."

"Thank you, sir."

"Alright, how are we looking? Fill me in, Scissors."

"It's not good, sir. They took Muscles's cans of sardines and Ray Charles's binoculars. He's been stumbling around blind ever since, running into practically everything. Big Ben hasn't ticked or tocked in days. Tea Bag's not allowed to use a British accent and Chopsticks can't speak Korean. They claim it's too un-American. They even made Compost Pile take a shower."

"Good God, man, it's worse than I expected."

"That's not all, sir. The Wiz's lab has been compromised. All weapons and explosives confiscated as contraband, but The Wiz has constructed a few mini potato guns. We're currently in search of ammo."

"What about the locked room for *The Cause*? Has it been compromised?"

"No, sir. They couldn't get it open. The Wiz had us spread false intelligence, claiming it was just a closet."

"Brilliant! Thank Hemingway."

"There's one other thing, sir. Some bad news I'm afraid. There's been a defection."

"A defection. Son-of-a-Hemingway! Who?"

"Wheelin' Dealin' Steven, sir. They put him in charge of toilet paper. He's currently Gunner Grape Juice's right-hand man."

"Why would he do such a thing?"

"It's been tough since you've been locked up, sir. I guess he just couldn't take it anymore. He broke prettily easily. A few of the others, the young ones, almost followed suit. But we've been trying to keep morale up. Colonel Sanders has been on the lookout for signs of POTS."

"Good, I'll deal with Wheelin' Dealin' Steven personally."

Just then, Muscles, with a fresh can of sardines on each arm, rushed into the rec room dragging Wheelin' Dealin' Steven by the neck. "I have the traitor, sir. He was hiding beneath a table. Didn't put up much of a fight, surrendered almost immediately."

"I'm sorry, sir. I'm so sorry. Please forgive me. I just couldn't eat another bread sandwich. It was too much. I'm so sorry. Please, I'll do anything. Just don't punish me too severely."

T.W. stood in front of Wheelin' Dealin' Steven and studied his face closely. He pulled the cigarette from behind his ear and placed it in his mouth. Scissors lit it for him.

"Nobody likes a turncoat," T.W. said. "For starters, I oughta kick the fillings out of your teeth, but that's just not my style. Until I figure out what to do with you I'm taking away all orphan privileges. That means no more selling on the orphan market and no PPSP-Douglas-Street- Affiliation vest. You're on probationary status until further notice and have to wear a Benedict Arnold headband at all times. Is that understood?"

Wheelin' Dealin' Steven lowered his head. "Yes, sir."

"Good. Muscles, keep a close eye on him."

Just then The Wiz came into the room, his big brow covered in sweat.

"We have a situation, sir."

"What is it?"

"Faygo, sir. Major Balls banned all caffeinated drinks and junk food. We've been able to hold him over with some coffee from the cafeteria, but he has been going cold turkey now for the past few weeks. He can't stop shaking and his vitals are down. He hasn't left his bed in two days, refusing any food or water. Colonel Sanders is with him for moral support. He needs sugar immediately. He's even speaking normal, sir."

"Good God. We need to get him some caffeine ASAP or we're going to lose him."

"Sir, I know where some Faygo and junk food are stored," Wheelin' Dealin' Steven said. "Gunner Grape Juice showed me."

"Good. Go and show Muscles where it is and make it snappy."

They left in pursuit of caffeine, while T.W. headed towards the second floor bedrooms. He found Faygo in bed, sweating profusely, his lips chapped and his eyes rheumy.

"He's going through some serious withdrawal" Colonel Sanders said.

"Sir . . . you're out ," Faygo barely managed to say. "It's so good to see you."

"How are you doing soldier?"

"I've been better. But look I can speak like a normal orphan now. Isn't that great?"

"There's nothing great about that, Faygo. We're going to get you fixed up right away, just hold tight."

Just then, Muscles sprinted into the room, carrying a six-pack of Grape Faygo. "Sir, Wheelin' Dealin' Steven came through. Everything was right where he said it would be."

"Good, Colonel Sanders hook up an IV. I want the Grape Faygo to go straight into his system. There's no time to waste."

An IV filled with Grape Faygo was hooked into Faygo's right arm. The men watched as purple fluid inched its way along the tube and into his system. Within seconds, Faygo shot up, his eyes fluttering like a butterfly.

"Ohyeahthatreallyhitthespot," his mouth raced. "Wooweeyowzer."

"He seems to be responding normally." Colonel Sanders held Faygo's wrist. "His vitals are up."

"Yummyyummyinmytummy."

"He's back," T.W. said. "Good job, men."

Just then Toaster sprinted into the room. "Sir, we have Gunner Grape Juice cornered in the kitchen."

"Let's go," T.W. said, leading the charge. They raced down the stairs and found Chopsticks and Gunner Grape Juice facing each other, standing like two gunslingers at high noon. "Wait." T.W. halted the men. "Let Chopsticks handle this, it's his kitchen."

The men stood down, while Chopsticks extracted a wooden spoon from the counter. Gunner Grape Juice wielded a long butcher's knife. He spat on the ground and then smiled at Chopsticks's choice of weaponry.

"You bring knifey to spoon fight," Chopsticks said. "Berry berry bad."

Gunner Grape Juice grinned, showing his few remaining teeth, which were the color of molasses. "Time to make some chopped noodles, Chopsuey."

Chopsticks charged, cursing in Korean. Before Gunner Grape Juice could say beets in a blender, Chopstick hit him with a barrage of spoon slaps to the face, knocking the chew right out of his mouth. His head bounced back and forth, while Chopsticks worked his wrist like a windshield wiper on high.

When Chopsticks finished, Gunner Grape Juice collapsed on the floor in a pile of his own spit. Chopsticks stood over him, twirling his wooden spoon before placing it in the side of his apron. He picked up Gunner Grape Juice's fallen knife and flung it across the room, where it landed on a magnetic knife rack.

"Alright, men," T.W. called. "This isn't over. We need to secure the perimeter, no one in or out. Chopsticks, tie up the prisoner, everyone else come with me."

They found Squirrel and Demmie in the mess hall.

"There you are, kid," T.W. said. "What's up with the lipstick and make-up?"

"Oh, right." Squirrel wiped his face clean. "Long story, sir."

"Save it for later. What's the status on Major Balls and Sergeant Breakfast?"

"They're taken care of, sir. The four Dobermans are currently making hamburger out of their behinds. It was all

Demmie's idea. She led them right into the trap. I think she has the making of a commander, sir."

"Very good. Just to be safe I'm sending a recon team out to assess the situation. Until they're both disposed of, it's better to take precaution. Muscles, form two teams, and report back to me in fifteen."

"Yes, sir." Muscles saluted before turning a corner. Just as he disappeared, there came the sound of a struggle, followed by a can of sardines rolling out of the hallway.

"What in the Hemingway?" T.W. said.

Major Balls entered the mess hall, his clothes in tatters. Visible scratches and bite marks covered his body like a severe rash. His muscles bulged and the vein on his forehead pulsed. He held a massive cup, half mixed with protein shake and steroids—a meathead's spinach. He gulped it down with one long swallow. When he was finished his body raged like the Incredible Hulk when angry. He stared at the orphans with clenched fists of rage.

"YOU MAGGOTS ARE DEAD MEAT!"

"Redrum, redrum, redrum," Monster muttered then wet himself and passed out. The rest of the men stood in place unsure of whether to fight or flee.

"Good God," Squirrel said. "He's roiding. Quick, Demmie, run and hide."

"Steady men." T.W. pulled out the Luger from the back of his pants. He placed a cigarette in his mouth and loaded the chamber, *chick-chick.* "I want everyone in attack formation. Stay low and keep moving. Scissors, how are we with those potato guns?"

"Locked and loaded, sir."

"Good. You and Matches provide cover fire. Everyone else to me. They may take our lives, but they can't take our orphanhood!"

T.W. led the assault. The men followed. Potatoes rained, bouncing off Major Balls's chest and forehead. His fury was so great he didn't seem to notice.

T.W. dodged Major Balls's first swing, but a second sent the Luger flying out of his hand. Crash crashed into Major Balls, but bounced right off, concussion number ninety-something. Ray Charles thought he was going right at Major Balls, but ran into a wall instead. Stone Age had his beard practically slapped off. Mike Tyson was judo-chopped before he could get a punch or bite in, Tea Bag was tea-bagged, and Cup Check was cup-checked. Duct Tape ran circles around Major Balls, attempting to wrap him like a mummy, but Major Balls just laughed and then broke free with one swipe of his arms.

Everything the men threw at him, Major Balls threw back, his steroid-induced rage making him invincible. Seafood attempted to bear hug him, Compost Pile tried to rub his armpits in his face, Super Soaker spat in his eyes, and Christmas Story kicked him with his good leg, but all failed.

"IS THAT THE BEST YOU MAGGOTS CAN DO?" Major Balls screamed as the last of the potatoes bounced off his chest.

The men were scattered all over the floor, some moaning, some bleeding, some unconscious, and all in pain. T.W. regained his composure and stood up. He pulled out his switchblade comb and pointed it at Major Balls.

"Major Balls, this is your last chance to surrender. Otherwise I'm going to open a can of Hemingway on you."

Major Balls laughed. He cracked his hands and then bunched them into fists. "I'M GONNA ENJOY THIS, MAG-GOT."

Squirrel, with paintbrush in hand, ran over and put his body between T.W. and Major Balls. Men still standing did the same. The only thing between them and utter destruction at the hands of Major Balls was Squirrel's lone paintbrush.

Major Balls's shadow fell over their faces. Just as he was about to strike, something jumped from the shadows and latched onto his tiny, steroid-reduced family jewels. Major Balls thrashed around in pain, while a dark mass of fur growled, refusing to let go.

"*Rosie!*" Squirrel called.

Major Balls tried everything he could to release himself from Rosie's grip. But the stubborn dog had his teeth sunk in deep, having found Major Balls's Achilles' jewels.

"Quick, while he's distracted," T.W. said. "Give him Hemingway."

The men rallied, jumping on Major Balls. They punched, kicked, bit, and scratched him into submission. Duct Tape used five rolls of duct tape to secure him in place. When they were finished Major Balls was wrapped up in a gray cocoon, withering around like a snake.

"Why you no good maggots," his voice screeched a decibel higher than Mike Tyson's, sounding like a record playing too fast. "I'm gonna get you for this."

"Duct Tape, silence him," T.W. said.

Duct Tape ran a piece of duct tape over Major Balls's lips. He continued to mumble and screech, the vein on his head threatening to pop. T.W. put a cigarette in his mouth. Scissors quickly lit it for him.

"That was a close one," he said. "Thank Hemingway for that dog. We couldn't have done it without her. What's her name anyway?"

"Rosie and it's a him." Squirrel bent down to pet his head. Rosie licked his hand. The poor dog had followed him all the way from Mayor Sharp's mansion. After years of living in an unwanted household, Rosie had finally found a place where he was wanted. The Row was perfect, seeing how he had always been an orphan kind of dog.

20

A Rebel without a Cause

WITH THE ROW RECLAIMED, the next order of business was securing the place, namely tying up the Triad of Terror. Major Balls and Gunner Grape Juice were detained in cells constructed out of parts of the electrified fence and welded together by Stone Age. Both suffered serious bouts of withdrawal, Major Balls from steroids and Gunner Grape Juice from chewing tobacco. A scouting party led by Muscles found Sergeant Breakfast two days later, deep within the dump, resting on top of a very high pile of trash and talking to herself.

"They don't eat pieces of crap for breakfast," Sergeant Breakfast muttered over and over again. Severely traumatized and dehydrated, she suffered from multiple dog bites and scratches. Her short dark hair had turned white. So white, in fact, it made Marshmallow jealous.

Colonel Sanders eventually coaxed her down. The Wiz gave her a large dose of "special" medication before she was placed in a cell. Day in and day out she stared at the walls, repeating "they don't eat pieces of crap for breakfast." Colonel Sanders diagnosed her as Section 8, all-out crazy. So crazy that she was more fanatical than Tom Travolta in his insane asylum dark comedy, *One Flew over the Dumpster Chicken's Nest.*

With the Triad of Terror squandered, there were only two pressing matters to attend to. The first was finding the men's PPSP-Douglas-Street-Affiliation vests and the second, returning the Row to its former glory.

"I tracked where they put the vests," Toaster explained, now a corporal after given a promotion for his contribution to Operation Reclaim the Row. "They're in garbage bags, just inside the dump. Thankfully no critters got to 'em."

"Very good, I'll put you and Muscles on it," T.W. said. "Make it a TP1."

Once recovered, they were distributed to all of the men, save for one. Wheelin' Dealin' Steven remained on probationary status, but it was later decided that he should be given a full pardon for his role in bringing back Faygo, after completing only forty hours of PAP detail.

"You heard 'em," Scissors said, "Pots and Pans detail."

Scissors was ordered to make a special dog-sized PPSP-Douglas-Street-Affiliation vest for Rosie, the Row's newly appointed mascot. As an afterthought, he also trimmed Rosie's bangs, which allowed him to see fully for the first time since being a puppy.

With the vests back in their proper place, it was only a matter of reorganizing the Row. It was tough and exhausting work, but the men pulled through, working around the clock for a week straight. They removed the boards covering the fireman pole holes, added toilet paper to all the stalls, thus putting a prompt end to the Second Teepee War, converted the holding cells back into Big Mama's office, threw out Major Balls's weight-lifting trophies from T.W.'s office, painstakingly reorganized the kitchen to Chopsticks's standards, returned all confiscated contraband to their rightful owners, and brought back all of the stuff from the dump and placed it in the rec room where it belonged.

Even Rosie did his part. He barked encouragement and followed Squirrel wherever he went. Sometimes he walked too close to an orphan's feet and was accidently booted out of the way, as was the case when Christmas Story's prosthetic leg sent him flying into the laundry chute all the way down to the basement where he stayed for the rest of day until a ticking Big Ben found him while looking for one of his missing watches.

T.W. hardly slept. He came and went so much that the shadows under his eyes appeared like coffee stains. Refusing to slow down, he drank more coffee and smoked more cigarettes than usual. Both Scissors and Squirrel couldn't help but notice.

"Sir, are you alright?" Scissors asked after T.W. had trailed off from one of his orders.

"Of course I am. Why in the Hemingway wouldn't I be?"

The next day, Squirrel found him staring out of the window of his office, his lit cigarette in desperate need of an ashtray and close to burning his finger.

"Jeez Louise, sir, you almost burned yourself," Squirrel said, bringing him an ashtray.

"Oh, right." T.W. continued to stare out the window as if Squirrel wasn't there.

Even Ray Charles, half blind and in constant need of adjusting his binoculars, could see that something was amiss with T.W.

"You wouldn't believe the orders he gave me," Ray Charles whispered. "He ordered me to fly. Can you believe that? I don't even have wings, well not yet, at least. He then said I could smoke real cigarettes instead of the candy ones."

"That doesn't sound like T.W.," Squirrel said. "Something's not right."

"Tell me about it. I didn't know what to do, so I just left. Told him I had an errand to run for The Wiz. I've been chewing candy cigarettes ever since. What's going on with him anyway, Squirrel?"

"I don't know."

"He was in the hole for a long time. I sure hope he isn't losing it. The Row would go straight to Hemingway if he did."

Squirrel agreed. He was half-tempted to speak with The Wiz or Colonel Sanders, but it was against Row protocol to go around a commanding officer. He hoped T.W. wasn't like the biblical Samson, powerless without his hair. Where was an adult when they needed one? Surely Big Mama would know what to do.

It took just over a week for the Row to return to a sense of orphancy. But with little to do, the men grew restless. They awaited further orders, but T.W. kept to himself, staying in his office most of the time. Scissors brought him his meals and took away the trays, the food barely touched. Whenever T.W. did leave his office, he was mostly despondent, saying quotes that made no orphan sense.

"'All things truly wicked start from innocence.'"

"'A casual stroll through the lunatic asylum shows that faith does not prove anything.'"

"'You cannot depend on your eyes when your imagination is out of focus.'"

"What's he talking about?" Ray Charles asked. "His quotes

used to have a purpose, a meaning, now they're just the ramblings of a madman."

The men were also starting to take notice of T.W.'s unpredictable behavior. Monster was terrified to go near him. There were whispers amongst the ranks that T.W. had stared into the orphan abyss and the orphan abyss had stared back at him. Squirrel met privately with Colonel Sanders.

"What are the symptoms of Post-Orphan-Traumatic Stress again?"

"Oh, you mean POTS," Colonel Sanders said, packing tobacco into his pipe. "Well, first there's erratic behavior, restlessness, despair, depression, lack of sleep, loss of interest in daily activities, detachment, difficulty concentrating, memory loss—"

"Okay, I get the gist of it. How do you fix it?"

"Well, I recommend medication first and then months, perhaps years, of psychotherapy and counseling. It's an ongoing therapeutic procedure that could span a lifetime. I'm thinking of writing a thesis on it."

"What's a short-term solution?"

"What do you mean?"

"Let's say a person doesn't have a lot of time and they need to be fixed real quick, any suggestions?"

"Hmmm." Colonel Sanders took a drag from his pipe. "Well, you can't unbreak an egg."

With T.W. in his own world, the routine of the Row became sporadic. The men came and went as they pleased. Classes were canceled, chores put off, and The Cause practically forgotten. Faygo drank as much Faygo as he wanted. Seafood moved his bedroom to the pantry where he made a bed out of Twinkies, so he could eat in his sleep. Matches nearly burned down the rec room when he used lit candles for pins and a water balloon full of gasoline for a bowling ball. It was fortunate he was playing with Super Soaker, who quickly doused the fire. Mike Tyson and Cup Check took turns punching each other in the orphan jewels. Compost Pile took to storing his collection of shopping carts in the hallway. Crash began riding his dirt bike up and down the stairs, crashing so many times and suffering so many concussions that at one time he believed he was Andy Kaufman recently returned from a trip to the moon. Rooster talked of getting the Flex Pistols back together again. And Ray Charles attempted to fill the leadership void left by T.W.'s intellectual absence.

"Tuck in that shirt, Peanut Butter!"

"Trim that beard, Stone Age!"

"That outfit is not Row appropriate, Belch!"

"Poop Stain, mustaches are only to be worn during combat!"

"If you swear one time, Potty Mouth, I swear I'll write you up!"

The men got so sick of Ray Charles's nagging that they talked The Ace of Spades into making him disappear to some disgusting and unpleasant place. Ray Charles was surprised to wake up one morning at a booth in a neighborhood White Castle.

The longer T.W. stayed out of commission, the more concerned Squirrel became. He tried staging an intervention with the other officers, but they were too busy doing their own thing. The Wiz tinkered with a space rocket, Scissors took inventory of bottles, cans, and marks, Muscles trained for a marathon, and Chopsticks sharpened knives and wooden spoons. With no one to assist him, Squirrel decided it was time for a course of action.

"Sir, may I speak to you?" Squirrel asked, entering T.W.'s office with Rosie at his side.

"Sure, kid, what's up?"

"Well, sir, I've been thinking—"

"Say," T.W. interrupted. "It's really jacked up what happened to all of your paintings. I'm really sorry about that."

"Yes, but it won't take long to paint again. As I was saying—"

"You know, we haven't played chess in a long time. What do you say, up for a game?"

"I don't know. As I was saying I am concerned about Big Mama. The Row's just not the same without her. Who knows where they took her or what they're doing to her right now. I think we need to get her back. I think it's time we put *The Cause* to good use, sir."

T.W. pulled out his switchblade comb and ran it over his head three times. "You're right. We have to do something. I just don't know what."

"What do you mean? You always know what to do. Isn't that why you have *The Cause* for moments like this?"

"I don't know, *maybe.*"

"What better time to use *The Cause* than to free Big Mama? It can't just sit there forever, not doing anything."

T.W. stared straight ahead. He suddenly looked like a scared, tired thirteen-year old boy rather than a fearless leader of men.

"You see that's it, Squirrely. There's something about *The Cause* you and the men just don't know."

"What's that, sir?"

"Come with me and I'll show you."

He led Squirrel out of his office and to the locked door, where no orphan had entered, save for T.W.

"What's in the room, sir?"

"See for yourself."

T.W. unlocked the door with the key from around his neck. Squirrel opened the door and climbed the constricted steps to the attic. Expecting something spectacular, outer-worldly, mind blowing, and strangely unique, Squirrel was disappointed to find—

"*Nothing,*" he said. "There's nothing in here."

The large, tapered room was completely bare except for some dust, cobwebs, and a few mouse droppings. Rosie sniffed the room and immediately sneezed.

"This can't be!" Squirrel said. "Major Balls must have found a way in here and taken everything."

"No, it's always been like this," T.W. said, joining him.

"But, sir that doesn't make a lick of sense. What about *The Cause*?"

"It doesn't exist."

"*What*?" Squirrel asked, staring in disbelief. Rosie whimpered.

"I'm sorry, kid, but it doesn't exist."

"Say it ain't so, sir!"

"I wish I could. You see, *The Cause* was just something I made up to give the men hope, something to strive for, to help them forget about the darkness of their life for a while. It was a safeguard to keep them from slipping through the cracks. It's just make-believe, like Santa Claus, the Tooth Fairy, or the Easter Bunny. You see, Squirrel, sometimes people, especially orphans, need something to believe in, even if it isn't real.

"*The Cause* doesn't exist. Never did. There you have it, the whole truth. I'm just a fraud, an imitation, a sham, a kid, not a leader. I'm not even a Teenage Wasteland for Hemingway's sake. I only preach *The Cause* to keep everyone in line. I don't know anything except for what I read in books. All I've done is lead these men into false dreams and false aspirations. Now I don't know what to do. Things have gotten so far out of control. I used to always know what to do. Call it instinct, gumption, or just plain gut feelings, but it's no longer there. I'm all dried up, a messenger without a message. You see, I don't have all the answers. That's why I created *The Cause* and now there just isn't cause for anything."

T.W. pulled his switchblade comb from his pocket, stared at it as if he didn't know what it was for, and then placed it back. Rosie whimpered and covered his face with his paws.

"But what about all of the mated socks from the sock room?" Squirrel asked. "What about all the junk scavenged from the dump or the collection of bottles and cans in the Treasury? I thought they all went towards *The Cause*."

"The socks, right." T.W. paced the room. "I sometimes just throw them back in the sock room or other times slip them in a drawer of an orphan who needs them. The money from the bottles and cans just goes back into the Row. Big Mama never asks where the money to pay the bills comes from. The junk always finds a place somewhere. Most of it ends up in The Wiz's lab or the armory."

"And the vehicles in the abandoned Ford plant?"

"They're just for recreational purposes."

"I still don't believe you, sir. What about all of the talk of revolution? What about Hemingway? He surely wouldn't talk like this."

"Hemingway was a drunk, a martyr to the craft. He was about as fit to lead as I am. I don't know why I'm telling you all of this. I haven't told a soul, not even Scissors or The Wiz. I guess it was just time to come clean. I'm not fit to lead anymore. I might as well throw in the towel and give it all up."

"That's ridiculous, sir."

"*Why?*"

"Because the Row needs you, the men need you, and I need you. You can't just give up because *The Cause* doesn't really exist."

"I can and I am. Look, Squirrel, I'm all washed up. I let three orphans, including you, get adopted on my watch and allowed the Row to be overrun by imbeciles. You might as well take over. I'm all finished for Hemingway's sake."

"Nonsense, you're just exhausted."

"No, I'm not. I'm . . . I'm . . . I don't even know what I am anymore, certainly not an orphan, that's for sure. Even Mayor Sharp, The Man, knows that. I . . . I . . . I just don't know."

Years of unselfishly leading and weeks of solitary confinement had done their number on T.W. who clearly suffered from POTS. Squirrel did the only sensible thing. He slapped T.W. hard across the face.

"For Hemingway's sake, get a grip man."

T.W. shook his head like water had just been thrown in his face.

"So what if *The Cause* doesn't exactly exist," Squirrel continued. "*The Cause* is what each and every one of us orphans decides it should be. For you it's an ideal, a belief, a great unknown. For me, it's Demmie and my paintbrushes. It's different for each orphan. Just because its make-believe doesn't mean we can't still believe in it."

"But what am I going to tell the men. They depend on me. How can they follow me if they know the truth? That my real name is—"

"I don't care what your real name is. You'll always be Teenage Wasteland to me. The men will follow you regardless because you are their leader—*my* leader. You helped them during their time of need and they'll do the same. Just tell them the truth and you'll see that they still believe. I know I do."

T.W. remained silent.

"I think you should get some rest, sir. You're worn thin. Sleep on it and we'll touch base in the morning."

"That's the thing, I can't sleep. Gosh darn insomnia has plagued me ever since the Triad put me in the hole."

"The Wiz has formulated a new sleeping gas. Perhaps that'll do the trick."

It did. T.W. slept for three days straight. Rosie made the mistake of sniffing the gas canister and was knocked out for two days, his body so inert and stiff it looked like the work of a taxidermist. There was talk among the men that T.W. was in a coma or worse yet, immobile like Tom Travolta in his caveman love story *While You Were Freezing*. When he finally awoke, T.W. seemed to have returned to his former self.

"Holy Hemingway, how long have I been out?"

"*Three days*, sir," Squirrel said.

"Three days, that's jacked up."

"I know, but it was needed. You look much better, sir."

"Thank you."

"I have something for you, sir. The Wiz put it together while you were sleeping."

"What is it?"

Squirrel handed him a black wig. "It's an Elvis wig, sir. It works like the mustaches and should stick to your head. You can use it until your hair grows back."

T.W. placed the wig on his shaved head. It added five inches to his height. He moved it around so that it sat right and then ran his switchblade comb through it three times. It stayed in place. Satisfied, T.W. put away his comb.

"Thanks. It fits like a glove. Now let's get down to business. How's the Row? Get Scissors and Ray Charles. I need a status report ASAP."

"Sir, the Row is fine. You need to eat first. You haven't eaten in three days."

"To heck with that." T.W. jumped out of bed. "Just give me a smoke and a cup of coffee and I'm good to go. Let's move, Squirrel, we got work to do."

"What are you talking about, sir?"

"We got to get Big Mama back. Quickly assemble the men."

"But, sir—"

"The only but I want to hear is your butt moving. Do I make myself clear?"

Squirrel smiled and saluted. T.W. was back.

Ten minutes later, T.W. was rejuvenated with coffee and cigarettes. He stood in the mess hall, facing his commanding officers and a few stragglers. "Where in the Hemingway is everyone? I thought I ordered you to ring the bell three times."

"I did, sir," a ticking Big Ben said. "But this is [alarm ringing] all that came."

T.W. scanned the heads in front of him and did a quick calculation. "It appears we're nine men short. Scissors, who are we missing?"

"Compost Pile . . . Seafood . . . Potty Mouth . . . Ray Charles—

"*Ray Charles, you say*! Good God man this place has gone straight to Hemingway in a handbasket. Wiz, hook up the loudspeaker. I want to make an announcement."

The Wiz did as instructed. A crackle followed by a high-pitched screech filled the airwaves of the Row. The Wiz handed T.W. a microphone.

"Listen up, men. This is your commander speaking. I don't know what in the Hemingway is going on around here, but if you're not dressed in your PPSP-Douglas-Street-Affiliation vests and in the mess hall for roll call in two minutes, I'll shove my boot so far up your behind you'll be tasting leather."

T.W. switched off the microphone and handed it back to The Wiz. "Big Ben, start the clock." It only took a minute for eight men to come running into the mess hall. Ray Charles led the charge, still adjusting his binoculars and nearly running into a table. Seafood was the last. He came huffing and puffing, a Twinkie in each hand, with only three seconds left to spare.

"Men this is unacceptable," T.W. said. "When that bell rings three times, I expect you to get your tails down here on the double. We're not running a day-care center here we're running an orphanage, and not just any orphanage, but the Row. Do I make myself clear?"

The men gave a thunderous yes.

"Good, now I have a special announcement to make. One that is difficult but needs to be said." T.W. paused and took a deep breath. "As you are well aware, I have not been myself of late. I've been out of it, not entirely there. The reason is there's something I've been keeping to myself, something I need to share with you right now."

T.W. looked to Squirrel who nodded back at him.

"Men, I have to come clean. *The Cause* does not exist."

A loud murmur rumbled through the ranks.

"There's no contingency plan. No end game. No higher purpose to our actions. In fact, the locked room across from my office is completely empty. It contains nothing but dust."

The men shook their heads in disbelief.

"*The Cause* is just something I made up. It's not real, except for in our hearts and in our minds. I'm sorry for deceiving you, men. The life of an orphan is rough and in order to make it he's got to be tough so I just thought you needed something to believe in, something to make this life worth living. That's why I created *The Cause*. For that I am truly sorry."

Silence filled the Row.

"So let me get this straight," Scissors said. "You're saying that *The Cause* is as made up and fictional as Tom Travolta's gender-confused character from the movie *Peter Pam*?"

"Wait—*Peter Pam* doesn't exist?" Ray Charles asked. "Wow that makes so much more sense now that I think about it."

"Yes, that's exactly what I'm saying. *The Cause* is complete fiction. It's about as real as the Boogeyman."

"But he exists," Monster claimed. "I've seen him."

"I've always assumed it was so," The Wiz said. "I calculated that there was a 67.88—repeating of course—percent chance that *The Cause* was just a figment of the imagination. However, I also calculated that there was a 77.29—repeating of course—percent chance that *The Cause* needed to exist or would exist under the right circumstances."

"I didn't even know there was a *Cause*," Seafood said, opening a Twinkie. "I just did what everyone else did."

"*The Cause* is the reason why I carry around this clipboard and keep track of everything," Scissors said.

"I thought my binoculars were a part of *The Cause*," Ray Charles said. "How else would I see?"

"Yeah, I thought everything I burned or blew up was part of *The Cause* too," Matches said.

"I work out and train for *The Cause*." Muscles adjusted the can of sardines on his arms. "So it must exist."

"Yeah*TheCause*iswhyIdrinksomuchFaygo," Faygo said.

"I WAS THINKING OF GETTING THE FLEX PISTOLS BACK TOGETHER FOR *THE CAUSE*," Rooster screamed.

"I-eck-burp-eck-for-eck-*The*-eck-*Cause*," Belch burped.

"I spit for *The Cause*," Super Soaker spat.

"I'm always in a pickle because of *The Cause*," Pickles said. "It has to exist or otherwise I wouldn't find myself in so many compromising situations."

"The only reason I ride a dirt bike and crash into so many things is for *The Cause*," Crash said. "If it wasn't for *The Cause* I never would have broken so many bones or suffered so many concussions."

"I don't shower for *The Cause*," Compost Pile said.

"I glow in the dark for *The Cause*," Marshmallow said.

"Why one of my main arguments for the origins of orhpanology stems from factors directly related to *The Cause*," Colonel Sanders said. "Without *The Cause*, there would be no orphan and without the orphan there would be no *Cause*."

"*The Cause* is the only thing I don't fear," Monster said.

"*The Cause* [sneeze] is my [sneeze] cure," Snot said. "Without it [sneeze] I would be [sneeze] dead of something [sneeze]."

"I cook berry berry dewicious food for *Cause*," Chopsticks said.

"%$#@!-bleep-bleep," Potty Mouth said, which translated to "I swear for *The Cause*."

"Why else would I carry all this bling if not for *The Cause*," Wheelin' Dealin' Steven said. "And by the way I have a Hemingway of a sale going on right now for international calling cards. Come and get 'em while they're hot."

"There'd be no magic without *The Cause*," The Ace of Spades said.

"I have a birthmark the size of *The Cause* on my face," Poop Stain said.

"I keep [alarm sounding] time for *The Cause*," a ticking Big Ben said.

"Why I wouldn't have a right leg if it weren't for *The Cause*." Christmas Story showed off his black-laced prosthetic leg, which caused a few of the men to whistle.

"I grow a beard for *The Cause*," Stone Age said. "Besides without *The Cause*, there'd be no need to make so many marks."

"*The Cause* is like a good roll of duct tape," Duct Tape said. "You never know when you're gonna need it, but it sure comes in handy when you do."

"I'd knock somebody into next Tuesday for *The Cause*," Mike Tyson squeaked.

"To *Cause* or not to *Cause*, that is the question, mates," Tea Bag said.

"I'm not feeling so well," Belly Ache said. "I don't know what's causing it, but I've just accepted that *The Cause* is always there even when there's nothing to diagnose."

"*The Cause* reminds me of the punch line to my latest joke," Cup Check said. "Why did the dodo bird become extinct?" No orphan took him up on it.

All of the men had shared what *The Cause* meant to them, save for two.

"Peanut Butter, what does *The Cause* mean to you?" T.W. asked.

The men turned their attention to their youngest member. "Hmmm—mumble, mumble—hmmm," was followed by a one second pause and then "Well, sir, it's like what everyone has been saying. Without *The Cause* no one would understand a word I say. I'm just glad *The Cause* is there even if it isn't, you know, *there*."

The men nodded in agreement.

"Squirrel, what does *The Cause* mean to you?" T.W. asked.

"It's painting and Demmie, sir. I love her. She's the reason why I do everything."

"And what are you willing to do for the girl you love?"

"Anything, sir."

"Be more specific."

"Well, for starters, I'd cross the highest mountain, swim the deepest ocean, and trek the driest desert. I'd fight each and every Wilson, and if it came to it, well, I'd even burn the city of Detroit to the ground."

"That's poetic. Sounds like something Hemingway would do." T.W. paused. "Now, here's what *The Cause* means to me, men. It means everything. It means no orphan is ever left behind. It means we stand together no matter what this world throws at us. It means we stand up for those who cannot stand themselves. It means we come out swinging with pistols blazing until all that stands in our way is kicked out of the way. It means we remember Snuggles."

"SNUGGLES!" the men said.

"And it means we're going to get Big Mama back. Men are you with me?"

The men gave a loud, thunderous yes.

"How are we going to do that, sir?" Scissors asked. "We don't even know where she's located or what they did with her."

"We're going to do what we should have done all along. This kind of situation calls for one thing and one thing only."

T.W. paused, his eyes sharp like pencils. "I'm calling a Code Black."

The men gasped. Scissors searched his clipboard frantically before scratching his head. "What does that even mean, sir?"

"*Revolution.*"

21

Prison Break

"ALRIGHT, MEN, WE MOVE by cover of night," T.W. said. "Three teams of four. We're going DEFCON 4. That means communication by hand signals and birdcall only. This is—"

"Sir, what birdcall are we using tonight?" Toaster asked. "Scissors?"

"Right, sir." Scissors scanned his clipboard. "Tonight is barred owl."

"You hear that, men, use barred owl. Now as I was saying this is a stealth mission, in and out. No need to cause a disturbance. The last thing we need is the police showing up again or worse yet, the National Guard. The Wiz is working on our Intel. He has some dumpster chickens hooked up with cameras acting as our eyes and ears over the prison. He'll report to us via walkie-talkie. I want everyone on channel 2. Toaster will be our man on the inside. He's to sneak in, administer sleeping gas, and open the front gate for the rest of us. In case we can't find a key, Matches has explosives. Now if you encounter a guard, make sure you use stun guns or CETM. We can't risk setting off the alarm."

"Close Encounter Tactical Moves!" Scissors shouted. The men nodded in agreement. A few of them used the moment to brush up on their judo chops and Jean-Claude Van Damme kicks, taking quick swipes and kicks at the air.

"The Wiz will hold down the fort with the reserves. I'm leading Easy Company, Muscles with Tango Company, and Squirrel with Bravo Company. Any questions?"

"But, what about me, sir?" Ray Charles asked. "I thought I was leading Bravo Company."

"Good God, man, how many times do I have to tell you? We need you to bring up the rear and be the lookout. Why else would you have those binoculars? Have your night vision ready."

"Yes, sir," Ray Charles said, adjusting his binoculars.

"Alright, enough beating around the bushes. I want everyone saddled up in full tactical gear—that includes vests, mustaches, and potato guns—in two minutes. Let's move people, operation FBMP is about to commence."

"Operation Free Big Mama from the Pen!" Scissors shouted. The men nodded in agreement.

Big Mama's exact location was discovered through interrogating Major Balls. He was uncooperative at first, but thanks to a protein shake mixed with The Wiz's latest batch of truth serum, he spilled the beans easily. Since the women's holding facility had been closed for over a year due to budget cuts, they had taken Big Mama down the street to the state pen and placed her in Cell Block F, the female wing of the prison.

Getting her location was the easy part, breaking her out the hard. T.W. met with his War Council to formulate an escape plan. After two hours of brainstorming and deliberating, their strategy was sketchy at best. It was so improbable that

The Wiz calculated their chances of success at only 21.65—repeating of course—percent. But sometimes *The Cause* worked in mysterious ways and an orphan just had to wing it.

T.W. led Easy Company, made up of Toaster, Matches, and Cup Check, down the front steps of the Row in the direction of the prison. He was closely followed by Tango—Muscles, Scissors, Duct Tape, and Mike Tyson. Bravo Company—Squirrel, Ray Charles, The Ace of Spades, and Compost Pile—brought up the rear.

They marched in single file and were halfway to the prison when they heard a stirring in a nearby dumpster. The men aimed their potato guns, ready to fire. Ray Charles accidently let out a shot, grazing the top of Mike Tyson's big head.

"Hey, what the . . .?" Mike Tyson raised his own gun.

"Hold your fire," T.W. called out. "Jeez Louise, didn't I train you two better? Don't fire until I give the order. Now stand down."

Ray Charles and Mike Tyson lowered their weapons.

"Who goes there?" T.W. said.

A shadow of a figure, cloaked in rags, a red hat, and smelling like garbage, emerged from the gloom. He was pushing a shopping cart full of clothes, cans, and junk, whispering, "Now where I'd put that bottle?"

"State your name and business," T.W. said. The man was too preoccupied with his missing bottle to give a reply. "Alright, men, fire on my command."

"Wait a minute, sir," Squirrel said. "I think I know him."

"Really? He looks like he's been dipped in garbage."

"Yeah, I'm sure. It's—"

"Stinky Pete," the man said. "How's it going fellas? Out for a late night stroll I see. I got me a half-eaten banana I found in the trash if anybody's hungry."

His left hand, the one offering the banana, was covered in a dirty glove with the tips cut off, revealing blackened nails and fingertips. Compost Pile moved in to take him up on his offer, but T.W. held him back.

"Never take a banana from a stranger," T.W. warned.

"Well, suit yourself then." Stinky Pete stuffed the banana in his jaw. He chewed with his mouth open, revealing teeth dark as coffee.

"Hey ain't you boys s'posed to be in bed? Ain't it a school night or something? I never did too good in school myself, just wasn't my strong suit. Problem was there were just too many numbers in math and too many words in English. I did the best at lunch, but I guess that doesn't really count as a class. Anyways, what are you boys up to?"

"We're breaking into a prison," T.W. said.

Stinky Pete rummaged in his worn-out army jacket, retrieving a cigarette butt. He placed it in his mouth. No one offered a light.

"Sounds like fun, mind if I join in?"

"But you're drunk as a skunk," Scissors said. "What kind of help could you possibly be?"

"Son, let me tell you something." Stinky Pete found a match in one of his many pockets and lit the cigarette butt. "I've been in and out of prisons more times than a baby's been in diapers. Heck, they even have a cell with my name on it. I'm practically like family with most of the guards. Some of 'em even sent me a Christmas card last year."

Stinky Pete paused to pull a bottle from his shopping cart.

It was almost empty, containing no more than a mouthful of a brown liquid the color of iced tea.

"I've gotten into more trouble than you boys have hair on your chests, which I know isn't saying a whole lot, but when it comes to a fight, ain't nobody better than Stinky Pete, just ask the Vietcong."

Stinky Pete had survived two tours of Vietnam. It was the reason why he mistrusted the government, was destitute, homeless, slightly crazy, and had two bullets still lodged somewhere in his lower back. "There's not a Charlie in Vietnam who doesn't cringe at the mention of the name Stinky Pete. Yes, sir, I used to be called Sneaky Pete before I took to wearing the streets of Detroit as my clothes."

"So you know of Charlie?" T.W. asked.

"Of course, more than I care to remember. Got two bullets right here on account of 'em." Stinky Pete lifted up his shirt, exposing his scarred back and causing the men to turn their heads in disgust. "That's right they gave me a Purple Heart for them ones."

"I got an Orphan Heart on account of two Charlies," Ray Charles said, his binoculars raised high.

"You don't say. I'll drink to that." Stinky Pete reached into his shopping cart for another bottle, finding one with only a few drops of something colored gravy brown.

"So what did you do before the war?" T.W. asked.

"Well, let's see, I was an orphan once, until the streets adopted me. Been living free as a dumpster chicken ever since."

That decided it. Stinky Pete was in. He celebrated by finishing off one of his bottles and bumming a smoke from T.W.

"I'll make you boys proud. Just you wait and see. Alright if we make a quick detour to my place before we head to the pen?"

"Your place?" T.W. asked. "I thought you were homeless."

"I am, but I constructed me a two-story cardboard house, even has a garage."

"But you don't have a car."

"Yeah, but I'm working on it, hoping to develop the first ever cardboard car. It won't run on gasoline either."

"What will it run on then?"

"I dunno. Haven't figured it out yet, but I'm thinking air. It's everywhere and free, you know what I mean?"

The men didn't but followed him anyways.

It was only a short distance. When they arrived, Stinky Pete parked his shopping cart in his cardboard garage. He stopped at the door and cursed after discovering his fourth eviction notice. He tore up the paper and stepped inside his cardboard house, which was no bigger than a newspaper stand. Hoping he had some important talisman, one befitting *The Cause* that would assist in their mission, the men were somewhat disappointed when Stinky Pete came out with another bottle, this one half-full and the color of the Detroit River.

"Well, don't know bout ya'll, but I'm ready to go," Stinky Pete said, taking a big swallow. He offered it to T.W. who shook his head no. Compost Pile waited until T.W. looked the other way before taking a pull from the bottle. He smiled afterwards, thinking he had found his calling in life. Stinky Pete patted him on the back, thinking he had maybe found the son he always thought he had but couldn't remember if he really did or not.

Five minutes later they arrived at the pen. They approached the front gate by walking with their backs against the wall commando style, carefully avoiding the huge spotlight that ran this way and that. Stinky Pete stumbled along, indifferent to caution, and more concerned about his bottle than he was with being seen.

"You're going to break our cover," T.W. said.

"What cover? They're more concerned with people getting out then they are with people getting in. Just trust ole Stinky Pete on this one. I got ya covered."

Stinky Pete took another swig from his bottle and stumbled along in the direction of the front gate. T.W. shook his head and wondered why in the Hemingway he had agreed to bring Stinky Pete along.

"Hey, I'll distract the guards for ya. That way your little fella, what's his name Toenail or something, can slip in unnoticed. Just leave it to ole Stinky Pete."

Before T.W. could order him to stand down, Stinky Pete was at the front gate, acting like he was late for a party.

"Stinky Pete, that you?"

"Sure is, Wilson, how you been?"

"Good and you?"

"Well, you know just living. Say you fellas still got my cell saved for me? I think I left something in there the last time I was here. Waddya say? Can I take a look for old time's sake?"

"Sure thing, Stinky Pete, anything for you."

The guard hit a button and the big gate rolled open. T.W. couldn't believe the ruse had actually worked. "Toaster, now's your chance—*move*."

Toaster, decked out in a black-and-white striped prison uniform reminiscent of Tom Travolta's wardrobe in his nursing home getaway thriller *Escape from Alzheimer's*, made for the gate and entered in after Stinky Pete. When the gate closed behind him, T.W. motioned to the men with his fingers. He pointed to his eyes, held up the number one, twirled it twice before pointing right, held up the number two, twirled it twice before pointing left, and finally held up the number three, twirled it twice before slapping his back.

The men nodded in silent agreement. T.W. led Easy Company in attack formation to the east side of the gate, Muscles moved Tango Company in attack formation to the west side of the gate, and Squirrel organized Bravo Company into a defensive measure towards the rear. Black PPSP-Douglas-Street-Affiliation vests were checked, mustaches worn as stylish and tough as Tom Travolta in his classic gym teacher undercover cop drama *Magnum P.E.*, and potato guns locked and loaded.

They were only in position for a few minutes before T.W.'s radio crackled.

"Breaker, breaker, Mother Ship copy this is HQ, over and out."

"Breaker, breaker, copy this is Mother Ship, over and out."

"Breaker, breaker, I have succeeded in jamming cameras and communication towers in and out of the red zone. Intel, via airborne dumpster chicken, shows that guards on both the north and south tower have been incapacitated. There appears to be an unspecified hostile roaming the yard. He's armed with a bottle of some sort, over and out."

"Breaker, breaker, disregard unspecified hostile. He is a friendly. I repeat he is a friendly, over and out."

"Breaker, breaker, roger that. HQ has recalibrated your chance of success based on recent Intel. You now have a 51.38—repeating of course—percent chance of success. Over and out."

Before T.W. could respond, a call of barred owl sounded from the other side of the prison wall. "Breaker, breaker, good to know. Switching to DEFCON 4. Preparing to assault the front gate. Over and out."

"Breaker, breaker, ten-four. Over and out."

T.W. turned off his radio and motioned to the men. He pointed to the sky, twirled his finger around his ear, and then brought his thumb across his throat. Next he pointed to his eyes, made a walking gesture with his fingers, and then made a pistol out of his finger and thumb pointed at the front gate.

The men raised their potato guns and got in position. They waited and waited, but nothing happened. T.W. called out barred owl, but there was no response. Five minutes went by and still nothing. T.W. was about to motion for Matches to set explosives, when the gate began to open. A lone figure stood on the other side, casting a dark shadow the length of a car.

"*Toaster*," T.W. whispered.

"The prison's yours, sir."

"What took you so long?"

"Sorry, sir. After I called barred owl I sent Stinky Pete to open the gate. He didn't make it very far." The men looked behind Toaster and saw Stinky Pete passed out at the bottom of a stairwell, one hand grasping his empty bottle.

"And the guards?"

"All the ones along the walls are debilitated. I've secured the control room. However we still have to clear out the cell blocks and locate the warden."

"Good work, Toaster. Alright, men, it's time for action. Easy Company will secure cell blocks A through C, Tango cell blocks D through F, while Bravo secures the perimeter. I don't want any surprises. Make every shot count. Big Mama's livelihood depends on it. We rendezvous in the courtyard. Move out."

The men moved into tactical formations and split off into three branches. Easy Company ran into little resistance while clearing A, B, and C blocks. T.W. stun gunned the first guard, Toaster popped up behind another and judo chopped him unconscious, Matches hit a third with a potato grenade, and Cup Check cup-checked the final guard into submission.

Tango was just as successful with D, E, and F blocks. Muscles knocked out a guard with a can of sardines, Mike Tyson knocked out another with his fists, Scissors Jean-Claude-Van-Dammed a third unconscious, and Duct Tape duct-taped the final guard.

There wasn't as much action in the courtyard, but Compost Pile found a stray guard and knocked him out with his stinky armpits, while Ray Charles thought he had a guard in a choke hold, but it turned out to be only a mop.

With all of the guards detained, there was only one last person to take care of—Barret Wilson, warden. They found him alone in his office. His large, robust frame was hunched over his desk, face deep in a hefty plate of fried chicken.

"W-what are you boys doing here?" he called out, spitting food everywhere. "I'm calling—"

Before he could finish, T.W. shot him with a potato gun. A spud the size of a hand grenade wedged in Warden Wilson's mouth, causing his eyes to bulge.

"Duct Tape, make sure he doesn't go anywhere," T.W. ordered. Duct Tape answered with a smile before holding up his roll of duct tape and pulling loose a fresh piece with a loud screech. Afterwards, the men rendezvoused back in the courtyard.

"Sir, we've located Big Mama," Muscles said.

"Good job. Lead the way. Squirrel, you come as well. Scissors, take inventory. Everyone else make sure the guards are locked up and scavenge anything that can be used for *The Cause*. Keep your fingers on your potato guns. We can't afford to let our guard down, not yet. Move out."

T.W., Muscles, and Squirrel hurried towards cell block F. They found Big Mama in her cell, dressed in a large black and white prison jumpsuit and reading the Bible.

"Oh Lordy, what are you boys doing here? Visiting hours ended already."

"We've come to rescue you, Big Mama," T.W. said.

"Oh, you shouldn't have, Lordy knows it. The last thing I need's is for ya'll to get in trouble over me, Lordy. I'm in the Lord's care now. Lordy knows he'll look over me. You boys best get out of here before you get yourselves in trouble."

"Nonsense. We're not going anywhere without you."

"Oh, Lordy. You're as persistent as Moses at the Red Sea. Lordy knows you are. Alright, alright, but we're heading straight back to the Row and you boys are heading straight to bed. Lordy knows it's past your bedtime."

T.W. and Squirrel nodded in agreement and then opened her cell. Big Mama grabbed each of them with a big, beefy arm and drew them in closer for a hug. Neither one could breathe, while Big Mama gushed. "Lordy, Lordy, Lordy, I've missed you so. How are the rest of my children? Please tell me they're alright."

She released the boys, who needed a few seconds to catch their breath. "Everyone's fine," T.W. managed. "The Row is ours again."

"Oh, Lordy, praise Jesus, Lordy yes."

Big Mama was still gushing and saying Lordy this and Lordy that as they made their way to the courtyard. They were halfway there when they encountered Scissors.

"Sir, we have a situation."

"What is it?"

"Come with me, sir."

"Alright, Squirrel, take Big Mama to the courtyard. Tell the others to prepare to fall back. I want us out of here in fifteen."

"I'm sorry for the intrusion, sir," Scissors said as they headed to cell block A. "But one of the prisoners wants to have a sit down with you."

"A prisoner? Why would a prisoner want to meet with me?"

"I dunno, sir. I'm just passing along the message. It sounded urgent and important. He said he used to be an orphan."

They came to a cell guarded by two burly prisoners. They were covered in tattoos and built like bulldozers. One of them grinned, revealing a single tooth. It was Sonny "One-Tooth" Paulson, the other was Mickey "No Dice" Sullivan. Both were serving twenty-five-year sentences for multiple counts of the illegal removal of tags from couches. Scissors was thankful for the set of bars between them.

"One of you guys called for a sit down," T.W. said.

"I did," a voice called from behind the two steroid-friendly hulks. They stepped aside, revealing a very old man seated on a bed. He was bald, save for a few long strands of hair that covered the top of his head like loose threads of string. His face had so many wrinkles it looked like a wet shirt straight out of the washer, in desperate need of an iron. He wore a silver cross over his black-and-white uniform. It glittered like a coin at the bottom of a wishing well.

"And who in the Hemingway are you?"

"Mafia Don, I run this joint."

At one hundred and five, Mafia Don was the oldest prisoner in the pen. He got his start during Prohibition, bootlegging from Canada when he was just a small orphan. By the time he was twenty he was head of his own family. Then, like all good things, organized crime went the way of the dinosaurs. The law caught up to him, and at the age of fifty-three, he was given a life sentence with the possibility of parole. He was most likely going to die in a prison, but his lawyer, Backseat Bob, was still optimistic, believing he could be eligible for parole in another ten years.

"I'm Teenage Wasteland, but you can call me T.W.," T.W. said. "I'm the oldest orphan at Desolation Row and I run this here operation."

Mafia Don nodded his approval.

"My sources tell me that you have control of the prison," Mafia Don said, his words slow and calculated, sounding like Tom Travolta in his action-packed underwater crime drama

The Codfather. "I was wondering if we could have a talk, from one orphan to another."

T.W. nodded his approval.

"Good," Mafia Don said. "I was hoping that maybe we could strike a deal."

"What kind of deal?"

"One mutually beneficial to both of us, one you can't refuse. You free me and my associates from this prison cell and we'll help you anyway we can."

T.W. brought out his switchblade comb and ran it through his hair three times. "I got your word you'll do as you say, Scout's Honor?"

"Scout's Honor."

"A word, sir," Scissors said.

"Give me a minute to discuss it with my second-in-command."

Mafia Don nodded. T.W. and Scissors walked to a faraway corner, out of earshot of the prisoners. "Sir, you can't be seriously considering striking a deal with him. He's part of the mafia, organized crime for Hemingway's sake."

"I'm well aware of that, Scissors, but in order to carry out a Code Black, we're going to need more men. Thirty-four orphans just isn't going to cut it. We need more manpower. We could use the prisoners."

"But what if they're dangerous? How can we trust them?"

T.W. pulled a cigarette from his ear. Scissors quickly lit it.

"Sometimes you just have to go with your gut. They need us and we sure as Hemingway need them. There's only one thing to do."

T.W. and Scissors came back to Mafia Don's cell. T.W. folded his arms. "Alright, Mafia Don, I'll roshambo you for it. If I win, you and the prisoners follow my orders. If you win, we release you from the prison, no strings attached."

Mafia Don thought on it. "Deal. Best two outta three, winner take all?"

"Agreed."

T.W. spat in his hand and Mafia Don did the same before shaking on it. Since they were in Mafia Don's territory, they played by prison rules. T.W.'s shank cut through Mafia Don's teepee, Mafia Don's bar of soap crushed T.W.'s shank, and finally T.W.'s teepee covered Mafia Don's bar of soap.

"You can roshambo with the best of 'em, kid," Mafia Don said afterwards.

"Thanks, boss. As a show of respect and a token of our appreciation we'll even throw in some loot and a bunch of letters accidently sent to the Row instead of the prison. That way you can tell your men you got something out of the deal."

Later that evening, Muscles transported all of the loot and letters from the Row to the abandoned textile mill where the prisoners made camp. It only took him one trip. He ended up carrying over thirty cartons of cigarettes, three dozen bars of soap, and two bags of unopened letters. The prisoners were so excited to have their lost mail returned they celebrated by passing around bottles of Listerine. Juan "AK-47" Martinez was brought to tears when he learned his pet Chihuahua, named 9mm, had given birth to six puppies.

The next morning, the men marched to the mill to get acquainted with the new ranks. Candy cigarettes were passed around and shared by all. As a show of good faith, T.W. gave the prisoners red shirts and hats knitted by Big Mama. Originally intended for orphans, they were a tight fit on the prisoners, but they didn't seem to mind, seeing as they were an upgrade to their black-and-white uniforms.

At first, the men were uneasy around the prisoners. They kept their fingers on the triggers of their potato guns, sizing up the much larger and bulkier prisoners who were real men, not orphans pretending to be men. Monster almost passed out, Belly Ache complained of being nauseous, and Mike Tyson had his fists clenched.

Mafia Don was given the title Commanding Officer of Prisoners, answering only to T.W. His capos included "Crazy-eye" Hopkins, Harry "The Menace" MacArthur, Juan "AK-47" Martinez, and Terry the Terrorizer. He had over one hundred prisoners, most of them former orphans, under his command. His soldiers were not sure what to make of their new boss, T.W., who was much younger and smaller than Mafia Don. They couldn't understand why the orphans wore ridiculous looking fake mustaches, but were somewhat impressed with their matching black PPSP-Douglas-Street-Affiliation vests.

The two groups faced each other with crossed arms. The prisoners big and intimidating with their muscles, tattoos, and grim faces. The orphans smaller and less intimidating with their fake mustaches and adolescent faces.

Ray Charles was the first to break rank. He stepped away from the men and stood steadfast with his arms at his hips and his binoculars staring straight ahead. After a long dramatic pause, he raised a single fist of solidarity. The unflinching prisoners didn't say a word or move a muscle in response.

Disappointed, Ray Charles was about to lower his arm when all of a sudden, the prisoners, acting as a collective unit, raised their own fists of solidarity.

Cup Check was the first of the men to actually approach the prisoners. For some reason he was drawn to Harry "The Menace" MacArthur.

"Hey, Harry 'The Menace' MacArthur, wanna hear a joke?"

"Sure."

"What'd the orphan say to the prisoner?"

Before Cup Check could get to the punch line Harry "The Menace" MacArthur cup-checked him in the orphan jewels. It appeared Cup Check had found his long lost father.

The other men followed suit. Ray Charles asked "Crazy-eye" Hopkins if he considered wearing binoculars. "Crazy-eye" Hopkins gave him the crazy eye as a response. Muscles asked Mickey "No Dice" Sullivan how much he bench-pressed and was surprised when Mickey answered, "About twenty-five cans of sardines." Poop Stain compared his birthmarks with the tattoos of Sonny "One Tooth" Paulson and was startled to discover they both shared good taste. Stone Age asked Juan "AK-47" Martinez what the current currency in the pen was and was surprised that toothpicks, matches, and bars of soap had equal buying power as the mark. Pickles made the mistake of asking Terry the Terrorizer what he was in for.

"Murder," Terry said, giving Pickles a deadpan stare. Pickles gulped and refrained from speaking to another prisoner.

At 1300, T.W. called the men and prisoners to attention.

"Listen up, men" T.W. said. "In case you don't know me, my name is Teenage Wasteland, T.W. for short. I'm in charge here. We go by my rules and my rules only. I don't know why most of you folks were locked up in the pen and don't really care. But get one thing straight, we don't kill people, we take prisoners—no offense, guys. That means blunt weapons only, no guns, knives, or shanks."

Some of the prisoners grumbled loudly. Mafia Don silenced them with one look, and the prisoners reluctantly nodded in agreement. This was followed by the sound of metal shanks falling to the concrete floor.

"Good. Now if you don't like the rules you can stay here or head back to the pen. But beyond these walls, it's my way or the highway. You can take it or leave it. Mafia Don has agreed to my demands. You report to him, while he reports to me. Any questions?"

The prisoners and the men didn't say a word.

"Good because today we fight for freedom, the end of tyranny, and most importantly *The Cause*."

The men gave a loud cheer, while the prisoners looked around like they had just missed the punch line to a funny joke.

"The revolution starts now. Today we put Detroit back on the map. We start by sticking it to The Man. It's payback time. We're gonna steal from the rich, give back to the poor, throw a wrench in the machine, and burn the city of Detroit to the ground if need be, starting with Mayor Sharp's office. Now are you with me?"

This was a language the prisoners understood. Most of them were in the pen thanks to men like the mayor, who made laws that favored themselves and exploited, mistreated, and abused the poor. The prisoners joined in with the men, sounding their approval. T.W. finally had his army. The city of Detroit was about to get the makeover it had desperately needed for the last fifty years. The time for *The Cause* had finally arrived.

22

The Men of Desolation Row vs. the City of Detroit

THE CITY OF DETROIT did not start out with a bang and it sure didn't end with one. Neglected for years by the national media, who only reported on violent crimes, political scandals, and bankruptcy scares, all it took to make headline news again was the reappearance of its buried skeletons, previously left unnoticed and hidden away beneath the shadows of urban decay. They were so far beneath the bottom of it all that no one saw them coming, especially the top brass whose vision was skewed by dollar signs.

It was true that you didn't need Bob Lennon to know which way the dumpster chicken flew, but from the outside looking in, the uprising that swept through Detroit like a pack of umbrella salesmen during a rainstorm was unexpected. For the forgotten residents who toiled daily beneath the clouds, it was a long time coming.

There was always smoke before there was fire.

For the men of Desolation Row, it was an opportunity of a lifetime, one for the ages, and a battle for all the marbles. It was the revolution T.W. had preached about since the day he first came to the Row, some two-and-a-half years prior. It was the reason why *The Cause* existed in the first place, and now it was ready to spread its wings and take flight, soaring high above the stench of the city's neglect.

On the day of the revolution, the city of Detroit started its day like any other. Normally vacant at night, it came alive by day as commuter buses, cars, and trains emptied the suburbs, bringing people to their daily jobs. Planes touched down, not with tourists, but rather passengers on their way to greener pastures in the neighboring cities of Chicago, Minneapolis, and Milwaukee. Restaurants opened doors for hungry executives and coffee shops offered steaming elixirs for groggy businessmen, while the disenfranchised did all of the serving, taking orders, wiping down tables, and mopping floors for minimum wage.

As the city awoke, the empty slums surrounding the highrises remained asleep and tired in their abandonment. Busted windows stared out into cracked brick walls, uneven sidewalks ran beside bumpy roads, cars with no wheels and more rust than steel parked besides buildings with more rats than residents, and the homeless with more cents than dollars begged for change from yuppies with more dollars than sense.

Out of this unsuspected gloom came a glimmering light of hope, easily missed by those expecting rain. It was just a tiny reflection bouncing off the black sunglasses of one young orphan whom the world had misplaced but was about to be reacquainted with.

"Full steam ahead." T.W. pointed his convoy forward. He stood on top of a very large black semitruck. On its grill, courtesy of Squirrel, was the painted face of a punk with a red

Mohawk and black sunglasses, his hand clinched in a fist of solidarity.

Chopsticks put the truck in gear and it lurched forward. The movement caused Ray Charles to lose his balance and his candy cigarette. He almost fell to the pavement below, but T.W. grabbed him by the collar of his vest.

"Watch where you're stepping, Ray Charles. That was a close one."

"Sorry, sir. See I told you it would have been better if I was driving, not riding."

"Nonsense, Ray Charles you ingest too many candy cigarettes to drive. How many times have I told you that?"

"I guess you're right, sir, but—

"The only but I'm concerned about is Mayor Sharp's butt, adding a nice good boot to it, you got that soldier?"

"Yes, sir."

"Good, now go check the munitions."

On the back of the semi was a very large catapult, one of The Wiz's finest creations, that had the ability to launch projectiles over 300 yards. It was dubbed the Orphan's Arm of Resistance, OAR for short. Muscles, with two shiny cans of sardines strapped to each arm, stood to its side, lifting a large tractor tire for exercise.

Behind the OAR was row upon row of dump trucks, all driven by former prisoners of the pen and carrying large loads of junk from the dump. Mafia Don sat in the passenger seat of the first truck, while Sonny "One-tooth" Paulson steered. The convoy accelerated slowly, going straight for the jugular—city hall, the majesty of Detroit.

Standing at ten-stories tall and constructed with new white marble, Detroit's city hall was a white rose in a field of ugly weeds. Whereas the rest of the city was dilapidated, crumbling, and sucked dry thanks to budget cuts, city hall was rejuvenated and refurbished with a seemingly endless supply of resources. Schools, fire stations, police departments, and orphanages were all put to the guillotine, while city hall continued to dazzle in yearly makeovers, receiving Venetian blinds, Persian rugs, mahogany desks, flat-screened TVs, new paint jobs, and the latest state-of-the-art modifications. It was Mayor Sharp's baby. His key to the White House, while the rest of the city remained locked away. For the men, it made an easy target.

Traffic was light as the convoy inched its way towards city hall, rumbling past cars that hadn't moved since the seventies and buildings that hadn't been renovated since the day they were built. A few homeless residents stopped to gape as the trucks rolled by, thinking the Thanksgiving Parade had come early this year. One stared with his mouth wide open, revealing teeth in just as bad shape as the buildings, before dropping his paper-bagged bottle to the ground where it smashed, adding to the discarded pieces of Detroit.

It was only when the convoy was within a few blocks of city hall that people finally took notice of what was at its doorstep, but by then, of course, it was too late.

High in city hall's tenth floor, Mayor Sharp sat in his three-windowed office and was halfway through a hearty breakfast of bacon, eggs, and coffee when he got the call. Not liking to be interrupted so early in the morning, he wiped his face with a napkin then tucked it back into the collar of his shirt as his campaign manager, Bartholomew Wilson, entered his office.

"Yes, what is it Bart?"

"Sorry, sir, but its urgent. We have a situation."

"Really, this early in the morning? What could it possibly be, Bart? Has part of the city finally caved in because of the old salt mines? Are the homeless overcrowding the food shelter again? Or, let me guess, crime is up? Better yet has Calloway dropped out of the Democratic primary? Oh wait, he already did."

"Oh no, sir, this is quite serious. I don't know how to explain it."

"Well, give it the good college try, Bart."

Bartholomew was about to speak, but before he could a large object came flying through Mayor Sharp's office window. It landed on the mayor's desk, crushing it to splinters and causing his breakfast to splatter all over Bartholomew's shirt. The statue of Alexander the Great cracked in two and the tiny red car, now missing two wheels, landed in Mayor Sharp's lap. Without even realizing it, he took it in his hand.

"Son-of-a-Calloway!" Mayor Sharp said. "What in the world was that?"

It was a ragged La-Z-Boy recliner that Bartholomew had bought over twenty years ago. After ten years of use it had been taken to the dump, at a discounted rate, of course, by his brother Baxter, and not seen again until now. Thanks to years of being out in the open and having suffered too many dumpster-chicken droppings, it was now too beat-up for Bartholomew to recognize.

"I don't know, sir."

"Well, find out! What else am I paying you for?"

Bartholomew was about to stand up, when a washing machine came through the second window. It was a Maytag, one

Mayor Sharp had purchased over twenty-five years earlier that had broken down and had been taken to the dump, for a discounted rate, of course.

"*Another one!* What in the world is going on here?"

"It must have something to do with what I was trying to tell you earlier, sir. There's been a report of an incident involving the police."

"Why didn't you say something?" Mayor Sharp asked, standing up from his chair; his napkin still tucked into his shirt. "Get my council together—*immediately*. I want everyone, including that pig-on-a-stick Captain Cornhole."

Bartholomew wrote down every word on his notepad.

"And I want to know more about this so-called incident," Mayor Sharp said, extending his arms as if in a greeting. "It has to be related to this."

The incident in question occurred just north of Michigan Avenue. A lone police officer—a Wilson in fact—was directing traffic when he noticed T.W.'s convoy barreling down Grand River. Never having to pull his gun out during the line of duty or having much to do besides direct traffic, Officer Wilson was as green as Tom Travolta in his dark, black-humored romantic comedy *Jack the Bean Stalker*.

"H-hey, you c-c-can't drive h-here," Officer Wilson said. "S-stop or I'll s-shoot."

Officer Wilson attempted to pull out his revolver but had forgotten to release the strap, so instead of pulling out his gun he managed to look like someone scratching his lower back. Some of the prisoners, feeling a little trigger-happy after so many years locked away in the pen, unloaded their potato guns. By the time they were finished, Officer Wilson was knocked unconscious and covered in so many potatoes it looked like the sky had rained taters.

"That's jacked up," T.W. observed. "Those men need to practice more self-control. They wasted half a sack of potatoes."

"Sir, would you like me to radio Mafia Don?" Scissors asked.

"That won't be necessary. I think we're within striking distance of city hall. Ray Charles, how are we looking?"

"I think I see it, sir," Ray Charles said, scanning the horizon. "It looks like a giant circle or oval or something."

"No, Ray Charles, that's Comerica Park, not city hall. Try looking to your left."

Ray Charles turned in the direction he hoped was his left.

"No, your *other* left, Ray Charles!"

Ray Charles turned in the right *left* direction, but still couldn't see anything because his binoculars had fogged up. "It's no good, sir. I'm as blind as Tom Travolta in his classic Aussie film from down under *Scent of a Wombat*."

"Well, since you can't see worth a Hemingway I want you to be my ears. You hear anything let me know. You got that, Ray Charles?"

Ray Charles couldn't hear anything besides the roar of the truck, but agreed anyways. T.W. ran his comb through his Elvis-wigged hair three times, before knocking on the top of the semi's roof with his boot. "Wiz, how are we looking?" he called. The Wiz popped out of a trapdoor and pulled a calculator out of his shirt pocket.

"I have two carrier dumpster chickens with cameras attached to their necks scouting the area ahead. So far we are on course and approaching the target. We are still about a half mile out of range. By my calculations we have a 64.69—repeating of course—percent chance of Operation AH being a success."

"Operation Animal House!" Scissors shouted. The men nodded in agreement.

"Very good," T.W. said. "Alright prepare the OAR. Big Ben, time the distances. Muscles, make it something heavy."

Muscles put down the tractor tire and lifted a cast iron oven. As soon as they were within striking distance of city hall, T.W. motioned for the convoy to stop. Phase 1—transport and convoy—was nearing completion. It was time to implement Phase 2.

"Make it rain." T.W. stood with his hands to his hips. The wind gently blew back his Elvis-wigged hair as the first shot went sailing through the air towards city hall. It was followed by a whole slew of junk scavenged from the dump, including couches, chairs, microwaves, washing machines, dryers, tread mills, engine parts, sewing machines, ovens, desks, chairs, car tires, etc.

The revolution was officially under way.

"Any sign of Stinky Pete?" T.W. asked.

"No, sir," Scissors said. "The radio has been quiet and no new dumpster-chicken carriers."

"I just hope he comes through. We'll need him if the National Guard shows."

On the eve of the big battle, Stinky Pete had volunteered his services, promising to recruit hundreds, even thousands to *The Cause*. He had just received his final eviction notice and had nothing to lose, complaining that a few of his homeless brethren had been shipped across the State line on a one-way bus ticket. There even had been talks of the mayor building a wall to keep them all in a state of Ohio.

Having to beg for a living for thirty plus years, Stinky Pete had all kinds of advertising experience of the cardboard variety. Some of his best cardboard signs included: Why live in a million dollar home when I can sleep beneath a 50 million dollar bridge? I'm not homeless. I just choose to sleep outside. I'll bet you a dollar you won't give me two dollars. Atlas shrugged, I begged, what's the difference? I'm a Vietnam vet that's homeless because Tom Travolta stole my role in *Born on the Fifth of Jack.*

"You can count on ole Stinky Pete," he reassured the men. "I'll recruit every vagrant, hobo, vet, and street dweller this side of 8 Mile. We'll be there when you need us. I've already got three or four ideas for a cardboard sign in the works. I just need to stop by my place for a few supplies if you know what I mean."

The men did. They just hoped Stinky Pete remained sober enough to do as promised.

"Any word from Delta Orphan Force yet?" T.W. asked.

"No, sir. They should be in position by now."

"Let's hope.

Demmie and Squirrel were put to the task of leading Delta Orphan Force's ground assault on city hall. Working as a small tactical unit, consisting of Toaster, Peanut Butter, Duct Tape, Wheelin' Dealin' Steven, and Mike Tyson, their mission was to infiltrate city hall and bug all lines of communication, thus giving the men viable Intel on the inside.

Posing as a group of Bible Study Students (BSS), they were dressed in their Sunday bests, the men in schoolboy uniforms and Demmie in a dark, plain dress. Wheelin' Dealin' Steven replaced all of his loot with Jesus memorabilia and crucifixes, selling them at a discount rate for the Lord. The rest carried heavy Bibles beneath their arms. While they waited for the signal, they lounged around the lobby of city hall, trying not to rouse suspicion.

"That's our cue," Squirrel said, shortly after the bombardment began. The men opened their Bibles and retrieved the weapons stashed between the torn out pages. Toaster popped up from behind a desk, a stunner in his hand.

"I've located the control room," he said. "There are five guards inside. We'll need a distraction to get them to come out."

"Right." Squirrel scratched his head. "We have to get in there ASAP."

"I have an idea," Demmie said.

"Let's hear it," Squirrel said.

"Peanut Butter and Mike Tyson, I'll need you to reenact a scene from *Sister Action 3*."

"The one where Tom Travolta is disguised as a nun and has to distract two guards while breaking into a bank?" Mike Tyson asked.

"Yes, exactly."

Demmie finished explaining her plans. Afterwards, Peanut Butter took off his Baby-Talk and asked the front desk for directions to the bathroom. Neither one of the secretaries could make any sense of his gibberish. Mike Tyson attempted to translate, but his voice was too high-pitched. He and Peanut Butter started to argue. It led to a pushing match. Security was called.

"Alright, now's our chance," Squirrel said. They made their way to the control room and disposed of the guards with judo chops and Jean-Claude Van Damme kicks. Demmie took out the remaining guards with perfume-disguised sleeping gas. Duct Tape secured the area with duct tape, while Toaster inserted The Wiz's high-tech infiltration gadget into a computer. In a matter of seconds, the control room was theirs.

Back at the OAR, Phase 2 was still under way. Ten dump trucks worth of junk had already been unloaded onto the city of Detroit. Within minutes, sirens could be heard in the distance, while police and TV news helicopters circled the sky above. T.W. decided it was time to up the ante.

"We need to do something about those 'copters," T.W. said, tilting his sunglasses. "Wiz, redirect the coordinates of the OAR. Matches, it's time to blacken the skies."

"Yes, sir," Matches said with a grin, holding out two red gas cans.

Matches doused a dump truck full of couches and chairs. They were then loaded one at a time onto the OAR and then lit with a match by Matches before being catapulted. Fireballs the size of golf carts soared through the air and crashed into abandoned building. The helicopters retreated as black smoke filled the air.

T.W. looked on, satisfied. However, he didn't have much time to relax. A few blocks ahead, police cars turned the corners and raced towards their location. T.W. triggered his radio. "Breaker, breaker, this is Mother Ship, Wrecking Ball, come in, over and out."

"Breaker, breaker, this is Wrecking Ball, over and out."

"Breaker, breaker, it's time to bring the thunder, over and out."

Off in the distance, Crash put down his radio and turned the ignition of a very large dump truck modified with a giant snowplow attached to the front and sharp metal spikes extending from the tires. It rumbled to life, sounding like a lion in the middle of dinner not taking kindly to an intruder.

Crash put on his seat belt, lowered the visor of his helmet, and put the truck in gear. Tires squealed as he made his way down Michigan Avenue. Police cars formed blockades along the city streets surrounding the OAR, hoping to disrupt the routes of the dump trucks and cut off any advances. Crash, beside himself with anticipation, giggled as he brought the truck to top speed and plowed through four police cars.

His helmeted head bounced off the ceiling—concussion number one hundred-something. He turned a corner and crashed through another barricade, this time sending two police cars rolling end over end. He was so ecstatic that tears of happiness rolled down his face. His parade of destruction looped around city hall and came back to the OAR. As he passed by he gave T.W. a thumbs-up before barreling down Michigan Avenue in search of other vehicles to destroy.

T.W. remained vigilant on top of the OAR, watching as dump truck after dump truck full of junk came and went. All around him the city of Detroit wept tears of smoke and crumbled concrete. T.W. thought it one of the most beautiful things he had ever seen.

A few hours into the revolution, Mayor Sharp met with his council to decide a course of action. They were seated in his office, where only one window remained unscathed. Six

Wilsons and Captain Cornhole surrounded Mayor Sharp. Captain Cornhole was so sweaty he looked like he had been out in the rain. Mr. Tidy served them refreshments.

Mayor Sharp was about to address his lackeys when a couch came hurtling through his third and final window. Barton Wilson, judge of the Detroit Circuit Court, was pleasantly surprised to discover it was the very one his wife had picked out years ago, which had been destroyed by their dog and then taken to the dump, at a discounted rate, of course.

"Son-of-a-Calloway!" Mayor Sharp complained. "Not this again."

"Sir, I think we should evacuate the city and call in the National Guard," Bartholomew said.

"Nonsense, Bart. It's an election year. We can't have that kind of negative publicity."

"But, sir, the city's in flames, buildings are destroyed, the police are outnumbered, and there's a whole army of ruffians roaming the streets. This is worse than the riots of—"

"*I don't care.* We'll deal with this."

"But how, sir?"

Every Wilson had an opinion on what should be done and soon filled the office with a ruckus of this and that. Mayor Sharp rubbed his eyes then slammed his fist down on his thigh. "*Enough already.*"

The room grew silent. The only noise to enter the room was the sound of explosions and sirens from outside.

"I'll tell you what we're going to do. We're going to reclaim the city. Captain Cornhole, I want you to organize your men and go out there and arrest every person that looks suspicious."

"But, sir, it's pandemonium out there. And since we closed down half the precincts because of budget cuts, I don't have the manpower or the resources. I can't—"

"What's that? *I can't hear you!*" Mayor Sharp said. "I thought I just gave you a direct order. Now go out there and get it done. If you need more men, call in the SWAT team or use the Tag Police. Heck take some Wilsons. There's plenty to go around."

The Wilsons began to complain. Mayor Sharp waved them into silence. "Go—*all of you*—get out of here and do something productive. Bart, you and Mr. Tidy may stay."

Captain Cornhole led the Wilsons out of the office like condemned men on their way to the gallows. Mayor Sharp mopped the sweat from his brow and ran his hand through his slick hair. He was about to bark an order to Bartholomew, but his wife, Betty, stormed into the room, her heavy bosom bouncing like a basketball.

"Oh, Albert, what in the world is happening? The news is saying we're being attacked. Is it true? Is it a terrorist attack?"

Mayor Sharp was about to console her, but a large mound of fur came flying through the open hole that was once his window and landed right on Mrs. Wilson. It wrapped around her like a towel in a windstorm. She was too busy trying to wrestle it off to realize that it was her long forgotten mink fur coat, one that had gone straight to the dump, at a discounted rate, of course, after being replaced by a family of fox.

"Get it off me, get it off me," she screamed, spinning in circles. Mayor Sharp was about to help her, but a small ball of fur flew out of the mass of coat like a spitball and landed on his lap. It was—

"*Rosie?*" Mayor Sharp said.

After not paying attention and straying too close to the catapult, Rosie was accidently kicked by Muscles into a pile of fur coats and launched out of the OAR. Luckily for him, Matches had run out of matches.

"What are you doing here?" Mayor Sharp asked. Neither he nor Mrs. Sharp had realized Rosie or Squirrel were missing, this despite the fact that they disappeared from their mansion weeks ago.

Rosie responded by growling and then biting him on the hand. Mayor Sharp howled with pain and tossed him away. He landed in front of Mrs. Sharp, who was still walking around in circles, trying to remove herself from the fur coat. She blindly booted Rosie into Mayor Sharp's mail drop box, which sent him all the way down to the control room where he landed at Squirrel's feet.

"Hey, boy, what are you doing here?" Squirrel bent down to pat him on the head. Rosie whimpered a reply. *It's complicated.*

"We got something over the radio," Toaster said, popping up from behind a desk. Large headphones covered his ears.

"What is it?" Demmie and Squirrel asked together.

"Something important," Toaster said. "The mayor's calling in the SWAT team and the Tag Police. They're organizing as we speak. We need to move ahead of schedule."

Back at the OAR, T.W.'s radio crackled. "Breaker, breaker, Mother Ship this is Moley Moley Moley, please come in, repeat please come in, over and out."

"Breaker, breaker, this is Mother Ship over and out."

"Breaker, breaker, we have reliable Intel that the SWAT team is en route and will be there momentarily, over and out."

"Breaker, breaker, roger that, engaging Phase 3 as we speak, over and out."

T.W. pulled out a flare gun from his back pocket, raised it to the sky, and pulled the trigger. A red flower burst into the sky. The men stopped what they were doing and looked skyward. Red signaled it was time to storm the gates. Men and prisoners alike abandoned trucks and took to the streets, carrying potato guns and taking up tactical formations. T.W. led the assault.

Captain Cornhole's ragtag posse of police officers, Tag Police, SWAT team, and Wilsons met them halfway. Dressed in riot gear, their faces were grim. They were out for blood. Captain Cornhole stood at their head, wiping his brow and chewing on a donut.

"There's so many," Pickles said. "What I would give for some reinforcements!"

The Wiz concurred. He pulled T.W. aside and said, "Sir, there's just too many. By my calculations we have a 77.04—repeating of course—percent chance of suffering severe casualties if we take them head on. I hate to say it, sir, but we're going to need some cover fire."

T.W. nodded and pulled out his radio.

"Breaker, breaker, come in Fish Guts, over and out."

Back at the dump, Compost Pile woke up from a nap, banging his head on the steering wheel of a large garbage truck. He was still rubbing his head when he answered the call.

"Breaker, breaker, this is Fish Guts, over and out."

"Breaker, breaker, it's time. Release the Kraken, over and out."

Compost Pile sat up behind the wheel and started the engine. He put it in gear and hit a switch that opened the tarp on the back. A repulsive stench as vile as rotten eggs mixed in a Porta-Potty filled the air. Compost Pile smiled as he took it in and circled the dump.

The back of the truck, filled to the brim with fish guts and rotten food, soon drew the attention of a few dumpster chickens. Within seconds they multiplied into a hundred. By the time Compost Pile pulled out of the dump, turned off Douglas Street, and headed down Michigan Avenue towards city hall, he had thousands of them trailing behind.

Back at the combat zone, T.W. held his men in position. They kept Captain Cornhole's men at bay with their potato guns but were quickly running out of ammo. Each man was down to his last potato when an unbearable stench filled the air.

"Bleep-bleep-%$#@!-bleep," Potty Mouth complained.

Captain Cornhole spat out his donut. A few of the police officers bent over and tossed up their breakfast.

"Alright, men," T.W. said. "Clothespins!"

The men did as instructed, placing clothespins on their noses. A few blocks down the street, Compost Pile's garbage truck barreled towards their direction. A dark gray cloud moved behind it.

"What in the name is that?" Captain Cornhole asked. "The weatherman didn't call for rain today." By the time he realized the cloud was a half million dumpster chickens, it was already too late.

"Umbrellas on my signal," T.W. said.

"Wait for it . . . wait for it . . . wait for it . . . *now*."

A hundred umbrellas sprung into action just as Detroit's runaway, dumpster chickens finally came home to roost. They covered everything in sight with three inches of whitish brown, putrid poop. Without the cover of umbrellas, Captain Cornhole's posse was splattered relentless. The city hall, once a sparkling pristine white, was now the color of a half-burnt marshmallow.

While Captain Cornhole's posse wiped the dumpster-chicken poop off their faces, T.W. ordered the men to charge. Rooster led with a loud war cry. Monster, Snot, and Bellyache took turns hiding behind each other. Poop Stain, Marshmallow, Belch, and Faygo threw potato-masher grenades. Cup Check teamed with his long lost father, Harry "The Menace" MacArthur, and together they cup-checked police officers in their family jewels. The Ace of Spades added some gray smoke as cover. Scissors commented later that it made for a beautiful touch. Super Soaker unscrewed fire hydrants and used the spray to send officers flying. The ones still covered in dumpster-chicken poop were thankful for the bath. Tea Bag and Colonel Sanders thought it a fine spectacle. They shared a cup of tea and a pipe while casually tossing a potato masher here and there.

In the middle of it all, Seafood and Captain Cornhole collided like two sumo wrestlers and pushed each other around like a pair of bulls with their horns locked. At a stalemate, neither one found an advantage until an orphan kneeled on all fours behind Captain Cornhole, causing him to fall down with a mighty thud cushioned by three inches of dumpster-chicken poop. Unable to get back up, Captain Cornhole was incapacitated, leaving the rest of his posse to retreat.

The men gave a loud, triumphant cheer, one that was short lived.

"We have an orphan down," Scissors called out. "I repeat an orphan down."

"Who?" T.W. asked. "Where?"

A cry sounded from beneath Captain Cornhole's collapsed body. A black-laced prosthetic leg protruded from its masses.

"Quick, lift him," T.W. ordered.

Muscles was the first to move. He rolled Captain Cornhole onto his side, placing him face-first in three inches of dumpster-chicken poop. Where his body used to be was indeed an orphan, but not Christmas Story who had lost his leg after slipping on a slick patch of dumpster-chicken poop. Instead it was—

"Ray Charles." T.W. rushed to Ray Charles's side and cradled his head in his arms. Ray Charles appeared badly hurt. His binoculars lay next to him cracked down the middle.

"Is that you, sir?" Ray Charles whispered.

"Yes, I'm here, Ray Charles, I'm right here."

"Good. It hurts real bad, sir. I'm sorry I let you down."

"Nonsense, Ray Charles. You didn't let anyone down."

"I got him good though, didn't I, sir?"

"You sure did, kid."

"I think I'm dying, sir." He coughed. "I'm not gonna make it."

"Nonsense. You're gonna make it, soldier."

Ray Charles was about to say something else, but his head fell feebly to the side. T.W. tried to shake him awake, but he remained as lifeless as a child's teddy bear.

"*Medic*," T.W. called out. "We need a medic."

No one responded.

"Everyone else has headed to city hall," Scissors said. "Including The Wiz. He's the only orphan qualified enough for a medic."

"We need to move. Quick, round up the rest of the men. We rendezvous in city hall."

"But what about you, sir?"

T.W. didn't have time to answer. He already had Ray Charles lifted off the ground and was racing towards city hall. "We need a medic," T.W. said as he entered city hall. He placed an unconscious Ray Charles on a nearby couch. A large group of both men and prisoners stood in the lobby, too stunned to move.

"Hurry, somebody get The Wiz. Ray Charles needs medical attention immediately."

Mafia Don stepped out of the crowd and approached Ray Charles. As a lifelong criminal, he had seen his share of wounds, having been shot seven times, stabbed another nine, and shanked three times while in the pen. All of his wounds he had tended to himself.

Mafia Don conducted a quick examination. "He has a steady pulse and doesn't appear to be bleeding internally."

"What's wrong with him then?" T.W. asked.

"I dunno. The boy appears to be comatose or something."

Just then The Wiz, Toaster, Squirrel, and Demmie entered the lobby. After another quick examination, The Wiz came to the same conclusion.

"He's beyond my expertise," The Wiz said, studying his calculator. "He needs to see a real doctor. By my calculations, Ray Charles has a 50.00—repeating of course—percent chance of making it."

Much to everyone's surprise, Demmie stepped forward and did the only sensible thing she could think of—she bent down and kissed Ray Charles on the lips. His reaction was instantaneous. Ray Charles jumped to life, rising like an upturned rake that had been stepped on, his eyes spinning.

"Hubba, hubba," he said then fell back onto the couch.

"Good God, man," T.W. said. "We thought you were a goner. Are you alright, kid?"

"I sure am, sir, but boy, I could sure use a candy cigarette right about now."

"Nonsense. Here take this, you deserve it." T.W. removed the cigarette from behind his ear and placed it in Ray Charles's lips. Toaster quickly lit it. Ray Charles had waited all of his life for this moment, and when it finally came, he couldn't help but cough.

"Hack-eck-ugh," he coughed. "Those taste terrible, sir."

T.W. took the smoke from his lips and placed it in his own mouth. "That'll put hair on your chest, Ray Charles. You're officially a man now."

Ray Charles coughed again. "No, sir, I think I rather remain a boy and just stick to my candy cigarettes."

"That an orphan." T.W. patted him on the shoulder. "Where's Duct Tape? We're gonna need to patch up those binoculars of yours."

"He's in the control room," Toaster said. "I'll go get him, sir."

Scissors came into the lobby with the rest of the men. "Sir, all men are accounted for," he reported. "The streets are abandoned. It's like a graveyard out there."

"Good. Bring in the supplies and secure the premises. Have the men take up their positions and round up all prisoners. I want this place locked up and secured by 1400."

"Roger that, sir."

"Squirrel, come with me."

"Where to, sir?"

"The seventh floor. It's time to cut the head off of the snake."

* * *

Mayor Sharp sat on the floor in the ruin of his office. In his hands was the red toy car from his youth. He toyed with its remaining two wheels, spinning them with his fingers. Staring out into nothing, he didn't even notice Bartholomew standing in the doorway.

"*Sir,* did you hear me?"

"Huh?" Mayor Sharp turned to Bartholomew. "No, what is it, Bart?"

"The city's been lost, sir. The whole police force has been wiped out. The . . . um . . . insurgents are storming the stairs as we speak. Everything has been compromised."

"Right," Mayor Sharp said, placing the toy car on the floor. "I guess there's only one thing left to do."

"What's that, sir?"

"Make the call. Use my personal line."

Bartholomew swallowed hard. "Yes, sir. I'll get right on it."

Mayor Sharp was still seated on the floor of his office when T.W., armed with his Luger, barged in with Squirrel.

He barely noticed them.

"Well if it isn't The Man." T.W. pointed the Luger at Mayor Sharp's chest. "We got you dead to rights. Surrender or we'll use lethal force."

"That won't be necessary. You got me, son, I surrender." Mayor Sharp turned to face his rivals, his face defeated. That's when he noticed—

"*Earl*, what are you doing here? Aren't you supposed to be home?"

"I haven't been there for weeks. My real home's at the Row. It's where I belong, sir."

Mayor Sharp smiled. "I was an orphan once. Probably didn't tell you that one did I, Earl? I was just like you two. Full of angst and disenchantment, but that was long ago. All I have left of those days is this tiny red car. Now it's missing two wheels instead of just one. I have no idea why I hung on to it through the years. I guess I should have tossed it aside like everything else, but oh well, here we are now, just me and you, two sides of the same coin, betting on different sides. What's the plan now that you've won? I bet you didn't think that far ahead, most orphans don't."

T.W. and Squirrel didn't know what to say. Mayor Sharp sensed their confusion and broke out into hysterical laughter. In his mania, he tossed the red car aside, which was down to its last wheel.

"I forgot to thank you—what's your name—T.W. is it? Is that what you go by? It was you after all who helped me get rid of my most bitter political rival. Calloway dropped out of his Democratic bid for Governor a few weeks ago. It didn't take much twisting of the arm once he understood the situation and saw what was at stake. After that it was easy taking care of my one and only obstacle, Big Mama. Her greatest strength was also her greatest weakness. That's just how it goes with people with big hearts. They're suckers for hope. I had everything planned out to a T, but I never saw this coming. Who would have thought you had it in you to come after the city the way you did. Now that took some gall, didn't it T.W.? Or do you prefer your other name?"

"I don't know what you're talking about."

"Of course you don't," Mayor Sharp said with a chuckle. "Now if you're going to shoot go ahead and pull the trigger. I'm finished here."

T.W. did just that, a tiny flame jutted out from the end of the Luger. He used it to light the cigarette in his mouth. This just made Mayor Sharp laugh even harder. Unsure of how to proceed, they left Mayor Sharp alone in his office.

"What was that all about?" Squirrel asked as they took the stairs.

"Nothing."

"It sure didn't sound like nothing."

"What do you expect from the ramblings of a madman?"

They made it back to the control room only to discover that a situation had arisen.

"Sir, you're not going to like this," The Wiz said, face deep in a computer screen. "The National Guard has been called in. We were too distracted with Ray Charles's injury to intercept the call. It was made on the Mayor's private line."

"Good God, man," T.W. said. "How much time do we have?"

"Not much. They're on their way."

"Son-of-a-Hemingway. We haven't a moment to lose. Quick call everyone to their stations. We need to take preventive measures and barricade the place. Wiz, I'll have—

"Sir, I think you need to see this." An out of breath Muscles stormed into the control room.

"Great, now what?"

"Follow me to the roof, sir."

The vantage point from the roof showed that the buildings around them were still smoking, while the city streets had been vacated, save for the police cars surrounding city hall. Below them were hundreds, perhaps thousands of Detroit's homeless crowded into the city center, using their shopping carts to form a large barrier between city hall and the impending National Guard. Stinky Pete had come through after all.

"Good God," T.W. said, "we just might have a chance."

* * *

The standoff with the National Guard and the men of Detroit lasted two days. Tanks, jeeps, artillery, a few thousand troops, and whatever resources the National Guard had available surrounded city hall. No one was allowed in or out of this heavily armed perimeter. All civilians, including the media, remained outside the green zone.

The men had come prepared bringing enough canned goods and canisters of Ovaltine to get them through the winter. The only thing standing between them and the National Guard was a large shopping-cart-constructed barrier, manned by a few thousand homeless who passed around paper-bag bottles and sang old Bob Lennon songs. The city had been trying to kick them out for years, now they reclaimed what had always been theirs to begin with, the streets of Detroit.

The National Guard refused to negotiate with what they claimed were Orphanized Terrorists, while the men refused to surrender to an organized government built on tyranny. They had only one demand—a New Orphan Order, shortened to NOO, a big fat *no* with an extra *o*. The men were hopeful and resilient, but nothing prepared them for the unexpected news that came on the morning of the second day of the standoff.

"Finnegan Winston Calloway, this is your father," a voice called from a bullhorn. "I'm here with your mother. We hoped staying at that orphanage would quiet some of your rebellion, but now you've taken it too far. This is enough already. We have come to take you home. Please come down and stop this nonsense."

"Who in the Hemingway is Finnegan?" Ray Charles asked. None of the men knew.

"Finn, we know you are in there. It's time for you to stop pretending you are an orphan and come out. Please show some reason. The National Guard is talking of retaking the building by force if necessary. Staying in there is only going to make things worse for everyone involved. Give this madness up before it turns violent."

"What's he talking about?" Squirrel asked. "Who in the Hemingway is pretending to be an orphan?"

"He must be trying to divide us," The Wiz said. "Conquer us from within, by turning on each other. It's a tactic often used by the military. By my calculations, it has a 16.32—repeating of course—percent chance of succeeding."

"That's jacked up," Ray Charles said. "We're all orphans

here. Who'd believe that load of bologna anyway? Guy's crazy, I tell you."

"No, he's not." T.W. took off his sunglasses, revealing pale green eyes.

"I knew it!" Muscles collected ten marks from Scissors.

"Son-of-a-Hemingway, I thought they were blue for sure," Ray Charles said, handing over twenty marks to Crash. All around the men were handing over marks or accepting them. Pickles bet his entire orphan's savings on brown, leaving him marks-less. Seafood was loath to part with his last Twinkie, betting on hazel.

"It's time to come clean," T.W. shouted, bringing order back to the men. "Everything he said is true. I should know. He's my father."

"*What!*" Squirrel gasped. The rest of the men were too shocked to speak.

"Don't you see? It's me he's talking about, kid."

The men let out a collective gasp. They just couldn't believe it was true.

"See, I told you," Colonel Sanders said to Scissors. "My Orphan Sense never lies. It can spot an orphan a mile away."

"But you're name's Teenage Wasteland not Finnegan," Ray Charles said.

"No, it's not. My real name's Finnegan Winston Calloway. I'm no orphan. I have a mom and a dad. I was born into wealth. In fact, my family's one of the wealthiest families in the state of Michigan."

T.W. pulled the cigarette from his ear and lit it himself. "Sorry, I lied to you boys. It wasn't fair of me, but now that the game's up, it's time to call it quits and go home. I can't let you men take the fall for my actions. I'm the only one totally responsible. I was always for starting the revolution, not what came after. I was too focused on tearing down the order of things to think much about the consequences of my actions. That's the problem with being a selfish idealist. Now all you men are in a jam and the only way out of it is for someone to take the fall and that's me."

"No," Squirrel said. "We're all in this together. No one forced us to come along. We came willingly and will go out unwillingly if that's what it comes down to. Remember your motto, no orphan left behind. If you go down, we go down with you, *together*."

"Sorry, kid, but it can't go down like that. Don't you see what will happen? They'll tear you apart and destroy all we created. They'll go easy on a rich kid like me, especially with my family connections and all, but they'll just stick it to the rest of you, give you the book and throw you all in detention centers. To them you're just future prisoners, animals in a cage. You think they care about adding more miles to your path to the state pen? You know I'm right. Remember Snuggles."

"Snuggles," the men whispered and then remained silent.

"There's got to be another way," Squirrel said.

"Sorry, kid, but this is it. The end of the road. Time for me to fly. I'm sorry I let you down, men. Alright, Wiz."

Without saying a word, The Wiz handed him a small backpack. T.W. placed it over his shoulders, approached the empty windowsill, and stared down at the ten-stories below. Crowds of people, a mix of reporters, National Guard, police, and civilians were all gathered around the shopping cart barricade surrounding the city center. T.W. spotted his parents standing on a police barricade, dressed in dark suits, as if ready for a funeral.

He turned to face the men, taking one last drag from his cigarette before dropping it out the window. He lowered his sunglasses back onto his eyes, gave a salute with his right hand, and then without saying a word leapt out the window. Stunned, the men rushed to the windowsill, while the crowd gasped below.

T.W. fell with his arms stretched out like a bird, his black Elvis-wig threatening to blow off his head. He was halfway down when he pulled a cord from the backpack, releasing a parachute. He floated out towards the crowd and landed somewhere in the middle. The National Guard was waiting to take him into custody.

As they carried him away, T.W. looked up at the men in city hall. Somewhere in the shuffle, he lost his sunglasses. The green of his eyes, running like a river, never left the men. Even in defeat, a martyr to *The Cause*, he maintained his dignity, the one thing The Man could never take away from him. He had earned his wings.

23

After the Flood

THE NEWSPAPERS CALLED it an "urban disaster."

Despite no natural occurrence, be it hurricane, tornado, earthquake, or wildfire, the damage totaled in the billions. Not since the white flight to the suburbs or the race riots of '68 had the orphan city of Detroit seen such destruction. Whole city blocks had to be leveled and rebuilt, while streets had to be torn up and repaved.

Whereas Detroit's decline had taken decades, it only took a matter of days for its destruction. Since the city was already in the red, the Federal Government stepped in to foot the bill. Things couldn't have worked out better for Mayor Sharp. He knew exactly how to take federal money and line his own pockets with it.

For the men, it was a devastating blow. Their optimistic ideals of revolution were squandered by reality—the hard truth that the good guy doesn't always win. They reluctantly threw in their towels shortly after T.W., or rather Finnegan, was taken away by a police car. With their leader gone, there was no longer a point to the uprising. *The Cause* was all used up. In the end, the city of Detroit just wasn't a place for a street fighting orphan.

With heads down, Squirrel and Demmie led the men out of city hall carrying white rags attached to broomsticks as flags of surrender. Tears fell from Ray Charles's duct-taped binoculars and trickled down his cheek. Snot sniffled and sneezed, Monster trembled, Bellyache rubbed his belly, Big Ben ticked, Marshmallow paled, Super Soaker spat, Compost Pile smelled, Christmas Story limped, and Potty Mouth was too depressed to curse.

The National Guard detained them and placed them in the back of a big yellow school bus. They were then driven to the Detroit Juvenile Detention Home where they were to stay until the day of their court hearing.

Stinky Pete and the vagrants were the next to go. Since they had not been part of the major fighting, they were told to disperse and head home, which for them meant just walking down the street. They had no reason to stick around anyway, now that their paper-bagged bottles were empty. Some of the police officers and National Guard attempted to give them a hard time, but Stinky Pete wasn't having any of it.

"Hey, I'm a Vietnam vet man and I got rights," Stinky Pete said. "If you lay a hand on me I'll call my lawyer Backseat Bob. He's the best lawyer under the bridge."

"'If the paper bag don't fit the bottle, you got to call a mistrial,'" Stinky Pete added, quoting Backseat Bob.

The prisoners were more hesitant to call it quits since prison cells were the only thing awaiting them. But Mafia Don was more given to reason than he was freedom. He convinced the men to throw down their shanks and potato guns, stating it would only be a massacre if they took on the National Guard. They were handcuffed, escorted to a bus, and driven back to the pen where they were all given an additional twenty years to their sentences. Mafia Don's lawyer, Backseat Bob, was still hopeful he could be eligible for parole in thirty years.

The media didn't know what to make of the men or the so-called "urban disaster." For starters, they had trouble deciding just what to call it. The right-wing *Detroit Freedom Isn't Free Press* called the men terrorists and their so-called revolution a plot to overthrow the government and undermine democracy. The left-leaning *Detroit Free Speech Press* called the men disenfranchised liberators, freedom-fighting insurgents who stood up for the common man and fought for social equality. The moderate *Detroit Free Press* simply called them misguided youth who had turned their rock 'n' roll angst into a billion dollar calamity.

Not one newspaper mentioned *The Cause.*

Some people called for justice, while others called for reform. Some called for their heads on a platter, while others wanted them released. Some wanted to make an example out of them, while others wanted their example to be followed.

Either way, the public wanted answers.

In the days after the disaster, Mayor Sharp and his Wilson cohorts devised the perfect way to give it to them. They put it all on the Calloways. After all, it was their own son who had initiated the whole thing in the first place. Thinking it the perfect ploy, Mayor Sharp quickly got over his military defeat and began working on his political victory.

They handpicked a reporter from the *Detroit Freedom Isn't Free Press*—a Wilson—to run multiple stories on both T.W./Finnegan and his wealthy father. The headlines included: "Millionaire's Son Burns City to the Ground Just Because He's Rich and Spoiled," "Calloway Put Son Up to It Just So He Could Undermine Mayor Sharp," "Enemies of Detroit: The Calloways," and "Why Should the Good Taxpayers Get Stuck with the Bill, When the Calloways Have Millions?"

"This is perfect, Bart," Mayor Sharp exclaimed, reading the morning paper with his breakfast. "Talk about good fortune. This is just another opportunity for us to turn trash into gold. Line our pockets with federal money and Calloways's. We can probably even make them pay for at least half of the damages. Their political career is over. Might as well start working on the first draft of my acceptance speech. The governor's house is practically mine now."

Bartholomew nodded in agreement.

"Let's celebrate tonight, Bart. Bottles of champagne, that fancy Mexican place I love, and cocktails afterwards. We deserve it, wouldn't you say?"

"I couldn't agree more, sir."

"Great. Have Mr. Tidy pick up my wife at five."

"Will do, sir."

Mayor Sharp chuckled as Bartholomew left his office. With no time to lose and anticipating a large government bailout, he had already ordered the reconstruction of city hall. Workers worked around the clock, replacing busted windows and scraping dumpster-chicken poop off the marble walls. His new desk was just as big as his old one. On it was a new and improved statue of Alexander the Great. Mayor Sharp stared into Alexander's eyes and felt that the Prince of Macedonia was sharing in his good fortune.

There was no way for Mayor Sharp to know that his cause for celebration was premature because unbeknownst to both him and Bartholomew, The Ace of Spades had made the entire contents of their safe disappear and reappear in the office of the *Detroit Free Press's* chief editor, who happened to be on a weeklong vacation in the Bahamas during the so-called "urban disaster."

When Upton Muckraker returned from vacation, he was surprised to discover a pile of the most incriminating evidence on record stacked on his desk. Someone had sent him the mayor's books that detailed every single illegal activity the mayor and Bartholomew had committed during the last twenty years. After years of wanting to stick it to Mayor Sharp, Upton finally had his ammo, a whole stockpile of it. Not since Watergate, had a politician had so much dirt on them out in the open. It took Upton and a small staff a few days to sort through it all. By the time they were finished they had a story worthy of the Pulitzer. In fact, it was both a career maker and ender.

The next day's headlines read as follows: "Mayor Sharp's Hand Caught in the Cookie Jar: Years of Extortion and Deception Drain the City of Detroit."

After a good night of festivity, Mayor Sharp was in good spirits when he sat down for his breakfast. His mood quickly soured as he read the morning paper.

"What kind of unsolicited garbage is this?" he asked. The garbage in question would become part of an ongoing investigation that the newspapers later referred to as Garbagegate, which detailed the millions of dollars Mayor Sharp and his cronies made by outsourcing jobs and insourcing garbage from neighboring Canada.

"Bart, get in here this instant!"

When Bartholomew didn't answer, Mayor Sharp stood up and threw down his napkin. "Bart, get in here. Bart? *Bart!*"

When his office door opened, it wasn't Bartholomew that came through, but rather a Federal prosecutor and four detectives, none of them named Wilson.

"What's the meaning of this?" Mayor Sharp asked.

"Albert Sharp, you have the right to remain silent."

Mayor Sharp did not remain silent, not for a single second, as he was escorted out of city hall and into a waiting police car. "I'm innocent. You got the wrong man. Do you know who I am? You're making a huge mistake. You'll hear from my lawyer. Your career will be over by the time I get through with you. You hear me? I'm going to be president someday and each and every one of you is going to regret this. You won't even be able to find a job sweeping streets by the time I'm done with you. I'm mayor of this city, you hear me *mayor*. I demand to be released right this instant."

He was still complaining and making threats as the police car pulled out of the city center and took the now Ex-Mayor Sharp to his new home, the pen, where he and the Wilsons took up an entire wing.

Ex-Mayor Sharp and his cronies were charged with twenty-seven counts of fraud, deceit, money laundering, and nepotism. Their tale of corruption garnered more headlines than the "urban disaster." The greatest backlash came from his former conservative supporters who felt betrayed when some of Ex-Mayor Sharp's tax write-offs—all from Mexican restaurants—were made public. They were under the impression he ate only American food, namely hot dogs, and found it blasphemous that he would indulge in something so un-American.

The biggest blow to Ex-Mayor Sharp was not prison or his bad reputation, but rather the truth. Upton Muckraker ran a whole series of articles aimed at spilling the beans on the mayor's greatest secret of all—that he was really an orphan. The headlines read: "Mayor Sharp Proves You Can Take the Orphan Out of the Orphanage, But You Can't Take the Orphanage Out of the Orphan." The articles included in-depth interviews with the Row's own Big Mama, who became somewhat of a local celebrity, the rock in Detroit Rock City.

With Ex-Mayor Sharp playing the villain, Mr. Calloway was the new hero. The citizens of Detroit unanimously voted him in as Ex-Mayor Sharp's successor—the new Mayor of Detroit. Mayor Calloway's first order of business was to pardon the men and reinstate funding to Desolation Row, overturning all phony charges handed to Big Mama. She was ecstatic, saying "Lordy, Lordy, Lordy, finally, we have a mayor with a heart as big as his voice, Lordy, yes."

Mayor Calloway also promised to decriminalize the cutting of couch and mattress tags, reducing sentences and freeing up the already overcrowded prison system. Next he put the homeless to work, namely Stinky Pete who was given a job on his campaign advertising committee. Stinky Pete was so ecstatic he went to work right away, writing down three or four new campaign slogans on a piece of cardboard.

Lastly, Mayor Calloway focused on urban renewal. The goal of his program was to bring the city of Detroit back into the national spotlight—this time for positive reasons. To kick-start his new initiative Mayor Calloway organized a massive benefit concert called *Detroit Now*. Its message was "Let's rebuild the city of Detroit before it sinks."

Detroit Now featured a whole slew of celebrities and live performances by artists such as Bob Lennon, fresh off a worldwide tour in Iceland, singing his new not-so-hit song "The Super Bowl Just Ain't a Place for a Detroit Lion," and Detroit's own The D singing his new song "Nothin' Says Gangsta Like an Orphan," the latest from his album *Straight Outta Detroit*. There was even talk of the Flex Pistols getting back together.

Tom Travolta acted as host. Tea Bag helped organize the production and all of the men were given front row seats and VIP passes. They sat starstruck, staring at their idols, Bob Lennon and Tom Travolta.

"Wow, Tom Travolta's mustache is just as impressive in real life as it is on the big screen," Ray Charles said. "I can't wait until mine grows in."

"Keep eating your onions," Squirrel said.

"Oh, I will, sir." Ray Charles pulled an onion from his vest pocket and took a large bite. "Look, he's about to give another speech."

Tom Travolta took the stage. "You know the last time I was in Detroit I was at the airport. I never did make it into the city, despite having a two-day layover. It must have rained the whole time I was there. I didn't see the sun once, but as soon as my plane took off that sun came out. It made me think about my stint in rehab shortly after filming *Lethal Injection 5*."

"One of my favorites," Ray Charles said, with tears in his binoculars, as he took another large bite from his onion.

"You know if I had a son I'd want him to be like Detroit— always there, but not always there. That way I could see him whenever I wanted and then when I didn't want to see him, he'd still be there out of sight and somewhat forgotten, but still waiting for me to show up. You know what I mean?"

The men didn't, but agreed anyway. Tom Travolta ended his keynote address by using the opportunity to promote his latest movie, *The Crass and the Curious 17*.

"I can't wait to see that one," Ray Charles said. "Best cat-racing series ever. I sure hope it's as good as the other sixteen."

Detroit's own The D closed out the event as the headlining act.

Ray Charles was so moved by his performance that he took to the stage, busted out some fresh dance moves, and even showcased a new break dance called the Detroit Shake, which involved spinning circles on his binoculars with his feet flying in the air.

"Go, Ray Charles, go. Go, Ray Charles, go," the crowd chanted.

But Ray Charles had more for the crowd than just his dance moves. He took the mic after his break dance and said, "My name is Ray Charles and I'm here to say, I smoke a pack of candy cigarettes nearly every single day. I got more rhythms than Big Ben has time. I'm not afraid to break some laws 'cause I'm down with *The Cause*. I got a bracelet that says what would Hemingway do, I got a pocket full of marks and all my orphans do too. Now we're the Proletariat Pistol-Swinging Punks of Detroit, we took it to the streets because the mayor tried to exploit. I don't have a mom and I don't have a dad, I'm an orphan up to no good because I was born to be bad. I don't have a home, no place to go, that's why you'll find me kickin' it at the Row. Now I'm down with the Row. Who's down with the Row? I said I'm down with the Row. Who's down with the Row?"

The whole crowd was down with the Row and waved their hands in solidarity.

Afterwards, Ray Charles concluded his act by attempting to crowd surf. However, his nearsightedness caused him to misjudge the distance from the stage to the crowd. He landed binocular-first on the ground. The crowd let out a gasp and then a cheer as Ray Charles popped right back up and waved his hands in the air like he was hailing a taxi.

After the benefit concert, The D was so impressed with Ray Charles's performance that he offered him a record deal. Ray Charles had to decline, stating he was already obligated to *The Cause*.

"Well, R to the Charles, if you change yo mind, you hit me up," The D said. "Here's my personal number. Call me or page me any time."

The benefit concert was a huge success, raising enough money to keep many of the city's previously closed programs afloat, Desolation Row included. There was enough money leftover that Big Mama was able to get an assistant. Only one person interviewed for the job, Ms. Mouse, who had quit her job at Detroit Public shortly after Principal Wilson had been let go for charges of embezzlement. It was only after she accepted the job that she learned of T.W./Finnegan's departure. She was often found crying in the bathroom during her lunch breaks.

After the big televised event a sense of orphancy returned to the Row. Leaderless, the men's first order of business was finding a new captain to helm the ship. In typical Row fashion it was decided by the ballot.

"Alright you all know the drill," The Wiz said. "Every man gets one vote and one vote only. And remember, no voting for yourself."

"Bleep-%$#@-bleep," Potty Mouth said, his political ambitions thrown out the window.

It was a close race. But in the end, Squirrel edged out Scissors by a narrow margin of two votes. After the results were read, the men gave Squirrel a salute and loud standing ovation. Squirrel was too taken aback to give a proper speech. "I'll do my best to keep you men proud," he said, knowing he had big shoes to fill.

"I knew it was going to be a close race," The Wiz said. "By my calculations there was a 51.19—repeating of course—percent chance of you narrowly defeating Scissors."

Squirrel was not sure what to make of his victory. The first one to congratulate him was Scissors. "You had my vote, sir."

"I voted for you as well. Will you be my second just as you were T.W.'s?"

"Of course, sir. It will be an honor."

After the election, Squirrel moved his things into T.W.'s former office. He placed the pickle jar containing his great-grandmother's dentures on the desk next to the typewriter and his paintbrushes in an empty tin can.

It felt strange sitting on the other side of the desk. No one had heard from or had seen T.W./Finnegan since the revolution. They had no way of knowing where he was or how he was doing. He was gone, and in his absence there was a part of the Row still missing.

"Where are you now?" Squirrel wondered, alone in the empty office.

As their newly appointed leader, Squirrel kept in place the same policies of his predecessor. The men returned to their daily schedules, classes, and chores. They toiled for *The Cause*, wore their black PPSP-Douglas-Street-Affiliation vests with dignity, and did whatever they could to prevent adoption.

With a new secretary, Big Mama had more time to stitch. She was often found outside on her bench, knitting new shirts for both the men and the prisoners of the pen, who stayed in contact and thought of her as a surrogate mother as well.

"Lordy, I sure hope Juan 'AK-47' Martinez likes these sweaters I'm knitting for his new puppies, Glock 9, Bazooka, Uzi, Beretta, Sawed-off, and Shotgun," Big Mama said, not concerned if anyone was listening. "Lordy, ain't them puppies cute."

The Flex Pistols even got back together, but their reunion was short-lived. After repeated calls for more kazoo from Rooster, they were forced to go on hiatus again. Ray Charles was devastated. He had been taking accordion lessons.

Squirrel became busy in the daily happening of the Row. So much so, that he didn't have time to dwell on the past. There were decisions to be made, men to command, and *The Cause* to live up to.

Since he still attended Detroit Public, he promoted Scissors to Dean of Orphans, putting him in charge of the handling of all classes and academia. This freed up Squirrel's time, allowing him to continue to study with Demmie after school at the library and to start the arduous work of repainting the walls of the Row.

"You miss him don't you?" Demmie asked one afternoon. Squirrel was staring at a blank page of his sketchbook.

"Yes, I guess I do."

"Well, you still got me."

Squirrel smiled. Demmie always had a way to make him feel better. He kissed her and went back to his sketchbook, adding more doodles than space.

Life was good, but as the weeks led to months, Squirrel couldn't help but feel a pang of longing that couldn't be placed. Some days he found himself seated at the chess table in the rec room, staring at nothing at all. The game no longer interested him, even when he played against The Wiz or Scissors. Other days he found himself staring out the window of his office, hoping to catch a glimpse of something he couldn't see, or perhaps something he didn't know to look for.

"Do you think he's out there?" Ray Charles asked one day, startling Squirrel from one of his daydreams.

"Who?"

"Him, you know T.W., I mean Finnegan or whatever his name is. Do you think he's out there somewhere?"

"Of course he is. It's just a matter of where."

Ray Charles adjusted his binoculars and left Squirrel with his thoughts. A lot had happened during the last year. Squirrel had suffered loss, isolation, torment, and anguish but found love, family, purpose, and direction along the way. From an outcast to an orphan, alone to in love, and a follower to a leader he had seen his ups and downs and everything in between. Through it all, he was still there, stronger in the parts that had felt broken and connected in the places that had felt missing. He had searched his whole life for a home, a place where he belonged, and now that he had it he only felt there was something more, something out there waiting for him to discover.

To ease his restlessness, Squirrel often took long walks, allowing his mind to wander along Douglas Street. Sometimes he thought about his old friend, wondering if he would ever see him again.

It was on such a walk, during a typical overcast Detroit day, that a voice from the past awakened him from a deep stupor. Squirrel was so distracted he didn't even hear the person sneak up behind him.

"Good God, man, it sure is a gloomy day. Would it kill the sun to make an appearance for a change?"

Squirrel turned to face his long lost friend, a smile spreading on his face. "T.W., I mean Finnegan, is that really you?"

"You can call me T.W. Finn never really suited me."

"What are you doing here?"

"I was just in the neighborhood and thought I'd walk my old stomping grounds, see how they're holding up."

"It's good to see you . . . sir."

"Enough with the useless formalities, I'm nobody's sir."

"But—"

"No buts about it. I'm a changed man now. Got my act together. Can't you tell?"

The orphan formerly known as T.W. was so different that he was almost unrecognizable. His hair had grown back, the Elvis wig long since retired, but was combed to the side instead of back. With no black sunglasses on, his pale green eyes gleamed like fields of clover in the sun. Instead of a white T-shirt, black leather jacket, blue jeans, and motorcycle boots, he wore a maroon schoolboy uniform. There wasn't even a cigarette behind his ear.

"What happened to you after the revolution? The men have been wondering. I didn't know what to tell them, so I just told them nothing."

"Same thing that always happens when I act up. Parents send me to Chuck Norris Boarding School. I did some community service, promised to never start a revolution again, and now here I am back to being a kid. What about you? I heard you're in charge now."

"How did you know?"

"I still got my sources."

T.W. didn't elaborate. Squirrel thought he understood, though part of him still didn't. "Can I ask you a question?"

"You don't need permission to ask a question, kid, just ask."

"It was your family wasn't it? They were the ones who donated monthly stipends to the Row, right?"

"Yes, I thought I had lost them for good this time, but they always find me. I think they were secretly hoping my time away would soften my rebellious side. I guess they were wrong."

"Well, at least you have parents to come looking for you. Why'd you pretend to be an orphan?"

"I don't know. I always felt like an orphan at heart, like I didn't belong anywhere. My parents were always pushing me to do this or do that. It made me feel like I was a square peg being forced into a round hole. Leaving my family was just a way for me to rebel and discover who I really was instead of who they wanted me to be. When I left home, close to three years ago, this street was where I ended up first. I was on my way to catch a bus to Chicago when I saw Scissors trimming the bushes over there. For some reason I was drawn to the place. Scissors spotted me staring at him and asked if I was a new orphan. I said yes without a second thought, and the rest is history."

"So you just winged it?"

"Yup, pretty much made it up as I went along. But part of me always knew I was destined for something great, even if that just meant starting a revolution and destroying half of a city."

"What will you do now that the revolution is over?"

"I don't know, maybe knock a few more things off my list, make a run for office or write another novel. I finished the last one, but it didn't feel like it went anywhere, just a bunch of words and characters, with nothing to tell. I want my next one to mean something, say something that needs to be heard. Perhaps a true story based on the Row and the Proletarian Pistol-Swinging Punks of Detroit. Now that would be a story to tell, *ours*. Wouldn't it?"

"Yes, yes it would." Squirrel smiled at the thought of it. "Do you think you'll fly again?"

"Not anytime soon, kid. Flying's a bit overrated. Besides I already got my wings."

T.W. looked to the sky. It was gray as smoke. His eyes searched for the sun, but it was nowhere to be found. He turned towards Squirrel and winked.

"Here take this," he said, offering Squirrel his prized switchblade comb.

"I can't take this, it's yours."

"Nonsense, you're the new punk, Squirrel. Keep it and stay cool."

"I will," Squirrel said, turning the switchblade comb in his hand. "Will I ever see you again?"

"Of course. I'll be around, always am, even when I'm not. See you later alligator."

"After a while crocodile."

"And one last thing, Squirrel."

"Yes?"

"Don't ever let The Man keep you down."

"An orphan can never stay down for too long . . . *sir*."

T.W. grinned and then paused to take in the worn out air of Detroit's Desolation Row one last time before walking away. He never looked back. Squirrel watched him go until he was out of sight. The new punk, Squirrel thought. He liked the sound of that. It had a ring to it. A name befitting *The Cause*, just right for an orphan who called the city of Detroit—the birthplace of punk—home.

He probably would have stood there until dusk, alone with his thoughts, if a voice hadn't called out from behind him.

"You know that kid's alright."

Squirrel turned around to see who spoke to him. "*Brown Sugar Man!*" Squirrel tipped his hat in courtesy. "What are you doing here?"

"Oh, you know, just moving along, strumming a song."

Brown Sugar Man stood next to the steps of the Row, his guitar strapped over his shoulder, hanging from his back. He brought it around and plucked a few notes that sounded like they had been to places not found on a map.

"I was thinking of a writing a song about him. He's the real deal, a true pistol that one. Just haven't figured out the name or melody yet. Got any ideas?"

"How about Teenage Wasteland?"

"You mean 'Baba O'Riley'? That one's already taken."

"Oh, well, how about 'The New Punk'?"

"Now that I can dig! Can you dig it, man?"

Squirrel could. He walked back to the Row with a big smile. Up in his office, Scissors met him with pressing news. It seemed the Row was blessed with its youngest newbie to date, a two-year-old named Knuckles who was left on the door-steps in nothing but dirty diapers and a small, ragged blanket.

"Why do they call him Knuckles?" Ray Charles asked, leaning into the crib to get a closer look at the teeny, two-year-old. A tiny fist shot up and smacked him right in the binoculars. Ray Charles stumbled back with his head spinning, while the youngster giggled.

"There's your answer," Squirrel said.

"He sure is a firecracker."

"'All things truly wicked start with innocence,'" Squirrel said, stealing a page from T.W. by quoting Hemingway.

"I'm sure he'll get along just fine with Cup Check and Mike Tyson."

Ray Charles left, rubbing his binoculars as he went. Squirrel smiled, tossed his bowler hat on the desk, and stared out the window of his office. He didn't have much time to think. Scissors came barging in with more urgent news.

"Sir, we have a situation."

"Yes, what is it?"

"We have an incoming Charlie. Toaster just intercepted the message."

"Sound the alarm," Squirrel ordered. He brought out his switchblade comb and ran it through his hair three times. When he was finished he placed it in the side pocket of his black PPSP-Douglas-Street-Affiliation vest and headed for the mess hall. The kitchen bell rang three times, sounding throughout the Row and reaching the ears of Big Mama, who sat outside on her bench, stitching. She smiled warmly, count-ing her blessings and said, "Lordy, Lordy, Lordy."

In a world of plenty and plenty without, Desolation Row stood somewhere in the middle, aware of its surroundings and steadfast to the directions. The city of Detroit sat beside her as a foundation of something tried, true, and tested. An ideal in constant need of a fresh face or a makeover, very much like Squirrel and T.W. and every other orphan who had come through the thick of it and stuck it to The Man. Together they were very much like the days that came and went, and in their passing, one thing held true: It was always a good day to be an orphan, especially at Desolation Row and in the city of Detroit.

October 6, 2013
Denver, CO

Acknowledgments

I WOULD LIKE TO THANK the following people for making this book possible:

To my mom, who gave me my creative side.

To my dad, who showed me how to have fun.

To my great-grandfather Russell, who taught me to enjoy life.

To Laurie, my heart.

To Jack, my artistic brother.

To Laura, Justin, and the kids, who gave me a place to stay when I needed it most and daily doses of inspiration, which allowed me to start this novel.

To Helena, my editor, who did a fantastic job in making this a better story and me a better writer.

To Kara, Samara, Honey Love, and Mel, my sisters from another mother.

To Andy (both of them), Pat, Kalu, Miguel, and Josh, my brothers from another father.

To Mark, who helped design my website. He and Oyster were the perfect roommates. To his father, Dave, who put me in contact with Helena.

To Nick, who designed the book cover and to Andrea for stepping in for Nick and finishing what he started.

To my South African friends, who gave me a family while away from home.

To Fred, co-founder of Dumpster Cat Cinemas.

To John, whose deep, late night talks drew inspiration.

To Stephen King, whose books taught me to love reading and opened the door for my own writing career.

To Bob Dylan, whose lyrics taught me how to be a poet first and writer second.

To everyone I've come in contact with on this road called life, inspiration is everywhere if you just look for it.

Dramatis Personae

The Adults of Detroit

Albert Sharp: Mayor of Detroit, The Man aka The Anti-Punk

Betty (Wilson) Sharp: Albert's wife

Big Mama: Head supervisor of Desolation Row, age 87

Maege Mackie: Squirrel's great-grandmother

Mr. Tidy: Mayor Sharp's butler

Ms. Mouse: Secretary, Detroit Public

Upton Muckraker: Chief editor of *The Detroit Free Press*

The Wilsons

Barret Wilson: Warden, Detroit House of Corrections

Bartholomew Wilson: Mayor Sharp's campaign manager and member of city council

Barton Wilson: Judge, Detroit Circuit Court

Baxter Wilson: Proprietor of the dump

Beasley Wilson: Principal, Detroit Public

Benedict Wilson: Agent of Tag Police

Brett Wilson: Chief of Detroit Fire Department

Byron Wilson: Member of Detroit Public Board of Education

The Cronies

Captain Cornhole: Chief of police

Gunner Grape Juice: Chewing tobacco enthusiast and cook (not so much)

Major Balls: Retired drill sergeant, US Marine Corp

Professor Bore: Ninety-year-old retired economist

Sergeant Breakfast: Major Balls's second-in-command

The Orphans of Desolation Row

Teenage Wasteland (T.W. for short): Anarchist and general commander of orphans and all matters related to *The Cause*, age 13

The Officers

Chopsticks: T.W.'s unspoken fourth-in-command and head chef, age 12

Muscles: T.W.'s third-in-command and heavy lifter, age 11

Ray Charles: T.W.'s runner and candy cigarette addict, age 8

Scissors: T.W.'s second-in-command, landscaper, and barber, age 12

The Wiz: T.W.'s first lieutenant, alchemist, genius, and chief scientist, age 11

The Men

Ace of Spades: Magician, age 8 ¾

Belch: Youngest twin and burp linguistic, age 9

Belly Ache: Oldest twin and hypochondriac, age 9

Big Ben: Logistics, age 10 ½

Christmas Story: Amputee, age 10

Colonel Sanders: Philosopher, age 12

Compost Pile: Vagrant, age 8

Crash: Stunt devil, age 9 ½

Cup Check: Comedian, age 8 ½

Faygo: Caffeine enthusiast, age 9

Marshmallow: Albino, age 8

Matches: Pyromaniac, age 10

Mike Tyson: Soprano, age 7

Peanut Butter: Youngest, age 5 ½

Pickles: Black sheep, age 10

Poop Stain: Tattoo specialist and make-up artist, age 9

Rooster: Human bullhorn and lead singer of the Flex Pistols, age 11

Seafood: Lazy procrastinator, age 12

Snot: Health risk, age 7

Snuggles: Thumb sucker, age 7

Stone Age: Blacksmith and welder, age 11

Super Soaker: The Human Hose, age 8 ½

Tea Bag: British transplant and theater director, age 10 ¼

Toaster: Master of disguise and spy, age 10

Wheelin' Dealin' Steven: Entrepreneur, age 11

The New Recruits

Duct Tape: Jack-of-all-trades, age 9 ½

Knuckles: Mixed martial artist, age 2

Monster: Scaredy-Cat, age 7

Potty Mouth: Sailor, age 11

Squirrel: Artistic virtuoso, age 13

The Children of Detroit Public

Demmie: Red-haired beauty, age 13

The Wilsons: Billy, Bobby, Benny, Bob, Bill, Ben, Benjamin, Bradley, Brandon, Braden, Brian, Blake, Boris, Barry, Barney, Buck, Burt, Buster, and Bird

The Prisoners of the State Pen

"Crazy-eye" Hopkins

Harry "The Menace" MacArthur

Juan "AK-47" Martinez

Mafia Don

Mickey "No Dice" Paulson

Sonny "One-Tooth" Sullivan

Terry the Terrorizer

Other Notable Characters

Backseat Bob: Lawyer for hire (all occasions)

Bob Lennon: Musician, illegitimate son of either Bob Dylan or John Lennon

Brown Sugar Man: Mysterious street musician

Rabies, Sick Boy, Snaggle Tooth, and Sir Barks-a-Lot: Dobermans of the dump

Rosie: Dog with many lives

Stinky Pete: Homeless man

The Calloways: Enigmatic benefactors of Desolation Row

The D: Famous rapper from Detroit

The Wilburys: Prospective parents

Tom Travolta: Famous actor of straight-to-video B-movies